TELLING SONNY

Telling Sonny

A novel
by

ELIZABETH GAUFFREAU

Adelaide Books
New York/Lisbon
2018

TELLING SONNY

A novel

By Elizabeth Gauffreau

Copyright © by Elizabeth Gauffreau

Cover design © 2018 Adelaide Books

Published by Adelaide Books, New York / Lisbon

adelaidebooks.org

Editor-in-Chief

Stevan V. Nikolic

For any information, please address Adelaide Books

at info@adelaidebooks.org

or write to:

Adelaide Books

244 Fifth Ave. Suite D27

New York, NY, 10001

ISBN-13: 978-1-949180-51-0

ISBN-10: 1-949180-51-4

Printed in the United States of America

To my father Elliott Gauffreau, whose stories brought the magic to my childhood. To my brother George Gauffreau, whose stories brought the laughter. May the best of you live on in me.

Chapter 1

After a year or so, the death knell marking the end of Faby's marriage lost its resonance—yet it continued to toll, as steady and devoid of feeling as a metronome set in motion for someone who can't keep time. Then in April of 1952, unbeknownst to Faby, the tolling unexpectedly stopped. For a week, she knew of nothing that should change her steady marking out of time. She walked to the telephone company in the morning to put in her hours at the switchboard; she walked home again at day's end to eat her meager supper.

As Louis's first wife, Faby would have been an afterthought to his family by this time, someone who probably should be notified of his death, seeing as she and Louis did have a child together—although he and the boy had not been close. In fact, from the time his divorce from Faby became final, Louis had see his first-born son a total of four times, one of those times, when Sonny was twelve, with the intent of introducing him to his half-brother Louis, Jr. so that Sonny could see up close that young Louis looked just like his father, while poor Sonny took after his mother's side of the family. Dark hair, brown eyes, French. But still, a first wife, a mother of a first-born son should probably be notified.

When the call came, Faby and her sister Josephine had just settled in for their weekly Saturday afternoon visit in Faby's small apartment overlooking Main Street, as an unseasonably warm breeze blew through the open windows. Faby almost didn't answer the call, but Josephine couldn't abide the sound of an unanswered telephone, so Faby picked up the receiver.

Even as Louis's sister was identifying herself, the prelude to news that could only be bad, Faby didn't recognize her voice, it had been so long since they had spoken. When Faby asked about the funeral, it had already taken place, and when she asked if anyone had told Sonny, Dorothy said, "No, we thought he would take it better coming from you."

"Of course you did."

Faby dropped the receiver back into its cradle without bothering to say goodbye. So Louis had reneged on one last promise, his promise to attend Sonny's wedding, now only two weeks away. She felt Josephine watching her from across the room, expecting some sign to indicate the nature of the call: a shake of her head that the funeral had been for an acquaintance, someone Josephine didn't know, or, that it had been for a distant relative from out-of-state who had merely died of old age. When Faby gave no sign, Josephine continued to wait, too polite, even with her sister, to ask outright, "Who was that on the telephone?" asking instead, "Is everything all right?" Then, when Faby continued to sit in silence, Josephine pressed her. "What's wrong? What's happened?"

"Louis is dead."

Josephine crossed the room to join her on the sofa. "When? What happened?"

Faby looked down at her hands in her lap. They lay palms up as if someone had dropped them there, the fingers curled and tingling. "Dorothy left it to me to tell Sonny."

Josephine took Faby's hands in hers. "What happened, Faby? Did he have a heart attack?"

"I don't know. I didn't think to ask."

"Dorothy didn't tell you?"

Faby shook her head. "No. I may have hung up on her."

"Oh, Faby."

"I don't know what to tell Sonny. They didn't tell him. They didn't tell him about the funeral. How can I tell him he wasn't even asked to his own father's funeral? Dorothy shouldn't have left it to me."

"No, she certainly shouldn't."

Faby squeezed Josephine's hands, grateful for the sympathy, then dropped them and stood up. "I'll need to call Dorothy back. Sonny will want to know how his father died."

Faby could not find Dorothy's telephone number anywhere in her desk—not written on the torn corner of an envelope tucked inside her address book and long forgotten, not loose in any of the drawers. When she dialed the operator to place the call, she gave Dorothy's maiden name and Louis's home town without thinking, and the call went through.

Dorothy answered on the first ring, as if she had been waiting for Faby to call back—so Faby didn't identify herself. "You didn't tell me how he died, Dorothy."

It had been a car accident, an inexorable hurtling of metal and glass against tree, Louis dead on impact. Faby could hear the collision as Dorothy was speaking, the grinding shriek of metal on metal, the pulsating explosion of glass, the instant before impact a never-ending moment of awareness, before his head smashed through the windshield and all his bones shattered.

The sound of Louis's final leave-taking didn't subside after Faby hung up the telephone, the grinding shriek of it so piercing it made her eyes hurt, the pulsating explosion of it so thunderous it made her chest hurt. How was she going to describe that sound to Sonny, two weeks before he was to be married?

"He was killed in a car accident. On a clear day, on dry pavement. How could he have been so careless?" After a moment, she murmured, "Thoughtless to the end," before lapsing into silence.

As the minutes went by, Faby remained silent, grateful for her sister's presence, hoping she would stay, both of them watching the curtains rise and fall at the open windows unbidden until the sound of Louis's accident left her head at last. There may have been street noises eddying in and out of the room with the unseasonably warm breeze—the sound of car doors slamming, shop bells tinkling, children calling after their mothers—but Faby didn't hear them.

As late afternoon passed into early evening, the breeze turned chill, and Josephine got up and closed the windows. Before leaving to prepare supper for her husband, she brought Faby aspirin and a glass of water, but that still didn't dispel the sound of the collision, which now had intensified to include the sound of the tree breaking apart, a splitting, tearing, rending that no tree should have to endure.

And what was she to tell Sonny about his father's death? What did Sonny know of his father, after all? Sonny knew what his father looked like, certainly, tall and blond, with an affable, lantern-jawed face. He even knew the basic facts of his father's life: high school athlete, veteran of the First World War, minor vaudeville player, master salesman. As far as Sonny was concerned, his father was a man of infinite charm, a man with that enviable quality, *savoir faire*. What was she to tell Sonny now?

Chapter 2

When Faby graduated from high school, she expected something to happen. After all of the essays were written, the equations solved, the exams taken, she expected that her life would be different—different in what way, she didn't know, but surely, after the embellished white dress, the carnation corsage, the scrolled diploma tied with ribbon—not to mention the class photograph—nine girls seated in a row, nine boys standing in a row behind them, not a one of them smiling, because they were the Class of 1924 and they mustn't demean the dignity of the occasion by smiling—surely, after that, Faby should expect her life to be different.

The summer immediately following graduation didn't count, of course, because it was summer, a time to spend out-of-doors with friends from morning till night, all piled into Clyde Geraw's flivver with a basket of cold meat sandwiches and rhubarb pie to sustain them as they tore over the rutted dirt roads surrounding the village, stopping only to eat, swim, and sing raucous songs no one could remember the words to.

When the summer ended, Faby watched from her bedroom window as Josephine set off alone on the first day of school, finding it hard to believe that she no longer had to traipse off to school every day, day after day, week after week.

Today, she could do as she pleased, and when today ended, she would have a lifetime of days to do as she pleased.

But first there were chores to do, she and Maman both coming under the increasingly resentful eye of Maman Aurore, now that there were three women to tend to the house and the meals, not two. Maman Aurore had lived with them for as long as Faby could remember, watching disapprovingly from her rocking chair by the window as she knit a never-ending series of sweaters-afghans-mittens-scarves-socks, as if the entire family could never be warm enough. Maman Aurore set such a fast pace for her needles that her finished scarves were long enough to tie someone up with—and have enough left over to strangle him in the bargain.

As Faby slipped an apron over her dress before beginning her morning chores, the thought occurred to her that the current state of affairs must actually be an improvement over what it had been when her mother first married her father, when Maman Aurore would have tried to run the household herself, moving the flour bin, crossing items off her daughter-in-law's grocery list, elbowing her away from the stove so that she could preside over the pot of soup simmering there, the two of them nearly coming to blows over a ball of bread dough to be kneaded. There must have been a spectacular blow-up between the two of them, with the rocking chair as the compromise.

After finishing her chores, Faby tossed a breezy *Bye-bye, now!* to her mother and grandmother and left the house. She gave little thought to where she was going as she set off down the sidewalk, just relishing the warm fall day—the sound of insects chirring companionably, the smell of wildflowers waning, a little acrid, a little poignant. The maple trees lining both sides of the street were just starting to turn yellow and gold—orange and red still several weeks away. A few of the leaves had fallen, detaching themselves gently from the branches that held them to drift through the air and land on people's lawns to form a pleasing random pattern, as if someone with a practiced eye had placed them there.

The houses Faby passed were as familiar to her as her own. Every house on the street had a porch, some on the front of the house leading to the front door, others on the side leading to the kitchen door. A few of the larger houses had both. On every porch was a tin box for the milkman to leave milk, cream, butter, and eggs, with the occasional quart of buttermilk, for those who had a taste for it. Being in the village, the houses didn't have mailboxes, Rural Free Delivery reserved for farms.

Halfway down the street, Mrs. Gibson's house had gone unpainted since 1910, the year her husband died, the window shades pulled down, as though Mrs. Gibson couldn't bear to look out and see that life on the street had gone on without him. Further down the street, the front porch of the Neales' house was nearly obscured by massive lilac bushes that reached to the second floor, keeping them trimmed having ended two generations of Neales before.

On sunny days like today, the Judds' dog, a grossly overweight beagle named Sally, would be sprawled in front of the door napping, too lazy to muster the strength to even lift her head when someone walked by. The Bergerons' house had a bay window in front, with a very excitable terrier resting uneasily on the window seat inside, breaking into fits of frantic barking whenever anyone passed by. Few, if any, of the neighborhood boys could resist stopping in front of the Bergerons' house and yelling something at the poor creature, sending it into hysterics while they pointed and laughed.

Walking at a brisk pace, Faby reached overstreet in just a few minutes, stopping briefly by Asletine's Dry Goods to see if there was anything interesting in the display window—there wasn't—before continuing on to Lincoln Park. The old biddies of the Ladies' Village Improvement Society had set out chrysanthemums in honor of the changing season, the yellow blooms vibrant against the backdrop of the park's evergreen shrubbery—and God forbid that any rambunctious boy from the school across the street should trample them or a heavy rain bend them or anyone criticize their color or arrangement. The fountain in the center of the park had not yet been turned off and drained for the season, the naked cherub still unable to keep the water in the pitcher he held above his head from overflowing into the three basins beneath him and splashing into the fountain below, poor fellow.

Directly across the street from the fountain stood the school, its solid brick bulk unchanged from the day Faby graduated, unchanged, for that matter, from the day she had entered the graded school on the first floor, knowing so little English that she didn't know how to ask permission to use the bathroom. How odd it was, to have spent so much time in that building, most of her life, in fact, and, just like that, to no longer belong there. If she were to enter the building and walk down the hall, the first person she encountered, whether principal, teacher, or student, would ask her what she was doing there.

She turned from the school to begin the walk home, stopping to get a drink of water at the new drinking fountain that been donated to the village by the L.V.I.S. the previous year. As she trudged back up Main Street, she idly wondered if they sent out clandestine patrols of their eldest members, stout, white-haired women wearing unfashionable hats, to make sure that the drinking fountain was not used improperly by the wrong people—despite the carved dedication announcing that the fountain was intended for use by "man and beast."

She found her mother and grandmother out in the back yard taking clothes off the line, working at opposite ends, each yanking the clothespin bag closer to her own end before releasing the clothespins from her hand.

"Where have you been?" Maman Aurore demanded, "wandering the streets like a vagabond?"

Maman gave a bath towel a sharp snap before folding it and setting it on the neat stack she'd made in the clothesbasket. "Leave her be. She's only been gone a short while."

Later, when all of the laundry was put away or hung on hangers for ironing, Faby wandered into the kitchen, where Maman and Maman Aurore were at the ironing board engaged in ironing one of Papa's shirts, Maman wielding the iron, Maman Aurore at her elbow sprinkling water on the cloth with the tips of her fingers from a bowl held in her other hand. Faby stood watching them for several minutes, wondering how Maman was able to maneuver the iron with someone constantly getting in her way, yet still avoid burning either of them.

After several more minutes had gone by, Maman Aurore looked up and said, "What do you *want*, child, just standing there like a witless sheep? Can't you find something to occupy your time?" Tears sprang to Faby's eyes, and she left the house by the back door, slamming it behind her. She knew that neither her mother nor her grandmother would come after her, first, because it wouldn't look good to the neighbors for either of them, or, even worse, for both of them, to go chasing down the street after her, scolding until they could get her back into the house to chastise her more thoroughly, and, second, neither would give up her appointed place at the ironing board with Papa's half-ironed shirt.

Throughout that fall, every morning when Josephine's alarm clock went off, in those first few moments of coming into wakefulness, Faby thought she too had to get up and get ready for school, moments later feeling the oddest mix of relief and disappointment when she realized that she didn't: the panic over homework left undone becoming relief, then disappointment that no one had assigned her any. Although she really didn't have to get right up, she couldn't bear the thought of staying in bed while the rest of the family was downstairs eating breakfast and preparing for the day ahead, as if she were some unwanted invalid whose needs would be attended to, dutifully, after everyone else's were met.

One unusually warm day in late October, Faby walked all the way down lower Main Street to the power plant, past all the blocks on Main Street, the Burt Block, the Perley block, the Billado Block, the Merrill Block, past the brick telephone building, where, inside, pale young women plugged and unplugged the telephone conversations of the village with bony fingers and tired eyes, while they waited for someone to marry them. When she reached the river, she stood on the bridge for a long time, looking over the railing at the water rushing over the falls, inexplicably glad for the movement and the rush of noise.

Even after the first snowfall of the year, the week after Thanksgiving, Faby continued her daily walk, now, however, unable to leave the house without Maman Aurore's fussing that she would catch her death, or fall and break a bone, or several bones, or get hit by a car while crossing a snow-covered street, the unfortunate driver unable to stop in time to avoid hitting her, poor man.

In December, Clyde Geraw asked Faby to the annual Christmas dance that the high school held at the Opera House, and she was sorely tempted to say yes, but she didn't. Two weeks later, watching Josephine, radiant in a red velvet dress, leave for the dance with Leonard Paradis, Faby didn't know whatever had possessed her to turn Clyde down, except that he was still in high school and she wasn't.

The winter was unusually hard that year, with more snow than even the oldest in the village could remember. Then, at the beginning of February, influenza hit the family, each one of them sick in turn, with Maman Aurore developing pneumonia and nearly dying, saved only by the grace of the Good Lord Above, according to her, which, Faby had to admit, could very well have been the case, her grandmother's abortive struggles to breathe as the illness progressed truly frightening. By the time the ice on the Missisquoi went out at the beginning of April, Faby was ready for spring. She was ready for warm days and tender green leaves, ready for the smell on the air that comes only in the spring and carries with it a poignant blend of melancholy and hope.

Once spring came, the days went by quickly, with spring cleaning and clearing out the flower beds and planting the vegetable garden and preparing for Josephine's graduation from high school. On the night before commencement ceremonies, as she lay in bed unable to sleep, Faby turned on her side and whispered, "What will you do, Josephine?"

Her sister didn't answer at first, and Faby thought she might already be asleep. Then Josephine whispered back, "I'm not sure what you mean, Faby. What will I do about what?"

"I mean, now that you're finished with school, what will you do?"

"What will I do? Why, I expect that I'll marry Leonard. Not right away, of course. I'll stay here and help out while he establishes himself and saves up enough money for us to get married."

"Oh." Faby saw in her mind's eye the image of *four* women in the kitchen wrangling over who would wipe the table and who would stir the stew and who would open which jar of vegetables, the four of them stumbling into one another like dancing bears, and she decided that she was best off just turning over and going to sleep.

Commencement exercises for the Class of 1925 were held in Lincoln Park, and the weather couldn't have been better: warm and sunny, with just enough of a breeze so that no parent, young sibling, or elderly relative got overheated sitting in the sun. The town band, a ragtag mix of old and young men who happened to be proficient at musical instruments, played "Pomp and Circumstance" at just the right pace, slow enough to afford the graduates their proper respect but not so slow that the business of the occasion lagged. The speeches weren't unduly long, although this year Faby found herself confounded by their theme of commencement. It had been a year since her high school graduation, and nothing had commenced for her, as far as she could tell.

Chapter 3

After the high school commencement ceremonies, the next big event for Enosburg Falls, Vermont took place at the beginning of July, when a traveling vaudeville show came to the Opera House. Moving pictures, with piano accompaniment provided by Mrs. Blanche Martin, were shown at the Opera House throughout the year, which was entertainment enough for young children and the elderly, neither of whom knew any better. However, Blanche's plodding arpeggios and stumbling glissandos in no way matched the action on the screen, and the flickering black-and-white images simply could not compare with the thrill of live performance, with its colorful costumes and feats of daring that held the potential of permanent injury for any performer whose attention wandered or whose sights were set too high. What's more, Faby knew from loitering in front of the Quincy Hotel, where the troupe stayed while the show was in town, when the performers were out of costume, these were people who wore impossibly stylish clothes, the men in suits with nipped waists and tight pants, the women with their skirts audaciously short. Once the performers were off-stage, their speaking voices, as they batted the latest slang back and forth like badminton shuttlecocks, reverted to the vowels of the states where they'd grown up, but whether California, New York, Michigan, or Tennessee, Faby had no way of knowing.

She looked forward to the vaudeville show for days, as soon as the playbills went up, stopping to read them on her way to Giddings Drugstore to buy *Bromo-Seltzer* for Maman Aurore, or the I.G.A. to buy sugar for Maman, delighting in the bold, black lettering, the profusion of exclamation points, the extravagant adjectives: "A spectacular lineup, stupendous, tremendous!! Rollicking comics! Kaleidoscopic tableaux! Altogether extravagantic!!!"

Even though she had been to the show every year since she was seven, it had never disappointed. Every year, the songs were always the catchiest she'd ever heard, the comics were always the funniest she'd ever seen, the dancers the most graceful, the acrobats the most nimble. And the performing animals—well, the performing animals were just the cleverest thing she'd ever seen. Every year, she talked about the show for days afterward, the worst third-rater just as memorable for her as the headliner. And after the show moved on, the images stayed with her until it returned the following year: her scrub brush on the bathroom floor becoming the lively patter of the headline comic, sheets on the clothesline becoming the most graceful of dancers, her own tuneless humming as she dressed in the morning transformed into a lilting melody sung by a willowy blonde in a white silk dress, the words and notes coming to her as effortlessly as her own name.

This year, she looked forward to the vaudeville show in a way she never had before. She and Josephine would attend the evening show for the first time unaccompanied, now that both were graduated from high school, Faby surprised at how little cajoling it had taken for Maman and Papa to agree to let them go alone. In the days before the show arrived in town, Faby played the performance inside her head every night before she went to sleep, taking each of the parts herself, in turn: The Acrobat, turning cartwheels, handstands, back flips, somersaults, each one more gravity-defying than the one before, the audience as they entered the Opera House halting in their tracks at the sight of her—The Escape Artist, no handcuffs too tight for her to slip from, no straight jacket too elaborate to hold her—The Athenian Dancer, running barefoot across the stage, evoking ancient ruins and hot Greek sun with nothing more than fluttering chiffon and graceful limbs—The Headliner, of course, singing or emoting to an enraptured audience, and, finally, The One-Woman Band to close the show, a big bass drum strapped to her back, a harmonica around her neck, a trumpet in one hand, a klaxon in the other, the audience in on the joke.

When the day of the show finally came, Faby stood in front of her open closet scowling, having decided that not a single one of her dresses was anything but old and shabby. Josephine stood in the doorway of the bedroom, already dressed, in her favorite blue voile, her hair neatly pinned up and waved in the front. "What's taking you so long, Faby? We don't want to be late."

"I can't decide what to wear."

Josephine entered the room and joined Faby in front of the open closet. "We're just going to a show, Faby. Wear your good dress."

Faby reached into the closet, pulled out her good dress, and held it against herself. "It's too long. They're wearing them shorter this year." She shoved the dress back into the closet.

"What about your green?"

"I wore that last year."

"For goodness sake, Faby, nobody's going to remember what you wore last year!" Josephine reached into the closet, pulled out a dress, and thrust it at Faby. "Here, wear the yellow. It looks good with your hair."

Faby slipped the dress over her head, and Josephine buttoned the back for her. "Do I have time to put a little polish on my shoes, Josephine? They're scuffed."

"No, you don't. Let's go."

"My hair!"

Josephine crossed the room to Faby's dresser and picked up her hairbrush. "Stand still." She ran the brush through Faby's hair, rubbed a spot of pomade between her hands, and smoothed her palms over Faby's dark cap of hair. "There, you're all set. I swear, Faby, sometimes you are just the silliest old thing."

Faby checked her hair in the mirror above the dresser for spite, catching Josephine's eye and making a face, before racing out of the room and clattering down the stairs, laughing, Josephine fast on her heels. Just as she was about to dash out the front door, tossing a breezy good-bye over her shoulder as the door closed behind her, she thought better of it and ran into the kitchen to tell Maman they were leaving, Josephine now two steps ahead of her.

Maman was at the sink washing the last of the supper dishes, while Maman Aurore sat in her rocker by the window knitting a sock. "Where do you two think you're going?" she said, looking up from her knitting as the girls entered the kitchen.

"To see the vaudeville show, Mémère," Josephine said.

"You're not going to any vaudeville show, either one of you. It's vulgar. Grown men telling dirty jokes for a living." Maman Aurore addressed her next remark to Maman's back. "How can you let those two young girls expose themselves to such vulgarity?" She continued to knit without looking down at her work, still addressing Maman's back. "You are just letting them run wild, Yvette. I don't know why you ever let Faby cut her hair."

"I decided on my own, Mémère," Faby said. "And my hair has nothing to do with going to a show."

"Don't be disrespectful to your grandmother," Maman said. She turned from the sink and wiped her hands on a dishtowel. "It's just harmless fun, Maman Aurore. Families take their children. Joseph and I have taken the girls ourselves, if you'll remember."

"Every year since I was seven, if you'll remember," Faby added, turning her head to avoid the disapproving look Maman shot in her direction.

"Young ladies should be accompanied when they go out in public." Maman Aurore's needles stopped clicking. "Perhaps I should go with them. To chaperone."

Faby glared at her grandmother, then quickly looked away before Maman Aurore could tell what she was thinking. *Meddlesome old biddy, suggesting that she spoil our evening out by going with us as chaperone, to sit in her rocking chair by the stage in front of everyone, knitting and carping about the performance: can't carry a tune, dances with two left feet, talks too fast, juggles too slow, far too old for ruffles and bows.*

"You don't need to do that, Maman Aurore," Maman said, taking a clean dishtowel out of a drawer and drying the last spots of water off a plate. "Faby is a grown woman after all."

"Nineteen years old is not grown," Maman Aurore sniffed.

Just then Josephine slipped out of the room. When she returned, she held a wrinkled program in her hand, declaring as she crossed the room to her grandmother's chair, "Lois Benoit gave me a program from the matinee. See, there is nothing vulgar in the show at all. I'll show you." She stood at Maman Aurore's elbow and began reading the program: "'Amazing Animals, featuring an acrobatic, well-dressed, fiddling baboon, a rope-jumping dog, and an ornery donkey and their trainers—'"

"A fiddling baboon, you say? A fiddling baboon? Why would a baboon want to play the fiddle?"

Josephine ignored that remark and continued reading, "'Ota Gygi, Court Violinist to the King of Spain'. The king of Spain, Mémère!"

"And I suppose the King of Spain taught the baboon to play the fiddle."

Just as Faby was about to shout at the old woman, Maman put the last plate away in the cupboard and made a shooing motion with her dishtowel. "Go on, now, girls, you don't want to be late. See that you come straight home afterward. Your father will be waiting up."

When they had gotten far enough down the street to be out of sight of the house, Faby turned to Josephine and said, "I can't believe they're letting us go alone." She half expected to hear their father's voice behind them telling them to return home immediately, with Maman Aurore's voice the chorus of reasons why.

"Why not?" Josephine said. "You're a grown woman after all."

Faby looked sharply at her sister to see if she was making fun of her, but Josephine's face, softly framed by her neatly waved hair, looked perfectly sincere. Faby almost responded, *I don't feel like a grown woman*, but stopped herself from saying it. She was the elder sister, after all, and there was nothing left for her to do but become a grown woman, particularly now that Josephine was graduated from high school, with plans to marry Leonard Paradis.

They reached the Opera House fifteen minutes before the show was to start, and Faby slowed her pace to take in the building's full effect. The Opera House was by far the grandest building in Enosburg, built by Dr. B.J. Kendall with Spavin Cure money in the 1890s—not so much in its ornamentation, which was simple, consisting of a dormered turret rising above the roofline and a series of large leaded glass windows across the front, but in its large proportions, made seemingly all the larger by narrow clapboards. The double doors through which Faby and Josephine entered seemed disproportionately small, the lobby also disproportionately small, the ceiling low, the ticket office barely two steps from the entrance.

Faby and Josephine handed over their tickets to Helen LaPierre, whose hair that evening appeared to have gotten on the wrong side of a henna rinse and a permanent wave. Faby couldn't help staring at it as Helen made a point of asking where their parents were—and she was just as glad that Josephine answered, "They're enjoying a quiet evening at home with our grandmother." Coming from Josephine, the response was polite. The same response coming from Faby would have been "fresh" and prompted an indignant telephone call from Helen LaPierre to their father the following day.

Leaving Helen LaPierre to make unpleasant remarks to the patrons behind them, they walked up the stairs to take their seats, the best seats in the house, Faby knew from previous years, in J-row, on the right, next to the aisle, not too far forward to spoil the illusion of the show but close enough to see well.

Settling into her seat, Faby tilted her head back to look up at the ceiling, a vast expanse of pale blue plaster set off by dark painted beams leading to a central painted medallion, from which hung a magnificent chandelier. The chandelier, as large as it was, with three descending layers of illumination, still seemed far too small for the great height of the ceiling.

Looking down from the ceiling toward the stage, Faby hoped to see that the curtain had parted; however, it still hung in its customary dusty folds. Although it was still too early for the show to begin, Faby knew that by leaning forward slightly, she could hear the sounds of preparations backstage: scenery being moved into position, props placed, urgent instructions whispered. If she leaned forward just a little more, she could also hear, from somewhere beneath her feet in the dressing rooms, those preparations as well, costumes donned, makeup applied, a singer warming up, a husband and wife team's kiss for good luck.

Shifting in her seat again, Faby looked around to see if any of the kids from school had come to see the show, but she didn't see any of them. She twisted around to look behind her. As she turned to face the front again, Josephine leaned over and whispered, "Will you sit *still*, Faby? You're fidgeting worse than a child."

Faby whispered back, "Sorry, Josephine," then, "I can't bear this waiting. What if the show doesn't start on time?"

"For goodness sake, Faby, have you ever known it not to start on time?"

Just then Faby's attention was diverted by a movement on the stage. Quickly turning to look, she saw that a short man in a checked suit had slipped out from the wings to position the easel on which the placards announcing each act would be placed. Faby leaned over and whispered to Josephine, "Finally!" and Josephine put her finger to her lips.

When Faby looked back to the stage, she saw that the easel wasn't positioned correctly. It was angled too far to the right: some of the people sitting on the left side of the aisle wouldn't be able to see the placards. Still fiddling with the legs of the easel, the man in the checked suit had not yet left the stage. Faby waited for him to look up momentarily, and when he did, she caught his eye and motioned for him to turn the easel. He paused, quizzical, then raised his hand slightly in a gesture of waving. Faby shook her head and again pantomimed that he should turn the easel to the left. After he made the adjustment, he pantomimed back to Faby—*Is it right now?*—and she nodded *yes*.

As the man in the checked suit slipped back into the wings, Faby couldn't help but think that she had averted certain disaster. It wouldn't matter how brilliantly an act performed, what benefit would it gain them if some in the audience didn't know what they were called? She was about to lean over to Josephine and tell her so, when the man in the checked suit placed the placard announcing the opening act on the easel: The Incredible Mulhaneys, Acrobatic Act.

The curtain parted, the orchestra began to play, and the Incredible Mulhaneys somersaulted onto the stage, all ten of them, one after the other, an assembly line of thin, rubber-jointed bodies, all topped with the same head of shocking red hair. The show had begun.

Faby watched the show as though she had never seen anything like it before—holding her breath for fear the smallest Mulhaney would plunge from his perch atop the pyramid of Mulhaneys to crack his head on the floor—struggling to swallow past the lump in her throat as the sweet strains of Ota Gygi's violin swept over her—laughing until the tears came at Hutchison & James's "Swell Meets Bum," as though she had not seen Hennessey & Fyne do the same sketch last year—marveling, truly marveling, at the fiddling baboon, Brownstone, whom she *would* describe to Maman Aurore, whether the old woman liked it or not.

In the end, it was the act following intermission that Faby was most captivated by. The performer was billed as Slim White, America's Favorite Hoofer—an apt description Faby thought at first—that by the time he shim-shammed off the stage to lively applause simply could not do him justice, "favorite" far too insipid a word to describe him, as though his talent for winning over an audience were on a par with the color blue or a well-worn sweater.

As soon as he bounded onto the stage, Faby could not take her eyes off him. She had never before seen anyone so tall and thin, with arms and legs longer than any she'd ever seen, yet completely coordinated. Nor had she ever seen a man as blond.

Slim White seemed to hold just the right proportions for the Opera House stage, as though he belonged there, as though the stage were his living room and the audience his neighbors, peering through the windows of his house as he did an elaborate riffle-timestep through his front door and, with a quick flick of his wrist, tossed his hat onto the coat rack, his overcoat following close behind, then travel-stepped through the living room and into the kitchen to prepare his supper, waltz-rolling from ice box to pantry to cutting board to stove, wielding a chopping knife with the panache of a swordsman, sautéing and stirring in two pans at once, both hands playing counterpoint to his feet, then double-timestepping from the kitchen to the dining room, his plate of food balanced on the fingertips of one hand, conveying each bite of food to his mouth with a flourish, signaling the end of his meal with his fork and knife executing a rim shot on his plate.

When the house lights came back up after the last act, Faby looked at Josephine and declared, "That was the best show yet, don't you think? I can't wait to see what they have next year!"

Josephine nodded and said, "You know, Faby, I think this year you may be right." She then stood up from her seat and nudged Faby to stand. "People are trying to get past us."

Faby stood up and stepped into the aisle to let the rest of the people in the row pass. As Josephine began following the crowd down the aisle toward the stairs, Faby reentered J-row and headed toward the side exit. Before she had gotten halfway down the row, she heard Josephine calling her. "Where are you going, Faby?"

Faby paused and turned to find that Josephine had re-traced her steps and was now right behind her.

"Where are you *going?*" Josephine repeated.

Faby pointed. "I'm going to wait for the performers when they come out so I can tell them how much I liked the show. They're staying at the Quincy, so they're bound to come out by the side door. And nothing else in town is open, so they have nowhere to go but the Quincy. Do you think maybe they would autograph our programs? Oh, that would be really something if we could get some autographs or even if we could get just one autograph. I would be satisfied with one autograph, wouldn't you?"

"Of course I should like an autograph on my program, but we need to go home. Papa is waiting up for us." Josephine turned around and walked back into the aisle. After hesitating a moment or two, Faby followed her. There was always next year to try for an autograph.

As they reached the lobby, Faby glanced at the box office and was surprised to see that Helen LaPierre and her startling hair were still there. When they were outside on the walk, she said to Josephine, "Did you see Helen LaPierre? She was still in the box office. Didn't she watch the show? Do you think she really stayed in the box office the whole time, watching the front door? Was she so worried that someone might try to get in without buying a ticket that she didn't watch the show? How could she miss the show?"

"Maybe she saw the matinee," Josephine said.

"Maybe, but still, the evening performance is always better than the matinee. Everybody knows that."

As they headed down Depot Street for home, Faby couldn't stop talking, she was so excited. She was practically skipping, she was so excited, twirling around to walk backwards, balancing on the curbstone with her arms out, jumping off, jumping back on, so it was several minutes before she realized that there were footsteps behind them. Josephine had already stopped walking and was motioning for her to be still. The footsteps behind them also stopped. Faby wondered which immature young man of her or Josephine's acquaintance might find it amusing to follow them, hide behind a tree, then leap out, and shout, "Boo!" There were so many immature young men of her acquaintance, and Josephine's, too—Peter Delorme, Sylvester Erno, David Irish, Johnny Leach—that she was at a loss to think which one of them it might be.

Josephine had resumed walking, and Faby skipped a step to catch up with her. It wasn't long before she heard the footsteps again. She was about to whisper to Josephine, *What should we do?* when Josephine stepped off the sidewalk and ducked behind a tree, motioning for Faby to follow her.

The footsteps continued until Faby could just make out a man advancing toward them. He was very tall, well over six feet, lanky, and walked with both hands in the pockets of his newly-fashionable baggy trousers. His blond hair was swept up into the most extravagant pompadour Faby had ever seen. Recognizing him now, she poked Josephine in the ribs and hissed in her ear, "That's Slim White! From the show! That's Slim White!"

Slim White stopped in front of the tree where they were hiding and lit a cigarette. "You can come out from behind that tree, girls. I can hear you giggling."

Faby stumbled out from behind the tree, bent nearly double with laughing, just managing to get enough breath to gasp, "Why are you following us?"

"Who else would I follow if not the prettiest two girls to come to the show tonight? Are you sisters?"

At that, Josephine stepped out from behind the tree, grabbed Faby's hand, and started walking. "Yes, we're sisters, and we're on our way home. We live just a couple of doors down."

Without thinking, Faby blurted out a correction to Josephine's fib. "Well, not just a couple of doors down. We live all the way at the end of the street."

"Our father is waiting up for us," Josephine said, squeezing Faby's hand hard enough to hurt.

"Well, then, I guess I'd better see you girls right home, hadn't I?" Slim White said, flicking his cigarette into the street and stepping between the two girls to tuck a hand under each of his arms, Faby so shocked at the feel of smooth fabric under her hand—and the solidity of an arm—that she let out a small gasp.

She couldn't believe that Slim White had sought her out and was actually talking to her. She wanted to ask him what it was like being in the vaudeville show, what it was really like being up there on the stage—but she wasn't sure if she should. People must ask him that all the time to the point of being a nuisance, like a child forever asking *why*? He might even consider it rude, like asking someone how much money he made. But when would she get another chance to ask an actual vaudeville player what it was like to perform? Never, that's when. And if she looked foolish, so what? She would never see Slim White again, unless he happened to be in the lineup next year when the show came through town—which was unlikely—so what did she have to lose?

She took a deep breath, tilted her head back to look up at Slim White as they walked, and asked him her question: "What's it like being in the vaudeville show?" When he looked down at her with apparent interest on his face, she took another breath and continued, "I've tried to imagine it so many times, what it must be like. What's it like to be up there on the stage?"

Slim White thought a moment, seeming to consider the question carefully before he spoke, seeming to know that for Faby the question was not an idle one. "Well, you know, when you're in a boffo show, there is no better feeling in this life than hearing that applause—no better feeling in the next life either, I'd wager. But then some night you'll find yourself playing to the morgue, and even though you've got the same line of patter as the night before, no matter what you do, what new business you add, you just walk off cold. And when that happens, you start thinking maybe it's time to take the veil and sell insurance for a living."

"Surely not!" Faby exclaimed. "You're so talented! You were the best act by far tonight—and I'm not just saying that!"

"Why, thank you," Slim White said, looking down at her and smiling. "Don't tell me I've got myself a fan—"

Josephine interrupted him. "Oh, we're sure you have many fans, Mr. White. Tell us, Mr. White, how do you like traveling? You must spend very little time at home."

Slim White managed to strike a pose without slowing his pace. "Yes, you might say that the theater is my home, although I don't know that I'd call the crummy dressing rooms I always seem to get much of a home. But I can't complain. Nothing beats the road for seeing the sights and meeting new people. Sure beats working for a living!"

By that time, they were just approaching their house, and Josephine pulled her hand free. "Here's our house. Our father is waiting for us."

Slim White stopped in front of the walk but kept Faby's hand tucked under his arm. Then he released Faby's hand, cocked a salute with a finger to his forehead, and sauntered down the street, Faby standing on the porch more imaging him than watching him as he walked down the darkened street, while Josephine hissed, *Come on,* from the doorway.

As soon as they entered the foyer, Josephine scolded her, "Oh, Faby, why did you do that?" but before Faby could answer her, Papa called out, "Is that you, girls?"

"Yes, Papa," Josephine called back, "it's us."

Faby started for the living room to tell Papa all about the show before he went upstairs to bed, when she felt Josephine's hand clamped on her wrist holding her back. "Don't you dare tell Papa that Slim White walked us home. Don't you *dare.*"

"Why not?" Faby said, shaking off Josephine's hand. "It's not every day we get to meet a vaudeville player." However, she acceded to her sister's wishes and made no mention of Slim White when she described the show to their father, except as one of many performers on the stage.

Chapter 4

The following day, Faby and Josephine were sitting on the front porch drinking iced tea as they recounted their favorite moments of the previous night's show when one of the older Neale boys, who washed dishes at the Quincy to earn money over the summer, sauntered up the porch steps with the smirk on his face typical for boys his age for which there was usually no good reason.

"What do *you* want?" Faby said.

His smirk approached the grotesque. "Why would I want anything from you, Faby Gauthier? Tall, skinny fellow staying at the Quincy paid me to give you this." He removed a folded piece of paper from his pants pocket, thrust it at Faby, and ran off.

"Well, I never," said Josephine.

"I wonder who it could be from," said Faby, knowing full well as she unfolded the note that the only tall, skinny fellow staying at the Quincy Hotel was the vaudevillian she had met the night before: *Meet me at the stage door after the show tonight. Slim White.*

"Slim White wants to meet me after the show tonight!" Faby passed the note to Josephine, who looked aghast.

"You're not going to do it, are you?"

"Of course I'm going to do it. I'll never get another chance to find out what it's *really* like to be in show business."

"Oh, Faby."

"Oh, ishkabibble."

Faby spent the rest of the day carefully crafting the best possible excuse for her absence late into the evening: Monopoly with the LaFlamme sisters, Monopoly being the most interminable game she could think of. She waited for Slim White by the side door of the Opera House, out of sight of the townspeople leaving by the front entrance at the end of the show. Although she was doing nothing wrong, there was no need for word to get back to her parents.

Slim White emerged from the Opera House looking freshly scrubbed. "Ah, there you are! I wasn't sure you'd come. Would you like to go for a walk, show me some of the town?"

"I'd love to!" Without hesitation, Faby took his arm and set off for Main Street.

"We had a full house tonight," Slim White said, after they had passed the IGA. "That's after a full house on opening night and at the matinee. I really expected it to be only half full, if that. In fact, when we got here, I couldn't figure out why we'd been booked for the entire week in such a small town."

"Oh, that's so all the other people will be able to see the show! The Opera House isn't anywhere near big enough to hold them all."

"What other people would those be?"

"The people from East Enosburg, West Enosburg, Enosburg Center, East Berkshire, West Berkshire, Samsonville, Bakersfield, Bordoville, Pumpkinville—"

"Oh, come on, now. You're pulling my leg."

"No, I'm not pulling your leg. The vaudeville show comes to town only once a year, so it attracts people from miles and miles around."

"I may need to punch up my act, then."

"Oh, no, you were wonderful! You shouldn't change a thing."

When they reached the Masonic Temple, Faby said, "Would you like to see Lincoln Park? Well, as much of it as you can see in the dark."

"Of course." He patted her hand resting lightly on his arm. "There's a doughboy, I see. You know, I'll bet there are enough bronze doughboys in parks across this great nation to form an army big enough to fight the war all over again . . . fountain, very nice . . . and a bandstand. You must have a town band, then."

"Oh, yes, they give a concert every Tuesday night in the summer."

"Any good?"

"Sometimes."

Slim White laughed and patted her hand. "I love a girl who can call 'em as she sees 'em."

They had reached the other side of the park and Faby said, "I'll take you back to the Quincy by way of School Street."

When she arrived home, her parents and Maman Aurore had gone to bed, but Josephine was still up, darning a stocking. "How was it? What did you do?"

Faby slipped off her shoes and lifted her dress to unhook her garters. "It was lovely. We walked to Lincoln Park."

"That's all?"

Faby nodded and slipped off her stockings.

"Oh. Well. I guess that's all right, then," Josephine said.

The next two nights, when Faby met Slim White at the stage door after the show, he was hungry, and he took her next door to the Quincy Hotel to keep him company while he ate, offering to buy her a meal, which she declined, having eaten supper at home. She knew she was in no danger of encountering anyone of her parents' acquaintance in the dining room of the Quincy Hotel, as they would consider eating out an unnecessary extravagance when they had perfectly good food to eat at home.

Faby loved listening to Slim White talk. He had done so many things in his life, and he was still a young man, not so much older than she. She asked him so many questions that more often than not he answered around a mouthful of steak or potato, yet with no loss of enunciation, so that Faby wondered if talking with a mouth full of food had been part of his stage training. After he finished his meal, he walked her home, asking for a circuitous route to give him a chance to see more of the village.

On Friday night, after the show closed, she took him up North Main Street, the weak light from the streetlamps barely illuminating their path, the branches of the maple trees that overhung the sidewalk so thick with leaves that little moonlight penetrated them, Faby feeling for the first time since she'd met him a little nervous to be walking alone at night with a man she didn't really know, so close to the road leading out of town.

When they reached the Spavin Cure factory, Slim White paused, and Faby wondered why he had stopped walking. He gestured expansively toward the building with both hands: "And what is this magnificent edifice?" Faby didn't answer him at first, taken aback by how he had phrased the question. While the Spavin Cure factory was certainly large, three times the size of the Opera House, with too much ornamentation for a factory—the same dormered turret rising above the roofline as the Opera House, with the addition of a large balcony over the front entrance—it could in no way be described as magnificent. It looked more like the place where Franklin County's indigent and infirm should be housed, along with the orphans, wayward girls, delinquent boys, and those who were not deranged enough to be sent to the state hospital in Waterbury but still too peculiar to live amongst others in the village.

"The Spavin Cure factory." The words sounded odd as Faby spoke them aloud.

"I can see that: Kendall's Spavin Cure. Is spavin some kind of disease that needs curing?"

"Sort of. Spavin Cure is a liniment for lame horses."

"Horse liniment." Slim White put his hands in his pockets and rocked back on his heels. "Well, how about that? I don't think I've seen any horses since I came to town. Is there much call for this stuff?"

Faby shook her head. "No. Not anymore."

They resumed walking. Now that Slim White was leaving town with the show the next day, Faby felt compelled to ask him the same question she'd asked him the first night they met, when he'd found her and Josephine giggling behind a tree: "What's it like being in the vaudeville show? What's it like being up there on the stage?"

Slim White stopped to light a cigarette, striking the match on the heel of his shoe. "You know, Faby, I've never had a regular job like other fellows." He snapped his wrist to put the match out and dropped it on the sidewalk. "I enlisted in the Army the day after I graduated from high school, shipped out to France two months after that. When the war ended, one of my buddies got me a job with the Shitty—pardon my French, *Sheedy* circuit—one of my buddies got me a job with the Sheedy circuit, and I've managed to stay employed ever since. I'm versatile, you see. I can dance like a house afire—tap, as you know, soft-shoe of course, although I prefer tap—it's the *sound* of fancy footwork that wows an audience. I have all the popular dances down pat just before they catch on—and I am a wonderfully graceful ballroom dancer—or so I'm told. I can play the comic or the straight man. I can do a patter act.

I can sing, play the banjo and the ukulele, the guitar, too, if someone else is playing over me. If I had to sit at a desk in an office for eight hours a day, I don't know how I'd ever stand it. I don't know how other fellows do it."

So, he had answered her question both times, honestly, she believed, thoughtfully, but she couldn't imagine what it must be like for him, or, more to the point, what it must be like for the women who were fortunate enough to be on the circuit, although she asked him about them, too. "Just imagine," he said, "folks clapping their hands and stomping their feet for you because you're such a doll, no matter how bad your singing is—or, imagine it the other way 'round, folks clapping their hands and stomping their feet for your beautiful singing, no matter how much of a Bug-Eyed Betty you are."

Chapter 5

The day after the vaudeville show left town was the Fourth of July, the annual parade a decidedly anticlimactic ending to the week: shuffling old veterans who should have been kept at home in the shade, wheezing Souza marches, farmers' wagons festooned with limp crepe paper streamers, Goofy Dolan dressed as Uncle Sam, and, inexplicably, a single Holstein clopping along with bunting draped over her back, led by a small boy also draped in bunting. As Faby stood on Main Street with her family watching the parade, she thought she saw Slim White in the crowd across the street, but as soon as she recognized him, she knew she had to be mistaken.

After the parade was over, the entire village trooped over to the ball field at the high school to eat barbecued chicken and limp coleslaw in the blazing sun. Faby and Josephine were lucky enough to overhear Chris Geraw at the table behind them making plans to take a group of kids swimming at Kidder's, and they invited themselves along. Nine kids ended up crammed into the small roadster, sitting on each other's laps and hanging over the sides, but nobody cared; swimming at Kidder's was worth the discomfort of getting themselves there.

After they'd returned home from swimming and eaten supper, Faby's mood had improved to the point of her agreeing to go with Josephine to listen to the band concert. There would be more Souza marches. Some old duffer would attempt to sing "America the Beautiful" through ill-fitting dentures as the microphone crackled and moaned. Then would come the inevitable polkas and worn-out ballads from the 1890s. However, Faby felt so relaxed from swimming all afternoon, her limbs lightened, her skin refreshed, she would listen to it all without a thought of complaint in her head.

No sooner had the band started to play the first number, than Faby felt a presence behind her and someone said, "May I join you ladies?"

Faby turned around, and there was Slim White, big as life, wearing a straw boater with a red, white, and blue band, which had obviously come out of a prop trunk.

"I thought you'd left town!"

Slim White lowered himself to the grass. "Overslept and missed my train, actually. Whoever heard of a train leaving the station *before* its scheduled time?"

"It happens all the time," Faby said. "When there's no one left in the depot, the conductor sees no point in waiting around, so he signals the engineer, and they leave."

"I suppose there's a certain balled up logic to that, although it would never pass in the city. Try that in Boston, and the station master would have a riot on his hands."

"You could have taken the afternoon train," Josephine said.

"Nah, I figured I may as well stay for the festivities. I hadn't seen a Fourth of July parade since I was discharged from the Army."

"I *thought* I saw you!" Faby exclaimed.

"You did? Why didn't you wave or do something to catch my attention?"

Before Faby could respond, Josephine said, "What did you think of the parade, Mr. White?"

"I enjoyed it. Very small-town. Although I didn't quite get the cow."

At that point, the band stopped playing, and there was a long pause as Sterling Judd slowly got to his feet, carefully set his cornet on his chair, and shuffled over to the microphone to launch a quavering rendition of "America the Beautiful," the sound of which appeared to stun Slim White into silence.

He found his voice again when the polkas started. "I once saw an act get booed off the stage for playing polkas with ten accordions. Billed themselves as 'Calvin's Accordion Cavalcade.' You never heard such a godawful racket in your life. They were so bad, people *backstage* were booing 'em."

"I don't understand," Faby said. "How could they be in a show if they weren't any good?"

Slim White laughed. "You're kidding me, right? You don't actually believe that an act has to be good to be booked for a show, do you?"

"Well, yes."

He reached over and squeezed her hand. "That's so sweet! If every audience could be like you, no player would ever be handed back his pictures, and everything would be jake for small-timers everywhere."

Faby smiled to herself at the thought of her enjoyment, her own enjoyment, giving people with big dreams and little talent employment and some measure of satisfaction.

When the band concert ended, to scattered applause and tooting car horns, Josephine scrambled to her feet and put out her hand to help Faby up. "We'd best be getting home. Our parents are expecting us."

Slim White looked at his watch. "It's only ten o'clock. Could I interest you in one last walk with me, Faby, to say good-bye?"

Josephine clamped her hand on Faby's wrist, Faby jerking at the unexpected gesture. "We need to be getting home, Faby."

"I'd like to go. We won't be gone long, will we, Slim? Please, Josephine? Make an excuse for me? I won't be long. I promise."

Josephine shook her head and turned to walk home by herself. Faby turned to Slim White. "Where would you like to go? I haven't taken you to Orchard Street yet."

"Actually, I've borrowed a car. I'd like to see a little of the countryside before I leave Vermont." He began walking, leading her to a Packard parked in front of the Masonic temple. Even in the weak light of the streetlamp, Faby recognized it immediately as belonging to the owner of the Quincy Hotel. It was the only Packard in town. She wondered how Slim White could possibly have talked Marvin Foote into loaning him his car. No one else ever drove Marvin Foote's Packard. No one. Slim White would have to have paid him.

"Oh, I don't know," she said. Strolling the village's residential neighborhoods with Slim White while most people were still up was one thing; taking a car ride with him, any kind of car ride with him, but especially a car ride with him at night, was quite another. "You're not going to be able to see much of the countryside in the dark."

Slim White gestured toward the sky. "Full moon tonight."

"Well, yes, but still—"

"Have you ever been for a drive under a full moon?"

Faby shook her head. "My father doesn't own a car. We take the train if we need to go out of town. If it's just in the village, we walk."

"So what do you say? I'll tell you more about the circuit. I'll tell you anything you want to know."

She hesitated, trying to decide if she wanted to offer an excuse, then said, "All right. I guess it will be all right."

43

As Slim White opened the passenger side door and helped her into her seat, Faby couldn't help but be impressed by the Packard's lavish interior: plush wool upholstery, carpeted floorboards, a shining wood dash set with gauges. When Slim White got himself settled into his seat and the car started, he tapped the gas gauge with his finger. "Full tank."

He headed up North Main Street, past the overhanging maples and the Spavin Cure Factory, out of town. As they left the familiar houses of the village behind and the scenery outside the car changed to the cleared farmland that surrounded the village on all sides, Faby could see that what he had said about the moon earlier was true. There was a full moon that night, a glorious full moon—but at the same time, there was something about it that didn't seem right. It was too large, too bright, too perfectly round, its cold luminescence spread too uniformly over the open fields and meadows that lay before them. The moon looked somehow out of place, as though it belonged in a different sky, not the sky under which she and Slim White were riding in a borrowed Packard.

They rode without speaking for several minutes, Faby knowing that he would break the silence soon enough but her own head as empty of small talk as if it had been tapped and drained. She watched his profile as he drove, surprised, in a way, that he kept both hands on the steering wheel.

When he spoke, it was to remark on the moon. "See what I mean? Isn't that the most glorious full moon you've ever seen?"

Faby hesitated before she answered him. "The most glorious? I suppose so. I've never seen any other moon but the one over Enosburg." As soon as she finished speaking, she wondered why she couldn't have just told him yes. She could have told him yes. She wanted to tell him yes—*yes, yes, yes, it's the most glorious moon I've ever seen or could ever hope to see.*

"You know what I've seen in the sky that is like nothing else?"

Faby shook her head without looking to see if he was looking at her or the road ahead.

"Lightning in the Florida Keys. In Key West, the horizon is so far away you can see lightning without hearing the thunder. It's the strangest thing. You see the lightning flicker and flash through the clouds, and you wait for the thunder because you know it's going to happen, because it's *supposed* to happen. You even wince a little as though you do hear it. But the thunder never comes, just more lightning."

Maybe that's where this moon belongs, Faby thought, in that strange Florida sky with the silent lightning.

"I think that's about the strangest thing I've ever seen as far as the sky is concerned," Slim White continued. "I run into a lot of strange people, naturally, in my line of work. People don't go into show business if they're happy being normal."

"I never thought of it that way."

"It's a fact."

Faby continued to look straight ahead as Slim White drove them farther and farther from the village, only turning to look at him when he slowed down and turned onto West Berkshire Road as if he had been on it before and knew where it led. Before she could ask him, he said, "I thought I'd see where this one leads."

She had no answer for that as he stepped on the gas again, pebbles and stones from the unpaved road soon making a racket against the undercarriage and fenders of the Packard.

"I'd better slow down," he said, easing up on the gas. "It wouldn't do for me to bring this splendid machine back to town with the paint all chipped."

The Packard continued to slow until it coasted to a stop by the side of the road. Faby looked out the window to see where they had stopped. From what she could see, if she were to open the door and step down, it would be into a tangle of weeds under a fallen barbed wire fence, solid ground an indeterminate distance beneath them. She turned to Slim White. He shut off the engine.

"We're not out of gas," he said. "I just wanted a chance to sit quietly and talk before we turn around and head back to town."

"Oh." She felt for the door handle with her right hand, curling her fingers around its curved surface; it felt small and flimsy in her hand, certainly not strong enough to open the door. She knew that if she attempted to move the handle it would snap off in her hand, and she would have no way out of the Packard, no way back from West Berkshire Road. She pulled her hand back and let it rest in her lap.

Louis turned slightly to face her. "You know, I'm so glad I met you."

Faby felt her face flush in the dark, and she moved her hand back to the door handle. "You are? Why?"

"Well, even though we've only known each other a few days, I think you're interested in me, genuinely interested in me. Not just as Slim White, but as Louis Kittell."

"Louis Kittell?"

"Yes."

"That's your name?"

"Yes. I didn't tell you my name? I must have told you my name. Slim White is a stage name."

"Oh. I thought 'Slim' was your nickname because you're tall and thin. But I thought your last name was really 'White'."

"Uh uh. Matter of fact, most of us on the circuit have stage names. When most folks name their infants, they don't try to come up with something catchy in case the kid decides to go into show business some day. They just name 'em after some relative or whatever name happens to be popular at the time."

"I never thought of it that way. But I guess I wouldn't have since I've never been involved in naming anyone."

Louis responded with a soft chuckle, although Faby saw no humor in what she had said.

Slim White's—Louis's—hands were now off the steering wheel, one resting on his thigh, the other resting on the back of the seat. Faby wasn't sure whether she wanted Louis's hand to inch its way over to her or not. She supposed not, although she supposed that it probably would.

What she really wanted at that moment was to ask him once more, *What's it like being in the vaudeville show? Can you tell me what it's really like? How do the stage boards feel under your feet? Do the footlights bother your eyes? Is it hot inside your costume? Can you move as freely as you do in your own clothes?*

Louis's hand had reached her shoulder. When he rubbed his fingers against her neck, she turned her head to look at his face. It seemed the same face she had grown accustomed to in the short time since she'd met him, nothing changed from his touching her, no narrowing of the eyes or twisting of the mouth, just his agreeable features and pleasant smile, the look on his face as though he were humming a song inside his head.

He leaned in to kiss her, and she closed her eyes. *What's it like to emerge from the darkness of the wings into the sudden light of the stage? Do you ever get stage fright?*

Louis continued to kiss her, slipping his tongue into her mouth and pulling her closer. *Do you get tired of saying the same lines every night? Dancing the same steps? Singing the same songs?*

When she felt his hand on her bare breast, she opened her eyes and pulled away. How had he gotten to it so quickly through the intricate workings of her clothes? Hadn't she been paying attention? "I'd better be getting home."

Louis's amiable expression still hadn't changed. "Sorry. I guess I was moving a little fast there." He looked at the luminescent dial of his watch. "It's still only eleven-thirty. Could we talk for a few minutes more before we head back? I don't know when I'll see you again . . . you know I'll write."

"You will?"

"I'll write you every week until the show comes back next year. Every week. I'll tell you about my adventures on the road. Do you know, I met Harry Houdini once? In a restaurant in New Jersey. He was sitting at the table right next to mine, eating spaghetti and meatballs. He was gracious enough to autograph a menu for me. I snuck it out under my coat."

Harry Houdini! Imagine that. "Do you still have it, the menu with Harry Houdini's autograph?"

"Of course. You don't think I'd lose something like that, do you? It's at my mother's. She keeps a trunk of mementoes for me." His fingers were brushing the side of her neck again. "Now, I'll bet that's something you'd like to see."

"Yes, I would. Very much. My family's mementoes wouldn't even fill a shoebox, much less a trunk."

Louis reached into the inside pocket of his jacket and extracted an envelope and a pencil stub. He handed the pencil stub to Faby and placed the envelope face down on his knee. "Here, you write down your address for me." Faby wrote her address, and Louis replaced the envelope and pencil in his pocket. "There. Now I can write you when I get to my next jump."

He cupped his hand around the back of her neck, and she felt her muscles relax under its warmth. Louis would write interesting letters, she was sure of it. She would have to work hard to make her letters keep his interest. Her life was as mundane as living with two parents, a sister, and a meddlesome grandmother could be, but she was sure she'd be able to be interesting if she were answering a letter from him. She felt Louis's lips brush her cheek, then brush her cheek again as he moved toward her mouth. As he kissed her, his hands didn't go inside her clothes or even on top of them. He unbuttoned his shirt with one hand and held Faby's hand with the other. When he had enough buttons undone, he tucked Faby's hand inside his shirt, gently flattening her palm against his chest, his hand still cradling hers. He wasn't wearing an undershirt, and his skin under her hand felt very warm. As he slowly moved her hand, she found that his chest was covered over with fine swirls of hair. He moved her hand down over his stomach, and the skin became smoother, the hair a single line disappearing into the waistband of his trousers. He unbuckled his belt himself, still keeping Faby's hand under his. He slid her hand down, down into a curly nest of coarse hair while his mouth stayed soft and wet on hers, guiding her hand down further still to touch flesh so stiff and unyielding it didn't seem to be part of him. Now his hands were inside her clothes, pulling her dress up and her drawers down. He maneuvered her onto her back, taking off his jacket and rolling it into a makeshift pillow that he placed under her head, all the while keeping his mouth on hers. She knew she could never say no now, and she wondered if it would hurt. Louis used his hand to guide himself inside her, and she felt pain only as a momentary pinch before he began a gentle rocking movement that ended with a shudder and a sigh.

He held his weight off her for the moment or two it took him to catch his breath. Then he sat up, zipped his trousers, and buckled his belt. Reaching to his left, he pulled the car door closed; at some point, he must have opened it. Faby lay sprawled on the seat as he had left her, unsure what she was supposed to do next. "Hand me my jacket, would you, doll?" Louis said, extending his arm. "I need a smoke." Faby pulled the jacket from where it had become crushed beneath her and handed it to him as she struggled to sit up. Louis's hand burrowed into the inside pocket of the crumpled jacket and extracted what looked like a silver cigarette case. Flipping open the lid, he asked her if she wanted one, and when she told him that she didn't smoke, he took one for himself, inserted it in the corner of his mouth, and shrugged his arms into his jacket. As Faby straightened her clothes, Louis helped her with buttons and hooks and, after first using it himself, loaned her his comb. She hesitated to use it at first, repulsed by the sticky brilliantine caught in its teeth, but then she thought the brilliantine could help tame the wild mess she knew her hair had become.

When she had her clothes straight and her hair combed, Louis lit the cigarette in his mouth and started the car. "I suppose it's time to head back. You can't stay longer?"

Faby shook her head.

"All right, then." Louis maneuvered the Packard back onto the road, Faby surprised that the car hadn't become ensnared in weeds and barbed wire in the time it had been parked by the side of the road, unable to stop herself from looking back to see if they were dragging tendrils of weeds or strands of barbed wire behind them.

As they drove back to the village the way they had come, for the first time since she'd met him, Faby had no certainty that Louis would break the silence between them with small talk, and he didn't.

When they pulled up to her house, Louis left the engine running, put it in neutral, and opened his door. "Let me get your door for you." He loped around the front of the car, opened Faby's door, and helped her out. "There you go." He offered her his arm. "I'll walk you to the door, and then I'm off." At the door, he kissed her lightly on the lips, and then he was gone.

Chapter 6

The next morning, when Faby awoke, she was alone in the bedroom. Josephine's bed was made, and the room was filled with sunlight strong and steady enough to hold dust motes along the entire length of its shafts. She could hear no sound of breakfast preparations, and the clock on the nightstand read 10:15. She had overslept, and for the first time ever, the family had left for Mass without her.

As she lay in bed watching the curtains rise and fall with the warm summer breeze through the open windows, Faby felt as if she had forgotten something, something important, but troubling, something she could ill afford to forget. A bird chirruped loudly, as if to jog her memory. Was it something she needed to do? Something she needed to tell someone? If she lay in bed much longer, the bedroom would become hot; it was already beginning to get stuffy, and she fell back asleep, only to be awakened a few minutes later by an urgent need to use the toilet.

As she sat on the toilet, she became aware of a peculiar smell that seemed to be coming from between her legs, slightly unpleasant and completely unfamiliar, almost an animal smell, like wet fur or urine. Louis. Louis Kittell. Slim White, America's Favorite Hoofer, had taken her for a ride in a borrowed

Packard, and she was not the same girl who had gotten up yesterday morning at a quarter to seven as usual, dressed in one of her everyday cotton dresses as usual, fussed with her hair as usual, until Maman Aurore, as usual, yelled up the stairs for her to come down and help her mother prepare breakfast. She was not the same girl who had left the bread on the toaster too long and, as usual, spent the next several minutes scraping blackened crumbs into the sink while Maman Aurore nattered at her for silly girl daydreaming.

Slim White had become a part of her last night, and she would never be the same again. If she were to marry—which she assumed she would, most people did—she would already have a secret to keep from her husband going into the marriage, a secret to keep from her fiancé before that, and from her beau before that. It was a secret to keep from any children she might have, but particularly her daughters. For now, though, it was a secret she would have to keep only from her family, which shouldn't be difficult because they would never expect it of her.

She went back into the bedroom and selected a dress to wear, a sleeveless blue chambray with a middy collar, her favorite for a hot summer day. After hanging the dress on the back of the bathroom door and starting her bath water, she went to the linen closet in the hall to choose the strongest perfumed soap she could find out of Maman Aurore's stockpile of soaps, bath salts, and dusting powder, all unopened in their original packaging, all given to her as Christmas and birthday gifts by people who seemed to think that getting old was just one constant battle to avoid smelling bad.

After her bath, Faby fixed herself a glass of iced tea and went out on the front porch to wait for the family to return from Mass.

Before even stepping foot on the porch, Maman Aurore was demanding to know when Faby had gotten home the night before and where she had been. Faby responded with the stock answer to that question from an adult, "Out with friends," and followed the family into the house to help with dinner.

Maman sent her to the pantry for a jar of pickles, seemingly satisfied with being given a reasonable response. Maman Aurore, on the other hand, was not. "And where were you?" the old woman demanded, grimly slicing into a loaf of bread.

"I told you, out with friends."

Maman Aurore tightened her grip on the knife. "Out where? What friends? Out with what friends where?"

Thinking that perhaps a complete sentence would stop the questions, Faby said, "After the band concert, I went to the Branch for a swim with a bunch of the kids from school."

"Not after dark, you didn't," Maman Aurore said, pointing the bread knife at Faby. "You were not at no Branch. You haven't been swimming at the Branch since you were in grade nine, and you came home with a bloodsucker on your toe screaming bloody murder until we could burn it off of you."

"Well, I *did* go to the Branch," Faby said, wishing Maman Aurore would just stop, because if Maman Aurore didn't stop, there was no way Faby would be able to stop thinking about where she had been last night and whom she had been with and what she had done—and at that moment she wanted to forget those things more than she had ever wanted anything in her life, more than a new dress, more than being asked to the senior prom, more than the vaudeville show she'd wanted to see so badly less than a week before.

Maman dropped a spoonful of butter into a bowl of riced potatoes and rapped the spoon sharply against the lip. "Never you mind about that. I'm about to serve Sunday dinner, and I don't want your father's meal to be unpleasant."

Faby flushed at the rebuke but at the same time felt a perverse sense of satisfaction that she and Maman Aurore had been chastised equally. Faby left the room to set the table in the dining room, and Josephine put down the trivets for the hot dishes. The three women put on a good face for the man of the house, and after dinner nothing more was said about Faby's late night.

When the day was over, after Faby and Josephine had washed and dried the supper dishes, they went upstairs to their bedroom and played cards, sitting cross-legged across from each other on Josephine's bed. The room was still overly warm from the hot summer day but not unbearably so. Faby had always found the stuffiness that the upstairs of the house took on at the end of a summer day somehow comforting, even soothing, as it enveloped her in a prelude to sleep.

When daylight began to fade from the room, neither sister turned on the light. Instead, as was their habit in the summer, they brushed their teeth, slipped on their nightgowns and lay down on top of the bedclothes to talk.

Josephine's voice was the first to drift into the empty space between the two beds. "You must have gotten back late from your walk."

"Did I wake you when I came in?"

"Just for a moment, but I went right back to sleep."

Faby hesitated briefly before setting her next thought free of her mind. "Slim White is not his real name."

"Well, of course it isn't."

"It's a stage name."

"Naturally. No one would name an infant 'Slim'."

"No. His name isn't 'White' either."

"Oh?"

"His real name is Louis Kittell."

"Hm, Louis Kittell. It doesn't suit him."

"No—hence the stage name." They both laughed softly, the laughter hovering briefly between the two beds before drifting out the open windows. Coming in through the windows was the high summer smell of cut grass.

"I wonder what the parents think when their child gives himself a stage name," Josephine said. "Think how hard they must try to come up with the perfect name for their baby, the disagreements between them, the hurt feelings on both sides of the family, names rejected because they're too old-fashioned, or too common, or so odd they would brand the child a misfit for life." She paused, and they both cried out in unison, "Badger Rasmussen!" turning their faces to their pillows to smother the giggles evoked by their oddly-named grade school playmate.

"Poor Badger," Faby gasped as she tried to catch her breath. "I wonder whatever happened to him."

"I don't know. I heard his parents moved to Highgate," Josephine said. "But that was years ago."

"Maybe he joined the Army, so he could go by just his last name."

"Maybe."

For the next several minutes, neither of them said anything else, and Faby was left thinking that nothing could ever make her happier than giggling with her sister in their darkened bedroom while their parents were downstairs doing whatever it was that parents did after their children went to bed. After several more minutes, Josephine's breathing became regular; she had fallen asleep.

Well, that's fine, Faby thought. *That's as it should be.* Josephine would lose no sleep over anything she had done with Leonard, which had to be nothing more than a little harmless necking before he walked her to the door: Faby was sure of it. There would be nothing more until they were married. Leonard wouldn't even try. Leonard would do nothing, *nothing,* that could possibly hurt his Josephine in any way. *And that's as it should be,* Faby thought. Josephine was a good girl, deserving of respect.

As the pent-up heat from the day gradually left the room through the open windows, the night noises coming in became louder. The modulated cheeping of crickets, as regular as synchronized metronomes, the plaintive *hoo? hoo?* of nocturnal birds, the rumble of a freight train passing through the village on its way to Canada, its whistle at the crossing that separated Main Street from North Main perfunctory at that time of night. From time to time, a cat yowled for no good reason, or a dog barked just because the other fellow did. Any of these sounds was usually enough to send Faby to sleep only moments after she heard a final murmur of thought from her sister, but not tonight. Tonight the crickets chirped *cheap, cheap, cheap, cheap,* the birds hooted *you, you, you, you,* and the train passed through the village without her.

After a time, unable to sleep, she heard her parents and her grandmother each in turn start up the stairs to go to bed, each coming to the door of the girls' bedroom and pushing it open to check on them, a habit that apparently died hard for those with children.

When they retired to their rooms, she listened to the sounds of their nightly routines as they settled themselves for sleep. Papa's sighing and shifting as he looked for a comfortable position to ease his sore shoulder. Maman's soft murmurs as she shared with Papa those thoughts that she didn't want to express in front of her mother-in-law. Maman Aurore's great grunting and groaning as she sought a comfortable position.

Faby had given up trying keeping her eyes closed. She rolled onto her side and looked at the alarm clock on the nightstand. The luminescent dial read 1:20. Would she *ever* be able to sleep again? She *should* be able to sleep. There was no good reason why she shouldn't. She had taken a hot bath, no one knew where she had been the night before, who she had been with, or what she had done, and Louis Kittell had left town, never to be seen again. It had been a mistake, that's all, a mistake of which no physical trace remained.

In the days that followed, Louis crossed her mind from time to time, but by the time he'd been gone long enough for her to wonder why he hadn't written, she had stopped thinking about him altogether.

*

Chapter 7

Faby awoke in a haze of nausea. So suddenly did it envelop her that at first she lay still, incredulous that she could come awake feeling so awful, before running down the hall to the bathroom in her bare feet, where she huddled on the linoleum next to the toilet waiting to vomit.

Saliva poured through her mouth, she retched several times, but she didn't vomit and the nausea didn't subside. Several minutes went by. Then her mother appeared in the doorway in her dressing gown, her hair still braided for sleeping. "What's the matter with you, *cher*? Are you sick?"

"I need to throw up."

"Other people have to use the bathroom. We've been waiting."

Faby closed her eyes and didn't move from her place by the toilet.

"I'll get you a basin, eh? If you have to be sick, you can use that."

Faby still didn't move from her place on the bathroom floor until Maman returned with a dented enameled basin, which she handed to Faby as she helped her up and led her back to her bedroom.

She lay back on the bed with the basin next to her, not daring to set it on the floor for fear she wouldn't be able to get to it in time, relieved that she could be in the room alone, Josephine having gotten up early to go on a Saturday outing with friends.

After a couple of hours, she began to feel better, and by noontime, she was feeling well enough to get dressed and go down to the kitchen for soda crackers and a cup of tea. By late afternoon, she felt back to normal, if a bit tired, and she ate some supper with the family, fully expecting to feel fine the next day.

The next morning, Faby was even more surprised than the day before when she woke up feeling just as sick, this time sitting on the floor by the toilet the whole time the family was at Mass, closing the bathroom door and opening the window all the way when the smell of the mutton her mother had in the oven for Sunday dinner began to creep up the stairs.

Later, after the family had eaten dinner and the mutton was safely inside the icebox, Faby got dressed and went downstairs to fix herself a cup of tea. As she passed through the living room, where her father was reading the Bible and her mother was darning socks, Maman Aurore got up from her chair and followed her into the kitchen.

As she ran water into the tea kettle, Faby turned to her grandmother, who was now in her customary rocking chair by the window, watching her. "I'm making myself a cup of tea, Mémère. Would you like me to make you one?"

"Yes," Maman Aurore nodded with a grimace. "Your mother's mutton is weighing heavy on my stomach."

Faby ran more water into the kettle and set it heavily on the stove. As she took a match from the holder and struck it on the burner, she could feel Maman Aurore eying her. Just as Faby was turning on the gas and touching the match to it, Maman Aurore spoke. "What's the matter with you, eh? Sick in the morning like that."

Startled, Faby jumped back from the stove as the burner burst on. She quickly turned down the flame. "Nothing, Mémère. I'm a little under the weather, is all."

A week later, Faby lay miserable on her bed, the dented basin by her side. Closing her eyes, she drifted off to sleep, only to wake up suddenly and vomit into the basin. When she stopped retching, she carried the basin down the hall to the bathroom to empty it into the toilet. As she was rinsing the basin, she heard her mother's voice at the bottom of the stairs. "Are you all right, Faby? Do you need me?"

"No, Maman, I'll be all right."

Faby wiped her mouth with a piece of toilet paper and sat on the edge of the bathtub until she stopped shaking, before washing her hands and returning to her bedroom with the basin. Remembering the night of the vaudeville show was no longer pleasant, as the thought of how excited she'd been as they had walked home afterward, unable to stop talking, twirling around to walk backwards, balancing on the curbstone with her arms out, jumping off, jumping back on, made her feel even sicker.

She eased herself down on the bed and lay as still as she possibly could, but it didn't help. Every movement of her body, even the slightest—turning her head, blinking her eyes—nauseated her. She closed her eyes and left them closed, but it didn't help. Even the simple, unavoidable act of breathing made vomiting seem immanent.

Another week went by, with Faby no better, waking up sick, then feeling better, only to wake up sick again. She had never been sick like this before. She was starting to feel frightened. She had never before had an illness that did not get better on its own as a matter of course. What if she had a cancer? If she had a cancer, it would not get better on its own, and she truly might die.

It got to the point where she became afraid to go to sleep, sitting up in bed with her eyes wide open, not daring to get up and prowl the house to stay awake, as Maman Aurore was a light sleeper still from nursing so many babies when she was young, and she would surely get up to find out what was the matter. But no matter how hard she tried, Faby was unable to stop herself from falling asleep—and unable to stop herself from coming awake in the morning so nauseated she wished she could die.

As the days went by, Faby gradually began feeling better sooner, particularly if she ate something bland, like soda crackers or dry toast. It took well over a month, however, before she dared trust her stomach to stay settled long enough for her to leave the house to see a doctor, first venturing overstreet to make the appointment from a public telephone. She asked the operator for the names of all the doctors in Saint Albans, then chose one with a foreign-sounding name, who wouldn't be as likely to ask questions, she thought. Even though he wouldn't know one way or the other, she gave herself a false name: Violet Sinclair, Mrs. Violet Sinclair, who lived at 134 North Elm Street. She made sure to construct a reasonably believable story for her family to explain not only her absence for an entire afternoon in the middle of the week but also her presence at the train depot when she purchased her ticket and waited for the train to arrive, should anyone of her parents'— or, more likely, her grandmother's—acquaintance see her and feel compelled to make a report. She was going to Saint Albans to see a movie at the Weldon Theatre. The Laurel and Hardy currently playing in the village held no amusement for anyone over the age of twelve, so it was only natural that she should seek out other entertainment. She would see "The Coming of Amos," which was frivolous enough for her parents to believe she was desperate to see it but not so risqué as to cause alarm.

Faustine Pothier had provided a detailed synopsis of the plot—actually more of a narrative than a synopsis; she had droned on interminably—one Saturday afternoon when she joined Faby and Josephine on the front porch to drink root beer and make snide remarks about passersby.

On the day of her appointment, Faby feigned sleep as Josephine got dressed, fixed her hair, and made her bed. Josephine had plans to go to Asletine's Dry Goods to see about a clerk's position to earn some money for her trousseau, although as yet Leonard had not popped the question. Leonard was not the sort of young man to ask his girl to marry him before he had the means to provide for her.

As Faby gnawed on a cracker and waited for the nausea to subside before getting out of bed to get dressed, it occurred to her that in all likelihood she looked too young to be Mrs. Violet Sinclair who lived at 134 North Elm Street with her lawfully-wedded husband, Mr. Edgar Sinclair. However, she could think of no way to make herself look any older, no way to make herself look anything but the age she was. From the back recesses of the closet, she found the frumpies of her dresses, a hideous, ill-fitting thing of mud-brown flannel, her best attempt at garment construction from grade ten home economics class. That, with a baggy brown cardigan buttoned over it, along with her wan face, would have to do. As she brushed her hair in front of the mirror, she noted that the outfit may not have made her look any older, but it did make her look as though she had a legitimate reason to see a doctor. Finishing with her hair, she gathered up her purse, stole down the front stairs, and slipped out the front door without a word to anyone, while Maman and Maman Aurore were occupied with punching down bread dough in the kitchen. She had the rehearsed excuse for her absence that she could deliver upon her return, if need be, but lying at the outset was simply too difficult to pull off.

After purchasing her ticket at the depot from Gardner Croft, who, true to form, asked her why she was going to Saint Albans, she felt painfully conspicuous as she waited for the train. Not only was she wearing the ugliest outfit imaginable, but sitting by herself waiting for the train was markedly out of character for her. She had never been on that train by herself—not once—and there was no one in the village who wouldn't know how out of character it was.

After arriving in Saint Albans and getting off the train, she sought out the station master and asked for directions to the street where the doctor's office was located. As the station master took the extra step of writing them down for her, the thought crossed her mind that she must look particularly young, befuddled, or pathetic, but she was grateful to have the directions in writing nonetheless. She found the doctor's office with little trouble and gave the receptionist her name, Mrs. Violet Sinclair, without her voice breaking. She hadn't thought about a wedding ring until she was undressed in the doctor's examining room and noticed her bare ring finger as she twisted her hands in her lap, waiting for him to come in and examine her. She still wore her class ring from high school, and she quickly slipped it off her right hand and onto her left, turning the signet around so that just the band showed. The doctor confirmed what she now knew, avoiding her eyes as carefully as she avoided his. "You should plan to see a doctor regularly," he said before leaving her alone to get dressed, he knowing full well that he would never see Mrs. Violet Sinclair again.

The two-hour wait for the afternoon train back to Enosburg was nearly unbearable, as the effort to keep from crying in public became more and more painful, making Faby's throat ache and her head throb. When she at last arrived home, after spending the whole ride back to the village with her face turned to the window, she came in the front door and went straight upstairs to her room because she couldn't stop the tears from spilling down her face. She couldn't bear it if Maman Aurore clamped a hand on her wrist and demanded to know where she'd been all day. She closed the bedroom door, sat on the edge of her bed, and took off her shoes and stockings. Josephine was lying on her bed reading from a book of best-loved poems. She sat up and let several minutes go by before whispering, "What are you going to do, Faby?"

Faby pulled her class ring off her left hand and set it on the nightstand. "How could I have been so foolish?" She had been saying it to herself the whole train ride home—how could I have been so foolish—*so foolish, so foolish, so foolish*—and Josephine was the only one she could say it aloud to.

Josephine closed her book without marking her place. "Do you know where he is now?"

Faby shook her head.

"Do you know how to get in touch with him?"

Faby again shook her head. "He said he'd write, but I haven't gotten any letters."

Josephine crossed her legs beneath her and leaned forward. "He didn't tell you what towns he'd be playing in? He must have mentioned some of them."

Faby looked down at her hands in her lap. "I don't think so." Her hands looked odd lying there, as though they belonged to someone else. "No, wait," she said, looking up. "He did say that he would be meeting up with another show in Boston. I remember because his mother and sister live in Bedford, and he said he was going to spend a few days with them before he joined the other show. I thought that was very considerate of him."

"Do you know where the other show was going, through what states?"

Faby looked down at her hands again and shook her head, not trusting her voice.

"Well, no matter," Josephine said briskly, like an adult. "You can send a letter to him in Bedford. You send it in care of General Delivery. The Post Master will give it to his mother, and his mother is bound to send the letter on ahead to the next town the show's scheduled to play."

"What if he doesn't check with the Post Office when he's on the road?"

"He'll check."

Faby had a terrible time writing the letter, not knowing what to say to Louis, not wanting to see the words for the condition she was in on paper, written in indelible ink by her own hand, unable now to remember the sound of his voice, barely able to remember what the man looked like. She finally wrote that she needed to speak with him right away on an urgent matter that couldn't wait.

Faby didn't hear from Louis for over a month, not until after Thanksgiving. Every time the telephone rang, the hope that it was Louis calling for her leapt into her throat. Every time the doorbell rang, she strained to hear Louis's voice asking for her, holding her breath for fear she wouldn't recognize it. She didn't know which she was more fearful of: that he hadn't picked up his mail in whatever town he was now in—or that he had received her letter and was staying away.

During that time, she tried to avoid her parents and her grandmother as much as possible, knowing that the trouble she was in showed as clearly on her face as the mark of Cain. She ate meals with her head bowed over her plate. She sat through Mass with her head bowed over her missal. She took long walks by herself, the crisp October air turning to the cold damp of November before the first snowfall, the brilliant foliage gone from the trees, burned in backyard incinerators, what leaves remained plastered to the sidewalks by the cold rain. On Saturdays, her walk included a stop at the library to return an armload of books and select an armload for the week ahead, her spending hours reading in her bedroom not at all out of the ordinary. Tuesdays and Thursdays, she stopped by Aseltine's to walk Josephine home, her sister's tales of righteous indignation at the high cost of hosiery, imperious demands for yard goods the store had never stocked, and persnickety old women selecting woolen underwear allowing her to walk through the door with a genuine smile on her face.

As the days went by with no word from Louis, Faby became increasingly frightened. If she didn't hear from him, she didn't know what she was going to do. Maman Aurore was watching her every move and hurling such knowing looks in her direction that she was afraid the old woman would make a pronouncement one night at the supper table in between bites of riced potatoes and gravy, and that would be the end of her.

She seldom went into the kitchen except to help with doing the dishes because she was still somewhat bothered by the sight of food, but early in November, on the day Maman was to put up apples for the winter, Faby decided that she would help her. Every year, Maman's older brother, Oncle Georges, would load five bushel baskets of apples into the back of his rattletrap truck and make the bone-jarring drive from his farm in Québec to deliver the apples to his sister, Faby marveling every year that there were still apples left in the baskets at the end of his trip. Oncle Georges had left this year's apples the previous day, and because they were mostly drops, they needed to be tended to right away.

It was a laborious and messy affair, what with the coring and peeling, boiling and pulping, mashing and straining, not to mention sticky apple leavings stuck everywhere, but Faby was glad for the chore, to keep her mind occupied and to show Maman that nothing was wrong. However, as she stood at the sink deftly working Maman's sharpest paring knife, she became aware that something about the sound of Maman Aurore's knitting needles was different. The clicking of her grandmother's knitting needles as she sat in her wide rocker by the window had been part of Faby's daily life for so long that it no longer registered as distinct, like the ticking of the mantle clock in the living room. But she heard the needles now, loud and deliberate, as though Maman Aurore were trying to call attention to whatever it was she was making. She had just finished casting on, and Faby noticed that the yarn was a pale green color she had never seen her grandmother use before, but she didn't pay much attention, thinking that Maman Aurore must be starting yet another pair of mittens. As the afternoon went on, however, the pale green yarn became foot-shaped. Foot-shaped and small. The hateful old woman was knitting a pair of booties.

That night, Faby had a terrible time falling asleep, the sound of Maman Aurore's knitting needles louder and louder in her head until she thought she would have to wake Josephine to see if she heard it, too. Finally, after several hours of it, Faby got out of bed and tiptoed down the stairs to the kitchen. Maman Aurore's knitting basket was in its usual place on the floor next to her rocker. The needles with the green yarn were right on top. Faby yanked out the needles and started to pull on the free end of the yarn to unravel it. The first row pulled out easily, and before too long, she had the whole thing unraveled, the green yarn cascading in kinks from her lap onto the floor. She piled it all into one messy heap on top of her grandmother's work basket, imaging her reaction when she came downstairs the next morning, to see her malicious afternoon's work in such disarray. But then Faby thought better of it: Maman Aurore would only find a way to blame Maman. Faby wound the green yarn into a tight, neat ball, which she thrust into the very bottom of the work basket, quickly snatching her hand back when her fingers touched the bottom of the basket, as if a trap were about to snap on them, realizing in that instant that she had never before gone into Maman Aurore's knitting basket, knowing even as an inquisitive child that doing so would be as foolhardy as putting her hand on a stove to see if it was hot.

Chapter 8

On Thanksgiving Day, Faby awoke feeling only momentarily nauseated, the queasiness gone by the time she awakened fully and opened her eyes. As she lay still, considering what her renewed feeling of normalcy might mean, she felt an odd sensation in her belly, a fluttering, almost a flickering, if that were possible. In the same instant, her heart started racing, and she wasn't sure whose blood she could hear pounding so loudly in her ears.

How would she ever be able to tell Maman and Papa? What would she say to them? What would they think of her? What would they say to her? She could probably hide any weight gain for a month at least, possibly two—and it appeared that she would be able to eat normally again. But of course Maman Aurore already knew, and she wasn't going to keep quiet indefinitely. Faby didn't know why the old woman had kept it to herself as long as she had. Even this morning, when her grandmother discovered that the previous day's knitting had been undone, Faby knew with certainty that Maman Aurore still wouldn't say anything. She would just make it a point to catch Faby's eye as she cast on stitches from the unraveled yarn and started the bootie all over again.

Would her parents send her away? Would they send her to stay with their only relative who lived by herself out-of-state, Maman Aurore's Tante Celeste in Maine, a thin, pitiless woman in her nineties who was not only too mean to die but too mean even for the customary infirmities of old age, still chopping wood for that black monster of a cookstove herself? Or, even worse, would they look to find some convent to send her to, to suffer an endless purgatory of praying and penance until at last her bastard child thrust himself into the world?

At Thanksgiving dinner, as Papa was saying grace, Faby thought, *I certainly have nothing to be thankful for*, wincing at the petulance in her inner voice. Cutting the slab of turkey Papa served her into small pieces that she could push around her plate when she didn't dare eat any more, she tried to imagine what being sent away would be like. First of all, there would be no familiar faces at the table when she took her meals; whether Tante Celeste or a room full of nuns, they would all look at her with the same condemnation in their eyes, as if every bite of food that she put in her mouth were going to nourish some unimaginable monster, unthinkably vile but equally unthinkable to destroy. There would be not a word exchanged among them as they grimly ate a meager meal of mashed turnips or pureed parsnips, no acknowledgement of each other's presence.

Louis finally called the next day, and Faby was startled when she took the call and found that she actually did recognize his voice. "Is it something you can tell me over the phone?" he said.

"No, I need to tell you in person."

"It's urgent, you said in your letter?"

"Yes."

"You're sure you can't tell me over the phone?"

"Yes."

"Well, all right then, I'll be there tomorrow."

"Tomorrow?"

"Yes. I'm at my mother's. In Bedford."

"Oh."

"I always spend holidays with my family." *Just like a normal person,* Faby heard Louis add, although his voice came from inside her head and not from the telephone receiver.

"You only just got my letter?"

"Oh, no, I got it a couple of weeks ago."

"But you didn't call." As soon as the words were out of her mouth, Faby regretted them. The last thing she should be doing was giving him an excuse for staying away.

"Fair enough, fair enough, I didn't. But, you know, I had to think things over." There was a slight pause on the line. "I'll be on the afternoon train tomorrow."

As Faby was wondering what she could say to ensure that Louis would come, he said, "Gotta ring off now, doll," and hung up.

Before she could get up the stairs to discuss this latest development with Josephine, Maman Aurore called out from the kitchen, where she and Maman were preparing turkey broth for soup, "Who was that, Faby? Who were you speaking with?" Faby gave her *pro forma* answer over her shoulder as she ran up the stairs, "One of my friends, Mémère!"

The next morning, as Faby brushed her hair in front of the mirror, she thought her face looked a little puffy, but she couldn't be sure and there was nothing to be done about it now even if it were. Josephine came up behind her and smoothed her hair. "When he gets here, everything will be all right. You'll see."

Two o'clock came and went with no Louis. Thinking the train might be delayed, Faby walked down to the depot, but Gardner Croft assured her that the afternoon train had gotten in on time, all of the expected passengers had gotten off without incident, and why did she want to know?

Two days later, after Faby had given up all hope, the doorbell rang, and Maman called up the stairs, "Faby, it's for you. It's Mr. White."

As Faby came down the stairs, she saw that Maman had let Louis into the house, where he stood in the front hall dressed in a respectable enough double-breasted suit with a lavender shirt, a startling patterned necktie, and a snap brim hat. He was smiling amiably, both hands in his pockets, flanked on either side by Maman and Maman Aurore, each of them with the same guarded expression on her face.

Faby felt such a rush of relief that she wanted to throw herself into Louis's arms, but she held back for fear that he would not get his hands out of his pockets in time to catch her. She waited for him to speak first, unsure how she should greet him in front of her mother and grandmother.

"Hello, Faby. It's good to see you. Mrs. Gauthier, could I please have your permission to take your lovely daughter for a walk?"

Faby was struck at how oddly sonorous his voice sounded, as though he were playing to an audience. As Maman nodded her head yes to his request, Maman Aurore arranged the strangest expression on her face, her customary disapproval now veiled by a scrim of pity.

Once outside, Louis tucked Faby's hand under his right arm and set off down the sidewalk, adjusting his pace to Faby's automatically, as though he'd been doing it all his life. Faby felt another rush of relief, but then thought better of it. He'd have to adjust his pace to anyone. He was taller than most people. She waited for him to start talking, but he didn't. He just strolled down the street with her on his arm as if he did it every day, smiling amiably, nodding agreeably when they met someone on the sidewalk. He walked on the outside, closest to the curb, which Faby remembered from some book or other was the gallant thing to do.

It wasn't until they reached Giddings Drugs that Louis began to speak, this time in the breezy tone that Faby remembered. "Sorry I haven't had a chance to write. When I signed on, I didn't expect to be doing a five-a-day. After the last show, I'm so beat I just fall into bed. Some nights I'm too tired even to eat. Do you think I've lost weight?"

Before Faby could respond, he continued, "I think I should change booking agencies. Those clowns really put one over on me this time."

Faby looked up at him, but she was so distracted by the image of an office full of clowns in rubber noses and floppy shoes conducting the business of typing contracts and shouting into telephones that she forgot what Louis had asked her. He didn't repeat the question, though, if he even remembered asking it himself.

When they reached Lincoln Park, Louis slowed his pace and led her to a bench. After they sat down, he didn't speak until Faby had turned to look at him. Then he said, "Are you in trouble?"

He asked the question as though he were asking a stranger for the time, casually, as if the answer wouldn't really matter much, regardless of what time he learned it was. Faby felt tears spring to her eyes at the same time she felt relieved that she hadn't had to think of a way to say the words herself. She nodded her head.

"I thought as much," Louis said, draping his arm across the back of the bench. He didn't say anything else, and Faby shifted her position, waiting, shivering a little inside her woolen coat, which normally kept her perfectly warm. When Louis still didn't say anything else, she said softly, "I didn't know if you'd come."

"Well, you know, Faby, the way I figure it, now's as good a time as any to settle down, and you're as good a girl to marry as any, so what the hell. Here I am."

A car puttered slowly past, Manfred Weatherbee and his wife Ida, on their way home from visiting Manfred's mother in

Sheldon, Manfred's hands locked to the steering wheel, Ida's eyes downcast.

Faby felt Louis's hand squeeze her shoulder. "Well, what do you say? Will you marry me?"

As Faby turned to face him, she felt her mouth go dry and she didn't dare speak. She felt as if she were seeing Louis for the first time, and seeing him sitting on a bench in front of Lincoln Park, facing Main Street Cemetery and The Park View Café, with no evening show at the Opera House to return to, he was just another fellow visiting from out of state, very much out of place in his natty attire.

"Yes," she said, "I'll marry you."

Louis jumped up from the bench and grabbed her hand, pulling her up after him. "Well, all right, then! Let's go tell your folks, and get this show on the road!"

Struggling to regain her balance as Louis set off at a vigorous pace, Faby almost responded, *What show?*, as she skipped a step to keep up with him, before realizing that of course he meant their marriage.

As they passed Giddings' Drugs, she thought what an odd word *marriage* was to be inside her head at that moment, a word that belonged with other people, with older people, adults, a word that really had nothing to do with her at all.

Louis was saying something. "Are you all right? You look a little pale. Do you need to sit down?"

Faby touched her hand to her head. "I think maybe I do. I'm feeling a little dizzy."

Louis turned her around with his hand at her elbow. "Sorry about that. I shouldn't have made you get up so fast." Opening the door to Giddings' Drugs, he led her to the soda foundation and helped her onto a stool. "Two Coca-Colas, that's a good fellow," he said to Lester Giddings, who was minding the soda fountain while his father counted out pills in the back of the store.

Lester took two glasses from under the counter as if he were about to toss them in the air and start juggling them, set them on the counter, and poured in Coke syrup. He then shot soda water into each glass with a perfectly-timed pull of the handle to fill it with not a drop spilled, and set the glasses down in front of them with a flourish. "There you are, two Coca-Colas."

He stood there waiting with an expectant look on his face, and Louis took out his wallet and handed him a dollar bill. However, when Lester returned from the cash register with Louis's change, Lester still stood in front of them with the same expectant look on his face. Louis reached into his pocket and passed Lester a dime. Lester said, "Thank you," but he remained standing in front of them with the expectant look on his face unchanged.

By then, Faby's dizziness had passed. She looked up at Lester and glared until he broke eye contact and moved down the counter.

Louis took a sip of his Coke and reached into his jacket pocket for his cigarette case. "What's the matter with that kid?"

"Nothing. We went to school together. He was waiting for me to introduce you."

Louis took out a cigarette, tapped it twice on the counter, and positioned it in the corner of his mouth. "Oh. I thought he was touched in the head or something, staring at us like that."

Faby bent her head to take another sip of her Coke. "No."

Louis lit his cigarette, turning his head to blow the smoke behind him. "So why didn't you?"

"Why didn't I what?"

"Why didn't you introduce me?"

"Just because we grew up in the same town and went to the same school together doesn't make Lester Giddings entitled to know all my business."

75

Louis leaned over to whisper in her ear. "I'd say you really do have something in the oven!" He tapped his cigarette on the ashtray in front of him.

Faby turned to look at him and out of nowhere felt the urge to put her hand to the back of his head and smash his nose into the ashtray. She bent her head to her Coke and waited for the urge to pass, unsure how long it would take, never having felt such an urge before in her life.

Just when the urge was about gone, Louis started talking again. "I'm not going to give you a cigar band."

Faby looked at him and frowned, unsure if she had heard him correctly.

"I'm not going to give you a cigar band," he repeated.

"What?" Her tone sounded rude, even to her own ears, and she immediately softened it. "Pardon me?"

"I didn't have time to get you a ring, but I'm not going to give you a cigar band to use when we get married. It's hokey."

"Oh." She hadn't thought about a ring.

"I'll use my signet ring." He held up his left hand. "It's fourteen-carat gold. Here, let's see how it fits you." He pulled the ring off his pinkie and held it up.

Faby looked at the ring, the monogram too elaborate to be recognizable. "We'd better be heading back. My mother will be wondering what's happened to me."

"Now, hold on a minute," Louis said, grabbing her left hand. "Let me see how it fits." He slid the ring onto her finger. "How about that? A perfect fit!"

Louis slipped the ring off Faby's finger and back onto his own. "I'll get you a nice wedding band *and* a diamond engagement ring, after I'm off this crappy circuit I got myself roped into. Those cheap bastards don't pay shit. Pardon my French. Those cheap bastards don't pay *peanuts*."

Faby smiled in spite of herself, and as they stood up to leave the store, she waved good-bye to Lester Giddings, who was just clearing away their glasses. "Come again!" Lester called as the door closed behind them.

"Feeling better?" Louis said when they were out on the sidewalk.

"A little, yes," Faby said, managing another smile without too much effort.

When they reached the house, Faby started feeling light-headed again. In front of the steps, Louis stopped her with his hands on her shoulders. "Now, I know you're nervous, so you let me do the talking, okay?"

Faby nodded her head, biting her bottom lip to keep it steady.

Inside the house, Faby hesitated on the mat. Louis leaned down and whispered to her, "Go find your mother and tell her that the two of us would like to speak with her and your father in the living room. This isn't something we should do standing in the front hall."

Maman was in the kitchen peeling potatoes for supper, while a pot of water steamed on the back of the stove and Maman Aurore stood at the stove tending to something in a cast iron skillet. Maman looked up from the potatoes as Faby entered the room. "Did you have a nice walk with Mr. White? What's he doing back in town? I thought he was traveling with the vaudeville show."

"He was, he is, he's with a different show now."

"Answer your mother's question, Faby," Maman Aurore said, pointing a turning fork at her.

"He came back to see me. He would like to speak with you and Papa in the living room."

"Now?" Maman said, not stopping her work with the potatoes, rinsing the one in her hand under the faucet and reaching for another.

"Yes. He's waiting in the front hall."

Maman wiped her hands on her apron. "I don't know why he should want to speak with us now, at the supper hour. Can't it wait? I need to speak with your father." She left the kitchen without taking off her apron.

Faby looked down at the floor as she waited for Maman Aurore to speak, trying to stop herself from flinching, but Maman Aurore remained silent, and when Faby looked up to see why, the same scrim of pity Faby had seen earlier still obscured the expression on her face.

Maman reentered the room, her hands behind her back untying her apron. "All right, Faby," she said. "Mr. White is in the living room with your father." Faby followed her mother into the living room, Maman Aurore's footsteps right behind them.

In the living room, both her father and Louis were smoking cigarettes, each of them rising as the women entered the room. Faby sat on the sofa next to Louis, and her mother and her grandmother took their positions in their customary armchairs.

Louis smiled at her mother and her grandmother and told them they were both looking well, at which they nodded without responding to the pleasantry.

Louis stubbed out his cigarette, set the ashtray on the table next to the sofa, and clasped his hands over his knees. "Mr. Gauthier, I'm here to ask for your blessing to marry Faby."

Faby looked from her father to her mother and back to her father. Both of her parents looked as shocked as if Louis had flung open their front door with no warning and burst into song. The next person to speak was Maman Aurore. "The man asked you a question, Joseph."

"Of course, Maman." Papa turned to Louis. "I'm sorry, Mr. White. I didn't mean to be rude."

"Quite all right, Mr. Gauthier."

"She's very young, Mr. White," Maman said softly. A handkerchief had appeared in her hand.

"Not so young, Maman," Faby said in French. "You said so yourself, I'm a grown woman now."

"Don't be disrespectful to your mother," Papa responded in French. Maman Aurore looked as if she were about to say something and then thought better of it, crossing her arms over her bosom instead.

"I'm sorry, Maman," Faby said in English without looking at her mother. She had barely looked at her mother's face since asking her to leave the kitchen to join Papa and Louis in the living room. She now could not bear to look at her mother at all, sitting so awkwardly in her armchair in the living room with a handkerchief becoming damp and wrinkled in her hand when she should be in the kitchen tending to the potatoes.

Papa's face looked strained, but Faby was unsure whether he did not know what he should say next or whether he knew exactly what he wanted to say and was struggling to find the right words in English. His cigarette was still between his fingers, the ash becoming longer and longer, until the lit end reached his fingers and he quickly stubbed it out and brushed the ash off his trouser leg.

As everyone in the room waited for Papa to speak, Faby became aware of the ticking of the clock on the mantle for the first time since she was a very young child, sitting on Papa's lap after Sunday dinner learning how to tell time. The clock's calm and steady marking out of time sounded completely unfamiliar, as though she were just now hearing it for the first time.

"I'll take good care of her," Louis said, putting his arm around Faby's shoulders, his bicep and his forearm applying a steady pressure, as if he were trying to fold her in half. "Believe you me."

"Yes, I'm sure you will," Papa said, "but isn't this sudden, Mr. White? Couldn't you wait a little while? You barely know each other."

Faby felt Louis pull his arm from her shoulders so that he could turn to see her face. The panic began rising in her throat, and she thought she might vomit before he could read the plea in her eyes, but read it he did, his arm going back around her shoulders, the puzzled look gone from his face as though it had never been there.

"Funny thing about love," he said, giving her shoulders a squeeze. "You can go along for years without ever giving it a passing thought, particularly a fellow like me, on the road all the time, never knowing from one year to the next where I'm going to be. Then one night you're up there on the stage and you look out past the footlights to see what kind of audience you have tonight and you see a pretty dark-haired girl in a yellow dress. She's the prettiest girl you've ever seen—and that's saying a lot, given the business you're in—and you know you have to meet her. So you arrange to meet her, and as soon as you start spending time with her, you know, you just know: This is the girl I'm going to marry."

Even though she had asked him to, Faby marveled at how well Louis could lie. Under different circumstances, one might even say he had a gift for it. She could see the strain slipping from her father's face, and, for a fleeting moment, she allowed herself the possibility that it was not a lie at all—until Louis took his arm from around her shoulders, reached into his jacket for a cigarette, stuck it in the corner of his mouth without lighting it, and continued talking. "So after the show left town, I found myself thinking about that pretty girl and how good it felt to be with her and how happy she could make me as my wife. I just couldn't get her out of my mind. So yesterday, I hopped on board a northbound train to ask that girl to marry me. She said yes, so here I am, hat in hand so to speak, to ask for your blessing."

Faby found it hard to read the expression that was now on her father's face. It was still dubious, to be sure, but there was something else she couldn't be sure of.

Papa stood up from his chair and extended his hand. "You have my blessing, Mr. White." Louis stood up and extended his hand. As they shook hands, he said, "Thank you, sir. I'll take good care of her." When Faby rose from the sofa to stand next to him, he reached into his jacket for a match and lit the cigarette that was still stuck in the corner of his mouth. "By the way," he said, squinting against the smoke, "Slim White isn't my real name."

Papa looked as if he wanted to take back his handshake and his blessing, the look on his face saying that no man of his acquaintance would ever consider asking a girl's father for his blessing to marry using anything but his own name. In fact, no man of his acquaintance would ever present himself to others as anything but who he actually was.

Maman and Maman Aurore also stood up, Maman Aurore looking to Papa expectantly, while Faby became suddenly lightheaded, fear nipping at her stomach. When Papa remained silent, Maman Aurore hissed in French, "Ask the man his name, Joseph." Still Papa remained silent, the five of them standing in an awkward tableau, not moving. "Ask the man his name, Joseph," Maman Aurore repeated, and Papa seemed to come to himself. "What is your name, then?"

"Louis Kittell. Your Faby is going to be Mrs. Louis Kittell."

Chapter 9

They were married the following day, and for Faby there was the same question of the dress as there had been the night of the vaudeville show, since there was no time for them to go to Saint Albans to get something new and certainly no time for Maman and Maman Aurore, even if they worked together, to make her one. Faby was just as glad of it so that she wouldn't have to struggle to conceal her altered shape as they fitted the dress.

So that morning, the four women of the house—Faby, Josephine, Maman, and Maman Aurore—stood shoulder to shoulder at the girls' open closet and determined that Faby would be married in her high school graduation dress, the only white dress she owned. Then they packed the rest of Faby's clothes and her few toiletries into the family's largest suitcase and snapped the latches. The suitcase would not be opened again until it reached its destination. Maman and Maman Aurore hurried out of the room to tend to the food.

Faby stood still in the middle of the room, not quite sure what she should do. She sat down abruptly on the suitcase and put her head down. After a moment, she heard footsteps and felt Josephine gently touch her shoulder. "Why don't you get into a hot bath, Faby, and I'll go press your dress." Faby looked at the clock on her nightstand. "Don't worry," Josephine said, handing Faby her bathrobe. "You have time. I'll call you if you're in there too long."

Faby slid into the hot water and closed her eyes. It was odd to think that after today, she would never bathe in this tub again. She would never again dry herself with one of her mother's big white towels, still stiff and fragrant from hanging outdoors on the clothesline. She would never again brush her teeth at this sink or fuss with her hair in front of the mirror above her dresser. She would never again sleep in her own bed or whisper her secrets to her sister in the dark after the rest of the house was asleep.

Too soon, she heard a light rap on the bathroom door and Josephine's voice telling her it was time to get dressed. After she got her graduation dress on, she was relieved to discover that it looked nearly the same on her now as it had on her graduation day. In fact, she looked so much as she had on graduation day she found it hard to believe that any time had passed at all, and harder still to believe how irrevocably she was changed.

Josephine came up behind her and smoothed her hair. "You look beautiful, Faby."

Faby put her hand to her head. "Thanks, Josephine. That's kind of you to say."

"I mean it, Faby. You look beautiful. You know what's missing, though?"

"Missing?"

"Yes. You should have a veil."

"I don't need a veil. I'm just getting married downstairs. It will be over before you know it, and I'll just have to change clothes anyway."

"No, you wait here. I have an idea." Josephine hurried out of the room.

Faby sat on the edge of her bed to put on her shoes and stockings. When Josephine returned, she held a piece of lace in her hand. Reaching down, she pinned the lace to Faby's hair and arranged it carefully over her shoulders. "There, doesn't that look nice?"

Faby got up and went to look in the mirror. "Thanks, Josephine. It does look nice. Where did you get it?"

Josephine put her finger to her lips and whispered, "It's Maman Aurore's dresser scarf."

"No!"

"Yes!"

"But—"

"I'll put it back while you change into your traveling clothes. Don't worry, she'll never know."

Faby smiled. "If she does find out, just tell her that I took it without asking, and you tried to stop me but I wouldn't listen. She'll believe that."

Josephine smiled and whispered, "You are a silly old thing," before turning to the mirror and putting the finishing touches to her own hair. After checking her hair one last time, Faby followed her sister downstairs to the living room to await Louis's arrival, both of her parents, as well as Maman Aurore, already keeping vigil, all three dressed in their Sunday best, with not a word passed among them. Maman's lips were moving, as if she were reading to herself or praying. After she and Josephine were sitting side-by-side on the sofa, Faby wondered if she were the only one of the five of them wondering if Louis might in fact not come, that the hokey melodrama she was caught up in had a surprise ending after all.

Father Messier arrived first, ten minutes before his appointed time, looking surprised when Papa ushered him into the living room, fetched him an extra chair from the dining room, and bade him to sit down. "The young man's not here yet, then?" Father Messier said in French.

Faby shook her head, unable to speak, while Papa responded, "No, not yet." Faby waited for Papa—or Maman or Josephine or even Maman Aurore—to chime in, "He'll be here any minute," but none of them did.

Louis arrived a half hour later, dressed as he had been the day before, his hair swept up in the extravagant pompadour Faby remembered from the night he'd followed her and Josephine from the Opera House. As he entered the living room, he smelled so strongly of bay rum that Faby wondered if he'd been drinking it.

"Sorry I'm late," he said, extending his hand first to Faby's father, then to Father Messier, but offering no explanation.

After an awkward silence, Father Messier rose from his chair and said, "Well, then. Shall we get started?"

"Now you're on the trolley!" Louis said before anyone else could respond.

After another awkward silence, Father Messier said, "All right, then, Faby and—?"

"Louis."

"Louis. Faby and Louis, you stand here in front of me. That's right. And Joseph, you stand here."

When the time in the ceremony came to "place the ring," Louis made a great show of taking his signet ring from his finger and sliding it onto Faby's, Faby at first pulling her hand back, she just as startled by her reflexive action as Louis.

After the ceremony, Papa ushered everyone into the dining room, where refreshments were laid out on the table— finger sandwiches, punch, an assortment of nuts and candies— and, on a glass pedestal, in the place of honor in the center of Maman's best white crocheted tablecloth, a small white cake covered over with elaborate whorls of frosting, Louis exclaiming when he saw it, "Well, will you look at that—a wedding cake! If that don't beat all." He picked up the knife resting on a plate next to the cake pedestal and passed it, handle first, to Faby. "Mrs. Kittell, will you help me slice the first piece?" Faby smiled as he put his hand over hers, then watched in horror as the knife sliced through the cake at Louis's touch, unbidden by her own hand. How could he? How could he evoke that night in Marvin Foote's Packard here, in her parents' house, with her entire family in attendance, not to mention Father Messier and the sacrament of marriage. How could he?

Louis leaned down and whispered in her ear, "What's the matter? Post-wedding jitters?"

She nodded her head, oddly relieved that at least he had noticed something was wrong. After she had eaten a few bites of cake, she went upstairs to change.

Papa borrowed Morris Draper's car to take Faby's suitcase to the depot, as the suitcase was too heavy for any of them to carry that distance. Faby rode in front with her father and Maman, while Josephine rode in back with the suitcase. Louis had left the house on foot and would meet them at the depot. Maman Aurore had been set to go to the depot as well but at the very last minute—stepping out of the house and onto the front porch, in fact—had developed a sick headache and gone upstairs to bed.

As Papa maneuvered the car carefully down their street, Faby watched as they passed each house, not sure if she would want to remember them, once she had left Enosburg behind to begin her life with Louis, but she took note of as many details as she could just in case she did want to remember: the Judds' poor fat beagle sprawled on the welcome mat waiting for any chance of the meager November sun's appearance from behind a cloud, Mrs. Gibson's pulled shades, a small group of children playing Tag in the Neales' front yard, oblivious to everything but their game. As they passed the Bergerons' house, the hysterical terrier as unhappy about people driving past in cars as it was about people walking past on the sidewalk, the thought crossed Faby's mind that Louis might not show up at the depot after all. She turned to look out the back window, but the car had outpaced him, and the sidewalk was empty, except for Mrs. Neale pushing a dilapidated baby buggy with the latest Neale safely bundled inside. Faby turned to face forward again. What if Louis were having second thoughts? What if he were thinking, *I don't want to be burdened with a wife and a child,* and left her behind, jumping on the train as it slowed down for the depot, yelling at the engineer to keep going, Louis hanging onto the side of the train car as it once again gathered speed?

When they reached the depot, Papa gingerly applied the brake and let the car coast to a stop, seemingly unsure of what to do next. Josephine leaned forward and pointed. "You can park right here, Papa."

Papa put the car in reverse and eased it into the space Josephine had pointed out. He turned off the engine. No one spoke, and no one made a move to get out of the car as it began making faint cooling off noises. The ordinary sounds of Depot Street—cars puttering by on their way to Main Street; snatches of conversations from passersby on the sidewalk and people arriving at the depot; a baby crying, bored and squirming in his mother's arms—sounded odd, as if Faby had never heard them before. She realized after a few more moments that she was holding her breath. She let it out and surreptitiously took in more air, certain that Maman, Papa, and Josephine were still holding theirs.

She made a move to open the door of the car, but no one else in the car moved, and she let her hand slip from the handle. She could think of nothing worse than opening that door and walking into the train depot by herself while her family remained in the car trying to decide which would be worse: saying their good-byes now and going home to make a clean break while they wondered if Louis would in fact show up, or going into the depot to wait with her, not speaking, too discomfited even for small talk.

A rap came at Faby's window, and all four of them jumped, startled, Maman even letting out a little yelp. It was Maman Aurore, rapping on the glass with her big red knuckles, her other hand clutching the neck of her winter coat closed. Faby could tell from the pinched look of her mouth that she still had the sick headache. Maman Aurore leaned into the driver's side window. "I must speak with Faby. Joseph, you go and buy her ticket." Papa got out of the car, followed by Maman. Faby looked to Josephine, who nodded her head and climbed out to join their parents. Only when Faby saw the three of them enter the depot did she leave the car. She turned to follow them, expecting Maman Aurore to join her, but her grandmother didn't move, her face gone pale, her mouth white. Faby wondered why Maman Aurore had not stayed behind in her bedroom with the shades drawn and a cold compress on her forehead. She looked about to vomit.

"What's the matter, Mémère?" Faby said, not understanding how her grandmother could risk getting sick in public, giving up punch and wedding cake in a stinking instant of humiliation.

"No one need know."

Faby's stomach dropped. She hadn't expected Maman Aurore to say it, not after keeping quiet for so long. Not after all the knowing looks, the telling glances, the baby-sized foot taking shape beneath the relentless knitting needles.

"No one need know," Maman Aurore repeated, clamping her hand on Faby's wrist, fumbling to get around her sleeve. "So you come back here to us when it's time for that baby to be born. People count the months one time." Maman Aurore ticked off months on her fingers. "Then they forget." Her face softened at the same time her grip on Faby's wrist loosened and her hand slid down to hold Faby's hand. "A girl needs her mother when her time comes."

Before Faby could respond, Maman Aurore turned and walked away, more quickly than was her customary old woman's gait. Faby watched her get halfway up Depot Street, at which point she stopped, leaned over, and vomited into the gutter. Faby turned from the train depot and ran up the street, putting a hand on her grandmother's shoulder when she reached her, gasping a little. "Are you all right, Mémère? Are you all right?"

Maman Aurore seemed to recover some, straightening up and taking a handkerchief from her coat pocket to dab at her mouth. "Go back, Faby," she said, turning her head to the side as she spoke. "Go back before your parents send your sister after you."

"No," Faby said. "I need to help you get home. You're sick."

"Go back, Faby. You'll miss your train. I'll be fine. It's just a headache." She tucked her handkerchief back into the pocket of her coat. "Lord knows, you've seen me with enough of them. I'll be fine."

Faby hesitated until Maman Aurore turned from her and began making her way up the street with her usual deliberate gait, seemingly recovered enough to get home on her own, although with old people, you never knew. Still, she always recovered from those sick headaches once she was able to sleep.

When Faby got back to the depot, Josephine stepped off the covered platform by the entrance and rushed up to her. "What took you so long, Faby? You don't want to miss your train when Louis gets here."

"He hasn't come yet?"

Josephine shook her head. "No, not yet. He should be here soon. Don't forget that he had to walk all the way from the house." Faby couldn't help smiling to herself as she followed her sister into the depot. That assertion of Louis's imminent arrival surely had to be as close to a fib as Josephine had ever come, except for the first night they'd met him, of course. With Louis's long legs and as gingerly as Papa had driven the borrowed car, Louis should have joined them at the depot by now.

"What did Mémère want?" Josephine said. "She can't even leave her bed when she gets one of those headaches. What did she want? Was she upset with you?"

"No," Faby said, as Josephine opened the door of the depot. "She just wanted to say good-bye. She was afraid my feelings were hurt when she changed her mind at the last minute about coming to see me off."

"I see," Josephine said, Faby feeling a pang of guilt that she'd lied to her—but there was no way she could explain what had just passed between her and Maman Aurore to her sister—or to herself, for that matter.

Inside the depot, it took a few moments for Faby's eyes to adjust to the dim light after being outside. She was surprised to see Maman and Papa standing awkwardly by the ticket counter instead of sitting on a bench, the suitcase with her belongings out of place on the floor in front of them. "There you are," Maman fussed, stepping forward. "We didn't know where you'd got to when you were away so long. Is Mémère all right? Joseph, you should go after her and drive her home. She's in no condition to be walking the streets by herself." Papa looked uncertain.

"She's all right," Faby said. "She just wanted to say goodbye, is all. Her headache's better."

Papa still looked uncertain. "If you're sure, Faby."

"She's all right," Faby said emphatically, at the same time her mother also said, "If you're sure—"

After that exchange, the four of them stood there not speaking, while the business of the train depot went on around them: Alvin and Mabel Blouin sitting placidly on a bench with a wicker basket between them, each chewing on a chicken leg as they waited for Alvin, Jr. to arrive home on leave from the Army; Marjorie Bashaw on the bench next to the Blouins, her baby Eugene no longer bored and squirming but stretched across her lap asleep, with his head nestled in the crook of her arm; Sylvain LaFlamme standing at the ticket window, looking very much the dairy farmer, even with his denim frock coat traded for a respectable enough suit jacket; Gardner Croft glee-fully selling Sylvain his ticket, as if taking the train the eighteen miles to Saint Albans were some indescribably thrilling adventure worthy of a sendoff with colored streamers and a brass band.

Her parents were whispering to each other in French, debating whether Papa should buy Faby's ticket or whether Louis would have already gotten it. Standing right next to her mother, Faby could hear the conversation perfectly well, and she couldn't believe that her parents were talking about her right there in front of her, as if by virtue of her getting married, she had lost all ability to understand her native language.

Papa spoke just then. "I was going to buy your ticket, Faby." He stopped speaking, then resumed. "But I didn't know your destination."

"No, Papa," Faby said, "Louis will buy my ticket." She had spoken more emphatically to her father than she had intended, but she couldn't very well tell her parents that she didn't know her destination either, that Louis would be just taking her along, almost as a prop packed into his theatrical trunk, arms and legs neatly folded to take up less room.

She looked from her father to her sister, unable to understand why Josephine wasn't trying to stop her, why the three of them weren't telling her that she didn't really need to go.

"Well, I guess we'd better all go sit down," Papa said, "before we get in people's way. I should tell someone about your suitcase." Faby watched him stop himself from saying, *but I don't know your destination.* He hesitated again and then said, "I'd better stay with your suitcase until Louis comes. You three go sit down."

They sat on the other side of Mabel Blouin, who had finished with her chicken leg and was now working on a massive brownie, as was Alvin, Sr. The Blouins both nodded and smiled as the three women sat down. "Would you like a brownie, girls?" Mabel said, opening the lid of the wicker basket.

Faby and Josephine shook their heads and said, "No, thank you."

"Yvette?" Mabel said, her hand still inside the wicker basket.

Maman smiled and politely shook her head.

Mabel wrapped her half-eaten brownie in a napkin, set it inside the basket, and closed the lid. "Well, then, I won't be impolite and eat in front of you."

"Where are you off to, or are you waiting for someone?" Mabel continued. "We're waiting for Alvin, Jr. He's coming home on leave from Fort Eustis in Virginia, although why he couldn't get leave to come home for Thanksgiving, I'll never know. It's not right."

Faby and Josephine nodded politely, and Alvin, Sr. said, "Now, Mabel," as he must have said a hundred times that day.

"Where are you off to?" Mabel resumed.

Before either Faby or Josephine could formulate a polite evasion, Eugene Bashaw woke up, and Mabel turned her attention to him, cooing at him mercilessly and chucking him under his fat little chin.

Louis had still not arrived. Maybe, just maybe, Faby thought, she would get to go home after all. If Maman Aurore had forgiven her transgression, surely Maman and Papa could, too. Maybe it would be all right. She would have to be sent away, of course—or maybe not if she took care not to leave the house. The baby would be born at home, and she would become Tante Faby to Maman's precious change-of-life baby.

Faby got up from the bench and crossed the room to stand by her father. Before she could say anything, however, someone swooped up behind her and planted a kiss on her cheek. "Well, hello, Mrs. Kittell." It was Louis. Louis had been drinking. "What are you doing just standing there? Go sit down while I buy your ticket and take care of your suitcase. You, too, Joseph, go sit."

Papa didn't move. "We've been waiting quite a while," he said carefully.

"Sorry about that," Louis said. "A man needs a little liquid courage as he embarks on this leg of life's journey." He winked, then turned to Faby. "Why so glum, dollface?"

He put his hand to her elbow and swept her along with him as he sauntered up to the ticket window and asked Gardner Croft to sell him two one-way tickets to White River Junction. Which of course didn't tell Faby anything. From White River, trains went everywhere: Boston, Albany, New York City, New Haven, and farther still, to Philadelphia, New Orleans, Chicago. Gardner had taken Louis's money when he seemed to just notice Faby standing at Louis's side, and the expression on his face said so loudly, *Who is this flashy young man asking for two one-way tickets to White River Junction, and what is Joseph Gauthier's daughter doing with him?*, that Faby could have smiled as long as Louis didn't blurt out the answer. Gardner passed Louis his change, but he held the one-way tickets to White River Junction in his hand as the expression on his face changed from natural curiosity to entitlement. Louis pocketed his change and with his other hand seized the tickets from Gardner, all the while smiling agreeably as he hooked his thumb over his shoulder and said, "Have a porter see to that suitcase, would you?" Without waiting for a response, he turned from the ticket window, walked up to Papa and told him that the suitcase would soon be loaded onto the train, so he no longer needed to keep watch over it. Papa hesitated, as though unsure whether he could safely relinquish the suitcase or whether it would be more prudent to remain by it, as if anyone in the depot—the two Blouins, still eating as they waited for Alvin, Jr., Marjorie Bashaw and baby Eugene, now sleeping again, or Sylvain La-Flamme, pulling papers and a packet of Bugle Boy from his inside jacket pocket to roll himself a smoke—would have bothered it in the first place.

Louis leaned down and whispered in Faby's ear, "What's with the gent at the ticket window?" and when she didn't respond, he shook his head and said something under his breath about "rubes" before taking out his cigarette case and exclaiming, "Well, then, Mrs. Kittell, let's take a seat and wait for our train."

Faby quickly turned to look at the clock above the ticket window. With the few minutes it would take for the arriving passengers and their luggage to be gotten off the train and the departing passengers and their luggage to be gotten on the train, she might still have enough time to think of a way out of this, some way to leave the depot and go back home with her parents and her sister in the borrowed car, never to return to the train depot again, unless a trip to the Sheldon Fair or shopping in Saint Albans were in order. Her suitcase could easily be put back in the car, its contents returned to their rightful places.

However, there was the question of whether she could find a way out of this that wouldn't cause her parents pain. And the answer to that question was no. She leaned forward to look at her parents and sister seated at the other end of the bench, waiting, Maman's face composed but the telltale lace edging of the handkerchief she held in her fist saying otherwise, Papa's face doggedly hopeful that his firstborn would be happy and well-cared for, Josephine already mentally composing the first letter she would send. Maybe Maman Aurore was right; people only count the months one time and then they forget—but that one time would be enough to hurt Maman and Papa in the way only a daughter can hurt her parents, and she didn't think she could bear it.

Louis leaned down, touched her arm, and whispered, "You look pale. Do you need to get some air?"

Faby nodded, so taken aback at his genuinely solicitous tone that she didn't trust herself to speak. He helped her up from the bench and kept his arm around her shoulders as he led her to her family. "Faby's feeling a bit woozy. I'm taking her out for some air." Maman started to get up, but Josephine stopped her with a light touch on her arm.

"She'll be all right in a few minutes," Louis said. "She just needs some air."

Faby stopped herself from looking back over her shoulder as Louis led her outside and away from the hot metal steam and cinders chuff and clang of the train.

"This is happening awfully fast, isn't it?" he said, his tone sounding thoughtful as he reached into his jacket pocket for his cigarette case, then put the cigarette case back without taking one out.

"Yes," she said, "awfully fast."

Several moments passed before he spoke again. "You know, I didn't just come up here and marry you on a whim. I wanted to do the right thing."

"Yes."

"I do care about you, and I'll take care of you," he continued. "You don't have to worry about that. I will take care of you and the baby."

Faby felt a rush of hope so intense that at first she didn't know what it was, as she stood looking at the Opera House across the street, trying to get her bearings. After a few moments had passed, she took Louis's arm. "I'm feeling better now. We don't want to miss our train."

When they entered the train depot, the waiting room was empty except for Faby's family and the Blouins, Alvin, Jr. struggling to balance his duffle bag on his shoulder with one hand, the other hand occupied with a brownie.

"Oh, there, you are!" Josephine exclaimed, rushing up to Faby and Louis. "They're holding the train for you!"

"Are you all right?" Maman said, putting her hand to Faby's cheek. Faby nodded and received a quick embrace from her mother, father, and sister in turn. Before she could cry out, *Good-bye!*, she was hoisted up the steps of the train and into a seat next to her husband. *It's just as well,* she thought, as the train started to move, *Just as well no time for long good-byes,* as the train picked up speed and quickly left Enosburg Falls behind. In no time at all, they would be in Sheldon Junction, then Saint Albans, then out of Franklin County altogether. Maman, Papa, and Josephine would be driving back up Depot Street in the Drapers' car, without the suitcase now. Arriving at the house, Papa would let Maman and Josephine out and continue on to Orchard Street to return the car to Mr. Draper, first stopping at the filling station to put two gallons of gasoline in the tank. Back at the house, Maman and Josephine would be seeing to Maman Aurore, who by now should be just dropping off to sleep.

Faby turned to look out the window, watching the landscape stream by as the train approached Sheldon Junction:

trees and cows, barns and pastures, farmhouses and fences, the Green Mountains always in view beyond them, a glimpse of the Missisquoi River from time to time. When the train stopped to take on more passengers, Faby and Louis got off to stretch their legs, returning to their seats a short time later to wait for the train to depart, Faby still wondering what their destination was.

Just as they were approaching Saint Albans, Faby felt Louis take her hand. Hope once again surged in her chest, until he removed his signet ring from her finger and replaced it on his own without saying a word. He stood up and made his way down the aisle, and she trailed after him onto the platform and into the station, where he smoked a cigarette and bought a newspaper. Back on the train, he gave a section of the paper to Faby and disappeared behind his own section until they reached White River Junction.

When the train stopped, Louis told her that they had time enough for a sandwich before they had to catch their next train. As they sat on a bench and unwrapped their sandwiches, Faby decided that asking one's husband where they were going on the train was a perfectly reasonable thing to do, particularly when they were already en route—so she asked him and he told her. "We're going to spend the night in Bedford, so I can introduce you to my mother and my sister. Then I'm playing a split week in Connecticut."

Chapter 10

When they reached Bedford and got off the train, Faby began scanning the faces of the people gathered at the platform, wondering if any of them could belong to Louis's mother and sister, or, if both of them in fact had come to the station to meet Louis's train. Just then, Louis pointed and said, "Ah, there they are," and took Faby's hand as he began moving through the crowd. When he reached the two women, he was still holding Faby by the hand, but his mother and sister didn't look surprised to see two people, so evidently he had already given them the news of his marriage.

"So this is Faby," Louis's mother said, with a perfunctory embrace. "We've heard so much about you." As Faby said, "I'm pleased to meet you," she took a small step back. How could the woman possibly have heard so much about her from Louis when they had gotten married suddenly in two days, and they barely even knew each other? Mother must be as practiced as son at telling lies.

Louis was nudging her arm. "Let's get a wiggle on. We're ready to go." Mother and Dorothy were already several paces ahead of them, striding purposefully in their stylish black pumps.

Dorothy drove them from the station in a shiny blue sedan. Louis's mother rode up front, while Faby and Louis sat in the back, Faby watching the tree-lined streets to see if they could tell her something about her new husband, what, she didn't know. They were just trees, after all. The houses were different from those in Enosburg, smaller, tidier, with no peeling paint and not a tin roof in sight. Except for a few grand exceptions built with Spavin Cure money, all of the houses in the village were some variation of a farmhouse. There were no such houses here.

As they pulled into a driveway, it occurred to Faby that she didn't know whether Louis's father was still alive. She couldn't even remember whether Louis had ever mentioned his father in their conversations, not that the subject of his father should have ever come up. Perhaps she would find out once they went inside the house.

"Here we are, Louis said." "This is the house where I grew up and the place I call home."

The place he called home looked nice enough, a little smaller than her home on Depot Street, painted a light grey with green shutters, the brick walk leading to the front door bordered on either side with low-growing ivy.

"We prepared a nice cold supper in case your train was late," Louis's mother said as she opened the car door and gracefully swung her legs to exit. "Dorothy and I will see to supper, Louis, while you bring in Faby's suitcase."

Louis's mother's house smelled like furniture polish and flowers. In the dining room, to Faby's right, Dorothy was setting out dinner plates and silverware. Other sounds of meal preparation, comforting in their familiarity, came from the kitchen at the back of the house. "It will be only a few more minutes," Louis's mother called from the kitchen.

"Okay, Mother," Louis answered. "I'm just taking Faby up to my room."

The front hall and the stairwell were papered in some kind of wallpaper that had a light background and a pattern of footbridges that looked vaguely oriental. The staircase had a beautiful banister of shiny dark wood. Faby followed Louis up the stairs, her hand gliding effortlessly along the shiny dark banister, even though she had no need to steady herself. At the head of the stairs was a bathroom, and Faby suddenly realized she that she had to go. As she hesitated, Louis nodded and said, "Go ahead. I'll just put your things down. My room is the one here on the right."

The small bathroom was painted a pleasant shade of yellow, with white tile. Crisp white curtains hung at the windows, a round, crocheted shade pull hanging between the curtains in case someone wanted extra privacy, even though the bathroom was on the second floor and faced nothing but tree branches and sky. After carefully turning the lock on the door and pulling down the shade, Faby slid down her drawers and sat on the toilet. She wouldn't mind a bath, she thought, as long as she could be absolutely sure that no one would walk in on her, that the lock on the door would hold.

When she went to the sink to wash her hands, she didn't see any shaving gear that would point to a man's presence in the house, although Louis's father could keep it in the medicine cabinet, she supposed. She thought about opening the medicine cabinet and looking inside but then thought better of it. Even if she were to just ease the door open and look, without touching anything, the next Kittell who got something out of that medicine cabinet would know that she'd snooped.

As she entered Louis's bedroom, she found him lounging on the bed smoking a cigarette. "Hey, there you are," he said, tapping ash into the ashtray on the nightstand, the finish of which had been ruined by cigarette burns and water rings. "I've put your things right here on the nightstand." He gestured with his cigarette to an open shelf below the single drawer of the nightstand.

That's odd, she thought. Why would he put her things in his room? "Where will I sleep?"

"Why, with your husband, of course! We're on our honeymoon, after all."

"We are?" Faby said and instantly regretted it. What a stupid thing to say. *But,* she wanted to tell him, *but, I've never thought of myself on a honeymoon. I'm not old enough for a honeymoon. I'm not really a grown woman at all. I'm really not.* Well, said a different voice in her head, *You've made your bed and now you'll lie in it, won't you?*

She kept looking at the room's only bed, a twin with modest wood headboard and footboard, neatly made up with a blue-and-white woven bedspread. How in the world were they both going to sleep in that bed, unless they lay touching all night long?

Before she could take that unwelcome thought any further, Louis's mother called them to supper, and Louis took Faby's hand and led her downstairs. As they entered the dining room, Faby wondered if he had told his mother and sister about her pregnancy. Probably not. There would have been no need to. There could be only one reason why a couple would marry so quickly and with so little fanfare, with no one from the groom's side of the family in attendance or even invited. And if that weren't enough, they would have surmised it as soon as they had laid eyes on her at the train station. She was not Louis's type. His type, she knew, was the flashier sort of girl, more like his sister—although a little younger.

In the dining room, Louis pulled out Faby's chair for her, with some awkwardness, as Faby at first didn't know what he was trying to do, fully expecting the chair to be yanked from beneath her as she hesitantly lowered herself onto it. As she got herself settled, she saw that the table was set for four, which in all likelihood settled the question of Louis's father—although not the question of whether he had died or absconded.

Supper was a relatively simple affair: sliced turkey artfully arranged on a platter, sliced bread in a napkin-draped basket, and cut-class dishes of various sizes and shapes holding mayonnaise, green olives, pickles, stuffed celery, and cranberry sauce. The largest bowl held gobs of some gelatinous substance the color of tomato soup, which Faby carefully avoided, putting some on her plate when it was offered but not eating it. Although she no longer had morning sickness, there was no point in courting disaster with unfamiliar food that questionable. Louis also avoided the stuff, waving his hand impatiently when his mother offered it to him. He asked for stuffing to go in his sandwich, at which his sister said, "Really, Louis, you shouldn't eat like that. You're not a stevedore, for Christ's sake." Their mother gave disapproving looks to both of them, but she didn't chastise Dorothy for cursing, and she got up and fetched Louis his stuffing.

After Louis's mother had seen that everyone had what they needed, she picked up her fork and said, "So, tell us a little about yourself, Faby. Your maiden name was Gauthier, I understand from Louis?"

"Yes," Faby said.

"I see." Louis's mother dabbed delicately at the corner of her mouth with her napkin.

"You must be French, then," Dorothy said from the other end of the table as she pushed food around on her plate, her face registering revulsion, although from Faby's heritage or what was on her plate, Faby couldn't tell.

"Brothers, sisters?" Louis's mother prompted.

"A sister. Josephine." Faby did not want to tell these people anything more about her sister than her name, for fear that doing so would cause some harm to come to Josephine— the same harm that would come to her if she told them anything about herself.

"What's your home town like, then?" Louis's mother said, cutting a bite of turkey without looking down at her plate. "It's in Vermont?"

"Yes." A wave of homesickness suddenly swept over Faby, a deep, painful yearning for *her* mother at the head of the table, *her* sister sitting across from her and, most of all, her *father* at the other end of the table, not Louis. She looked miserably down at her plate as her husband began to answer his mother in her stead. "Yes, Mother, Enosburg Falls is only ten miles from the Canadian border. It's a quaint little town, very picturesque, wouldn't you say, Faby?"

She nodded, grateful that her mouth was full of celery, so she could politely not answer him.

"Let's see, what else can I tell you about Enosburg Falls, Vermont? It has a splendid opera house, which of course is where Faby and I met. She was gracious enough to show me around town. Quiet streets, as I recall, with rambling houses. Just outside of town are a number of dairy farms, more cows than people, as they say. Um, what else? Oh, yes, the main industry in town has something to do with horses. What was it now, Faby?"

"Spavin Cure. Horse liniment."

"Ah, yes," Louis's mother said. "Spavin Cure. The wagon used to come through town when I was a child. Is there much call for it up your way?"

Faby shook her head. "Not anymore."

When they had finished eating, Dorothy cleared the table and brought in a double-layer cake on a glass pedestal, which she set in front of her mother. Someone—probably Louis's mother—had taken the time to pull the thick white frosting into small peaks all over the cake, even on the sides, unlike Maman Aurore, whose cake-frosting technique was more like troweling mortar on bricks: slap a load on, spread it, slap on another load, and be done with it. They must have cake only on special occasions.

When they were finished with dessert, Louis's mother announced that they would have their coffee in the living room after the dishes were done. Without thinking, Faby got up and started clearing the dessert plates from the table.

"What is she *doing?*" Dorothy said to Louis before turning to Faby to address her directly: "In our family, we don't expect our guests to work in the kitchen."

Louis's mother gently took the stack of dessert plates from Faby and said, "Thank you for offering, dear. I do appreciate the thought. Now you and Louis go into the living room and relax while Dorothy and I do the dishes. We'll bring in the coffee when we're finished. We won't be long."

Faby looked down, trying to hide her tears as Louis put his arm around her and led her from the room, leaning down and whispering, "Don't mind Dorothy. She was a mean little girl, and she's never grown out of it." He led her to the sofa in the living room and sat next to her, still with his arm around her shoulder. When he offered her his handkerchief, she decided that she could go ahead and cry. Louis kissed the top of her head, and, after a bit, she felt better and handed Louis back his handkerchief.

When Louis's mother entered the room with a silver coffee service, he got up and took the tray from her. "I'll serve," he said, bending over to hold the tray at the right height for each of the women to serve herself before setting the tray on an ottoman and serving himself.

"Well," he said as each of them sat in place with cup and saucer in hand, "This is nice, isn't it, all of us together for the first time?"

No one responded, not even to nod or say, *Mmm,* and Faby thought it was as stupid a thing for Louis to say at that moment as her unthinking expression of incredulity earlier when he had said that they were on their honeymoon.

Thankfully, the cups were dainty, and the coffee was soon gone. Louis stood up and took Faby by the hand. "We're off to get some sleep. It's been a long day, and it's going to be a longer one tomorrow."

When they reached the top of the stairs, Louis let go of Faby's hand to enter the bedroom; however, she hesitated on the threshold. How long would it take after she entered the room for Louis to remind her that, her feelings to the contrary, he was on his honeymoon and there were certain things he had a right to expect? Certain things he knew a great deal about. Certain things about which she, for all intents and purposes, knew nothing. Certain things that would take place on his narrow bed under the woven blue-and-white bedspread. She wondered what he would do if she resisted. The first time, he had snuck up on her unawares, but this time she knew better.

Turning her attention to what Louis was actually doing, she saw that he was not turning down the bed covers as she was expecting but instead was crouched on the floor pulling at something, which he hauled onto the bed. Settling himself next to it, he said, "Would you like to see my mementoes?"

"Oh, yes!" She had actually begun to think that the trunk of mementoes, and in particular the signed photograph of Harry Houdini, had just been so much talk to impress a small-town girl. She entered the bedroom and sat on the bed, facing Louis over the trunk. "I've never seen a trunk like that before."

"Oh? It's a cabin trunk. You know, for on board ship. It will fit under a bunk." He snapped the latches. "It was my father's."

Faby waited, but Louis didn't elaborate, and she thought it best not to pry. Obviously, the man must have either abandoned his family years ago or died a death too horrific to bear thinking about.

"Let's see what we have here," Louis said, lifting the lid halfway and pausing for a moment to catch her eye until she smiled. Lifting the lid the rest of the way, he reached into the trunk and took out a stack of well-worn sheet music, which he began sorting through. "Ah, yes, 'The Trail of the Lonesome Pine.' I remember it well. A guaranteed crowd-pleaser, sure to bring a tear to the eye of man and woman alike." Louis rose from the bed and began to sing, delivering the song directly to Faby in a queer affected tenor, accentuating every vowel in the most unnatural fashion and trilling every 'r'. Faby could do nothing but gape at him as he sang all three verses, each one more overwrought than the last. When he was finished, he changed the expression on his face from poignant yearning to anticipation, as though he truly expected Faby to applaud his performance. When she didn't, he sat back down on the bed and set the sheet music aside. "Okay, I can see that m'lady is not in a frame of mind for musical stylings this evening."

"Oh, no, Louis," Faby protested, "it's not that—"

"No, no, don't apologize. That's the whole point of vaudeville-—variety. If one act doesn't suit your fancy, the next one will or the one after that. I am a versatile performer, you'll remember." He paused to give her a wink. "And I have the hide of a rhinoceros. Have to, in this business." He turned his attention back to the contents of the trunk. "I know you'll be interested in this." He reached into the trunk and took out a large scrapbook, which he laid across Faby's lap. "Now this, this is my treasure, what I'm saving for my grandchildren some day. It has the program from every show I've been in, along with a ticket and a postcard from each town where the show played. I also have reviews from the small town newspapers, which tend to be enthusiastic in the most gratifying of ways." He began turning the pages of the scrapbook slowly. "When I first started out, I got signed pictures from everyone in the show, just in case they hit the Big Time one day and became famous."

"Have many of them have become famous?" Faby said, looking up from the airbrushed face in her lap expectantly.

Louis shook his head and rolled his eyes. "I stopped collecting those a while ago now. None of us on the circuits I play, myself included, is going to become famous. For us it's a job, a way to keep body and soul together without dying of boredom before we're forty. It also gives us a chance to make people laugh and forget about their troubles for a while, and in my book, that's not small beer."

"I suppose not," Faby said, feeling inexplicably crestfallen. "I never thought of it that way."

"Now, *this* fellow," Louis said, catching her eye with a smile and turning the page with a flourish. "*This* fellow is famous."

"Harry Houdini!" There he was, The Great Houdini, in a staged crouch, nearly naked, festooned with chains and padlocks, his arm muscles flexed, Harry Houdini on an eight-by-ten glossy. On the facing page was a wrinkled menu for Luigi's Italian Ristorante with blue ink scrawled across the pasta entries: *To Slim White—Harry Houdini—3/25/23.*

"He really signed your menu!" Faby exclaimed.

"That's right," Louis said. "I met The Great Houdini in a restaurant in Camden, New Jersey. He and his wife were eating spaghetti and meatballs, and when she got up to go to the ladies' room, I took my menu went over to their table, introduced myself, and asked him for his autograph. "I never met a more gracious fellow."

"Why did he sign it, *To Slim White?*"

"Well, that was at the time when I thought I would become famous one day." Looking a little sheepish, Louis turned the next page of the scrapbook to a photograph of a performing dog, a wiry terrier up on her hind legs, dressed in a full, vaguely Spanish-looking skirt with a lace mantilla somehow affixed to her little terrier head.

"This is Trixie," Louis said. "For a brief time, Trixie was a real up-and-comer. She could swing on a trapeze, walk a tightrope, ride a unicycle, play the piano. But she was best known for her "Bohemian Dance" performance. You should have seen her, dressed in a gypsy skirt and mantilla, twirling and leaping in time to the music. Well, everything was co-pacetic until one day Trixie just up and refused to perform, for no apparent reason. She wasn't injured, and, according to Jake's story later—that's Jake Meyers, her trainer—he had done nothing that would cause her to refuse his commands.

"So that afternoon—it was a matinee performance—she let Jake put her costume on her as usual. She made her entrance on her hind legs as usual—but when the music began to play, she sat on her haunches and refused to dance. Not only did she refuse to dance, she refused to get up. She just sat there on that stage looking at Jake while he went through every command for the entire act—twice—at which point, she flopped down and played dead. The audience of course thought it was all part of the act—why wouldn't they?—as long as you weren't Jake, it was hilarious—and they laughed and clapped; you might even say appreciatively. Then the laughter died away as one by one they began to realize that Jake had no more control over that dog than you or I have over the phases of the moon. As soon as Jake sensed the audience's realization, he flew into a rage and lunged at Trixie but she, being a dog, was too quick for him. He began chasing her around the stage until he was able to grab one of her hind legs and pull her to him while he began hitting her with his other hand. Then, still holding her by the hind leg, he hurled her offstage into the wings, with her yelping bloody murder. It was utter pandemonium. Trixie yelping, Jake cursing, the children in the audience crying, and the women shrieking. Then the men in the audience got up from their seats and began advancing on the stage. There was no salvaging the show after that. The stage manager dropped the curtain, and the emcee directed the audience back to the box office for refunds." Louis paused for a moment, seemingly lost in thought. "Needless to say, Jake's contract was cancelled and he was sent packing. As far as I know, he was never heard from again. Sad, in a way. There's not much a fellow can do with a dog act without the dog."

Faby sensed someone watching her, and she turned to see his mother standing in the doorway. "Louis, you've told Faby enough stories for one night. Let her get some sleep. The poor girl needs her rest. Faby, he will go on all night if you let him."

"Oh, no," Faby said, "I'm not tired at all."

"That's all right, Mother," Louis said, putting the scrapbook back in the trunk. "We'll have plenty of time for stories later."

Faby had two simultaneous thoughts at that moment, and she didn't know which frightened her more: the thought that she would have to lie on that narrow bed with him now, for an entire night, or the thought that he believed their marriage was actually going to last.

"Well, good night, then," Louis's mother said. "I've laid out fresh towels for both of you in the bathroom." She turned, and Faby heard her footsteps going down the stairs. Faby didn't move from her place on the bed as Louis got up to slide the trunk under the bed. "Oh," he said, as she moved her legs, "I almost forgot. I have something for you." He opened the drawer of the nightstand, reached inside, and held up a gold ring pinched between his thumb and forefinger. "This was my great-grandmother's."

Remarkably, the ring was a perfect fit, so there was nothing to be done but wear it. Faby looked down at the ring on her finger. This was no family heirloom. This was a utilitarian circle of gold that had, for whatever reason, not been interred with its owner when she died, instead dropped carelessly in someone's jewelry box, with the misshapen bracelets, rings with missing stones, and brooches deemed too ugly or old-fashioned to wear.

"You can use the bathroom first," Louis said. "Just leave me some hot water."

Faby warily entered the cheery yellow bathroom, taking care to lock the door behind her. As she eased off each piece of her clothing, she became more and more fearful that someone would walk in on her, even though she had turned the lock. She ran a scant two inches of tepid water in the bathtub, washed herself as quickly as she could, and wrapped a towel around her torso before she stepped out of the tub. With the towel, she didn't feel as exposed, so she was able to spend the proper time brushing her teeth.

After brushing her teeth, she slipped her nightgown on over her head and brushed her hair. Then she brushed her teeth again. When she was finished with her teeth for the second time, she examined her face in the mirror above the sink. The thought occurred to her that in all likelihood she would not be the first young bride to lock herself in the bathroom on her wedding night and refuse to come out. What she didn't know was how those bridegrooms would respond to being denied in such an obvious fashion. As tempting as it seemed at that moment to remain behind a locked door, her safety assured, if in fact she were to stay in the bathroom, with the door locked, in the end there was nothing to be gained by it. She would spend several miserable hours cowering on the closed toilet seat lid while Louis and his mother stood outside the door trying to persuade her to come out. And when at last she did come out—she would have to—one couldn't very well stay locked in a bathroom indefinitely—the look of, what? anger? pity? impatience?—on the faces of Louis and his mother would be just too humiliating. There was nothing for it but to turn the lock, turn the doorknob, and walk the four short steps back to Louis's bedroom, where he was, once again, sprawled on the bed smoking a cigarette. When she hesitated on the threshold, he squinted through the haze of smoke and smiled as he stubbed out the cigarette. "Ah, there you are. I won't be long."

As she waited for Louis to finish in the bathroom, she gradually became aware of a soft but insistent sound, a rhythmic pulsing that sounded almost familiar, but that she couldn't quite identify, given that she was hearing it in a strange house. It took her several moments, looking this way and that around the room, before she realized that what she was hearing was the sound of her own blood pounding in her ears.

Louis's tall frame filled the doorway, his legs white and hairy beneath a shiny striped bathrobe. His hair was wet and tousled, falling over his forehead and into his eyes. Except for the fact that he was over six feet tall, he could have been a ten or twelve year-old-boy. Faby got up off the bed as he hung his bathrobe on its hook in the closet. When he closed the closet door, she saw that he was wearing a sleeveless undershirt and striped boxer shorts: the sandy brown hair in his armpits filled her with dread. Then he was in bed and under the covers and waiting for her. Then he was laughing.

She couldn't think what he might be laughing at except that he had to be laughing at her. "Why are you laughing?"

"I'm sorry. You should see the look on your face! You look absolutely terrified. Come to bed. I'm not going to do anything tonight. Really. Come to bed. You need to get some sleep." When she got under the covers, trying as best she could to keep her nightgown from riding up above her waist, Louis kissed her on the forehead, and she lay there not knowing what to do, holding herself as stiffly as she could against his lean flank as the minutes ticked by.

Louis appeared not to have moved since Faby had gotten into bed, and she held her breath for a moment, trying to determine if he had fallen asleep. Downstairs in the hall off the kitchen, in its own little alcove in the wall, was a telephone. If Louis were in fact asleep, she could get up, slip out from beneath the covers, and go downstairs to use the telephone to call Josephine. All of the bedrooms were upstairs, so as long as she spoke softly, no one would hear. She could make her way to the telephone in the alcove and give the operator the number, the operator not finding it at all unusual that someone would whisper a number for long distance in the middle of night. At the other end, in her parents' house on Depot Street, the telephone would ring. Papa would answer it, of course; as man of the house, he always answered the telephone when he was home.

Faby turned to look on the nightstand, but there was no alarm clock. However, she didn't need a clock to tell her it was the middle of the night. She could no more call her parents' house in the middle of the night, waking the entire family into a panic, simply to ask for Josephine, for no good reason other than wanting to hear Josephine's voice, than she could wake Louis to tell him that she was going to do it.

"Can't sleep?"

Faby jumped at the sound of his voice. "No."

"Strange house, strange bed?"

Stranger for a husband? "Yes."

"Well, it takes a little getting used to. After a while, you become accustomed to it."

Louis didn't say anything else, but now that she knew he was awake, Faby once again held herself very stiffly, holding her breath, afraid that he was about to go back on his word not to do anything. When at last he began to snore, she slowly started to relax, easing the tension out of each muscle bit by bit until her body lay against the length of his, and she fell asleep, just before the faint lavender of first dawn light became visible through the windows.

Chapter 11

Faby opened her eyes to unfamiliar wallpaper in shades of red, green, and cream, perfectly symmetrical flowers neatly arranged on vertical stripes, windows of the wrong size and the wrong placement on the walls, a closet door on the wrong side of the room. She looked around the room, trying to get her bearings. Of course. Louis had married her the day before, and they had spent the night at his mother's house in Massachusetts. At some point today, she and Louis had to catch a train.

Judging from the sounds and smells of breakfast wafting up the stairwell, she was the only one in the house who hadn't yet gotten up. When she entered the dining room, where Louis, his mother, and his sister sat at the table, she had the oddest sensation of making an entrance that was much more important than simply coming into a dining room to eat breakfast.

Louis looked up from his eggs. "Well, there you are, sleepyhead, joining us at last!" Faby felt her face flush with embarrassment, and she put her hand to her hair. Louis got up and pulled her chair out for her. "I drew the shades, so that you could sleep a little longer. You had a long day yesterday." Louis's tone of voice seemed oddly, inexplicably, genuinely kind.

Louis's mother smiled. "What can I get for you for breakfast, Faby? We have scrambled eggs." She pointed to a covered dish. "Or, I could make you poached or fried, or would you prefer corn flakes?"

"Scrambled eggs will be fine, thank you."

Louis's mother motioned for Faby to hand over her plate. When she received it back, it had bacon and toast on it that she didn't want, in addition to the eggs, but she didn't say anything. She turned to Louis. "What time's our train, Louis?"

"It leaves at two this afternoon."

Before Faby could ask when it would arrive at their destination, his mother said, "That will give us just enough time for you to see the doctor and have some lunch before we have to be leaving for the station."

Faby wasn't sure she'd heard her correctly. "I beg your pardon?"

Louis's mother gave him a look, a look that clearly said, *You didn't tell her?* and Louis looked down sheepishly at his half-eaten scrambled eggs. When he looked up again, a brief moment later, the sheepish look was gone, and he said, "I'm sorry, Mother. It completely slipped my mind when I was showing Faby my mementoes." Now turning to Faby, he said, "Mother suggested that we take you to get checked out by our family doctor, to make sure everything is all right with you and the baby, seeing as we'll be traveling before it's born." Louis paused, his mother gave him another telling look, and he continued, "You know, if you think it would be easier with the baby, you don't have to come on the circuit with me. You could stay here while you're waiting for it to be born." Tears sprang to Faby's eyes, which Louis must have seen because he quickly said, "It was just a thought. Of course I want you to come with me."

Later, after a brief, uncomfortable car ride, they arrived at the doctor's office and sat down to wait in the small waiting room, which looked to be a converted sunroom or porch of some kind, with mismatched dining room chairs arranged around the perimeter of the room. There was only one other patient ahead of them, a dumpy woman of indeterminate age with rheumy eyes and a barking cough. She held a handkerchief to her mouth as though expecting at any moment to expel whatever it was in her lungs causing her such misery.

Before long, a harried-looking woman emerged from the examining room holding two pale children by the hand, one child clutching his ear, the other with his finger up his nose. The door to the examining room opened; a nurse poked her head in the waiting room, and called out a name. The coughing woman got up. The nurse waited for her to enter the examining room and then closed the door behind them.

After several minutes had passed, the coughing woman emerged from the examining room, clutching a small piece of paper in her hand, the expression on her face still miserable but with a thin overlay of triumph, the doctor having acquiesced to her demands for the treatment of what ailed her. When the nurse poked her head into the waiting room a few minutes later and called for "Mrs. Kittell," Faby made no move to get up, and Louis whispered in her ear, "That's you."

In the examining room, the nurse directed Faby to stand behind a screen and remove her drawers, her garter belt, and her stockings. Her other clothing was loose enough that she didn't need to remove any of it, for which she was grateful, feeling that same fear of exposure as she had the night before when she took a bath. The nurse helped her onto the examining table, draped her lower half with a sheet, and arranged her legs for the examination, while Dr. Harris washed his hands and slipped on a pair of short rubber gloves.

Although Dr. Harris appeared to be in his 70s, with a deeply-lined face and gray hair changing over to white, his posture was erect, his hands were steady, and he had a face that did not appear to suffer fools, or patients, gladly. As she watched him tug at the gloves, Faby noticed a small table on which had been set a tray laid out with several metal instruments, the purpose of which, she decided, she really did not want to know, and she quickly looked away.

The nurse wheeled the table to be within easy reach of Dr. Harris's right hand. She then stood by the examining table and smiled reassuringly as Faby lay on her back with her knees spread wide and both hands clenched into fists while he slipped things inside her which should never have gone inside her—or inside anyone else, for that matter—the only consolation being that Louis and his family didn't have ringside seats to her exposed privates.

When Dr. Harris was finished, he stripped off the rubber gloves and the nurse rearranged the sheet, Faby's clothing, and her legs to get her ready for the next part of the examination, which involved much poking and prodding and thumping of her belly and murmurs of *Hmm, good, good,* from Dr. Harris. Then the nurse laid a thin towel on Faby's exposed belly, and Dr. Harris leaned down and put his ear to it, at the same time putting his two fingers on Faby's wrist. Faby jumped, startled. The nurse once again smiled reassurance. "It's all right, dear. He's listening for your baby's heartbeat." Listening for it? Did that mean there might not be one? "Very good," Dr. Harris said as he straightened up, before she could take that thought any further. "No cause for concern here. There's a nice strong heartbeat. Are you feeling much movement?"

Faby nodded and said, "Some," as Dr. Harris motioned for the nurse to help her sit up. "You look to be twenty weeks along," Dr. Harris informed her, in a definitive tone that Faby found oddly comforting, given that she could pinpoint the moment of conception herself, to the month, day, and hour, if not the minute. She was twenty weeks along. That meant that in four months, her baby would be born. In four months, no more, no less.

"Now, you're young and healthy," Dr. Harris said, washing his hands at a small sink on the other side of the room, "nevertheless, you still must take scrupulous care with your personal hygiene to ensure no accidents of pregnancy."

Faby didn't like the way he said "personal hygiene," as if it were a given that she existed in a perpetual state of filth—and "accidents of pregnancy" sounded downright ominous. "You must drink plenty of fluids," Dr. Harris continued, his tone now taking on a tinge of kindliness, "to eliminate waste products from the body. You must also attempt a bowel movement every day; even if you don't succeed in having one, you still must make the attempt." Faby started to feel panic rising because there were too many instructions to remember them all, and she had no way of writing them down. "You must keep yourself evenly warm at all times to promote excretion of waste through the skin. You must then bathe every day to remove it: a sponge-bath is preferable, and shower-baths are strictly forbidden. Every day, you should take some light exercise in the fresh air. You must avoid heavy lifting or straining and, most particularly, you must not use the sewing machine."

That particular restriction, although it didn't seem to make a whole lot of sense, gave her no cause for concern until she realized that there would be no one else but she to prepare the baby's layette. Louis couldn't very well be expected to do it. The thought of Louis hunched over a dining room table surveying all of those little pieces of yellow flannel, nightgown pieces and diaper shirt pieces and bonnet pieces, trying to figure out what went with what was ludicrous.

"Starting in your seventh month," Dr. Harris was saying, raising his voice, as though he knew she had not been paying attention to what he was saying after he delivered the sewing machine restriction, "you will need to begin preparing for the birth. No more riding on the train or in a car unless absolutely necessary. No marital relations. And starting in your eighth month, you must see a doctor once a week to have your urine and your blood pressure checked." The tinge of kindliness in his tone now replaced by officiousness, he paused, as though expecting Faby to respond with either assent or a question. When she didn't, he opened the drawer of a cabinet and handed her a pamphlet. "Here, this will give you guidelines to follow to keep yourself healthy and deliver a robust baby." Faby thanked him politely as she looked at the front of the pamphlet. It was entitled "Prenatal Care," with a publication date of 1915. Obviously, if he had given out so few of the pamphlets in ten years that he still had one to give to her, his other patients must have been more receptive to his instructions. Well, no matter, it would give her something to read on the train.

As Louis drove them back to the house in silence, his mother in the front seat beside him, Faby couldn't recall ever having seen the back of someone's head look so smug. Back at the house, they ate a light lunch of turkey salad sandwiches cut into triangles, followed by fruit cocktail. When they were finished with lunch, Louis took Faby's suitcase out to the car, and she used the toilet one last time before leaving, Louis calling up the stairs before she had even she washed her hands, "Let's get a wiggle on—we have a train to catch!"

As they rode to the station, with Dorothy driving this time, Faby was surprised at how strange the streets of Bedford looked, as if she had never seen them before, even though she had ridden this way the previous day. Dorothy dropped them off at the entrance to the station, waited without turning off the engine while Louis unloaded Faby's suitcase, and then promptly drove off.

After Louis purchased their tickets and saw to Faby's suitcase, the train was boarding, so they didn't have to sit and wait for it, good timing obviously coming naturally to America's Favorite Hoofer. Louis guided Faby up the aisle with his hand on her shoulder until he found an empty seat toward the rear of the car, motioning for her to enter first and sit next to the window. As she got herself settled, slipping off her coat, Faby noted that the smell of the car—stale tobacco, competing colognes, wool, dust, and sweat—was admittedly unpleasant— but at least there were no over or undertones of manure.

Before getting a good look around, Faby had the immediate sense that the car was larger than the passenger cars of the Missisquoi Railroad that served Enosburg and the rest of Franklin County—which was to be expected, given the difference in size between Vermont and Massachusetts—and nearly full, with no empty seats and only a handful of people sitting in seats by themselves. All of the men wore fedoras and tailored suits or overcoats. They looked prosperous, in a way that even the most prosperous farmer, conveying his wife and many children to church in a new Ford, never could. She wondered where these men could be going as they busied themselves snapping open their newspapers. Somewhere that had something to do with business, most likely, and money.

As the train began to move, Faby turned to the window to watch the people remaining on the platform. In the foreground, a young couple, the girl holding a small, long-haired dog in the crook of her arm, stood waving goodbye to someone they were obviously very glad to see the last of, both of them waving enthusiastically, if not exuberantly, and grinning from ear to ear. Even the dog looked happy, his little black dog lips curved into a smile, his plumed tail waving from side to side beneath the girl's elbow. Without thinking, Faby nudged Louis and whispered, "Good riddance to bad rubbish!" Louis said, "What was that?" and when Faby pointed, he lightly kissed the top of her head. She smiled up at him, then immediately felt embarrassed for having done so, as though she were flirting with a stranger with whom she had no business flirting, and her parents would be duly informed.

As the train began to pick up speed, Faby twisted to get a last look at the Bedford station—the platform now empty except for a forlorn-looking fat man in a double-breasted suit—before turning around to see what lay ahead.

"Don't get too excited," Louis said, reaching into the inside pocket of his jacket, taking out a comb, and quickly running it through his hair. "This just takes us to Boston."

"We're just going to Boston? I thought you said we were going to Connecticut." She had never been to Boston, of course, but, still, Massachusetts was an adjoining state, and even though *she* had never been to Boston, she knew of people in Enosburg who had, each and every venturing out of Franklin County being duly reported in the next issue of *The Enosburg Standard.*

"We are, but we're taking the train into Boston because neither Mother nor Dorothy likes driving in the city. We'll get the Pennsy at South Station for our jump."

"Jump?" Faby turned from the window to look at him.

"Yes, traveling to my next booking. I guess I'm going to have to teach you the lingo, aren't I? I don't expect that you've spent any time with fellows in my line of work except for me, right?"

"That's true, you're the only one." Faby paused, considering. "I don't think there has ever been anyone from Enosburg who has gone into show business. Well, except for the town band, and I don't think that really counts as show business because no one pays to see them. We just bring blankets to the park and sit on the grass while they play."

"True, no one pays to see 'em—but don't sell those boys short. You can find some damn fine musicians in a town band."

No sooner had the train picked up speed, flashing past residential neighborhoods, the outskirts of one town quickly becoming the outskirts of the next, than it began to decrease speed. The train yard was soon in sight, a labyrinth of tracks and switches even more dizzying than the junction at White River, if that were possible. As soon as the covered platform came in sight, as if on cue, the men in the car snapped their newspapers closed and folded them neatly to tuck under their arms as they stood and began a slow shuffle to the front of the car before it had even stopped.

Faby made no move to get up, assuming she and Louis would wait their turn politely until those already standing and those in the seats in front of them had gotten off the train, but Louis jumped to his feet. He snatched their coats from the overhead rack, tossed them over his shoulder, and, in nearly the same motion, grabbed Faby by the hand to thrust himself, and Faby along with him, in front of the two people who blocked the aisle by their seat, one a middle-aged man holding a briefcase in addition to his newspaper, the other slightly older, holding a small valise, neither of whom seemed the least bit bothered at being treated so rudely by a stranger and his mortified young wife. When Louis reached the door of the car, he turned to help Faby step off, then grabbed her hand and began loping for the station, Faby running to keep up with him, as he shouted an explanation back over his shoulder, "We don't have much time before our train, and I have to see to our bags!"

Inside the station, he led Faby to a bench, dropping her coat next to her. "I'm going to see to our bags. Now, I need you to stay here. Understand? I need to be able to find you in a hurry so we don't miss our train. Do you hear me? *Don't move.*" He rushed off before giving Faby a chance to answer, quickly disappearing into the crowd, Faby desperately trying to keep him in sight, the only person she knew in a city of thousands upon thousands of people, most of whom looked to be in this vast space, milling about, striding purposefully, waiting determinedly, unaware of any concerns but their own.

She was now alone, which was probably just as well. She needed a few moments to catch her breath and compose herself after the sprint from the train. Her hair, she was sure, was a mess, and anyone looking at her would know instantly that she was on the verge of tears after being treated like a child by her new husband—not only treated like a child, but treated like a dim-witted child, a child who wouldn't have sense enough to come in out of the rain, or, in this case, didn't have sense enough to know how easily she could become lost in a place as large as this to which she had never been. Of course she wasn't going to move.

She didn't think she had ever seen so many people in the same place at the same time. There couldn't possibly be any people left in the City of Boston to occupy the buildings and drive the cars and jostle one another on the sidewalks. In this cavernous space, the number of people to fill the Opera House, the place that accommodated the most people in Enosburg, would be no more than the number of people now at the newsstand in the center of the concourse, browsing newspapers and magazines, smoking cigarettes, waiting their turn to pay.

While the Opera House had a coffered ceiling, it didn't begin to compare with the coffered ceiling of the South Station Terminal, the elaborate network of polished wood so high above the floor that looking up made her dizzy. Looking down made her equally dizzy, the mosaic marble floor unimaginably intricate. Everywhere she looked, dark mahogany gleamed, polished granite glowed, and shining brass shone. The enameled brick and plaster walls were bright with electric lights. In comparison, the Opera House, with it unadorned plaster walls, utilitarian sconces, and wood floors looked like the plainest of farmhouses, lived in by a family just eking out a living with a small herd of scrawny cows and a meager farm stand in the summer. Compared with the South Station Terminal, the train station on Depot Street was a mere *attempt* at a train station, one small room with varnished wainscoting, in places discolored and scratched, with a comfortable pot-bellied stove in one corner and a hopeless rube of a ticket master at the window, who exclaimed in genuine delight every time he sold a ticket.

Now that she had caught her breath, Faby became aware of a disturbance in her belly, a quick, random bumping, like a ricochet. She hoped that her running into the station with Louis hadn't harmed the baby, causing one of those "accidents of pregnancy" Doctor Harris had warned her about, the accidents in question too dire for him to describe to her, not that she knew what an accident of pregnancy even was. Some occurrence, seemingly harmless at the time, that weeks or months later produced a defective infant, a cripple or an idiot? Or some kind of damage to her own insides that would bring pain and bleeding? Or—an accident of pregnancy might bring an end to it altogether. She held her breath, waiting for another ricochet. None came.

What did come was pressure. Pressure on her bladder. She shifted in her seat to ease it, first this way, then that, but the pressure remained constant. Pressure *from* the bladder, not on it. She had to use the toilet. Just the thought of how long it had been since she had last emptied her bladder intensified the pressure all the more. What was she going to do? Obviously, there would be a ladies' room in the building, several of them, in fact, but she had no idea where they would be, if any were in sight of the bench where she was sitting, where Louis had left her and told her not to move. If she left to look for a bathroom and Louis came back to an empty bench, she had no idea what he would do. Would he stand there and call her name, softly at first, then louder, until he was shouting, his face turning red, the cords in his neck standing out, pacing the area around the bench as people stared at him, sniggering at the nattily dressed man who had managed to lose his ninny of a wife when he went to tend to her suitcase so that she could have clean underwear in Connecticut? Would he enlist the aid of a porter, necessitating the expenditure of a tip? Or, which was much more likely, would he simply shrug, board the train to Connecticut alone, and leave her here?

She craned her neck to see if she could see him coming back—he had been in a hurry, after all—but there were too many people obstructing her view. She then stood up to get a better view, which intensified the urgency in her bladder. She took another few seconds to look for a sign for a ladies' room—if not the entrance itself, at least a sign with an arrow pointing the way—with no luck. She sat back down. Surely, Louis would be back any moment now, and she could go use the toilet. He would have to ask the conductor to hold the train for her, but he would have a ready quip to save face, she would empty her bladder, and they would be on their way to Connecticut.

It was no use. She had to go to the bathroom, and she had to go *now*. Louis could be angry with her, or Louis could leave her behind, but she was going to leave the bench and find a ladies' room. Wetting herself was simply not an option.

She got up as slowly and carefully as she could, aware that she had waited long enough for any sudden movement to prove disastrous. Taking a few steps away from the bench, she stopped to scan her immediate surroundings, but there was no ladies' room in sight. She took a few more steps, no ladies' room. When she took a few more steps and turned back to make sure she could still see her bench, she couldn't, so she gave up trying and quickened her pace on the loud marble floor until she found a ladies' room at last and made it to the toilet in time, not knowing whether to rejoice or weep in relief as her waste, along with the baby's, streamed from her body. After quickly washing her hands, she left the bathroom and stopped, not knowing whether to turn right or left.

To the right, in the middle of the concourse, a group of young women stood talking loudly and laughing. To the left, a man in a homburg hat was getting his shoes polished. Another two women brushed past her from the ladies' room, shrugging on their coats as they walked. Obviously, they knew where they were going.

Well, she couldn't very well stand here indefinitely. She had to get back to the bench before Louis came for her. Or maybe she didn't. She'd always been told that if she were to get lost in the woods, she should stay where she was until someone found her. She looked across the concourse for any kind of seat where she could wait for Louis, but then thought better of it. The lost-in-the-woods rule was based on the premise that someone wants to find you.

She began walking. Nothing looked familiar, and everything looked familiar. After she had gone far enough to come upon another ladies' room, she thought about turning back and going the other way, but that normally got a lost person even more lost. She would just keep walking until she reached the end of the building or the waiting room where Louis had left her. With this decision, she felt a little better—until she heard the announcement for the train to Providence. Whether she had missed the train with Louis or without Louis, she had missed the train.

Someone touched her shoulder, and she started. "Sorry, miss, begging your pardon," the porter who had touched her shoulder said, his dark face oddly deferential. "Do you need assistance finding your party?"

They had both stopped walking. "Oh," Faby said, turning to face him, "My husband, yes. I need to find my husband. He's tall with blond hair. He was carrying a camel's hair overcoat, although he may have put it on—"

"Oh, no, ma'am," the porter said, smiling, "I'm not going to go look for him. I'll have an announcement put on the public address. What's his name?"

"Oh," Faby said, flushing. "Louis. Louis Kittell."

"All right, ma'am. Now you go stand over there, and I'll have the announcement put on. Your husband will be here to fetch you in no time at all. Now, you stay put, ma'am, until he comes."

The porter walked off, and in a few moments the announcement came on. Before too long, she saw Louis coming towards her. "Where the hell have you *been*? I've been looking all over for you. We've missed our goddamn train. I *told* you to stay in the waiting area. I *told* you not to move. We've missed our goddamn train."

People were staring at them, she knew, at this urbane young man and his ninny of a wife. "I had to,"—she was already crying—"I had to go to the bathroom." Sobbing now, she tried to explain how she wasn't able to wait, but she was crying too hard to speak. Louis put his arm around her shoulders and drew her aside. "All right, all right. None of that, now. I'm sorry. I was worried, is all. I didn't know what had happened to you." He put both arms around her as she sobbed against his chest. She could imagine the pitying looks of passersby and Louis's wry smile as he met their eyes—*Well, what's a fellow to do?*—and she didn't care. She was newly married to a man she barely knew, pregnant with his child, and leaving everything she had ever known and everyone she had ever loved behind. It was time to cry.

Chapter 12

Louis let her cry herself out, for which she felt oddly grateful. He handed her his handkerchief. "Missing the train isn't the end of the world. It will give us a chance to get some supper. Are you hungry?"

She hadn't thought about being hungry. She handed him back his handkerchief. "Yes, I guess I am."

"Good, good. We'll have ourselves a nice supper while we wait for the next train to Providence. Ready?"

She nodded, wondering where they would find a restaurant, skipping to catch up with his long strides. She briefly considered asking him to slow his pace, then decided against it. She had caused him enough aggravation as it was. Louis looked down and offered her his arm, smiling that amiable smile she remembered from his time in Enosburg. After several minutes of walking, they arrived at a lunchroom, yet another feature of the South Station Terminal on a grand scale, the long marble counter set atop more gleaming mahogany, with enough stools for ten Giddings Drugs soda foundations.

Louis found two empty stools next to each other, and they sat down. "Ham and cheese on rye okay?" he said when the counter attendant, a short, chinless man who looked more bored than attentive, came to take their order. Faby nodded as

Louis ordered the sandwiches, coffee for himself, and milk for her. "And two pieces of cherry pie, if you've got 'em," he added as the attendant turned away. "It's best to order everything you want at once," Louis said to Faby, in what seemed like a stage whisper for the attendant's benefit. "Once you've given your order, they're done with you 'til you're ready to pay the check."

As she ate the sandwich and drank the milk, Faby felt a wash of gratitude toward Louis for buying her something to eat. She'd been hungry and tired, and the food made her feel better. Her next thought was how wrong that seemed. The husband provided the money to stock the pantry, of course, but the women in the family provided the meals. They planned the meals, shopped for the food, prepared the food, served the food—and there was never, *ever* any doubt that at the appointed time for breakfast, lunch, or supper, a meal would be on the table, like the sun coming up in the morning and going down at night. She reached for her cherry pie and ate it thoughtfully. The crust wasn't as flaky as Maman Aurore's, but it didn't matter—*any* cherry pie was good cherry pie. Louis lit a cigarette and motioned to the counter attendant for more coffee. The attendant avoided making eye contact, thereby avoiding the need to take five or six steps to the coffee pot and another five or six steps to Louis's cup, until Louis stood up, leaned across the counter, and snapped his fingers.

When Louis had his coffee, Faby said, "What time does our train leave?" He looked at his watch. "Another ten minutes." After he'd finished his cigarette and gulped down the last of his coffee, he stood up, fished in his pocket for a handful of change, and picked out two quarters and a dime, which he dropped on top of the grease-spotted check left by the attendant. Helping Faby off the stool, he looked at her, then the stool, then the floor, then her again. "Faby, where is your coat?"

Her coat. She didn't have her coat. She thought back. She had left it in the waiting area when she went to look for the ladies' room. Thinking she'd be coming right back, she'd left it on the bench. Before she could answer him, Louis said, "You left it in the waiting area, didn't you?" She nodded, not trusting herself to speak. "It's all right," Louis said. "I'll get it." He took her hand and headed off in the direction of the platform. Finding a porter, he said, "Could you see that my wife gets on the train, then ask the conductor to hold it for a few minutes while I go get her coat?"

"Yes, sir," the porter said as Louis pressed a coin in his hand and rushed off, his overcoat flapping behind him. "Tall fella, ain't he?" the porter said. "Look at them long legs. He sure can hoof it."

"He's America's Favorite Hoofer," Faby informed the porter, to which he responded, "You don't say."

The porter helped Faby onto the train and, she hoped, went in search of the conductor as Louis had instructed. She sat in the first empty seat she found so that Louis would at least not have to hunt for her on the train. She wondered how long it would take them to get to their destination. The other passengers in the car seemed to be settling in for a long ride, stowing their coats and belongings securely in the overhead racks, adjusting their clothing so that it wouldn't tug or bind as they sat, and chatting with their traveling companions, trying out this topic and that to find one that would help pass the time.

Louis had returned with her coat, which he folded neatly and placed in the overhead rack, followed by his own. As the train began to pull out of the station in a raucous swirl of steam and cinders, the thought occurred to Faby that she and Louis would be spending a great deal of time together riding on trains, which would give her an opportunity to have private, intimate conversations with him—about his school days, his time in the Army, how and when he had learned to dance—as the landscapes and the cityscapes unfolded before their eyes. She couldn't help but feel a surge of excitement in her stomach, with some trepidation, of course, but excitement nonetheless. She was going on the circuit.

Looking out the window as the train pulled away, Faby was surprised to see how few people had remained on the platform to see their loved ones off on their journeys, just a cluster of surly-looking young men smoking cigarettes who looked as though they had no business being there in the first place, several bedraggled women holding equally bedraggled children by the hand, and an old woman so infirm that she obviously couldn't leave the platform unaided. She would remain there, on the South Station platform, leaning on her cane, clutching her worn satchel until whomever had left her behind came back to fetch her.

As they left the train yard behind, Faby looked out the window and strained to see as much of Boston as she could in the rapidly falling twilight, street after street of identical three-story houses unlike any she had ever seen before, three bay windows set one atop the other, three small porches set one atop the other, each house the same as the one set next it with the only variation she could see being the houses' states of repair.

Soon, they left the city behind, then the outskirts of the city. Louis reached into the inside pocket of his jacket and extracted a deck of cards. "How about a game of gin rummy. Do you play? I'll teach you if you don't know how."

"Oh, no, I know gin rummy."

Louis shuffled the cards deftly. When he cut the deck, he drew a queen and she drew a seven. Looking at her first hand, Faby saw that he had dealt her a run of five clubs. When she looked up from her hand, he was chuckling. "Watch it, there, dollface. You have a tell."

"What do you mean?"

"A tell. I can tell by the expression on your face that you have a good hand."

"Oh." She felt a little deflated. When she won the first hand, she wondered if he let her win, as if she were a child who couldn't bear to lose. However, when she won the next three hands, she didn't think so. Louis was not the type of man to lose at anything four times in a row.

City lights came into view, and Louis put the cards back in his pocket as the other passengers began gathering their belongings. "Providence."

"Oh? We're not continuing to Connecticut? I thought you said your next engagement was in Connecticut."

"It was, but while you were sleeping in at Mother's, I got on the blower and managed to finagle myself a spot on the bill at the Majestic to break the jump to Ridgefield."

"That was fast!"

Louis winked. "I know a guy."

Chapter 13

When Faby awoke the next morning in Providence for her first real day of married life, the view through the grimy window of their hotel room didn't look worth getting out of bed for. The room itself was unlike any she had ever seen before, very small with a high ceiling and wallpaper that looked as though it had been deliberately designed to be drab, rather than acquiring its drabness naturally over time.

She scrambled out of bed, dug into her suitcase for her robe, and left the room in search of the toilet, which she found at the end of a long, narrow corridor. The bathroom smelled strongly of Breath o' Pine, as though it had just been cleaned, and she thought she might like to take a bath. Setting the plug in the drain and turning on the hot water tap, she dashed back to the room for her clothes before someone else could claim the bathroom. After returning, she waited until the water had reached just the right level in the tub before undressing, sliding in, and closing her eyes. No city sounds made their way into the room as she lay there, just the undertone of exchanging air as she breathed and the beating of her heart.

She opened her eyes to see that her body was not fully-immersed in the bath water, as she had thought, but her breasts and her belly had formed three little islands, just cresting the surface of the water. She poked at her belly, which seemed to have formed a hard little mound some time in recent days without her having taken notice of it. Now that the dreadful nausea and vomiting seemed to have gone for good and the initial soreness of her breasts had subsided, the only change she had been aware of throughout the day was the baby moving around in her abdomen, which was more of an unknown companion sharing her body with her than actual changes to her own body.

When the bath water began to cool, she turned the hot water tap back on, then thought better of it. There would be other guests on the floor who needed to use the bathroom. She dressed reluctantly and returned to the room. As she made the bed, she found a note on the nightstand laid out with two quarters and what looked like a ticket of some kind under the quarters. The note was addressed to her, from Louis:

Faby—
I've gone to rehearsal. Here's money to get yourself something to eat and a ticket to the evening show. We'll have a late supper after the show.

—Slim
How wonderful! Money for food—and a ticket to the show! Things had happened so fast over the last few days she had completely forgotten that she would be able to see the vaudeville show not just once a year but whenever she liked. Why, when they weren't traveling to the next town, she could see the show every day if she liked. Imagine that! The show Louis was playing in was different from the one that had come to Enosburg those many months before, so of course the acts would be completely different, except for Louis's, but she could watch him dance for hours and hours and never tire of his style

and grace, not to mention the intricate impossibility of his footwork. She wondered who the headliner would be—a musical act with piano, singing, and banter? a magician, perhaps? a witty monologist? an opera soubrette? She had seen a singer billed as an opera soubrette only once and found her more annoying than enchanting, with verbal frills, trills, and histrionics that were, really, not completely necessary. She smiled at the thought and wondered if she could have the makings of a theater critic. Well, why not? She was certainly capable, having seen every vaudeville show in Enosburg since she was ten and read Chandler Mason's review in the *Enosburg Standard* the following week, and of course her good grades in English. As she set the note back on the nightstand, she was surprised at Louis's Palmer-perfect penmanship. She would have thought him to have more of a slap-dash hand.

At the theater, Faby checked the playbill first and found Louis billed as "SlimWhite and His Fantastic Flying Feet," no longer America's favorite, it would appear—or perhaps the alliterative new billing was a step up for him. Smiling at her own pun, she hesitated in front of the box office and took the ticket Louis had left for her out of her purse.

When it came time for Louis's act, there was a slight delay before the curtain rose. Then Louis strolled onto the stage to piano accompaniment with a huge grin on his face that she didn't remember from his performance in Enosburg. Could that smile be his knowing that she was in the audience, and he was playing to her for the first time as his wife? She smiled in response, as he began a slow, graceful soft shoe, still accompanied by only the piano. She had assumed that he would do the same routine as he had in Enosburg, and she was a little disappointed that she wouldn't get to see it again, but this must be that versatility he had mentioned when he showed her his scrapbook at his mother's house. Suddenly brass blared, and

Louis was doing the Charleston, the fastest and wildest version of the Charleston Faby had ever seen, arms and legs flying, smile widening into a genuine grin. As the Charleston ended, saxophones took over for Louis to do the Black Bottom. As he began his foot stomps, Faby heard a gasp from the elderly woman seated next to her. When Louis's arms pinwheeled to slap the floor and then his own bottom, the elderly woman exhaled an *Outrageous!*, stood up, and walked out. Faby would have to remember to ask Louis if anyone else had ever walked out on his performance before. "Black Bottom" wasn't "Shine On Harvest Moon," but it certainly wasn't anything to get steamed up about. Looking back at the stage, Faby saw that Louis was actually laughing. He must have seen the woman get up and walk out. He ended his performance with a broad wink, and it was time for intermission.

Faby didn't wait for the curtain to come all the way down before getting up and heading for the ladies' room, the location of which she had taken care to identify when she first entered the lobby of the theater. There was a line, but one she could wait with little risk of an accident. As she stood waiting, the baby shifted within her, seeming to stretch, and Faby wondered if he had been able to hear the show through her belly or, at the very least, feel the rhythm of the music. She liked the thought of telling him when he was old enough that he had attended his first vaudeville show before he was even born, and his father, yes, *his* father, had wowed the crowd with his performance of the two most popular dances of the day. She would hold back the detail of the elderly woman taking umbrage at the Black Bottom and walking out, to tell him later, when he was old enough to appreciate the folly of the older generation's outrage at the younger generation's having a good time.

When the three of them were spending a leisurely Saturday together at home, when the weather was too cold or wet for picnics, Louis would teach him the Charleston and the Black Bottom, his little toddler limbs so stumpy and abbreviated in their movements that no one but his father and mother would have any idea what he was doing, just like when a baby first learns to talk, and his speech is gibberish to everyone but his mother, who understands every utterance, every babbled syllable perfectly. They would have a phonograph and lots of records so they could play music and sing and dance whenever they liked.

After the show as they walked in search of a place for Louis to get something to eat, he confirmed that he had indeed seen the elderly woman walk out on his act and that no one had ever walked out on his act before. "I wonder what she was doing there. I would wager that she's never been to a vaudeville show before, although that seems hard to believe in this day and age. If you don't like an act, you just wait for the next one. And if you absolutely *hate* it, you don't get up and walk out. You sit on your hands and then applaud the following act twice as hard as it deserves."

Chapter 14

Outside the window, the cityscapes of southern New England filled Faby's field of vision to the point of disorientation, a dizzying hodgepodge of brick factories, smoke stacks, stone spires, bridges and trestles, rows of roofs, miles of crazily crisscrossing electrical wires—and buildings—buildings everywhere, the only open spaces between them streets, which weren't in fact open at all but filled with cars and trolleys and buses and trucks—and cemeteries jammed full of headstones, the people packed as closely in their graves as they had been in their dwellings.

They had to change trains in New London, and once they had gotten themselves settled again, a couple who looked to be older than Louis but younger than Faby's parents sat down in the seat opposite theirs. The wife was laden with several parcels, which she handed over to her husband to stow in the overhead rack. She was wearing a particularly unflattering cloche, of brown felt, with an oversized felt flower emerging from one side. Faby looked over at the husband, who, having finished with his wife's parcels, had sat down and pulled out a pocket watch to check the time. "We should be leaving momentarily," he announced.

Louis introduced himself to the couple after adjusting his trouser legs to preserve the creases. "How do you do? I'm Louis Kittell, and this is my bride Faby. We're on our honeymoon."

After the husband had introduced himself as Harold Jackson and his wife as Hildred, he said, "So, you're newly-weds. Well isn't that nice," and Hildred echoed, "Isn't that nice. Harold and I have been married for seventeen years."

Faby turned to Louis, expecting him to tell Harold and Hildred of the intimate family wedding, the overnight stay in Bedford, playing Providence, the theater where he would next play. "Yessiree Bob, it's nice!" he exclaimed, putting his arm around her shoulders and squeezing. He picked up her left hand, placed it on his knee, and put his hand over hers. He directed his next remarks to the Jacksons. "We had such a fine wedding. The exquisite music, the magnificent flowers, the sumptuous food, mountains in the background, our friends and family all in attendance, Faby a veritable vision in white."

Faby was so startled by Louis's description of their wedding that she nearly objected; however, she wasn't about to embarrass him in front of others, regardless of how foolish he sounded. He reached into his jacket pocket and took out his comb. "Well, that's enough about us!" Faby was unsure whether she should remove her hand from his knee, now that his hand was no longer on hers, seeing as he'd been the one to put it there. Louis ran the comb through his hair. Replacing the comb in his pocket, he once again covered Faby's hand with his. "So, what can you tell us about yourselves?"

Harold and Hildred looked at each other as if no one had ever asked them that question before. As she watched Harold's face, Faby thought he was about to ask Louis why he wanted to know, but he proceeded to answer the question instead. It was, after all, a harmless question, Faby told herself, asked more out of politeness than a selfish need to pass the time with idle conversation.

"Well, let's see," Harold said, looking at his wife, who nodded encouragement. "We're from Schenectady. We've lived there for the past, ten is it now, no, eleven years. And before that, we lived in Lowell."

"Schenectady, you say," Louis murmured. "How do you like it?"

"Oh, we like it well enough. We own our own home, and the children can walk to school."

"You have children, do you?" Louis prompted when Harold stopped speaking. "How old?"

Harold answered without hesitation. "Mary is fifteen, Alice is nine, and James is four."

"He's our baby," Hildred added needlessly. "Harold, won't you show Louis and Faby the picture in your wallet?"

Harold dutifully pulled out his wallet and took out a small snapshot, which he handed to Louis. "A fine-looking lot," Louis said. He passed the snapshot back to Harold.

"Why, thank you," Harold responded.

"What's your occupation?" Louis asked Harold as he replaced the photograph in his wallet.

"I manage a shoe factory."

"A shoe factory, you say."

"Yes," Hildred interjected. "He worked his way up from the assembly line to foreman and from foreman to manager."

"Shoes," Louis said. "How about that. Shoes."

"He makes a very good living," Hildred said, but she stopped short of announcing how much money he made. Several moments of silence went by until Harold broke it. "You haven't told us your occupation, Louis."

"Haven't I?"

Both Jacksons shook their heads, and Faby wondered what he would tell them.

"I'm an accountant," he announced. Faby stopped herself from exclaiming, *What?!* and then exacerbating his lie by clapping her hand over her mouth.

"Now, Faby, here"—he patted her hand—"doesn't understand the attraction of tallying columns of numbers all day long, but she's never had a good head for figures, have you, dear?"

"No. No head for figures."

"You see, accounting is such a satisfying occupation. It's clean and quiet, relatively speaking, and you're the fellow who holds all the answers to what's important to the company."

"True enough," Harold murmured.

Faby turned to look out the window at the passing landscape. Where were they now? They must be halfway through Connectocut by now. She turned to Louis. "Do you know where we are?"

Louis looked past her out the window. "Oh, yes, we've just passed through Westbrook, and that's Guilford up ahead."

Hildred said, "Oh, my! How can you tell? I don't think we've passed through many stations, have we?"

"I've very well-acquainted with the Boston and Maine line."

Harold frowned. "But I thought you said you were an accountant."

"I am. Accounting is my *current* occupation. I was a drummer for a while before I took up accounting."

"I see. What did you sell?"

"Adding machines, of course. That's how I got into accounting. They're really quite a marvel, adding machines."

Faby's breath caught in her throat. As luck would have it, however, Harold turned out to be enamored of office machines, and he burbled on happily about adding machines and typewriters, the Dictaphone, the Graphotype for addressing envelopes, ending with the mechanical pencil sharpener and its invaluable contribution to American efficiency, productivity, and prosperity.

When Harold at last ran out of office machines, Louis changed the subject to the merits and detractions of East Coast railroads, with which he was most intimately acquainted. As Louis enumerated the merits of the Boston and Maine Railroad, Harold looked interested enough to be taking notes, if only he'd had the foresight that morning before leaving for the train station to have tucked a notebook and pencil into one of the jacket pockets of his neatly-pressed brown suit.

Listening to Louis go on so, Faby was struck by how much he reminded her of Tommy Snyder, the biggest know-it-all in her class, who could never let any question go by, regardless of the subject, without answering it himself, who insisted on one-upping people to the point of nearly getting himself punched in the nose. At the same time she noted the similarity, Faby was surprised to realize that it really didn't bother her. Was it so wrong to help people to pass the time with interesting conversation on a long trip? Wasn't what Louis was doing just a form of entertainment? Perfectly harmless entertainment, even useful entertainment, you could be justified in saying?

After a while, Faby began to feel herself getting drowsy at the same time she knew that she would need to get up and go to the bathroom before too long. Louis had changed the subject to the news of the day: the growth of radiotelephone commercial service, some governor's ties with Tammany Hall, football. She turned her head to the window so that no one would see her eyelids flutter and close—which they would, when an adult started in on the news of the day— no matter how hard she tried to stay awake. She began to doze, her head bumping gently against the window glass with the train's movement. Just as she fell asleep, she heard Hildred say, "The poor thing must be worn out," and Louis respond, "It's been a whirlwind."

When Faby came awake, a short while later, her head was resting against Louis's shoulder. She jerked upright as quickly as if her head had been resting against the shoulder of a stranger, which, in point of fact, was really the case. Not counting the past forty-eight hours, she had known her husband for less than a week. Her parents had known each other all their lives. Their childhood memories always included each other. She couldn't imagine a childhood memory of hers including Louis Kittell, except, perhaps, as a friend's slightly dangerous older brother. The trunk of vaudeville mementoes aside, she knew next to nothing about him. Why, she knew more about her former teachers' husbands than she knew about her own. She knew that Mrs. Pillsbury and her husband Kenneth were third cousins, and he owned his farm free and clear. She knew that Mrs. Randall's husband Willard had arthritis in his hip, and it would flare in damp weather. She even knew that Mrs. Aikin's husband John had only a sixth grade education. An advancing tightness in her throat signaled that tears were imminent.

Think about it, the voice inside her head continued as the ache in her throat spread to prickle her nose, *you know more about the merchants in Enosburg than you know about this person you married.* Rodney Dolan had been known as Goofy Dolan as a boy because of his over-fondness of bad jokes, and he was still known as Goofy Dolan, successful furniture store or no. Franklin Giddings hadn't spoken with his brother George in over ten years, the two of them having fallen out over their parents' estate, George getting the house to live in and Franklin getting the store to make a living.

In fact, Faby had to admit that she knew more about the neighborhood *dogs* than she knew about her husband: their temperament, their parentage, and all their likes and dislikes. Her eyes were brimming, and she didn't dare blink for fear blinking would force the tears out of her eyes and down her face but she needed to blink to hold the tears in and the train's wheels just repeated, *How could I have been so foolish, so foolish, so foolish, so foolish?*

Faby. Someone was saying her name. *Faby.* She turned her head just enough to glance at Hildred without jostling her brimming eyes. "Faby," Hildred was saying, "come help me find the ladies."

Louis immediately said, "Oh, it's right—" but Hildred shot him such a look that he cut his sentence short and shrugged his shoulders. "You'll get used it," Harold said.

Louis got up and stood in the aisle to let Faby out of her seat. Harold got up to let Hildred out, while Faby stood uncertainly in the aisle, until Hildred touched her on the elbow and said, "This way." Faby kept her head down as she and Hildred made their way up the aisle. Still not used to the movement of the train, she felt unsteady on her feet.

After they had each used the rest room, Hildred put her hands on Faby's shoulders. "Are you pregnant, dear?"

Faby nodded her head, Hildred's use of Maman's term of endearment setting off sobs.

"I thought as much," Hildred said putting her arm around Faby's shoulders. "It's the hormones that are making you weepy. You just let it out, and I'll help you fix your face before we go back to the men."

Faby continued to cry, but letting it out didn't make her feel any better. If only it were that simple, a simple release of pent-up emotion, and equilibrium would be restored. Her chest heaved. "I don't know him."

"Who don't you know?" Hildred said.

"Louis. My husband. I don't know him." Her chest heaved again.

"Oh, that's a normal feeling for newlyweds," Hildred said. "It does take that first year of marriage before you really get to know each other. Living together takes some adjustment, as you get used to each other's quirks. Why, when we were first married, Harold refused to use the same towel twice, and I was doing wash three times a week. He wouldn't eat mashed potatoes; they had to be baked. He always saved one section of the afternoon paper to read after we'd gone to bed, and the rustling of the pages irritated me so I wouldn't sleep for hours."

"No," Faby said, "it's not that. I really don't know him." She tried to pull more air into her lungs, with little effect. "I don't know him. I'd known him for less than a week when I married him."

"Less than a week?" Hildred said, sounding surprised but not judgmental.

"Yes," Faby said, "I had known him for less than a week when I married him. How could I have done such a thing? I'd known him for less than a week, and he didn't write like he said he would until I wrote him about the baby. And then it took him weeks to respond."

"Well," Hildred said slowly, "if he was willing to marry you, he must be a decent man. Even though he barely knew you, he cared enough about you to preserve your reputation."

"How could I have married someone I barely knew? I knew nothing about him except that he was in the vaudeville show."

"The vaudeville show?" Hildred said. "What do you mean? I thought he was an accountant."

Faby shook her head. "No, he's not an accountant. He's America's Favorite Hoofer."

"So, that's how he bills himself, is it?" Hildred said. She didn't say anything else for several moments. "Well, the important thing is that he's giving your child a name. You can decide what to do about the marriage once the baby is born. Nowadays, nobody has to *stay* married. There is no shame in divorce."

No shame in divorce. Maybe in Schenectady, New York, there was no shame in divorce, but there still was shame in divorce in Enosburg Falls, Vermont—and always, always with blame assigned. Take it from Maman Aurore, there was blame assigned: He ran around; she turned a blind eye. He drank; she drove him to it. He beat her; she asked for it. Oh, there was shame, all right, and it lived in the telephone wires connecting all of those horrid old biddies who had nothing better to do with their time than gossip and snipe and belittle and judge.

Faby's sobs began to subside, and after a few more minutes, her breathing calmed. "Feeling better?" Hildred asked, and Faby nodded her head.

"Well, then, let's wipe your eyes and splash some cold water on your face."

Faby did as she was told and followed Hildred back down the aisle to where Louis and Harold were waiting, both with expectant looks on their faces as though an explanation were their right. As she was taking her seat, Hildred exchanged such a disapproving look with Harold that Faby was afraid Louis would see it and ask what it was about, but he showed no reaction when he stood up to let Faby resume the window seat, so it must have passed by him unnoticed. When he sat back down, he leaned over and asked Faby if she was all right.

She nodded, feeling strangely calm, but whether the calm was from Hildred's reassurances or just the aftermath of a good cry, she didn't know and she didn't care. She would sit here in her warm oasis of calm thinking of nothing at all as the landscape passed by and the train rocked gently and the conversations of the other passengers eddied around her and her husband did his best to keep their traveling companions entertained.

Chapter 15

After their time in Providence, Faby developed a routine for herself. She spent the first day exploring the new town they were in, taking care to note the location of the library so that she could pass the remaining days in that town reading, taking care to shelve the book in the wrong section of the Dewey Decimal System, so that someone else wouldn't check it out. After being forced to abandon the ending of *Gentle Julia* in Ridgefield, Connecticut, she became much better at selecting books she would be able to read in their entirety before the next jump.

She attended the opening night performance in each new town Louis played, sometimes telling the person sitting next to her that Slim White was her husband, other times relishing her special status privately. She would then write her review of the performance the following evening in a notebook she entitled, *Reviews from the Road*. When she was satisfied with her review, she would go in search of the day's newspaper. One of the towns was too small to have a daily, but the rest did, and she could compare her review with that of the local theater critic. The remaining evenings in the town she spent writing letters home. The fact that one could receive mail while traveling from town to town was really quite a marvel.

Opening night in Pine Plains, New York, Louis performed the same act Faby had seen him perform in Enosburg. She was pleased to see that his act was as effortless and ingratiating as when she had first seen it in the Opera House, and she applauded his performance so long and so hard that her hands were stinging long after the curtain came down on his last curtain call, but still, she wondered why he'd gone back to it. The audiences in Providence, Ridgefield, Norfolk, East Hadaam, and Hamilton had all responded so enthusiastically to his new act.

After a brief delay, the curtain rose, and there was Louis again, with an undersized derby perched atop his head and a goofy grin on his face befitting a seventh grade boy with a peashooter and a supply of spitballs. He gave a slight bow, dislodging the derby, which he caught in midair and deftly flipped back onto his head. "With all due respect to Mr. Bud Purdy, who is unable to perform for you this evening due to losing his train fare in a pool hall, I will be performing his number in his place. And with my deepest and sincerest apologies to Mr. Eddie Cantor, I give you, "'The Dumber They Come, The Better I Like 'Em.'" Prancing about the stage, Louis gave a very energetic if uneven rendition of the tune, laughing and adding some extra cross-overs and turns whenever he forgot the words.

A ventriloquist act followed Louis's second turn on the stage, Mr. Abernethy sitting on a chair with Joe, his dummy, on his knee. Mr. Abernethy and Joe were dressed in matching brown suits, each with the same figured tie, pocket handkerchief, and homburg, as though about to set off for a day at the office. Next to Mr. Abernethy stood a small table with a telephone on it. Mr. Abernethy began the conversation by asking Joe if he had a sister. Joe replied that he did, but she had died and gone to heaven. As he gave his condolences, Mr.

Abernethy offered to telephone St. Peter in heaven so that Joe could speak with his dear, departed sister. As Joe was expressing wonderment that such a thing could be possible, Mr. Abernethy lifted the receiver. The receiver made the customary tone signal, immediately followed by a woman's voice asking for the number. Mr. Abernethy asked for *Heaven, please,* whereupon the operator said *Hold the line, please,* the tone signal sounded, and a man's voice came on the line. While St. Peter was occupied looking for Joe's sister in the book, Joe and Mr. Abernethy filled the time with small talk, until St. Peter came back on the line and said he was sorry, but Joe's sister wasn't in heaven. The receiver clicked as St. Peter hung up, and the tone signal sounded again. Mr. Abernethy and Joe the dummy looked at each other and said at the same time, *Could she have gone to the other . . .* Ever the obliging fellow, Mr. Abernethy got the operator back on the line to be connected with the devil in Hades. The devil confirmed that Joe's sister was indeed in Hades; however, she was unable to come to the telephone because she was busy shoveling coal. Joe burst into tears and began sobbing as Mr. Abernethy hung up the telephone and tried to comfort him as he snuffled and sobbed. The scene ended with Mr. Abernethy whipping his handkerchief out of his jacket pocket and giving it to the dummy, who blew his nose with great honking blows.

Halfway through the following act, someone tapped Faby on the shoulder, and when she turned, startled, to see who it was, there was Louis in the seat behind her, leaning forward to whisper in her ear, "I thought I'd watch the rest of the show with you, but there wasn't an empty seat next to you."

Faby turned around to smile at him, and the smile stayed on her face for the rest of the show, just knowing he was behind her. When the curtain came down on the last act, which featured two stout women flailing at one another with boxing gloves, Louis helped Faby on her with coat and led her out the stage door.

"What say we find a place to get something to eat before we go to the hotel? I'm starving."

Less than a block from the theater, they found a late-night diner. Through the steamed windows, all the seats appeared to be taken, but when they entered, Louis spotted two empty stools at the far end of the counter and hustled Faby over to grab them before someone else could. "I'm in the mood for pancakes tonight. How do pancakes sound to you?"

"Pancakes sound good."

They'd barely had time to get their coats off when a counterman appeared with coffee pot in hand, to which Louis said, "Yes, for me and milk for the little lady." After he ordered their pancakes and put cream and sugar in his coffee, he said, "So, how did you like the show?", adding before she could respond, "You needn't bother with the boxing fat women. They don't count."

"I thought they were quite strange, actually."

"I'd go so far as to say downright indecent. Women of a certain age and heft have no business donning abbreviated costumes and punching each other in the head. But what about the rest of the show?"

"I was so impressed by Mr. Abernethy! I don't see how he could sound like so many different characters *and* a real telephone tone signal. And how could he be speaking to Joe and crying at the same time? Was it some kind of trick?"

"Oh, no, the act is real, but damned if I know how he does it. I know the basics, but the really good vents have an exceptional talent. What did you think of my act? How did I do?"

"Oh, your act was as good as the first time I saw it! Your dancing is so effortless."

"Thank you. That's the highest compliment a hoofer can get. Effortless it ain't, believe you me. Ah, our pancakes have arrived and about time, too, I'd say." He sliced through his stack and took a bite. "I hope no one confused me for Bud Purdy, or the poor fellow is going to have to bill himself as somebody else to keep working."

Faby poured syrup on her pancakes. "You forgot some of the words, but you weren't so bad. I thought you were quite funny, actually."

"Thanks. I did get a few yocks, didn't I?"

"Did Bud Purdy really lose his train fare in a pool hall?"

"Yes, he did." Louis shook his head and took a sip of his coffee. "I've never seen a fellow love a game so much and play it so badly. You'd think at some point, he would have learned not to bet on himself."

After they'd finished eating, Louis said, "Are you up for walking back to the hotel? The streetcars aren't running, and I'd rather not spend the money on a taxicab."

Out on the sidewalk, the air felt cold and raw after the heat of the diner, and they walked quickly, the sound of their shoes striking the pavement echoing loudly in the empty street, Louis's arm around Faby's waist so that she could keep up with him.

Back at the hotel, she felt oddly relaxed when Louis joined her in bed. He lay on his back with his fingers laced behind his head.

"Tell me about yourself."

"What?" Faby turned to look at him. The room's only window had no shade, and the dim light from a streetlamp cast shadows on his face. "Tell me about yourself," he repeated.

"What do you want to know?" She couldn't think of anything she could tell him about herself that could possibly be of interest to him.

"Well, I showed you my scrapbook, so you know all about me. But I don't know a thing about you except that you're from a French family, and you're a fan of the vaudeville show. I don't know your birthday, I don't know your favorite color, I don't know what you like to do on a Sunday afternoon."

Faby tried to think whether she had ever been asked that question before in her life. *Tell me about yourself.* She really didn't think so. Everyone in Enosburg knew everything there was to know about her. Her favorite thing to do on a Sunday afternoon was spent time with her sister in their bedroom. Her favorite color was purple. She had been born at home on May 5, 1907, in the same house on Depot Street where her family lived now, her mother attended by Dr. Ballard, for an uneventful arrival at seven pounds, nine ounces.

Without consciously willing it, Faby began to envision the scene of her birth, something she had never done before. The scene would have taken place in Maman and Papa's bedroom, the window shades drawn against prying eyes, never mind that the room was on the second floor, Maman propped up in bed with pillows, in pain but not overcome, Papa waiting anxiously downstairs. Dr. Ballard was at Maman's bedside, comforting, encouraging—and standing immediately behind Dr. Ballard, peering over his shoulder at poor Maman's exposed private parts, waiting for the arrival of her first grandchild, as if it were her right, was Maman Aurore. How *horrible* for Maman, and there would have been nothing she could do. Once her labor had progressed, she'd been as trapped as if shackled to the bed posts.

Without thinking to whom she was speaking, Faby blurted, "I think my grandmother was in the room when I was born watching me come out, and my father would have done nothing to stop her."

Louis turned his head to stare at her for a long moment and then started laughing. "Jeez Louise, I just asked you your birthday!"

"Sorry," Faby said, her face flushing in the darkened room. "I don't know what made me say that."

Louis was still laughing. "No, that's all right. Tell me more."

"Well, my birthday is May fifth." She didn't bother with the year because she'd already told him how old she was when they'd first met after the show. "My sister Josephine is only eleven months younger than I. It was just the two of us growing up. Josephine graduated from high school in June. She'll marry Leonard, I suppose." Faby stopped speaking. Of course Josephine would marry, she would make such a good wife and it was expected, but, still, it was impossible to imagine her younger sister marrying for years and years.

"Leonard?" Louis prompted

"Leonard Paradis. He and Josephine have been steadies since grade nine."

"Grade nine, eh? Is this Leonard a nice fellow?"

"Oh, yes. He never loses his temper, and he always keeps his word."

"A good catch?"

"A very good catch! His father owns the insurance agency, and Leonard knows the business already."

"So is that all there is to Leonard?"

"He's very good-looking."

"More good-looking than me?"

"Oh, yes!" Faby immediately clapped her hand over her mouth. How could she have *said* such a thing?

"Don't worry. You didn't hurt my feelings. I know I'm no Valentino. But I'm not exactly an Airedale, either!"

"Oh, no, of course not. You're quite attractive."

When she didn't resume speaking, Louis said, "Go on, tell me more."

"If Josephine weren't so sweet, the other girls would be envious of her. Most of them will marry farmers. It must be just *horrid* to live on a farm. The house smells like manure, your clothes smell like manure, and if you step foot outdoors, you're done for. The worst part is that it's the wife's responsibility to wash the husband's barn clothes, and if they have sons, then it's just that much worse. So, even though many of the girls at school *expect* to marry farmers, they're envious of anyone lucky enough to marry someone who doesn't come with a farm."

"I see."

"My Oncle Georges owns a farm in Québec, outside of Coaticook."

"Coaticook?"

"Yes, that's where my father's family is from. Maman Aurore and Grandpère Gauthier came to Vermont in the 1880s, shortly after the got married, because Maman Aurore refused to marry him if he stayed on the farm. I never knew my grandpère. He died before right before my father was born, in a logging accident. The rest of Papa's family didn't have any reason to leave, so they stayed in Québec. When I was little, we used to go up there every year for Thanksgiving until enough of the old people had died so that we didn't have to anymore. I *hated* going to Oncle Georges' for Thanksgiving, and not just because of the manure. He has an apple orchard, so there was plenty of hard cider with the dinner, and before it, too, and every year one or two of the grown-ups would get drunk and get into a fight at the table. It was awful because it wasn't just the drunk people that were fighting. The rest of them would join in *because* the other two were drunk. The wives would start crying because their husbands were shouting and wouldn't listen when they told them to stop, and then the little kids would start crying because their *mothers* were crying, and some years there were babies in their mothers' laps or in baskets on the floor if they were too young to sit up, and they skipped over crying and went right to shrieking. It would get so loud that Oncle Georges' hound dogs tied up outside in the dooryard would start barking and howling until you felt like your head was going to explode if you couldn't get out of there, but you were a little kid, so even though your parents were yelling or crying, you couldn't leave the table without getting their permission. One year, when I was six or seven, I *did* leave the table without permission and went outside and sat with the hounds, but they wouldn't stop howling, and I got cold, so I went back inside."

Louis turned on his side and stroked Faby's cheek with his finger. "You are a pretty girl, Faby. So young." His hand moved lower to stroke her neck before he kissed it. "I hope you'll always stay just the way you are." His mouth moved to her breasts, and the farm and the cold and the hounds and the fighting faded away.

Chapter 16

On Christmas morning, Faby awoke to the sound of two men talking directly behind her head. ". . . ladies' corsets, Fred. There was this one dry goods merchant, older fellow, used to place a small order with me every year—but he refused to examine my samples, wouldn't even look at 'em. He'd bring his wife to the hotel with him, and he'd stand out in the hall while the wife came into the sample room with me to examine the goods and tell me what styles and sizes to put on the order. Then she'd take the order out to her husband for him to look it over and sign. The old fellow passed away three or four years ago, and his son took over the business. And I'll be jiggered if he won't look at the samples either! Brings his mother to the sample room, same as his dad did. It's the queerest thing."

Faby opened her eyes to a cozy wallpapered room tucked beneath the eaves. Muted winter sunlight came through a small dormered window, but she couldn't remember whether they were in the front of the house or the back. Louis was still asleep, lying on his back with his fists tucked under his chin.

"That is a queer thing, Bob. You'd think that a man in the business of selling wouldn't have such a delicate sensibility. To make a living, ya gotta be able to sell anything. Although, truth be told, I found myself to be a man of delicate sensibilities when I went on the road selling a line of medical supplies: hernia trusses, enema kits, hemorrhoid cushions, and the like . . . ladies' sanitary belts. I lasted only one season. I made a good living, but setting up my sample room and writing up the bill of goods just gave me the willies. I could barely ask for my sample trunks to be delivered from the train station, I was so afraid their contents would be known to all and sundry. The following season, I found a place for myself at a house that carried a nice line of shoes."

Faby felt Louis stir beside her. He would soon awaken if Fred and Bob didn't lower their voices. As thin as the wall was, the four of them had to be in an attic room that had been partitioned into two bedrooms.

"All in all, I'd say that if a fellow wants to be successful on the road he can't go wrong with shoes, ladies' shoes in particular—because for some people of the feminine persuasion—and you know the ones I mean, Bob—last year's shoes may as well be last week's boyfriend. Time to cast 'em aside and get a new pair! Now, for the average merchant, particularly for those out in the sticks, this year's kitten-heeled pump looks no different from last year's kitten-heeled pump—so if you can make yourself out to be the expert on the latest styles, you've got your order in the bag."

"All right, Fred, I'll give you ladies' shoes, but, for my money, I'll take a nice line of baby shoes any day of the week. That's the line I'm in right now, as a matter of fact. Why, a merchant has to have a heart of stone to refuse the finest, softest kidskin just waiting to cradle those precious little feet. However, seeing as a merchant with a heart of stone is not unheard of, I hedge my bets with a little salesmanship. When I set up my sample room, beside each pair of shoes, I put a framed photograph of the cutest little nipper wearing that very same style taking his first step into the outstretched arms of his loving mother. And for every style the merchant orders, he gets a bronzed pair of those self-same little shoes for his store display."

"Now, that's salesmanship! I tip my hat to you, Bob."

"Weren't we supposed to be going down for breakfast, Fred?"

"Why, yes, Bob, I believe we were."

After Fred and Bob had gotten dressed and taken themselves down the stairs, the room was quiet except for a low hum that Faby hadn't noticed before and an odd smell she couldn't quite place, almost like dust burning. She looked around the room as she waited for Louis to wake up. A small chest of drawers with a cloudy framed mirror attached to it was positioned in one corner of the room. In the opposite corner a small table held what looked like a large copper bowl set on a stand with an electrical cord coming from it. Set into the copper bowl was a glowing red tube, the heat source for the room apparently.

The bedsprings creaked, and Louis leaned over and kissed her nose. "Merry Christmas, Mrs. Kittell. Our first Christmas together." He smiled down at her while she wondered why it didn't feel anything like Christmas at all but just another day.

"I got you a present," he said. "Wait here." He jumped out of bed, dug into his suitcase, and came back to bed with a wrapped package in his hand. Faby made no move to take it from him.

"What's the matter? Take your present."

She continued to look at the gaily-wrapped package, stricken. When she finally looked up, she whispered. "I can't. I didn't get you one."

"No, no, I got this for both of us—and the baby, too! Open it. You'll see what I mean."

"I didn't get you one."

"You'll get me one next year. Come on, open it. It's been burning a hole in my suitcase since East Hadaam, and I want to know if you like it."

She took the package from his hand and slowly pulled the ribbon to undo the bow. "It's so pretty, I almost hate to open it. Should I save the paper?"

"No, you shouldn't save the paper—just open it already!"

When Faby had the paper off, she found that Louis had gotten her a Brownie camera outfit, complete with two rolls of film, a portrait attachment for pictures at arm's length, a tube of photo paste, and a fifty-page photo album.

"See?" he said. "It's to start our family album! Do you like it?"

"I think it's the best Christmas present I've ever received. I've always wanted a Brownie camera of my own."

Louis grabbed her and kissed her hard on the mouth. "I'm so glad! We'd better be getting ourselves down to breakfast. If Fred and Bob eat as much as they talk, the food will be gone in very short order."

"You heard, then."

"Oh, yeah, I heard 'em all right. I awoke this Christmas morn to visions of enema kits and hemorrhoid cushions dancing in my head."

When Faby and Louis found the dining room, the two drummers were already well into their breakfast. The person seated at the head of the table, a sturdy woman of indeterminate age whom Faby vaguely remembered from the night before, beckoned them to the table. "Come, eat. I've prepared a nice Christmas breakfast, and there's plenty to go around. I'm Mrs. Thompson, if you don't remember from last night. You got in very late."

"We're sorry about," Louis said, pulling out Faby's chair. "Regrettably, our train was delayed for many more hours than we care to remember."

159

Two men sat together on the other side of the table, Bob and Fred, presumably. They both looked to be in their early forties, one with thinning sandy hair, the other already having lost his. "Merry Christmas!" they cried in unison, looking up from their plates and saluting the new arrivals with their forks.

Mrs. Thompson said, "Watch what you're doing," and snatched a clump of scrambled egg off the patterned tablecloth and dropped it onto the saucer under Fred or Bob's coffee cup. "Pay these two no mind. They've stayed here so often, they think they're at home."

"Every year since 1915," Fred or Bob affirmed.

"That's not exactly something to brag about, Fred," Mrs. Thompson said. "A man your age should be married by now with a house full of little ones."

"I'm Fred Young," the drummer with the thinning hair said. "Pleased to meet you."

"Likewise," Louis said. "I'm Louis Kittell, and this is my wife Faby."

"Faby. That's a pretty name. I've never heard it before."

The bald drummer interrupted him. "Faby is a French name. If I may introduce myself, I'm Bob Ingalls."

Thinking it must now be her turn to greet their breakfast companions, Faby said, "How do you do?"

"Very well, thank you!" Bob and Fred crowed in unison.

She looked at the serving platters covering the table to see what she might like to eat; she had not eaten since the previous afternoon, when they had gotten off the train in Scranton for a quick bite. However, there were still two people at the table who had not introduced themselves, a man with a bad haircut at the other end of the table and a thin woman wearing spectacles. The woman, who looked as though she might be a teacher, set down her fork and patted her lips with her napkin. "I'm Miss Bowdoin. Pleased to make your acquaintance."

"Likewise," Louis said, smiling and nodding his head.

The man with the bad haircut harrumphed.

"And this fine gentleman," Mrs. Thompson said, "is my husband Melvin. He owns a feed store."

"Indeed I do. If you own livestock, I'm the man to see!"

"Oh, we have no livestock, sir!" Louis said, laughing. "The wife here wouldn't stand for it." He speared a pancake. "No offense."

"None taken. So what brings you to Mercersburg on Christmas? Why aren't you home with your own Christmas tree and a turkey in the oven?"

The platter closest to Faby held muffins of some sort, and she took one rather than ask for the French toast and bacon she wanted at the other end of the table. Biting into the muffin, she tasted canned pineapple and coconut. She didn't think she had ever experienced such an exhausting breakfast.

"Vaudeville dates," Louis said.

"Vaudeville? You don't say! Should I know you?

Louis shook his head. "Oh, no. Strictly small-time."

"But still," Mr. Thompson said, "you have to have some talent to get up there on the stage in front of hundreds of people. What do you do?"

"I'm a hoofer."

"A hoofer, you say. I have two left feet myself. I've always wondered how you fellows make it look so easy. What's your secret?"

"Melvin!" his wife scolded. "Let the poor man eat his breakfast in peace. He and his wife got in very late last night. And it's Christmas." She turned to Faby. "Would you like some coffee to go with that muffin, dear? A muffin's not much of a breakfast by itself. How about some oatmeal? It's not Christmas morning without oatmeal and brown sugar." She started to reach for the bowl, but when Faby looked up at her, she drew back her hand and exclaimed, "Oh, my dear, I'm so sorry! What's wrong?"

Faby looked back down at her plate, unable to answer.

"It's her first Christmas away from her family," Louis said. "Maybe I should take her upstairs." He pushed back his chair. "Excuse us, please."

Faby was crying in earnest by the time they got back to their room. "I'm sorry. I didn't mean to embarrass you. All those introductions, it just got so overwhelming. I've never eaten breakfast with strangers before. It's always just the five of us for breakfast on Christmas morning."

Louis bent down and slipped off her shoes, then his own. He guided her onto the bed so that he was propped up against the headboard and she was resting against his chest. "You know," he said, wrapping his arms around her, "now that I think about it, Christmas breakfast with two drummers and a schoolmarm could be considered pretty grim, not to mention the feed store man. I'll wager before this day is out, he will have told us the price of chicken feed *and* fertilizer. Shall I tell you about Christmases of childhood past?"

Faby nodded her head against his chest.

"Before I do, did you get enough to eat? Shall I go back down and get you something else?"

She shook her head. "Uh uh. Tell me about Christmas."

"All right, then! My favorite Christmas tradition when I little was when Dad would take the whole family into Boston to see the lights. I liked the stores on Tremont Street best. To me, they weren't stores at all but huge houses where rich people lived with their children. The children had the best toys, and they did nothing but play with their toys all day, and they could do whatever they liked with no one bothering them or demanding that they put the toys away. And the toys would wondrous, so intricate and mechanical they would never get tiresome. How I wanted to be one of those lucky boys!" He stopped speaking, rubbing Faby's shoulder absently. Faint sounds of movement and dishes being cleared came from downstairs. "I was rather a greedy child, I suppose. Perfectly content until I saw what the next fellow had. Then I just had to have it for myself."

"You sound spoiled."

"I was—until I stopped being cute. Then Mother stopped indulging me."

"You were cute as a child?"

"Of course I was cute as a child. Aren't all little children cute?"

"Oh, no. I didn't mean it that way. I just can't imagine you as small and not . . . "

"Gangly?"

"Well, yes, I suppose you could put it that way."

"I think that started happening when I was nine or ten. Before that, I was the same as the other boys my age."

Faby doubted that Louis Kittell had ever been the same as the other boys his age. There would always have been something that set him apart.

"Now, my *least* favorite Christmas tradition," he went on, "was the mean older sister telling the innocent little brother that there is no Santa Claus."

Oh, no!" Faby said, looking up at him. "Did she really do that to you?"

"Indeed she did. Took great pleasure in it, too. She learned it in a school lesson one year, and she couldn't wait to tell me when she got home. She didn't even wait to get her *coat* off before she went running through the house to find me and see how quick she could make me cry. When I stopped crying finally, Mother took to her bed for the rest of the afternoon."

"I guess my mother had it easy. Josephine and I always got along; she was my best friend growing up . . . still is."

"Do you miss her?"

"Terribly."

"It must be particularly bad today, being your first Christmas away from home."

"Yes."

"I thought as much. Every family has its own Christmas traditions, and while other families' traditions may be similar, they're just not the same. We'll have to start our own traditions, you and I, once the baby is born." He stopped speaking, seeming to gaze into the glowing copper heater for a vision of the future. "I think our Christmas traditions will have to start with telling the story of Mother and Dad's first Christmas together, when they were stuck up in the attic of Mrs. Thompson's boarding house with two drummers trying to one up each other."

A knock came at the bedroom door, and they both jumped as Mrs. Thompson pushed it open and stuck her head in the room without waiting for a response. "We're about to get Christmas music on the radio. Would you like to come down and listen with us?"

To make up for her earlier rudeness at the breakfast table, Faby nodded and said, "Yes, thank you. That sounds lovely."

Mrs. Thompson's living room was decorated for Christmas, a tabletop tree with glass bulbs placed in front of the window and an evergreen garland entwined with red ribbon draped across the mantelpiece. The radio, an enormous cabinet model positioned next to the sofa, was draped with a garland of its own. Fred, Bob, and Miss Bowdoin were lined up in a row on the sofa. Mr. Thompson sat in an armchair that looked as though it had been moved out of place to be closer to the radio. Miss Bowdoin's face held a decidedly pained expression, while Fred and Bob looked as jovial as ever.

"Glad you could join us!" Mr. Thompson shouted over what sounded like an army of French horns. Mrs. Thompson descended on the radio and adjusted the volume. "There, that's better. Mister seems to think that the louder you play the music, the better it gets."

"I've run into a few pit leaders of like mind in my travels," Louis said "It didn't work for them."

"I should think not," Mrs. Thompson said, settling herself in a small rocking chair by the fireplace.

Louis guided Faby to the only free armchair in the room and sat on the floor with his back against the chair. When the French horns surrendered to a vocal number, he wrapped his hand around one of Faby's ankles, running his thumb back and forth across the bone.

As the program progressed, the smell of roasting turkey began to fill the room, and Faby felt her spirits lift. There would be a real home-cooked Christmas dinner to look forward to.

When the program ended, Mrs. Thompson got up to turn off the radio and go into the kitchen to baste the turkey. Mr. Thompson took a pipe out of his shirt pocket, filled the bowl with tobacco, and settled back in his chair for a smoke.

"I think I'll go to my room and rest until dinner," Miss Bowdoin said, getting up from the sofa and smoothing the wrinkles from the lap of her dress.

Fred and Bob hadn't moved from their places on the sofa, looking across the room at Louis as though expecting him to now entertain them.

He scrambled up from his position on the floor and put his hand out to Faby. "How's about a walk? I could use some fresh air."

After excusing themselves, they put on their coats and slipped out the front door, leaving Bob and Fred to entertain themselves.

There was no snow on the ground, but the air felt cold and raw as they stepped off the porch and began walking down the sidewalk at a brisk pace. Mrs. Thompson's boarding house was on a residential street of mostly large Victorian houses interspersed with some smaller ones of more recent vintage, not a single house without an elaborately decorated evergreen wreath on its front door. Several of the houses had multiple automobiles parked in the driveway, families spending Christmas together.

They walked several more blocks until the residential streets gave way to the downtown area.

"I think there should be a hotel around here somewhere," Louis said, slowing his pace.

"A hotel? Are we going to leave Mrs. Thompson's?"

"Oh, no, we're staying at Mrs. Thompson's for the duration of the run. It's the cheapest room in town, and we get our meals included. Don't you worry—I know a good thing when I see it."

After they'd walked another block, he stopped and said, "Ah, here we are. The Hotel Mercer." He peered through the plate glass window. "And yes, they have a pay telephone." He pushed open door and strode across the lobby with Faby trailing behind him.

"I'll call Mother and Dorothy first, and then we'll call your folks." Louis stepped into the phone booth, leaving the door open as he placed a collect call with the operator. "Hello, Mother, Merry Christmas. . . . We're in Mercersburg, Pennsylvania spending Christmas at Mrs. Thompson's fine boarding establishment. . . . She's fine, the baby's fine. . . . Smyrna, Delaware. . . . . Let me speak to Dorothy. . . . Merry Christmas, Sis, gotta ring off now!" He hung up the receiver and ducked his head to leave the booth. "Your turn." When Faby didn't make a move to enter the booth, he said, "Would you like me to place the call for you? What's the number?"

Louis reentered the booth, placed the call, and spent the next several moments explaining who he was and convincing Faby's father to accept the charges. Once he'd accomplished that, he bellowed, "Merry Christmas!" and handed the receiver to Faby as he exited the booth. Entering the booth, she put the receiver to her ear and gingerly stepped up to the mouthpiece. "Papa?"

"Faby, is that you?"

"Yes, Papa, it's me. . . . I'm fine . . . . Mercersburg, Pennsylvania . . . . In a boarding house. . . . I don't think so. We're headed south. . . . I will."

She then had the same conversation with Maman, Maman Aurore, and Josephine in turn, although she could hear in Josephine's voice that she was unable to ask Faby what she wanted to ask her with the entire family huddled around the telephone wanting to hear.

Chapter 17

Five days later, as the train pulled out of the Mercersburg station, Faby couldn't stop thinking about her new Brownie camera, which now held the first photographs for their family album: Christmas at Mrs. Thompson's boarding house. When the film was developed, there would be an exterior shot of Mrs. Thompson's boarding house, another exterior shot of the boarding house, this one with her and Louis standing in front of it smiling, and the Christmas tree in the living room. Faby wasn't sure whether the interior shot would come out, but the room had been sunny when she took the picture, so she was hopeful that it would.

Opening night in Smyrna, Delaware, Faby was surprised at the lackluster response of the audience to the show, which Louis attributed to "post-Christmas blues." When she wrote up her review of the show the next day, she wasn't sure how to work in "post-Christmas blues," so she just left out the audience response, except for her own enthusiasm and delight, which she referred to as "this reviewer's" for the sake of honesty if not full disclosure.

The following evening, after she'd gone out to get herself something to eat, she took a bath and tried to wait up for Louis, but the warm room and the comfortable bed and the thought of lying next to him proved to be too much, and she fell asleep.

Several hours later she was awakened by the sound of a key in the lock, and she opened her eyes to see Louis taking off his coat and hat. "Sorry," he said. "I didn't mean to wake you. You must have fallen asleep with the light on." He crossed the room to the bathroom and flipped on the light, then walked over to the bed and turned off the bedside lamp. "There, now the light won't be in your face."

"Thanks. How was the show tonight?"

"Great! We had a much better audience tonight. Every act went over with 'em, even the dumb acts."

"Dumb acts?"

He nodded as he began to undress in the dim light from the open bathroom door. "Acts without dialog. Acrobats and jugglers and such, scenic tableaux."

Faby watched him undress until he turned his attention to unbuckling his belt, at which point Faby turned her head away.

"I'm just going to take a quick bath," he said. "Do you think you'll be awake when I'm finished?"

"I expect so, yes. I'm wide awake now."

He nodded and slipped off his boxer shorts before Faby could look away, and she caught a glimpse a very pale backside, concave on the sides. She didn't know quite what to make of it.

As he splashed in the bathtub, Louis sang a medley of popular songs, none of them all the way through, as though he either couldn't remember all of the words or he'd decided to sing just his favorite part of each one. Faby sat up and fluffed her pillow. She had never heard anyone sing in the bathtub before, the goal being to wash as quickly as possible and get out before the water cooled. She rather liked that Louis was singing in the bathtub. She would have liked to sing along, but she had no way of knowing when he would switch to another song or what it would be.

After Louis finished his bath and brushed his teeth, he emerged from the bathroom with a towel wrapped around his waist. He dropped the towel to put on a clean undershirt and boxer shorts, and Faby looked at his manhood full-on before he pulled on his boxer shorts. Her face flushed as she wondered whether he had seen her look.

In bed, Louis put his hand on her belly and looked up her expectantly. "Does the baby kick you much? Or is it not big enough yet?"

"Oh, I get kicked plenty. Punched, too, I imagine. I can't really tell the difference between hands and feet."

"I don't feel anything."

"Just be patient, you will."

Louis put his other hand on her belly, so that both hands covered it. Several minutes went by, and Faby could feel herself getting drowsy. Just as she was dropping off to sleep, Louis shouted, "There, I felt something!" and she jumped, startled. "What's wrong?"

"I felt something—there it is again! What's he doing?"

"Shifting, I think. He gets restless sometimes."

"Oh, he's stopped." Louis took his hands from belly. "My shouting must have frightened him."

Faby turned on her side so that her belly rested on the mattress, easing the pressure on her insides. "I don't know. His movements are pretty random."

Louis turned from his back to his side, resting his hand on Faby's hip and whispering, "Good night, sweetheart."

Sometime later, she came awake to someone's hand on her belly, a smooth, warm hand passing over the mound the baby had pushed out, passing smoothly, warmly over her skin as she lay curled on her side. She opened her eyes momentarily to confirm that the room was still fully dark, closing them again as the hand continued to stroke her belly, warmly, smoothly. A sigh escaped her lips as the hand moved to her breasts, with the same smooth, warm stroking, first one breast, then the other. Then, he was inside her and moving until he shuddered and she fell back asleep.

The next day, when Faby left the hotel to explore Smyrna, she took enough snapshots of the town to give the entire family—and anyone else in the village who might be interested—the perfect sense of what Smyrna, Delaware had been like, on this day, New Year's Day 1926, when she was pregnant with her first child and her husband couldn't bear to leave her behind when he went on the road the play vaudeville.

Chapter 18

Chintz curtains framed the view of an overcast winter sky through the window of their hotel room in Atlantic City. Under the window, a chipped radiator gurgled and hissed, and Faby was quickly reminded of how raw the air outside had been the night before. Swinging her legs over the side of the bed, she rushed to the window for her first look at Atlantic City. It was unfortunate that her first visit was in the winter, with such a biting wind, but surely, America's Favorite Hoofer would play Atlantic City again, when the weather was nicer. For all she knew, they might come back every year! But first things first. She would take a bath in their private bathroom.

Kneeling down by the tub, she set the drain plug and turned on the faucet to run her bath. While the bath water was running, she went into her suitcase to find her favorite winter outfit: a heavy woolen skirt Maman had made over from one of Maman Aurore's before she had become very stout and a matching pullover sweater. She smiled as she laid the clothes out on the bed. Maman had surprised her by dyeing them both the perfect shade of purple.

Returning to the bathroom, she turned off the faucet, pulled her nightgown over her head, and eased herself into the hot water. After she had soaped herself, she slid down, rested her head on the edge of the tub, and closed her eyes. There was not a sound in the room except the beating of her own heart.

After several minutes had gone by and she had become aware of other sounds—faint, muffled street noises, voices, a vacuum cleaner running—she drained the bath water and got out of the tub to dry herself off and get dressed. Her chemise was quite snug, and when she went to button her skirt the ends of the waistband didn't meet, and there was no way they would be joined, no matter how hard she tried to tug at them and suck in her stomach. There was nothing for it but to pack away her favorite skirt, put on a roomier flannel dress, pull the mismatched sweater over it, grab her Brownie camera, and venture out to explore Atlantic City.

In no time at all, she found a pharmacy with a lunch counter, where she ordered her favorite breakfast of cinnamon toast and milk, the toast fixed just the way she liked it, hot, with the cinnamon and sugar melting into the butter.

Back out on the sidewalk, she paused momentarily. To think—she was really in Atlantic City. Old Orchard Beach was the ocean vacation spot of choice for Franklin County families who didn't have farms they couldn't leave, and the honeymoon destination for most Enosburg girls was an overnight stay in Saint Albans with a picnic on Lake Champlain the next day before heading back to Enosburg in time for supper. And here she was, Faby Gauthier, in Atlantic City! Why, *The Enosburg Standard* would actually call it news. If a visiting aunt from Saint Albans, a school trip to Montpelier, or a rabid raccoon all rated as news—which at one time or another they had—a trip to Atlantic City would rate a two-column article of the traveler's exploits, *and* a photograph with a caption! She must find the Boardwalk.

Trying to get her bearings, she stopped walking and was nearly sideswiped by a woman pushing a baby carriage, who must have been walking close behind her. She quickly stepped out of the woman's way and backed into a display bin in front of a grocery store, nearly losing her balance. Luckily, the proprietor had not yet filled it with the shiniest of his apples and the smoothest of his oranges, so at least there was no avalanche of bouncing fruit to pretend she hadn't caused. What were all of these people doing on the sidewalk in the middle of the morning? In this part of the city, there weren't any attractions—just regular pharmacies and movie theaters and grocery stores and shoe stores, with apartments above them and hotels beside them and trolley tracks on the street in front. The ocean was nowhere to be seen.

There was a line of parked cars at the curb—seven or eight of them—with drivers behind the wheel. Faby wondered what they were all waiting for lined up in a row like that, then realized that they must be taxicabs. Imagine that. You want to go somewhere, and there is a man in a car just waiting to take you. Of course, you have to pay for the ride, but still, it must be convenient.

As she walked, she was surprised at how straight and flat the streets were, how one led to another at regular intervals, with no meanderings for cemeteries or hills or the Missisquoi River. The sun felt warm on her face, and the wind had died down some since she'd left the hotel earlier. It felt good just to walk.

In addition to stores and restaurants, there were countless hotels, block after block of them, with gables and turrets and spires, many more hotels than at Old Orchard Beach, which was definitely small—time compared to Atlantic City. Gradually, the stores and restaurants and hotels gave way to a more residential area, with large shingled houses set chock-a-block, their vast front porches not even four feet back from the sidewalk. Some of the porches had what must have been entire suites of furniture, chairs and tables and settees and chaises, each piece encased in its own canvas cover to protect it from the weather. How grand it must be to buy an entire suite of furniture just for your front porch!

One house had what looked like a type of porch on the roof, a large flat area with a low balustrade all the way around open to the sky. Faby wondered if people actually went up there or if it was just for show. It would be a shame if this magnificent rooftop were just for show. You must be able to see all of Atlantic City from up there, even to the ocean.

She began to wonder how far she'd walked. Surely, she must be getting close to the ocean by now—although she didn't feel the least bit tired, and she had walked blocks and blocks and blocks. Two men in long, brown overcoats sauntered by her and tipped their hats. Several cars puttered past, each with a man driving and a lone passenger in the back. Then more cars, several with multiple passengers, and more people on the sidewalk, women holding children by the hand, young men smoking cigarettes, animated young women walking arm in arm. Could she be getting close? Unless it was her imagination, there was a hint of salt in the air, and the wind had picked up. Then in the distance, she heard the cry of a gull, then another. There was no mistaking the hue and cry of seagulls. She was getting close! She passed by a church with a tall, narrow spire, then several very large houses featuring domed turrets. Finally, the Atlantic Ocean came into view and the distant horizon beyond it, water and sky both in winter shades of slate.

On the other side of the street stood a very large hotel, taking up at least a full city block. She slowed her pace and took several steps back, craning her neck to find the name of the hotel: The Seaside. A two-story veranda ran the entire length and width of the Seaside Hotel, with a series of rocking chairs conveniently set out, more rocking chairs in one place than she had ever seen in her entire life. Although the veranda was deep enough to be well-sheltered from the wind, there was not a single person to be seen in any of the rocking chairs, not even one hardy soul in overcoat and lap robe taking in the ocean air.

Two women wearing camel's hair coats with immense fur collars brushed past her, and she realized that she was standing stock-still in the middle of the sidewalk gaping. She quickly resumed walking, and there before her was the Atlantic City Boardwalk, a number of people strolling along it in their winter coats, a few being pushed in elaborate wicker chairs large enough for two people. Immediately in front of her stood an immense arcade built onto a pier over the sand and extending out over the water. As she hurried to reach the Boardwalk, she saw *another* arcade right next to the first one. She couldn't imagine what the different varieties of amusements could possibly be that *two* arcades would be needed to house them all. She stopped to take a picture of each one.

Reaching the Boardwalk, she immediately went to the railing to look out at the ocean, choppy and muted under the gray winter sky. She stood there for several minutes, her hands on the railing, looking out at the horizon, finding it remarkable, really, that she could even see it. Vermont was all mountains, valleys, hills, and trees, effectively obscuring all that lay beyond.

The sand immediately below her looked cold and damp, as though walking through it would not be a soft, warm sinking but a struggle. The high water mark was littered with strong-smelling clumps of detritus, seagulls wheeling above it uttering raucous cries. More people were on the beach than she would have expected, given the season, men and women, alone and in pairs, bundled in coats and scarves, walking along the sand looking pensive, their hands shoved deep into their pockets.

She resumed walking, unsure where to look first, afraid she would miss something important, an Atlantic City landmark that anyone who had ever been there would be sure to know about. Everywhere she looked were billboards—Lucky Strike Cigarettes, Coca-Cola, Velvet Pipe Tobacco, Van Raalte Silk Gloves, Fatima Cigars, Bromo Seltzer, Sqibb's Dental Cream, Konjola: The *New* Medicine, for When You're Not Feeling 100%—all adorning the buildings and the skyline like pictures hung to brighten the walls of a drab room.

And shops—were there shops on the Atlantic City Boardwalk! Shops selling magazines for the wives to read as they sunbathed on the beach and newspapers for their husbands to keep up with the news of the world. Shops selling toys and novelties to keep the children occupied in the evening while their parents relived the day's adventures as they relaxed on the veranda of the Seaside Hotel and waited for the sun to set. Shops selling all manner of confections: ice cream, cotton candy, chocolates, jelly rolls, Eskimo Pies, Cracker Jack, fudge, enough sweets to give a person bellyache just walking past them. There was even a photography studio where you could get your photograph taken and put onto a picture postcard to send back home to your friends and relations. Imagine that! Faby Gauthier's face on a picture postcard with *Atlantic City!* emblazoned on the front. Her breezy salutation on the back would be the talk of the village before the recipient had even retrieved the postcard from the Post Office.

Continuing on, she passed by the Hotel Knickerbocker, a massive brick building with pennants flying from the roof and more windows than anyone could ever count. Here, there would be no washing of upper-story windows balanced on a ladder with the scowling face of Maman Aurore on the other side of the glass looking for streaks. Here, there would be machinery and apparatuses and an army of window washers to keep all those windows clean and sparkling.

Across from the Hotel Knickerbocker was Central Pier, a large building spread out over a city block, with a lofty arched entrance flanked by turrets and massive billboards on the roof. Faby couldn't tell what actually went on inside the building behind the plate glass, and she didn't stop to take a picture or slow her pace, passing by another candy shop, another ice cream parlor, an optician's shop just in case one lost one's spectacles on the beach. She was surprised to come upon an antique shop with an ornate mirrored breakfront in the window so massive it filled the entire display space and so ugly it was a wonder the hideous thing had survived long enough to become an antique without someone putting it to good use by chopping it up for firewood. She couldn't imagine anyone who would come to a vacation city to purchase awkward, hulking pieces furniture when they could just wait for a relative to die, and they'd be stuck with more awkward, hulking pieces of furniture than they knew what to do with.

Several doors down from the ugly breakfront, a large store sold an inexplicable combination of merchandise: rugs, diamonds and art. A shop called Thérèse French, its wares shielded by deep candy-striped awnings, featured a display of impossibly stylish clothes behind the plate glass, all asymmetrical closures and geometric embellishment, clothes meant to be seen in. As Faby tried to imagine herself in one of Thérèse French's outfits, all thoughts of rich women's clothes were pushed out of her head by the sight of the RCA Radiola building and Victor Radio, complete with the Victor dog listening to the gramophone, just like on Papa's records! She took two pictures of the Victor dog, one for her own family album and one to give to Papa. She advanced the film and resumed walking.

More shops, more billboards, more ice cream. Fralinger's Salt-water Taffy, massive pyramids of candy boxes displayed in the window and throughout the store, thousands upon thousands of individually-wrapped chewy gobs.

When she realized that she was walking past the façade of the Ritz-Carlton Hotel, she took it as a sign that she had come far enough. After taking a picture of it, she turned on her heel and headed back up the Boardwalk. A small storefront she had previously missed caught her eye. "LIVING INFANTS," it proclaimed in gold lettering on the plate glass window. She stepped up for a closer look. "COME AND SEE BABIES THAT WEIGH LESS THAN THREE POUNDS 25£" How could a baby weigh less than three pounds? Babies who were born that early didn't survive. If they survived the birth, they died within a few days, unable to nurse, barely able to breathe. She peered through the plate glass but was unable to see any living infants, so she resumed walking. She reached Steeple-chase Pier sooner than she expected and left the Boardwalk by the Seaside Hotel to walk back to the hotel to get ready for Lou-is's opening night at Nixon's Apollo Theatre in Atlantic City.

She found the theater easily enough, although she was surprised to see that it was not at all grand. It had a large lighted sign, but other than that, the building looked more like a storefront than a theater, not at all like the Opera House in Enosburg. Inside, the lobby was mostly taken up by the twin easels, one displaying the playbill, the other displaying a poster of the headliner, one Eliza Christie, and the glassed-in cage housing the box office. Inside the cage was a young woman not much older than Faby, whose face was set in an expression halfway between boredom and disgust: if every single person in the theater lobby were to drop dead in front of her, she would only roll her eyes. "Pass?" she said.

"Yes, my husband—"

"Well, go on, then." She jerked her thumb in the general direction of Faby's right.

"Thank you," Faby said automatically, knowing she would get no "You're welcome" in return.

The usher, on the other hand, was of another sort entirely. He was also young, but with an open, smiling face covered in freckles. "Hello, there!" he exclaimed as Faby approached him. "You are in for a treat tonight! We've got Eliza Christie head-lining, the greatest protean artiste the world has *ever* known *and* the best juggling act you've *ever* seen and *three* animal acts, not to *mention* Slim White! There is not a single flop on the whole bill! Not a one! Believe you me, I've seen a lot of acts come and go through these here doors, and these are the crème de la crème!"

What a strange fellow this usher was. Faby wondered if he spoke only in exclamations in his everyday life: "Of *course* I'll go to the store for you, Mother! They've got the best-rising baking powder *ever* and Post Toasties *and* canned peas! I'll carry them home in a sack *and* bring you your change!" She smiled at the back of his head as he led her to her seat.

While the house lights weren't bright, they provided enough light so that she could see a barrel ceiling with deco-rative medallions and three sections of upholstered seats. The stage itself was quite large, larger than the stage in the Opera House, with an elaborate curtain concealing the wonders to come. She looked around to see what type of people came to the vaudeville show in Atlantic City, middle-aged couples with children old enough to stay up for an evening show, el-derly couples who would strain to hear, asking each other, *what? what did he say?* during the comics' patter, young couples flashily dressed for a night on the town, the vaudeville show only the beginning of their good time.

When the houselights dimmed and the show began, who came tumbling onto the stage but The Incredible Mulhaneys!

The second act was billed as brother and sister, Fred and Elsie Baynes. The curtain opened on a nighttime scene, with Fred and Elsie dressed in old-fashioned clothes, their faces of indeterminate age under greasepaint. Seated on a bench under what looked to resemble a willow tree, Fred and Elsie made googly eyes at each other as they warbled their way through "Shine on Harvest Moon" and "By the Light of the Silvery Moon." They took their bows to lukewarm applause, and Faby made a point of applauding till her hands stung, so that their feelings wouldn't be hurt.

The third act on the bill, Joe and Norma Hennessy performing the comedy sketch, "After the Shower," was better-received, although it, too, focused on young love, even using the same bench and willow tree, the nighttime backdrop replaced by a lake in summer. Unlike Fred and Elsie, the Hennessys were obviously as young as the characters they played, and even from a distance both were incredibly attractive. The sketch consisted primarily of banter and flirting, with a flimsy but amusing plot of mistaken identity arising from each person having been caught in the rain, which necessitated borrowing dry clothes from a friend. The flirting was so outrageous that if an Enosburg girl's parents had caught her at it they would have packed her off to the upper reaches of the Northeast Kingdom to live on a farm with elderly relatives until she learned how to behave.

Before Faby could take that thought any further, the stage was occupied by the same ventriloquist act she had seen in Pine Plains, Mr. Abernethy and his dummy Joe, calling first St. Peter, then the devil so that Joe could speak with his sister who had died. After the curtain came down on Mr. Abernethy and Joe, it rose on Louis, tall and dapper in what looked like a new suit, looking as close to handsome as she had ever seen him. Still asleep when he left early for rehearsal that morning, she hadn't seen him all day. As she watched him move his hips for the Black Bottom, she felt something go through her womb that she was certain had nothing to do with the baby, a stirring she had never felt before.

There was no time for Faby to speculate as to what it could have been, however, because the orchestra was already playing the overture to the next act, listed in the program as, "The Inimitable Jack Munroe Performing 'Darktown Strutters' Ball' and 'Alexander's Ragtime Band'." Jack's singing voice was loud, enthusiastic, and as charming as his smile. When he encouraged the audience to sing along with him on the chorus of "Alexander's Ragtime Band," Faby sang as enthusiastically as he did and just about as loud.

After the intermission, Charlie the Chimp wowed the audience with his bow-legged adaptation of style and grace; then it was time for the headliner, listed in the program as "Eliza Christie: Protean Artiste in 'The Trial of Margaret Fagin', a courtroom drama." As Faby waited for the curtain to rise, she found herself holding her breath, wondering what a "Protean Artiste" could possibly be. The curtain rose slowly, more slowly than for the other acts. The stage was completely black, except for a single dim spotlight that gradually brightened to reveal a balding middle-aged man in a suit coat and matching vest, who was only visible from the waist up. Faby leaned forward and peered ahead as hard as she could, but she could see nothing else on the stage, only the middle-aged man's upper half. Just as she was wondering whether this was some kind of a magic act, a disembodied male voice came from out of the darkness:

"Please tell us the cause of death, Dr. Straub."

"Ronald Fagin died of arsenic poisoning, Your Honor."

"Could the arsenic have been accidentally ingested?"

"That would be highly unlikely. The amounts found in his stomach contents were too high."

"Could he have taken the arsenic himself, to commit suicide?"

"Of course, it's possible, but highly unlikely. I've been a medical examiner for thirty years, and in all that time, I've never seen a man commit suicide with arsenic. They usually go for a gunshot to the head or a fall from a tall building or a bridge. *Madame Bovary* aside, arsenic poisoning is a terrible way to die."

"Death is not instantaneous, then?"

"No, it is not. Arsenic causes severe stomach cramps and vomiting that can go on for several hours before death."

"I see. And this would be an ugly death to witness? A painful death?"

"Yes, it would."

"Thank you, doctor. Next witness, please."

The stage went completely dark for a mere second or two, and when the spotlight came back on, it revealed a rather stout woman with a plain face, her gray hair done up in an old-fashioned bun, who also was visible only from the waist up.

"Describe to us, Mrs. Briscoe, your role in the Fagin household."

"I'm the cook, Your Honor." Mrs. Briscoe's voice was soft and a little gruff, as if she didn't do a lot of talking, but it was definitely a woman's voice, just as Dr. Straub's voice had definitely been a man's. Mrs. Briscoe went on to describe how she had been employed by Mr. and Mrs. Fagin since they were first married, ten years before, and since that time she had cooked all of their meals—although she did have to concede that on the day in question, Mrs. Fagin had sent her home early because her bunions were bothering her, so she had no direct knowledge of who would have prepared the meal that had killed Mr. Fagin.

After Mrs. Briscoe's testimony had concluded, the stage again went completely dark, again for a mere moment or two, and when the spotlight came up again, it revealed a slender young woman in a sleeveless orange dress, with blond hair, penciled eyebrows, and very red lips. *How can this be?* Faby thought. *How can only one actress play all of the parts? There is no time for her to change costumes. How lucky Louis is to be on the same bill with such a talent.*

The judge asked the woman for her name.

"Velma Valente, Your Honor." Velma Valente's speaking voice was high-pitched but pleasant, not at all shrill as if someone were pitching her voice unnaturally for effect. Her voice remaining consistent as she delivered her testimony that she and Mr. Fagin were close friends, but she had not been after anything more than a bit of fun.

There were five more witnesses: a twelve-year-old boy that Mrs. Fagin had sent to buy rat poison the week before her husband's death; the jaundiced, adenoidal store clerk who sold it to him after reading the note she had sent with him; the Fagins' colored chauffer, who had heard them arguing to and from the Congress Hotel on the day in question; Mrs. Fagin's red-haired best friend Lucy Trethewey, who swore the Fagins' marriage was a happy one with nary a cross word between them; and the elderly liver-spotted principal of Velma Valente's high school at the time she attended, who proclaimed in a booming voice that Edna Goldfarb had been an inveterate liar from childhood, and a leopard doesn't change its spots, now, does it?

Last on the stand was Margaret Fagin herself, a striking woman of about thirty with delicate features and a peaches-and-cream complexion framed by dark hair covered with a veil. She was dressed in black, so that only her face was visible against the dark void of the stage, adding to the dramatic effect as the judge began to question her.

"Now, Mrs. Fagin, you understand that you are under no obligation to testify?"

Margaret Fagin responded in a clear voice that would have been musical under other circumstances. "I understand, Your Honor. I need to clear my name so that I can properly mourn my husband." Her testimony involved an argument with her husband about an ugly green dress, a sick headache and a strong sedative, an explanation of why it appeared that she had purchased rat point when in fact she hadn't, and her discovery of her husband's body:

"I found him on the bathroom floor. His eyes were open, and when I touched his neck for a pulse, he was stone-cold dead!" She began sobbing in earnest, a handkerchief pressed to her mouth, as the single spotlight slowly dimmed, then faded away entirely. The curtain came down to utter silence from the audience and then exclamations of disgust all over the theater. *What?!* They're not going to say if she *did* it?! We sat through all of that, and we don't know if she *did* it?! What kind of a courtroom drama is *that?!*

After the show, Faby waited for Louis in the lobby, which was pleasantly awhirl with the sounds and smells of other people—chatter, laughter, perfume, cigarette smoke—people who had just spent several hours in one another's company enjoying themselves. Louis hurried up to her before all of the patrons had even left the theater, his face still shiny from cold cream. He put his arm around her shoulders and kissed her on the cheek. "Hey, there, dollface!" As Faby smiled up at him, the thought unexpectedly crossed her mind that she had missed him. Kissing her again, he said, "Let's stop by a deli and get some supper to take back to the room."

As he led her out of the theater with his arm around her waist, he said, "How did you like the show tonight? While I was in my dressing room changing during the headliner's act, I heard from a couple of people who had seen it that the audience wasn't too keen on her act."

"No, they weren't. They were pretty mad that they didn't find out how the trial ended."

"Missed the whole point of the protean act, eh? Well, let that be a lesson to her. If you get up on the stage and start telling a story, you'd better give the audience an ending, or there will be no sweet hand to hand music for you!"

There were several open delicatessens in the vicinity of the theater, and Louis stepped into the first one they came to without looking at the menu posted in the window. Inside the delicatessen was a strong smell of meat: raw meat, cooked meat, smoked meat. Men with half-eaten sandwiches in front of them were seated in pairs at small tables placed throughout the room, talking loudly with their mouths full. Several more men perched on stools at the counter, eating pie. Faby waited by the door as Louis made his way to the counter to place his order.

Back in their room, as soon as they had taken off their coats, he removed a brown bottle from the deli sack and asked her if she had ever had cream soda. When she shook her head, he said, "You are in for a treat, m'dear." He pulled a set of keys out of his pocket, popped the bottle cap, and handed her the bottle. She cautiously sniffed the contents before taking a tentative sip. An unexpected taste of vanilla filled her mouth, sweet, like cake. "What did I tell you!" Louis crowed. "I just knew you'd like it."

He waited to eat his pastrami sandwich until Faby had gotten ready for bed; then he undressed and joined her under the covers in his underwear. "Want some?" he said, offering her the sandwich. As they'd shared the sandwich, as well as the big slice of coconut pie he had bought for dessert, Louis clicked off the light, and Faby tried to settle herself for sleep.

Just as she was about to drift off, she heard Louis's voice say dreamily, "I remember my first time in Atlantic City. Dad thought it would be a swell idea to take the family with him to the Office Appliances Convention. It wasn't. I spent the entire first day on the beach, and I got such a bad sunburn, my face blistered as if it had been thrust into a blast furnace."

"You didn't use sunburn cream to prevent it?"

"Of course not. I was a ten-year-old boy. I was not about to put cream of any sort on my face."

"What happened?"

"What happened? I had to spend the entire four days in the hotel room with Mother standing guard over me so I couldn't sneak out, that's what happened. I played so many games of solitaire I thought I would go off my nut. Playing endless rounds of rummy with Mother wasn't much better. The worst of it was Dorothy coming in at the end of *her* time on the beach with a tan, although Mother would chastise her for starting down the road to her complexion's ruination. Nowadays, I do use a little cream, and I *never* go out in the sun without a hat." He paused. "You will need to watch for that when the baby is born."

"I will," she murmured and went to sleep, not the least bit worried about it, given her family's French coloring.

Chapter 19

As soon as she opened her eyes the following morning, Faby decided that she must go back to the Boardwalk, and she set off as soon as she finished her breakfast. Leaving the pharmacy, she walked purposefully, now that she had a definite destination, recognizing the grand hotels and shops and restaurants she had passed the day before but not taking particular note of them. She soon reached her destination, and after paying the admission fee, hesitantly entered the large room where the incubator babies were displayed.

The incubators were set against two walls of the room behind a railing. Each incubator appeared to be some sort of glass box with various tubes and pipes attached, set on metal legs. Two of the incubators were empty, but the others each held a small form resting on a cushion, with a barely perceptible head poking out of spotless white swaddling. A woman in a nurse's uniform, who had been doing something on the other side of the room, pushed a small metal stand on wheels to the first incubator, then brought over a stool. She spoke to Faby over the railing. "It's feeding time, if you would like to watch."

Faby nodded. The room was quite warm, but she left her coat buttoned, clutching the front of it with both hands.

"We'll start with little Arthur here," the nurse said. She opened the door of the first incubator, removed the tiny form from inside, carefully positioned him in the crook of her arm, and whispered, "Arthur came to us only last week. He weighed just two pounds, five ounces. He is still very, very weak, and we must feed him with an eyedropper." Arthur parted his lips when the tip of the eyedropper touched them; the drop of milky liquid went in, and it didn't come out. The nurse continued to feed him, one drop at a time, until he had consumed what must have been little more than a teaspoon of milk. "He did well today," she said. "When he came to us, he was having trouble swallowing." Arthur let out a little mewling cry as she placed him back in the incubator. If he hadn't been swaddled, Faby was sure his tiny arms and legs would have been flailing.

"Is he all right?" Faby asked the nurse as she secured the incubator door.

"Oh, yes. They just prefer to be held; it makes them feel safe."

Maybe that's why the babies were swaddled, so the people coming in to see them couldn't see the baby's panic when he was reminded that he had left the womb too soon—a glass box on metal legs, even a warm glass box, no substitution for a mother's warmth and beating heart.

With the nurse occupied on the other side of the room washing her hands, Faby leaned over the railing to see if she could get a look at the infant in the next incubator, but the tiny bundle didn't look any different from the tiny bundle named Arthur. When the nurse returned and opened the incubator door, she said over her shoulder, "Usually, there are two of us, but it's just me today. Two of Irma's kids are down with the grippe, and if we even *think* we've been exposed to *anything*, even a case of the sniffles, we don't take a chance." She gently removed the infant from the incubator, positioned it in the crook of, and performed the same ministrations with the eye dropper as she had with Arthur. "This is Carole," she informed Faby in a soft voice. "She's much stronger than when she came to us. Why, she'll be able to take a bottle very soon. Won't you, sweetheart?" The nurse lowered her voice to a whisper. "Her mama died giving birth to her, poor mite, and her daddy is so broken up about it, he's never been to see her, not once."

"Her mother died?" Faby said.

The nurse nodded. "She hemorrhaged. By the time the doctor got there, she was beyond saving." She paused with the eyedropper in her hand. ". . . although, even if she'd been in a hospital, it might not have made a difference." She shook her head. "When they hemorrhage like that, it's nearly impossible to stop it." After she finished the feeding, she laid Carole back in the incubator, and Carole let out the same mewling cry as Arthur.

Left by herself as the nurse washed her hands for the next feeding, Faby thought about leaving the Incubator Babies Exhibit. She had seen the incubator babies; she had learned how they were cared for; she had even heard two of their stories. That should be enough.

But she stayed. She almost wished she could offer to help the nurse, since she was working by herself, but of course Faby would be no help at all. Even the smallest element of the infants' care required specialized knowledge and training.

The next infant, Marcel, took his feeding from a bottle, a very small bottle, but a bottle. He looked to be almost the size of a newborn, and his face didn't have that blank, almost fused look about it that had given such a sense of immateriality to Arthur and Carole. "It's graduation day for Marcel tomorrow," the nurse said, smiling.

"Graduation day?"

"Yes, that's what we call it when a baby becomes strong enough to go home with his parents."

"Oh, I see," Faby said. "That would be a milestone day."

The nurse set the bottle down and raised Marcel to her shoulder, patting his back ever so gently to bring up a nearly imperceptible burp before laying him back in the incubator.

A thin but sustained cry came from one of the incubators further down the row, soon joined by a cry from the incubator next to it. "That's the twins," the nurse said, "right on cue." She hurried to the other side of the room, her movements made urgent by the cries. When she returned and opened the incubator door, she said, "If I could feed them both together, I would." Once comfortably arranged in the crook of her arm, the infant stopped crying while its twin continued unabated. The nurse held the eyedropper to the infant's lips. "I hate that they have to be separated. Twins are born early often enough that you'd think there could be double incubators for them . . . although oftentimes only one makes it through the birth."

The nurse replaced the infant in its incubator and removed its twin from the incubator next to it. As soon as the infant was comfortably arranged and ready for feeding, its twin started crying. "See what I mean?" the nurse said. "They need to be together."

Hesitantly, Faby asked, "What are their names?"

"Oh!" the nurse said. "George and Georgina."

"They're not identical, then?" Faby said, surprised.

The nurse shook her head. "No. They're brother and sister. This is Georgina."

How very odd, Faby thought, *to give your two children the same name*—that thought immediately followed by the realization that they must be namesakes of their father or perhaps a grandfather, and they were both named the same in case one died. She again thought of leaving the Infant Incubator Exhibit, which shouldn't rightly be called an exhibit at all. The room seemed to be getting increasingly warmer, but she couldn't bring herself to remove or even unbutton her coat. The nurse fed two more infants, James and Ronald, without incident, but the next one was different. It seemed somehow limper in its swaddling than the other infants and gave no sign of awareness that it had been removed from its enclosure. Faby watched as the nurse picked up a length of narrow tubing and began threading it up the infant's nose. She must have gasped because the nurse said, "I'm sorry. I should have warned you. What I'm doing is called *gavage* feeding." She picked up a small syringe, held it above the infant's head and slowly began depressing the plunger. "Florence isn't able to swallow yet, which is why she has to be fed this way. The tube doesn't bother her because her gag reflex isn't developed."

Faby nodded that she understood but didn't say anything. The nurse set the empty syringe on the stand, slowly pulled the tubing back out through Florence's nose, and placed her back in her incubator. "One more," the nurse said, picking up Florence's feeding apparatus and hurrying to the other side of the room.

The last infant to be fed, Roger, was able to take a bottle, Faby was relieved to see. Perhaps he was getting close to his graduation day. "You know," the nurse said as Roger settled into sucking, "Most of the parents don't come to see the babies while they're here. A few do, like Marcel's, but most don't. I've never been able to understand it, myself." When she was finished with Roger, she turned to Faby. "Now it's time for diapering. Would you like to watch?"

"Oh, yes," Faby said. The nurse returned with a different rolling cart, this one with sides and a shelf underneath for stacks of diapers and a pail to put the soiled ones in. The nurse wheeled the cart to Arthur's incubator. She placed him on his back on the cart and undid the blanket he was swaddled in, revealing a bulbous, bony torso that appeared to be mostly ribcage and tiny arms and legs that couldn't have been bigger around than Faby's thumb. It was perfectly obvious why his parents weren't coming to see him. Faby waited until the nurse had finished changing Arthur's diaper before blurting, "I think I'd better go now," and rushing out the door.

As Faby began to walk the now interminable distance back to the hotel, she could barely breathe. She walked over to the railing to appear to be looking out to sea instead of leaning on the railing trying to catch her breath. The baby stirred within her and went still. She looked at her wristwatch to see how long she had been at the Incubator Infants Exhibit. Nearly two hours! As she continued to walk, the thought occurred to her that for those two hours, no one else had been in to see the exhibit. Maybe she was the only one young enough and naive enough not to have known that this exhibit was in no way an amusement.

Back at the hotel, she lay down on the bed, but as much as she wanted to sleep she couldn't. The baby had roused himself with a series of kicks and punches before pitching and rolling as though he were trying to beat his head against the wall of her womb. She spread both hands across her belly and pushed as hard as she could to get him to stop, but he wouldn't.

Maman had been barely into her seventh month when she fell down the cellar stairs while carrying a basket full of empty Mason jars, Faby arriving home from school with Josephine to find Dr. Ballard's Model T parked in front of the house, Papa and Maman Aurore sitting together on the sofa in the living room, tears running down Papa's face, Maman Aurore repeating, *If I'd known, I would have stopped her. If I'd known, I would have stopped her,* and Maman propped up in bed with pillows, her face dead white, looking down at the tiny bundle she held in her arms.

Dr. Ballard sat in a chair at her bedside. When he saw Faby and Josephine standing in the doorway, he ushered them out of the room, whispering, "I want her to sleep," as he closed the door softly behind him. In the hall, he said, "Your mother has taken a fall and delivered early. She'll be all right, but she is going to need a lot of rest, and you girls will need to help your grandmother and not cause your mother any trouble. Do you understand?" Faby nodded and said, "What about—?" Dr. Ballard turned to reenter the bedroom. "He was born too soon." Faby stood in the hall, not knowing what to do, not knowing whether she and Josephine should go downstairs to Papa and Maman Aurore, or whether they should go to their room and stay out of the way. Sitting on her bed with Josephine, Faby whispered, "I wonder if they will let us see him."

Josephine didn't respond. They sat that way without speaking for what seemed like a very long time until they heard the doorbell ring, then the sound of heavy footsteps coming up the stairs, and Papa, Maman Aurore, and Father Messier on the landing. Papa appeared in the open doorway of their bedroom and said, "Father Messier is here to baptize your brother; please stay in your room."

"What's his name?" Faby whispered.

"Guillaume, after your grandpére."

Faby sat back down on the bed with Josephine and waited, leaving the door open. She wondered what could be taking so long, then realized that after baptizing him, Father Messier would be giving Guillaume last rites. She never did get to see Guillaume, forever a tiny bundle in their mother's arms and a name, nothing more.

After finally falling asleep, Faby dozed fitfully, waking a short time later to go out and get something to eat. When she returned to the hotel, she picked up a discarded newspaper from a chair in the lobby to pass the time until she could go to bed for the night.

Later, after Louis had returned from the show and was getting ready for bed, Faby wondered how she could tell him about the Infant Incubator Exhibit, how she could describe those faceless little creatures in glass cases, bound from head to foot, no longer part of their mothers, but not yet part of the world they were intended for either, only allowed to enter it for the drops of nourishment forced upon them to keep them alive and afterwards for their private parts to be cleansed of the resulting waste.

"I went to the Infant Incubator Exhibit today," she said when Louis got into bed and she felt the warmth of his body next to hers and the soft touch of his lips against the back of her neck.

"Oh? I haven't seen it. What was it like?"

"It's set up like an exhibit with the babies in glass incubators behind a railing where you can watch while a nurse cares for them. Most of them have to be fed with an eyedropper because they aren't able to suck. If they're born before they can swallow, they have to be fed with a tube up their nose and down their throat." She stopped speaking. Louis was lying so close to her she could feel his heart beating against her back, and she whispered, "Their faces had almost a desperate look, like their features had been fused. I don't know how to describe it." Again, she stopped speaking while Louis's heart beat quietly against her back. "The babies were so tiny it's a miracle they were alive when they were born, and it's an even bigger miracle they continued to live."

Louis moved away from her to lie on his back. "I saw some of that in the war, fellows with injuries so bad you couldn't fathom how they could possibly have survived long enough to even be loaded into an ambulance, much less survive the trip to the field hospital. In some cases, it would have been better if they hadn't. "

Neither of them spoke for several minutes until Louis broke the silence. "You would be huddled in a trench for days on end with the artillery pounding and the fellow next to you bleeding to death and screaming for a medic or his mother, whichever one he believes can get to him first."

Faby saw the image of little Arthur's unbearably frail arms and legs, now grown to maturation through meticulous care only to be ripped from their torso and thoughtlessly flung across a field in some foreign country he had never intended to go to. She had thought it was just the accidents of pregnancy she would need to guard against, practicing good hygiene and avoiding rickety stairs. Then would come caring for the baby properly, keeping him clean, well-fed and free from illness, protecting his tender skin from the sun. But this was only the beginning of the harm that could befall him, whether protected within her body or having passed from her body to join his family. And when he was at last ready to join them, Maman would not be there. Faby's lying-in would be in some unknown hotel in some unknown town, with only Louis there to tend to them and keep them from harm.

Chapter 20

The day they were to leave Atlantic City, Louis took Faby to a sit-down restaurant for a late breakfast after checking them out of the hotel and arranging to have their bags delivered to the train station. Although it wasn't yet time for lunch, the restaurant was full and they had to wait for a table. Most of the tables were occupied by families, all dressed in their Sunday best, the mothers hovering anxiously over their children, ever vigilant to prevent them from staining their clothes, the fathers looking down at their plates, glumly chewing.

"Church must have let out a little while ago," Faby said.

After they'd been waiting for ten minutes or so, the hostess led them to a table for two by a large plate glass window overlooking the Boardwalk and the ocean beyond it. Faby couldn't believe their good luck, to have an ocean view at a sit-down restaurant, the movement of the water creating an ever-changing display of muted slate tones randomly embellished with white.

As they left the restaurant, Louis said, "What say you and I take a stroll on the Boardwalk before we go to the train station, see the sights so to speak?"

"Oh, could we? Do we have enough time?" Faby took his arm before he could offer it. "I didn't think we'd get a chance to see it together."

As they set off for the Boardwalk, she felt oddly buoyant, the heels of her shoes striking the sidewalk with the confident sound of someone who knows where she's going. When they reached the Boardwalk, they encountered a series of men in topcoats and homburgs striding purposefully, seemingly intent on getting somewhere important, where, she couldn't imagine. It was too cold for ice cream, and eating saltwater taffy would be undignified for a man of substance. Women in long woolen coats scurried along in twos and threes, while younger women wearing fur and fashionable hats walked at a more leisurely pace. Faby smiled and nodded greetings to the other young couples they encountered strolling along as they were, the husband's gait shortened to his wife's, his arm around her shoulders.

As they passed by each of the grand hotels on the Boardwalk, Faby tried to imagine what the grounds would look like in the summer, when they came into their own after lying dormant and brown all winter, the lush carpets of grass, the carefully tended beds of colorful flowers, weeds plucked as soon as they breached the surface, deadheads and wilted petals instantly removed. And what must the ocean look like from the vantage point of the grounds of a grand hotel in the summer, how blue and calm, the sunlight glittering and glancing off the waves, the horizon far, far away but still somehow within reach?

Oh, she and Louis must come back to Atlantic City in the summer! Surely, he would play here again. He was such a good performer, and the audience loved him. There was no reason why he couldn't hit the Big Time, and when he did, he would perform in Atlantic City all summer long, and they would stay in the grand hotels, the Seaside, the Traymore, the Marlborough-Bleinheim, the Knickerbocker, and of course the Ritz-Carlton, a different one each week. After a sumptuous breakfast in bed ordered from room service, Louis would be off to rehearsal, and she would dress in her swimming suit to spend the day on the beach, swimming in the ocean and sunbathing with a good book until she was brown as a nut.

Just then the baby listed and reeled in his confined space, and Faby dressed him in a cunning blue romper and sun bonnet. He was filling a pail with wet sand to make a turret for the sand castle he and his father were making. When it was finished, they would rinse their hands of sand in the ocean and the family would eat a picnic lunch.

Across from the grand hotels stood a pier built out over the ocean offering amusements after a day at the beach: dancing, concerts, movies, aquarium exhibits, and a twice-daily fish haul. While Louis paused to look at the colorful broadsides, Faby looked out over the vast colonnaded pier, and her eye was caught by what looked like some sort of European villa near the end of the pier. She hadn't noticed it previously, and from a distance, she couldn't tell what its white façade was made of, but from the look of the statuary positioned about, it was probably made of marble. From what she could see, all of the statues were naked women: naked women perched on lions, naked women holding small children, naked women clutching drapery, naked women just standing there for no apparent reason.

"Look at that." Louis said. "Eddie Cantor is playing here next week! "Hmm, let's see who else is playing at Young's Million Dollar Pier in Atlantic City. Elsie Janis, sweetheart of the AEF, very nice, very nice. Fred Allen, one of my personal favorites. Fanny Brice, a doff of the hat to an immensely talented lady. And Eva Tanguay, the Queen of Vaudeville, although she's getting rather long in the tooth." He paused as though considering. "Yeah, it would have been swell to have made the Big Time, to be on the same bill as Eddie Cantor, although I would prefer Sophie Tucker over Eva Tanguay. Aside from her getting on in years and that dreadful red hair, I couldn't handle hearing her voice night after night—whether from the wings or from my dressing room. That screech of hers could wake the dead, and once awake the dead would beg for someone, anyone, to kill them to escape it."

Faby laughed. "Her singing can't be *that* bad."

"Oh, yes, it can! And you only have to hear it once to be shell-shocked for the rest of your life. Advantage, Small Time."

"I think you still have a chance to make the Big Time. You're the best dancer I've ever seen."

Louis looked down at her and smiled. "I know better, but it's sweet of you to say so."

They resumed their stroll, Louis's arm still around Faby's shoulders. As they walked by the antique shop window displaying the mirrored breakfront, Louis let out a low whistle. "That has got to be the ugliest piece of furniture I have ever seen. It's hideously ugly, shockingly ugly, *astoundingly* ugly. Why, I would call that thing the Eva Tanguay of breakfronts. I'll bet if you were to open it up, it would be stuffed full of the most outlandish costumes ever to blight a stage, feathered appendages and all." Louis shook his head and resumed walking. "Gotta give her credit, though. She may be on the downhill side of forty now, but in her heyday, she sure knew how to get people's attention."

Louis kept Faby entertained with more Eva Tanguay stories—choking a fellow chorus girl unconscious, breaking a fiddle over a pit leader's head, cancelling engagements for spite—and before she knew it, they had reached Steeplechase Pier, the maniacal clown's maw poised to swallow up anyone who had a quarter to spare.

"Jeez Louise," Louis said, shaking his head "That thing's enough to give a grown man nightmares; I'd hate to think what it would do to a child." He reached into his pocket for change. "We still have some time to kill before our train. Let's take a look inside." Before Faby could respond, she was inside an enclosed space, the floor was rotating beneath her feet, and Louis had grabbed her to keep her from falling. Once they were on solid ground again, Louis passed two quarters to the ticket booth attendant, who seemed oddly overdressed for the job, a homburg on his head, a red carnation in his lapel, a two-point handkerchief square in his pocket. After he had tipped his hat to them as he handed over the tickets, Louis leaned down and whispered in Faby's ear, "He's just happy to be in show business!"

They were so many amusements, Faby wasn't sure where to look first, but just then her attention was caught by the sound of something breaking, as though someone had dropped a piece of china or knocked over a vase and it had smashed. Another crash sounded, louder than the previous one, then a whole series of crashes.

"That must be one clumsy waiter!" Louis said.

As they drew nearer to the sound, Faby saw that it came not from a restaurant but a booth with rows of dishes set up on shelves: plates, bowls, cups, and, saucers. A determined-looking woman in a patterned dress was hurling balls at the dishes, while her companion held her coat and pocketbook. The sign advertising the booth read, "'If you can't break up your own home, break up ours.'"

When all of the dishes were broken, the woman in the patterned dress retrieved her coat and pocketbook from her companion and walked away without claiming a prize. The shelves on which the broken dishes had been displayed rotated to reveal a set of intact dishes; another woman stepped up to the pile of balls and began hurling them at the dishes. Faby stepped closer to get a better look. She could see no prizes displayed: no painted Kewpie dolls, no stuffed animals, nothing to be gained but the satisfaction of breaking the dishes.

"Who would have thought people would pay good money to break dishes?" she said, to which Louis responded, "Who would have thought people would pay good money to see a regurgitation act? *Chacun a son gout*, as the French like to say."

Faby laughed and tugged on Louis's hand. "Let's go find the scenic railway. I love the scenic railway!"

When they found it, the cars were just starting to move along the track. She counted all of five people in the cars, two young couples bundled into overcoats, hats securely settled on their heads, gloved hands grasping the safety bar in front of them, and a man who looked to be of her father's age and stature sitting in the middle of a car by himself with a pipe clenched between his teeth, a tiny puff of smoke seeping from his barely parted lips. Faby watched as the train cars gradually picked up speed. How she would love for Louis to take her on the scenic railway, but if a scenic railway wasn't an accident of pregnancy waiting to happen, she didn't know what was. No matter. She was certain they would be coming back to Atlantic City, many times over, as Louis danced his way up to the Big Time.

After the scenic railway, they stopped to watch a stout woman in an elaborate dress go down The Slide, ending in an unceremonious dumping into a large wooden bowl. She was quickly followed by a young couple sliding together, the girl sitting between the boy's legs, his arms around her waist so they wouldn't get separated.

The unmistakable sound of a band organ diverted Faby's attention from The Slide. There must be a carousel nearby! She wondered how large it would be. To be on Atlantic City's Steeplechase Pier, it would have to be very large indeed, with all manner of animals one could choose to ride, not just horses, but lions, tigers, zebras, ostriches, roosters, giraffes, rabbits, and a pair of swans with a seat between them for the elderly and sedate. As they drew closer, Faby saw that far from being the largest, most magnificent carousel she had ever seen, the one in front of her was the smallest she had ever seen, a carousel in miniature, with a hefty adult perched awkwardly atop every horse but one, a dapple gray with a little boy splayed across it, his arms in a stranglehold around the horse's neck. When the dapple gray came around again, Faby tried to smile encouragement to the boy, but he had closed his eyes.

"Look at that poor little nipper," Louis said. "He's terrified. He's too small to have gotten up there himself. His dad must have put him on the horse and then walked off and left him. I can't imagine anyone doing that to a child."

When they left Steeplechase Pier, the wind had died down, and the sun felt momentarily warm on Faby's face. The cries of the seagulls sweeping and wheeling across the sky sounded hopeful, and she looked forward to boarding the train for their next destination.

Chapter 21

As the train pulled out of the station, Louis settled into his seat and said expansively, "Ah, Atlantic City, 'The Playground of the Nation.' So, what did you think of your first visit to Atlantic City, Faby? Was it everything you expected?"

"I didn't know what to expect, really. I thought it might be like Old Orchard Beach, being a vacation spot at the ocean and all, but Old Orchard doesn't have half the amusements of Atlantic City. Why, Steeplechase Pier alone has more amusements than Old Orchard."

"Small beer, eh?"

"And how! Although Old Orchard is very popular, particularly with people from Québec. In fact, it's so popular with Québécois you'll hear more people on the beach speaking French than speaking English. How Josephine and I loved Old Orchard Beach when we were kids! Papa would take us for a week every year when he had his vacation, and we'd stay in a small cottage only a block from the beach, all of us in one room together, Maman and Papa in the double bed, Maman Aurore in the single bed, and Josephine and me on cots that we folded up during the day—although we never stayed indoors during the day. As soon as we were finished with breakfast, Maman and Maman Aurore would pack up our picnic lunch in a big basket, and we would all set out for the beach, Papa leading the way with the beach umbrella, blanket, and towels, Maman and Maman Aurore behind him carrying the picnic basket between them. Josephine and I carried our sand toys of course. Occasionally we'd have to dart ahead of the grown-ups for fear of giggling and not being able to stop at the sight of Maman Aurore in her bathing costume."

"I don't think I can picture Maman Aurore in a bathing costume," Louis said thoughtfully, as though he were really trying to imagine it. "She's a little on the stout side."

"It was quite a sight," Faby said. "It had bloomers, and she'd had it so long it was all blotchy and faded from the sun. Believe it or not, Maman Aurore is a very good swimmer. She taught Josephine and me how to swim, as a matter of fact. Papa tried, but he was too afraid that whichever one of us he was holding up would sink to the bottom if he took his hand away. Maman Aurore had no such qualms. If we floundered, she would just stand there and shout, "Kick your *feet,* child, kick your *feet!* Do you want to drown in the Bay of Fundy?"

"Drown in the Bay of Fundy? What did she mean by that?"

"I don't know. She always said it; I think it's just some kind of expression."

"I saved Dorothy from drowning once," Louis said. "She got caught in an undertow at Menemsha."

Faby turned to him and frowned. "Do you think someone Maman Aurore knew drowned in the Bay of Fundy?"

"I would expect so, wouldn't you?"

"I don't know—although she was dead set on making sure we could swim in water over our heads." Faby didn't say anything else for several minutes, watching out the window as the train left the view of open water, then quiescent winter marshland behind, the vestiges of Atlantic City. She really didn't want to think about people drowning. She turned away from the window. "You know, I can't remember it ever raining the week of Papa's vacation. Not once. Papa would check the *Farmer's Almanac* the day before we were to leave to see what the weather was supposed to be for that week, and depending on what *The Almanac* was forecasting, he would say, *Looks like beach weather, girls!* or just shake his head and tell Maman to pack the playing cards and the cribbage board. As soon as we got to the cabin and Papa put our bags inside, he would leave Maman and Maman Aurore to unpack our things while he took Josephine and me for a walk to the Pier to buy a kite to fly on the beach. We'd have the hardest time trying to remember what we'd bought the year before, so we could pick something different: it wouldn't do to fly the same kite two years in a row. Papa would fly that kite on the beach until the wind ripped the paper to shreds or the string snapped, whichever came first."

"I never cared much for kite-flying," Louis said. "Too much bother getting them down from trees and telegraph wires."

"Papa would buy five tickets apiece for Josephine and me to go on the rides. When we were little, we'd stick to the Caterpillar ride and the merry-go-round, but when we got a little older, we were allowed to be more adventuresome, and the Dodgems became my favorite. Josephine liked the Ferris wheel best."

"I was a demon on the Dodgems," Louis said.

"Oh, your family went to Old Orchard Beach, too?"

"No, no, I'm talking about Revere Beach—although Mother would not be caught dead in the place of course. We had to go to Martha's Vineyard every year." Louis paused and shook his head. "Dorothy always threw up on the ferry. I don't know why. Now, she regularly goes sailing with her friends in the summer—but back then she always threw up on the ferry. We'd stay at my Uncle Clarence and Aunt Ida's house in Edgartown while they vacationed in the Adirondacks. Mother would go bird watching in the morning and then spend the afternoon sweeping sand from Uncle Clarence's floors and beating sand from Uncle Clarence's rugs. Dad would lie on a chaise lounge on Uncle Clarence's front porch for the entire day reading *Office Appliances* magazine. That was really the name of it: *Office Appliances: The Magazine of Office Equipment.* Can you imagine anything duller?"

Faby was sure she couldn't.

"He'd bring all twelve issues from the previous year in his briefcase, so he would have something to do on vacation and not have to talk to anybody."

"That doesn't sound like much fun."

"It wasn't. Dorothy would stay on the porch playing with her dolls, and when she became too old for dolls, she would lie on her own chaise lounge reading a week's worth of library books. That left me on my own to go swimming and ramble around the dunes. I like swimming as much as the next fellow, but that water is too cold to stay in all day, and sitting on the sand in a wet bathing suit waiting for it to dry is pretty darned miserable. When I turned fifteen, I just refused to go with them. There was quite a to-do, let me tell you. Mother was furious because Dad sided with me. She seldom raised her voice, but that day she let Dad have it with both barrels—not loud enough that she could be heard by the neighbors, of course—but she was as close to full volume as she could get."

"What did your dad do?"

"He told her the matter was settled and she needed to make sure that there was enough food in the icebox that I could eat decently for the week. Then Dorothy tried to get in on the action and stay behind as well, but Dad told her it was out of the question for an underage girl to stay in a house without adult supervision for a week. She tried to argue with him and got sent to her room for her trouble." Louis paused for a moment. "I could see how Dorothy would think it unfair that I could stay alone in the house and she, a year older than me, couldn't, but Dad knew she'd bring dates home, and he knew what they would try to do. That didn't appease Mother, however. Dorothy told me that Mother refused to speak to him for the entire week on the island. And when they got back, she *still* wasn't speaking to him. As you know, I'm a pretty easy-going fellow, but there was too much tension in the house even for me, and I talked my way into staying with a cousin in Lexington until Dorothy called to give me the all-clear." He stopped speaking and brought both hands down on his thighs. "Well! I need to visit the gents." As soon as he left, Faby stood up and made her way to the ladies' room.

When Faby returned from the ladies' room, Louis had taken the window seat. He smiled as she took the aisle seat. "Having the house to myself for a week was glorious. It was the first time in my life that I was able to do whatever I wanted without having to answer to anybody. I could get up when I wanted and go to bed when I wanted. I could eat what I wanted, go where I wanted."

Faby wondered what doing whatever one pleased whenever one pleased could possibly be like. As Louis said, it must be glorious.

"And where I wanted to go," Louis continued, "was Revere Beach. I needed some excitement after being stuck at a school desk all year. In fact—and don't you dare breathe a word to Mother—I had been planning my vacation mutiny the entire school year. I'd had a paper route since seventh grade, but that year, instead of spending my earnings on baseball cards and jawbreakers, I saved my money, every last penny, so that I would have plenty to spend at Revere Beach. And spend it I did, every last penny. At that time, Revere Beach had fifteen roller coasters, *fifteen,* and I rode every one of them that week, every day, multiple times. I could throw my arms in the air and holler until I had no voice left at all. Up and down and all around, nothing beats a roller coaster."

"I've never been on a roller coaster," Faby said. "Josephine and I would beg Papa to let us go on the roller coaster, but he always said no. It was much too dangerous."

"Statistically speaking, riding a roller coaster is safer than riding in an airplane. As a matter of fact, riding a roller coaster is safer than train travel. Fewer derailments."

"Derailments?"

"Not that we have anything to worry about, of course," he continued, poking a stray bit of hair back into place. "In any event, nothing beats a fast roller coaster to make you feel alive." His hand went back to his hair. "Speaking of fast, I read in the paper a while back that Revere Beach is building a new roller coaster that will be the tallest and fastest in the *world.* Can you imagine? It's going to reach speeds of forty-five to fifty miles an hour. They're calling it 'The Cyclone'." Louis stopped speaking, and when he didn't resume, Faby looked past him to see what was outside the window. They appeared to be traveling through the outskirts of a town, some open fields, a narrow road, a cluster of houses, a steeple, soon left behind. Sitting in the aisle seat, she was not at the right vantage point to see where the train was going or where it had been.

"I spent my days at the beach," Louis said, "Hours upon hours lounging on the sand, looking at girls in their bathing suits, keeping a sharp eye out for the more daring girls who eschewed their stockings." He paused, and Faby wondered how pretty the girls were whom he was watching in his mind's eye. Judging by the expression on his face, very pretty, very pretty indeed.

"I lost my virginity to one of those girls," Louis mused a few moments later. "I don't remember her name. She had very curly hair. Rosa, Rita? Something like that. I was surprised at how easy it was. A little banter, a little flattery, and I was in. I will always remember Revere Beach fondly."

Faby didn't know what to say. Did Louis expect her to respond? What was she supposed to say to something like that? What would anyone say to something like that? And why in God's name would he tell her this?

Chapter 22

Rockaway Beach was bitterly cold with an unrelenting wind blowing icy needles of spray off the ocean, the boardwalk empty save for a miserable-looking man being pushed in a rolling chair by an equally miserable-looking female companion, her face pinched from the cold, her eyes squinted against the wind. Louis had taken into his head that they must see the sights of Rockaway before their train left for his Buffalo engagement, even though the sights were shuttered for the season, his Rockaway Beach engagement having been for the much smaller audience of year-round residents.

A husband and wife juggling team had opened the show, juggling as they made their entrance onto the empty stage, Mr. Johnson from stage left with red balls and Mrs. Johnson from stage right with yellow balls. Their entrance was remarkable enough, but when they met in the center of the stage, their movements were completely synchronized, each rapid hand rising and falling at the same time, each red ball at the same place in its arc as its yellow counterpart. The Johnsons then switched places while the balls were in the air, so that Mr. Johnson was juggling the yellow balls, while Mrs. Johnson had the red. Then, in the blink of an eye, the balls were in their hands, the curtain closed and opened, and they were sitting at each end of a kitchen table set for breakfast, pantomiming an argument. Suddenly, they both got up from the table, knocking over their chairs, and Mrs. Johnson snatched up objects from the table and hurled them at Mr. Johnson—sugar bowl, cream pitcher, egg cup, tea pot, toast rack—in rapid succession as Mr. Johnson caught each one and tossed it in the air—until he was juggling the entire contents of the kitchen table. He then stopped each object in its downward arc and tossed it to his wife who put it back on the table before the next object arrived. At the end, all of the objects were back in their original places on the table, Mr. and Mrs. Johnson were seated in their righted chairs, and Mrs. Johnson was pouring actual tea from the pot that only moments before had been in the air. Faby turned to the patron seated next to her to remark on the magnificent trick, but the elderly woman's thin lips were pursed in such an unexpected expression of disapproval that Faby quickly looked back to the stage.

The Johnsons were now standing next to each other with a little girl on their shoulders, one foot on each parent as she juggled two balls. The child looked to be about five years old, her hair cut in bangs and an enormous pink bow on her head. She kept the balls in the air, as well as her balance, with apparent ease. Suddenly, Mr. and Mrs. Johnson each took a step to the side, and Faby gasped, but as the girl fell, each parent caught her under the arm with one hand while the other hand caught the ball she'd been juggling, and the three of them exited all smiles to good applause. The elderly woman next to Faby grunted in disgust and muttered that those people ought to be ashamed of themselves—not for endangering the little girl's safety but for keeping her up past her bedtime.

Faby found herself unable to shake the force of the elderly woman's disapproval until well after intermission, when Floyd and Charlie the Chimp made their appearance.

Floyd made his entrance to piano accompaniment, leading Charlie by the hand. Charlie was fully-dressed in a navy blue blazer, shirt and tie, and white flannel trousers, with a Panama hat on his head and some version of two-toned spectators on his long, flat chimpanzee feet. Floyd was nattily-attired in the human version of the same outfit. Still holding Charlie by the hand, Floyd began to lead him in a slow and easy soft-shoe, which Charlie the Chimp mimicked to the best of his stumpy, bow-legged ability. When Charlie and Floyd finished their routine, as the last piano chord faded away, Charlie plucked the Panama hat from his head and tossed it to the orchestra leader, who caught it with one hand, and set it on the music stand in front of him. The audience erupted in laughter, with a spontaneous smattering of applause. Charlie took a quick, jerky bow and clapped his own hands, at which the audience laughed even harder. Suddenly, brass blared, and there was Charlie the Chimp center stage doing the Charleston. Not until saxophones replaced the brass for the Black Bottom did Faby realize that Charlie the Chimp had stolen Slim White's act.

After the show, Louis had been furious, and now, four days later, as he grimly hustled Faby down the boardwalk at Rockaway Beach, he was still fuming. "That goddamn son-of-a-bitch, stealing my act for an ape. It would have been bad enough if he'd stolen it for himself, but the no-talent bastard had to steal it for a goddamn flea-bitten ape that should have been left in the goddamn jungle flinging feces where he belonged."

By the time their train pulled out of Rockaway Station and they'd left the tangled cityscapes and competing smokestacks of the New York City boroughs behind, Louis seemed to have recovered his equilibrium, and when he returned to his seat after his first trip to the smoker, he entertained Faby with some show business stories.

"Obviously, vaudeville players are notorious for stealing each other's acts. In fact, that's the only reason a vaudevillian will go to see a show that he's not in. Certainly not to be entertained. But the good ones avoid being too obvious about it, taking the idea for the skit and changing the dialog and the props, taking dance bits from several routines and putting them together. While we're always on the lookout for anything we can use to wow an audience, at the same time, you need to be careful who you borrow from. There are some people in this business, even in Small Time, that you just don't want to cross because you never know who they may be connected to—if they're connected to someone who can prevent you from getting bookings, you can kiss your show business dreams goodbye. Even worse, though, is when the audience is on to you. I remember this one sap, Gus Hovitch was his name, who stole an entire comedy routine lock, stock, and barrel from a guy who had never played the town where Gus was next booked. Unbeknownst to Gus, however, *that* guy had actually stolen it from someone else who had played that self-same town just the week before and absolutely killed the audience. So, opening night, Gus comes out on stage and starts doing the act. He delivers the first punch line. Nothing. He gets to the second punch line. Still nothing. He ratchets up the business. *Still* nothing. He mugs. No one in the audience is laughing, not even a chuckle. Those of us in the wings waiting our turn are terrified. What a bunch of stiffs! If they're not gonna laugh at one of the funniest acts we've heard in ages, how are they gonna react to *our* acts? There is a river of flop sweat flowing backstage, believe you me. So he gets about halfway through the act and you could see that he's thinking, *How the hell am I gonna get out of this?*, because the worst thing you can do when your act flops is run off the stage before it's even finished. Only rank amateurs do that, and it's curtains for them for a career in show business, pardon the pun.

"By this time, the audience has started talking to each other, completely ignoring him. But he soldiers on, right to the bitter end, when what should have been a wow finish met with complete silence. Since the audience had seen the same act, word-for-word, pratfall-for-pratfall only the week before, they knew exactly when to stop chatting with each other and just freeze him out. I have to say, I think that audience did him a favor. Gus Hovitch never stole another act, even threw away his standard joke book. Every act he puts on now is a complete original, and last I heard he was on his way to the Big Time.

"There was another fellow—what was his name?—I don't remember—who stole so many other acts, he was known on the circuit as Larry Lightfingers. Odd-looking fellow, as I recall, wore a large mustache to hide a harelip. Kept changing his name, too."

"Really, why?"

"So he could stay employed! He wasn't very good. Anyway, this particular time, Larry decided that he wasn't going to do the comedy routine he'd been booked for in the deuce spot. Nobody wants the deuce spot—it's the worst spot on the bill, but it had taken him so long to even get that, he was bound and determined he was going to make an impression. Old Lightfingers decides he's gonna try out a new act, which he'd stolen from a headliner in Detroit. During rehearsal, Larry gives no indication of what he has planned for opening night, just goes through his routine, doing pratfalls and mugging to beat the band. Come opening night, the dancing dogs have pranced off the stage, the curtain comes down, the curtain goes up, and there is Larry dressed like some kind of country squire all in tweed and carrying a walking stick. He launches into this monologue about English country life with the most preposterous British accent you've ever heard. His timing is totally off, and the audience just sits there gawking at him, trying to decide whether they should laugh or cringe. Then, about halfway through the act, the curtain suddenly comes down, there is a sound of scuffling and then Nellie Baker is positioned in front of the olio singing, "I Love You Truly." Before she gets halfway through the first verse, the scuffling behind the olio gets louder, and now cursing has been added to the mix, nearly drowning out poor Nellie, who is still singing, desperately trying to carry on with the show, God love her. Now, a fellow would have been able to take advantage of the hullabaloo going on behind him, with all manner of double takes, playing it up big for the audience, but not that poor young girl. Well, she stumbles into the second verse of "I Love You Truly," and there is the sound of a fist hitting a nose and breaking it. There is no mistaking the sound of someone being punched full-on in the face and breaking his nose. After you hear it once, you'll never fail to recognize it. The audience gasps, and Nellie starts to cry, but she never stops singing, and she gets a huge round of applause from the audience for being such a trooper. Of course, the nose in question was Light-Lightfingers', and the fist belonged to the headliner of the show, from whom Larry had stolen the monologue *and* the costuming, right down to the silver bulldog head on his walking stick. Turns out that in addition to being light-fingered with his material, Larry was also really unlucky. He had stolen the monologue from Digby Bennett, who was actually headlining the show with that very mono-logue. However, Bennett hadn't been at rehearsal because he'd missed his train, and it never occurred to Larry to read the playbill to see who else was on it. In addition to having no talent, Larry was not very bright."

Louis paused, and Faby looked out the window as the train passed through Allentown. "That incident finished him in vaude, of course, and he went crawling back to whatever hick town he'd come out of to milk cows or pound sand or weigh nails at the hardware store, or whatever it was he did before he took it into his head to follow his show business dreams."

Louis looked past Faby at the passing landscape, which appeared to consist mostly of alternating farmland and factories. She followed his gaze, thinking he was finished with his story, but he turned back to her and continued, "For some people, it just doesn't pay to follow their dreams—and it's too bad they don't have sense enough to just stay where they are. Following a dream that will never come true will bring you nothing but heartache."

Faby continued to watch the passing landscape, shifting in her seat from time to time, trying to find a comfortable position as the baby fidgeted in his confined space, unable to settle himself.

"Now that I think about it," Louis said, "We were playing Scranton when Larry Lightfingers misappropriated the headliner's act. Or it might have been Wilkes-Barre. In any event, that girl singer Nellie was the prettiest little thing you ever saw, light brown curly hair, blue eyes, and a figure that wouldn't quit. After the show was over, when I got back to the hotel, I went up to her room to see how she was doing. Poor bunny was sitting on the edge of the bed in her bathrobe crying. I comforted her, of course, and when we were finished, I gave her money for a train ticket home. Do you know, Faby, six months later I received a letter from her with the train fare I'd given her, paying me back. She'd given up on the idea of going into show business and gone ahead and married the boy she'd been going with in high school. That was a couple of years ago, so she's probably had some babies and gotten fat."

"Not all women get fat after they've had babies," Faby interjected. "And those who do probably can't help it."

"If you say so," Louis said.

As the train rumbled through Pennsylvania, the baby continued to fidget and squirm, until Faby began to wonder if there was something wrong with him.

Chapter 23

Opening night in Pottsville, the show went over big, with Louis receiving three curtain calls for his act—which Faby hoped would put an end once and for all to the subject of Floyd's stealing his act on behalf of Charlie the Chimp.

The following night, she didn't hear him when he came in after the show, and she woke up the next morning with him in the bed beside her, up on one elbow looking down at her. "How was the show?" she said when was she was awake enough to have her wits about her.

"Well," he said, flipping the covers aside and getting up. "If I said we had a boffo show last night, I'd be lying. My act wowed 'em, though. If I do say so myself. And I *do* say so myself." He went into the bathroom, and from behind the closed door, she heard his stream hitting the toilet. Then the toilet flushed, and the door opened. "And just in case you're wondering, I did *not* milk the applause. No siree Bob. I am *not* that kind of fellow." Faby got out of bed, found clean drawers and stockings in her suitcase, and retrieved her clothes from the day before where she'd carefully draped them over the bureau. "Now the Vincent sisters, you want to talk about milking the applause, standing there all simpering and blushing and refusing to leave the stage. Shameless, utterly shameless." His voice became muffled; he must be talking around his tooth-brush. "Kids are the worst, though, the little bastards, with their goddamn parents egging 'em on from the wings. I can't *stand* kids." He spat, once, twice. "Well, regardless, a *discerning* audience knows *genuine* talent." He popped his head out the door as Faby was pulling on her jersey dress. "Sorry about that. Pay me no mind. I just need to blow off a little steam now and again. It's not all sweetness and light backstage. No siree Bob." Faby heard the sound of running water and a razor tapping against the sink.

After he had finished shaving, he came into the room to get dressed. As he was buttoning his shirt, he paused and looked hard at Faby. "You're wearing that dress again?"

"None of my other clothes fit me. I've gotten too big."

"I can see that." He shrugged on his overcoat. "I should see if one of the girls with the show can make you a couple of dresses, so you don't have to wear the same dress every day. There must be something in a trunk someone could make over for you. Come on, get your coat on, so we can get some break-fast. It'll have to be just coffee and a doughnut, I'm afraid. We're running a little low on cash."

The diner where they had their coffee and doughnuts looked a little down at the heels, and when the young count-erman asked for their order, Faby saw that he was missing one of his front teeth.

"That's a beaut of a shiner," Louis remarked to the count-erman when he plunked their breakfast down in front of them.

"Got in a fight," the counterman responded, his tone sounding as though he had answered the same question for every single customer he had served since the diner opened for breakfast several hours earlier. Faby could see how that could quickly become tiresome, and she hoped Louis would have sense enough to drop the subject—but of course he didn't.

"Did you win?"

The counterman ducked down to retrieve a bin full of dirty dishes, saying as he straightened up, "Does it *look* like I won?"

"Maybe, depends on whether you gave as good as you got."

The counterman slammed the bin of dirty dishes down on the drainboard by the sink. Louis started laughing, saying to Faby in a stage whisper, "Touchy fellow, isn't he?"

If Faby had dared say what she wanted to say, she would have said, *You should leave him alone. It's bad enough he had to come to work looking that way without people the likes of you making fun of him.* But she held her tongue.

As they left the diner, Louis said, "I'll come back to the hotel with you; we should both try to catch a little more shuteye. Our train for Buffalo leaves at two a.m., and I can't afford to pay another day for the room. You're going to have to come to the show or wait in my dressing room." This wasn't the first time he hadn't been able to pay an extra day for her to rest before they had to catch the train in the middle of the night for his next jump. "Is there a couch or a daybed in your dressing room?"

"'Fraid not, just a lumpy armchair this time."

When they got back to the hotel, Faby slipped off her shoes and lay down on the bed, turning on her side so that the sagging mattress could take most of the weight of the baby. Louis took his shoes off and lay down facing her. "You've been a real trooper so far." He reached out to stroke her cheek. "I have to say, it's been nice having the company. But after the baby's born, you'll need to stay home. Life on the road isn't healthy for an infant."

"But some of the wives are traveling with babies."

"Yes, but those wives are in the act, or they have acts of their own."

"Oh. I guess I hadn't thought that far ahead. I haven't even begun to put a layette together." As soon as she said "layette," she remembered the sewing machine restriction from the accidents of pregnancy pamphlet and mentally counted the months from the fourth of July. She was now in her seventh month and restricted from using the sewing machine. She would be unable to sew the layette, not that she had access to a sewing machine to begin with. The pamphlet also restricted her from riding on trains and having marital relations, but there was no helping either of them.

"Do you really want me to go back home after the baby's born?"

"In fact, we should think about getting you back home *before* the baby's born, so that you can be properly looked after. I'll wire Mother to start getting my old room ready for you and the baby."

"No."

The bedsprings squealed as she turned to face away from Louis. He gave no response and was soon snoring, as she lay awake until it was time to go to the theater. Deciding that she couldn't face seeing the show, she waited for him in his dressing room, huddled in the lumpy armchair in the chill damp as the familiar sounds of gaiety ebbed and flowed around her unseen.

Chapter 24

They were on the train again. After being pulled out of the lumpy armchair, pushed into a taxicab, and dragged through the Pottsville Station to be deposited in a seat, Faby had hoped she would be able to sleep, having become used to the incessant rattle and shake of train travel, even in the middle of the night, but the baby was fidgeting so that she couldn't get comfortable now matter how she shifted her position. It was as if he were trying to right himself, having decided that he had spent long enough living his life upside down.

Louis of course was oblivious to her discomfort, lounging in his seat as the train careened through the darkness, as if he were sitting on the beach daydreaming a Sunday afternoon away.

"I'm thinking I should add something to my act, something for a real wow finish. I don't know—what do you think?"

Glad for the distraction, she turned to look at his profile in the dim light. "I don't think there's anything wrong with it."

"I know there isn't anything *wrong* with it. It's just getting harder and harder to impress. One fellow does a backflip, the next fellow has to do a whole series of backflips, and if one fellow somersaults off the stage into the aisle, the next fellow has to somersault off the stage into the pit orchestra. Big Time,

Small Time, it doesn't matter. You have to wow the audience to keep getting bookings."

The baby gave Faby such a hard kick that she gasped.

"What's wrong?" Louis said.

"The baby kicked me. Hard." Faby couldn't be sure which of her internal organs had taken the blow as another kick landed on the opposite side.

"Oh?" Louis rested his hand on her belly as the baby kicked twice more in quick succession. His face broke into a grin. "Atta boy!"

Faby shifted in her seat so that he would have to move his hand. "You want the baby to be a boy?"

"Of course. Doesn't every fellow want a son to carry on his name and tell the stories of his adventures to? After all, there are just some stories a fellow can't tell a daughter." Louis winked, and Faby turned away from him, hoping with all her heart that that baby would be a girl.

Later, as the train pulled into Williamsport, a cloudy winter dawn broke, the sun appearing to cast more cold than warmth over the barely visible landscape. Faby got up with Louis when he left the train to stretch his legs, hoping the movement of her walking would settle the baby.

As the train was pulling out of the station, Louis said, "We should think about names."

Faby managed a rueful smile. "You know, after seven months, I've not once thought about what we might name the baby."

"Neither have I, which is why I mentioned it."

"I think I should like to give a baby girl Josephine's middle name, Collette. It's such a pretty name. I've always envied her for it."

"Have you, now? What's your middle name, then?"

"Marie."

"Ah, I see. The all-purpose middle name for little French girls everywhere."

"What's *your* middle name, then?"

"Phillip."

"Phillip, is it? Well, if the baby is a boy, I would like to name him after my brother Guillaume."

"Oh, no, Mother wouldn't stand for any French names."

"William, then?"

"William's a good respectable name, but I'm thinking Louis, Junior. Louise if it's a girl."

"Of course you are."

"Indeed I am."

Faby could see that there was no point in taking the discussion any further. Apparently, the child she was sharing her body with was destined to become Louis Phillip or Louise Philippa, and she had no say in the matter. She turned her attention to the landscape outside the train window, snow-covered trees and snow-covered open spaces, fields and bodies of water indistinguishable from each other, the occasional snow-covered town which lay beyond, the buildings huddled together against the wind, a lone steeple brave enough to pierce the lowering sky.

After a while, the train began slowing down. Louis glanced past Faby out the window and said, "Ah, looks like we're coming into some kind of station. Seneca."

The train screeched and huffed itself to a stop at the Seneca station. Louis stood up. "I'm going to find a lunch counter and see about getting us a couple of sandwiches for our lunch. You'd better come with me."

Faby hesitated, but she got up and followed Louis off the train. As they left the platform, he grabbed her hand and set off on his search for a lunch counter. He found one within a matter of moments, ordered two turkey sandwiches without asking Faby what she wanted, and loped back to the train, dragging Faby behind him. Stowing their coats in the overhead rack, he said over his shoulder, "I'm not about to pay the prices the dining car charges. Damn chiselers try to take advantage of the traveling man every chance they get." He stopped speaking and sat down. "Sandwiches will have to do. I would have preferred tuna fish to turkey, but they'd have stunk up the entire car." He quickly ran a comb through his hair, which had become disheveled from his dash through the station. "I once saw a fellow get punched in the face for eating tuna fish on a train."

Faby wasn't sure whether to believe him about the sandwich-inspired fracas or not. As if reading her thoughts, Louis continued on, "Nasty business. The tuna fish fellow's nose was broken. His wife went into a fit of hysterics and had to be restrained by the other passengers. Needless to say, the fellow who threw the punch was taken off the train at the next station by the police and arrested. You had to feel sorry for the poor sap with the broken nose. After it healed, he wouldn't have a manly story to explain his crooked nose. If I were he, I would just make one up. Even crashing to the floor in a drunken stupor is more dignified than getting punched over a tuna fish sandwich." Louis settled back in his seat, seemingly pleased with his story, even if his audience hadn't responded to it.

Faby gradually became aware that there was something different about her surroundings: it had begun to snow. As her eyes adjusted to the muted light coming through the window, she realized that the train was heading straight into a snow storm, the snow a swirling, mesmerizing cloud of white, the landscape beyond indiscernible, muffled in drifts.

How she and Josephine used to love snow days when they were in school, tucked up in their bedroom with cups of cocoa, a plate of molasses cookies still warm from the oven, and a stack of borrowed *Photoplay* magazines, while the storm hurled itself against the rattling storm windows, school cancelled only for a blizzard, nothing less.

Louis craned his neck to look out the window. "I don't like the looks of this."

"You don't? Why not?"

"Why not? Because it's damned inconvenient, that's why not. I should have *known* better than to take a booking in Buffalo this time of year—but the money was too good to pass up. I really don't like the looks of this." He stood up. "I'm going for a smoke."

The train appeared to be slowing down, the sound of the wheels clacking over points in the track coming at decreasing intervals. Peering into the swirling, windblown snow, Faby couldn't make out any shapes that looked like buildings or any kind of a town. The train jolted with a great screech of metal on metal, and Faby put out her arms to brace herself on the seat in front of her as the metal screeching went on and on. Finally, with another jolt, the train stopped. There was a brief interval of silence in the car as the passengers absorbed the fact that the train hadn't hit anything or derailed; then the hubbub of voices started. *Why have we stopped? What's happened? Why have we stopped? Has the train broken down? Why have we stopped? Where's the conductor? Why have we stopped?* Faby wondered if Louis was still in the smoking car and whether he would come back for her or continue to leave her here alone with the crying children, frightened mothers, and impatient drummers, distraught at the thought of losing a single potential order to a weather delay. She got up and knelt on her seat to look for him. The door of the car opened, and he came through it scowling. He sat down next to her and shook his head. "The storm's even worse up ahead. We're going to have to wait until the tracks are cleared. The drifts are too deep for the locomotive on this train to get through."

"How long will that take? Do you know where we are?"

"We're still two hours out of Buffalo—under the best of circumstances. I should have *known* better than to take this booking. I wish I had someone who could've talked me out of it."

Faby held her breath, trying to make herself as small as she could. Louis lapsed into scowling silence in his seat. After several minutes, he retrieved their sandwiches from the over-head rack and handed her one. "Here, let's eat. Since we're not going anywhere for a while, we might as well try and make the best of it."

Faby nodded as she took her sandwich from him and unwrapped it, so relieved that he had come out of his funk she didn't dare trust her voice to speak.

"Kinda dry, isn't it?" Louis said with a grimace after they'd been working on the sandwiches for a few minutes.

Faby nodded, chewing determinedly, not about to let the food he'd paid for go to waste.

"Well, that's life on the road for you," Louis said. "You never know what kind of food you're gonna get, just that it's not gonna be very good. I say keep your expectations low, and you won't be disappointed—and occasionally you might be pleasantly surprised. In point of fact, the best steak dinner I ever ate was in this grubby little place in some godforsaken backwater that I couldn't recall the name of if I passed through there a hundred more times. Talk about a ptomaine palace! I didn't even want to sit down in there, much less put anything that had come into contact with the premises in my mouth—but I was famished. I hadn't eaten all day, and it was the only restaurant in town, so I decided to take the chance. Well, let me tell you, that was the best T-bone steak I have ever had, before or since, perfect medium-rare, seared on the outside to hold in the juices, and so tender you barely needed a knife to cut it. I don't know who the cook was, but he sure knew his steak. Just the memory of that steak dinner kept me going for weeks." He paused to take a bite of his sandwich before continuing. "Seriously, though, Faby, you need to know that food poisoning is an occupational hazard for traveling performers that we try to avoid at all costs. Besides being hell on earth while it's happening, it can have lasting effects. In point of fact, I know personally of a fellow who lost his one and only chance at the Big Time from eating bad clams. A Keith scout was in the audience specifically to see his act—it had been wowing the Small Time for over a year—and this particular night it was headlining the bill. Jimmy was flying high. The house lights came down, the curtain went up—and where was poor Jimmy? Doubled over in his dressing room puking into a wastebasket. He was able to go on the following night, but by then it was too late. The Keith scout had moved on, and the poor bastard never got another go at the brass ring. Excuse my French." Louis took another bite of his sandwich as Faby wondered why he was telling her such an unpleasant story when she was trying to eat and, which, moreover, appeared to be in direct contradiction to his ptomaine palace steak story. "Jimmy was never the same after that, nor was his act. Those clams had broken him. Last I heard, he was giving piano lessons to children whose talents are disproportionate to their mothers' judgment of same." Louis swallowed the final bite of his turkey sandwich. "I may not be destined for the Big Time, but you will never catch me trying to teach some fat kid with two left feet and a harridan of a mother to do a buck-and-wing. Not me, no siree Bob!"

Louis left for the smoking car, and Faby rested her head against the seat back and closed her eyes. The baby had settled down at last. Perhaps he'd just been hungry. As the turkey sandwich grudgingly began to digest, Faby began to wonder how long they would be stranded or, more to the point, how long they *could* be stranded. On the other side of the window glass, the storm only seemed to have intensified. Whatever town they were stranded in was in full white-out. How could the townspeople even know they were stranded and needed rescue? They were on a train, just passing through, after all.

At home, there was nothing to fear from a storm, not even a blizzard. Papa strapped on his snow shoes and walked to the Spavin Cure Factory to earn his pay as usual, with Maman holding supper for him in the evening to allow for the additional time it would take him to return home. There were more Mason jars in the pantry than you could ever count, filled with vegetables, fruit, and ground venison from Papa's annual buck, with still more jars in the cellar. There was plenty of wood for the furnace, and there was coal for the small pot-bellied stove in the living room. When the electricity went out, there was a supply of kerosene in the cellar to light the lamps Maman Aurore had brought with her from Québec. There would even be water if the pipes froze, in an array of pitchers, jars, crocks, and jugs, prepared when Maman Aurore's bones signaled that the coming storm would be a particularly bad one.

What would happen when the food in the dining car ran out? There would have been only enough put in to feed the passengers for the number of meals it took to reach their destination, and when it ran out, there would be no more and no way to get any more. The same must be true for the coal; it was being used to heat the passenger cars, but the supply would run out at some point, and there would no heat and no way to power the locomotive either.

"What's the matter, Faby?" Louis had returned from the smoking car. "You look like someone just walked over your grave."

"Are you sure someone is coming to get us? How do they know we're here?"

"Of course someone is coming to get us. I told you, they're sending another locomotive to clear the tracks."

"Are you sure? How do they know we're stranded here? How do they know where we are?"

"Not to worry, little lady," a voice behind her said. "The engineer telegraphs a distress call to the next station." Just as she was turning around to who had spoken, she was stopped by a glare from Louis, who informed her that the New York Central Railroad knew what to do when it snowed, for Christ's sake, and she decided she had best keep her questions to herself.

By the time the train began to move again, it was well after dark, and they didn't reach the Buffalo station until nearly midnight, twelve hours behind schedule, Faby blinking in the light of the station, stumbling after Louis as he went in search of a taxicab to take them to their hotel. When they reached their room at last, Faby used the toilet, got into her nightgown, and crawled into bed, beyond the point of caring whether Louis joined her in bed or not.

Chapter 25

When Faby next opened her eyes, she was alone in the bed, and the covers weren't keeping out the chill of the room. She could see through one of the room's tall windows that the snow appeared to have stopped, but she couldn't tell what time of day it was. The room was unimaginably quiet. Just as she was wondering where Louis was, a key sounded in the lock, and he burst into the room, slamming the door behind him. "God damn it! God damn it all to hell!"

She struggled to sit up, clutching the bedclothes to her chest as he slammed his hat and overcoat on the floor and continued to curse. "Do you want to know what happened? Do you want to know what happened?!"

Faby nodded, not knowing what he expected her to say, what she was supposed to say.

"After missing opening night, we finally get to this wretched shithole of a city, I get myself to the theater, thinking I can give the pit leader my sheet music and get in some re-hearsal time before the first performance, and the goddamn door is locked . . . the goddamn door is locked! There's just some phonus-bolonus sign on the door, 'Closed for death in the family.' So, I'm thinking, okay, all right, they've closed to attend a funeral. I'll miss out on the first two shows, but they'll open after the funeral, and the rest will go on. But when I ask around, I find out that they're closed for the rest of the week, and our contracts are canceled, kaput." He paused to take a breath. "And do you know why? Do you want to know why we're stuck in this dump cooling our heels for three days before my next jump with no pay whatsoever, not a single measly dime to recoup my expenses? Do you want to know why?" He stopped speaking, his normally pale face flushed red. Faby hesitated, then shook her head. "Why?"

"The owner's brother-in-law dropped dead of a heart attack shoveling his neighbor's front walk, that's why. The owner's brother-in-law! They cheat me out of three days' pay for a goddamn brother-in-law. Not even immediate family—a brother-in-law for Christ's sake. And not even the brother-in-law's own front walk but his neighbor's! The way I see it, if you're stupid enough to live in goddamn Buffalo, New York, then you deserve to drop dead shoveling snow." As soon as he stopped speaking, he walked over to the window and turned his back on Faby to look out at the snow-covered street below.

She watched him from the bed for several minutes, shivering, wondering if she should try to say something to him that would make him feel better or whether she should get up and take a bath, leaving him alone to cool off. His arm moved, and she heard a match strike. "Now that I'm not going to be paid, we should move to a cheaper hotel, but I say the hell with it. Maybe I'll just do a bunk in the middle of the night. Serve the chiseling bastards right."

At that, Faby slid out of bed and went into the room's tiny bathroom to use the toilet and draw a bath. While the bath water was running, she returned to the room to gather up her clothes.

Louis crossed the room to flick the ash from his cigarette into the ashtray by the bed. "I'm sorry I got myself into such a lather. I don't usually get so worked up when faced with a setback. Having a wife with a baby on the way sheds a different light on things, I suppose. You'd better get back to your bath before the tub overflows."

Faby had no sooner taken her clothes into the bathroom and gotten into the bathtub than the door opened and Louis poked his head in. She bent forward to cover her breasts and distended belly as best she could with her arms.

"Do you know Five Hundred?" Louis said.

"What? Do I know five hundred what?"

"The card game. I thought I'd see if I could round up a few people to play cards with us to pass the time."

"Oh!" She shivered in the draft from the open door, her teeth chattering. "Yes, I know how to play Five Hundred."

"Good. You take your bath, and I'll see who I can find." He shut the door, but she didn't move to expose herself until she heard the latch click, taking her bath and dressing as quickly as she could, to be ready when Louis and the others came back to the room. As she put on her wristwatch, she was surprised to see that the time was nearly noon; she had missed breakfast. She idly wondered why she wasn't feeling hungry after having missed breakfast, and last night's supper, as well, when the train was delayed.

After brushing her teeth to freshen her breath, she made the bed. She wondered what could be taking Louis so long. She had never found it difficult to round up a group of people for a game of cards—it was the most natural thing in the world—but then again, perhaps hotel guests would be leery of a tall lantern-jawed stranger wearing a loud sport coat and an equally startling necktie come knocking at their door asking them to leave the safety of their rooms for a game of unknown stakes.

She crossed the room to the windows and looked out to see what Buffalo might look like in daylight, the taxicab ride from the station the night before having been a surreal, stuttering progression of snow and streetlamps. Across from where she stood was an uninterrupted block of three-story buildings, their flat roofs covered with drifting snow, random patches of snow still clinging to the brickwork façades where the storm had flung them. Whether the buildings housed offices, apartments, or other hotels was impossible to tell. Looking down, she saw that the street below appeared to have been plowed, after a fashion. With huge piles of snow heaped on either side, the street looked barely passable, and she could see no vehicles even making an attempt, nor could she see a single person making the attempt on foot. The residents of the city, and the merchants as well, were probably still shoveling their walks and driveways, which, she well knew, was easier said than done, every pass of the snowplow necessitating yet another round of shoveling. Perhaps when the new day had dawned after the storm, the residents of Buffalo had all dropped dead shoveling snow, the men at any rate, leaving behind the women and children, as well as any elderly men weak of limb and short of breath, too frightened to move away from the stove or furnace grate around which they were huddled.

She was about to take this morbid line of thought just a little further when the door of the room opened, and Louis came entered the room, shutting the door behind him.

"You weren't able to find anyone to play cards with us?"

"Shirley and Ed are coming. They went out to find a deli to pick up some food."

Although Faby had always wanted to try deli food, never having eaten any except for the coconut cream pie Louis had shared with her in Atlantic City, for some reason, the thought of food was not at all appealing.

"Ah," Louis said, "here they are." Louis opened the door to reveal a man and woman who looked to be about his age, give or take a couple of years, Shirley and Ed, presumably. Ed held a paper sack in one hand. From the other, a small box done up with string dangled from one finger. Shirley relieved him of the food and crossed the room to set it on the dresser.

"Well, that was an adventure," Ed said, shedding his overcoat and bending down to reach his feet. "I hate wearing these damn things. But I'm not about to ruin a five-dollar pair of shoes tromping around in the snow." As he slipped the rubbers off his shoes, Faby couldn't help staring. She had never seen such a pair of shoes on a man, two-tone wing tips with the most elaborate perforated design. No wonder they had cost Ed five dollars! The rest of Ed, in striped socks, cuffed trousers, striped tie to match his socks, was equally snazzy. As for Shirley, well, after slipping off her dainty overshoes and dropping her coat and hat on top of Ed's on the chair, perfectly marcelled Shirley was decked out for a game of cards in a red wool two-piece with an elaborately-plumed parrot at the hip, a long beaded necklace ending in a beaded tassel, and drop earrings to match. "Do you like my parrot?" Shirley said, running her fingers over it. "It's all hand-embroidered."

"It's beautiful," Faby said. "Did your mother make it for you? My mother made me a red wool dress; it's my favorite."

"Good heavens, no! I wouldn't be caught dead in anything my mother made. Perish the thought." Shirley gave a stage shudder, as though the dreaded thought would continue to live in her mind if she didn't physically drive it out.

Louis now made his presence known by crossing the room to Faby and thrusting her in front of him. "Let me introduce you to the wife here."

"The wife?" Ed said, laughing. "Did I hear you right?" He put his hand to his ear. "Did I hear you say 'the wife'?"

"Yes, indeed you did, Ed. This beautiful little doll is my wife Faby."

An odd expression passed over Shirley's face, but it was gone so quickly Faby couldn't be sure she'd even seen it, much less try to interpret what it meant.

"Married," Shirley said. "That's certainly unexpected. How did you two meet?"

"Yeah," Ed chimed in. "How *did* you two meet? I never would have figured old Slim here as a fellow to travel with excess baggage."

Faby looked over at Louis, wondering how he would respond to the question of how they had met, whether he would make up some perfectly plausible but ridiculous story or tell Shirley and Ed the truth.

In fact, he did neither. Instead, he pulled the bedspread off the bed with a flourish befitting a magician about to reveal the illusion of a lifetime and asked Shirley to help him spread it on the floor.

"Oh, a picnic!" she exclaimed, clapping her hands before reaching down to grab two ends of the bedspread, then lifting them in perfect unison with Louis to arrange the bedspread on the floor without a single wrinkle. Faby frowned. How could Shirley and Louis possibly have done that? No one ever spread the blanket for the picnic perfectly the first time. There was always much maneuvering and billowing of fabric, losing one's grip on one's end, and chastising from one's partner.

Louis and Shirley sat down on the blanket, Louis sitting awkwardly cross-legged, Shirley with her legs tucked gracefully to the side. "Come on, Ed," Louis said. "Let's see what you've brought us. I'm famished. Come on, Faby, time to eat."

Faby sat on the bedspread facing Louis, while Ed knelt down and began removing the contents of the paper bag and placing them in the center of the blanket. "Well, let's see, shall we? We have a ham-and-cheese on rye, a ham-and-cheese on white, a ham-and -cheese on wheat, and a ham-and-cheese on pumpernickel."

"So you think you're a comedian, now?" Louis said. "Nobody likes a ham."

Ed acknowledged the cleverness of the pun with a cocked finger in Louis's direction. "No joke. I didn't like the looks of the other meats, so I got four ham-and-cheese."

Faby's stomach gave a lurch as the image of poor Jimmy puking into a wastebasket flashed into her mind.

"There are plenty of dill pickles to go around," Ed continued, reaching into the bag and extracting a waxed paper packet. "And for snacking later, crullers! By the way, you owe me two simoleans, sport. I'll kick in the extra two bits."

"You're a prince among men," Louis said, bending forward to unwrap the sandwiches, looking for the one with the bread he wanted, which turned out to be white, the one Faby wanted. She hesitantly reached out and took half of the sandwich on wheat bread. "Take the other half," Ed said. "There's enough for everyone."

Faby shook her head. "Thanks all the same. I'm not very hungry."

"Neither am I," Shirley said, reaching with an elegant manicured hand and taking the other half of the ham-and-cheese on wheat. She wore what looked like a diamond ring on her right hand, if the stone was real, but her left ring finger was bare; apparently Shirley and Ed were not a couple, or if they were, they weren't a serious couple. "We girls have to watch our figures," Shirley said, and Faby blushed, knowing just how obvious her pregnancy now was. Despite her marriage to Louis, the thought of anyone knowing the condition she was in was embarrassing, if no longer mortifying.

"You never did answer Ed's question," Shirley said, going for a dill pickle. "How did you and Faby meet?"

Louis motioned that his mouth was full, gaining a few seconds before he needed to speak. "It was love at first sight, of course—totally unexpected, as love at first sight always is. Faby is from a small town in northern Vermont, and once a year to celebrate the Fourth of July, they book a show to play in the town's opera house. It plays for an entire week to give an opportunity for everyone from the surrounding towns a chance to see it, seeing as the opera house is quite small."

"It's not so small," Faby said softly, all the while knowing she should keep the remark to herself.

"What part of Vermont?" Shirley interjected. "I played Brattleboro once, in '22 or '23." She paused to take a delicate bite of her sandwich. "Had to be '22 'cause I was still playing with Whatshisname. Boy, did our act wow 'em in Brattleboro! We took five curtain calls on opening night." She put up her hand and spread her fingers. "Five! First time I'd ever gotten that many curtain calls. Although not the last, of course."

"Of course," Louis said dryly, giving Shirley a look, which she immediately returned. "As it happens," she continued, "I've gotten more curtain calls as a single—not that that's either here nor there. Whatshisname and I had been working on this flirtation act for months on the Pantages time, and by the time we played Brattleboro, we were killing them—nobody could touch us. Not even Seeley and Fields could have touched us that night. I wore the cutest little summer dress, with the skirt shortened so that you could see my legs when I danced, but still demure, of course, to make Whatshisname in his horn rim glasses and bow tie look even more the bashful admirer. He wrote all the banter, but I worked out the business for both of us, and we worked out the dance routine together. In one of the first towns we played, the pit leader couldn't keep time, and he kept speeding up the tempo toward the end when he was supposed to be slowing it down for the finish, and we had to double-time it to keep up with the music. When it got some yocks from the audience, we decided to keep it in. I worked in some more business from there, and for the wow finish—"

Louis interrupted her. "I thought you wanted to hear how Faby and I met?"

Shirley looked a little distracted at the interruption. "Oh, yes, I did, didn't I? Do tell."

"As I was saying, I was playing a small town in northern Vermont over the Fourth of July last summer, nowhere *near* Brattleboro, when I saw the prettiest little dark-haired girl in a yellow dress sitting in the audience, right in my line of sight. Lucky she wasn't sitting further back, or I wouldn't have been able to see her."

Faby murmured, "Row J gives the best view in the Opera House."

"As she watched my number, she couldn't take her eyes off me, which is always gratifying, of course, but even more than that there was a glow about her face that I'd never seen from an audience before. She was *entranced* by the performance. A fellow hoofer can appreciate your technique, because he knows what it takes to come off a seven and execute an entire series of perfect knee drops, particularly if he has yet to fully master an over the top step, while for most audiences it's more like watching a magic show. They sit there with their mouths agape wondering how it could be humanly possible for someone to move his feet so fast. With Faby, it was different. She appreciated the *artistry* of it."

Faby almost blurted out, "I *did?*" when she was stopped by the realization that Louis was actually right. It *was* the artistry that had entranced her so.

"After the show ended, I didn't even wait to take off my makeup. I just had to meet this girl, so I hung around by the stage door—"

"Three-sheeting, were you, Louis?"

"*No*, I wasn't three-sheeting. Seeing as she enjoyed my performance, I thought she might like to have her program autographed. No such luck, though. When I caught sight of her walking down the street with her sister, I decided to follow them."

"You probably scared the poor girls half to death," Ed interjected.

"Naw, just startled 'em a bit."

"He jumped out from behind a tree," Faby said.

Louis winked at her. "After that introduction, how could she resist me? She met me at the stage door every night after the show and kept me company while I had my supper."

Shirley mouthed, "three-sheeting" at Ed, who rolled his eyes in return.

"After the show moved on, I decided to court her with a series of letters," Louis continued in a dreamy voice. "No matter where I was, no matter how tired, when my last performance of the day was over, I would go back to my hotel and pour out my heart to Faby in a letter. I wrote her every single day. Heaven knows what the mailman must have thought of so many letters with so many different postmarks, all going to one house."

"There is no mail delivery in the village," Faby said, wondering why she felt the need to correct Louis's minor factual error. "We go to the post office to pick up our mail."

"And you wrote me the loveliest letters in return," Louis said, looking directly at her, "filled with the most charming details of village life. Band concerts in the park, picnics with friends, babysitting the neighbors' rambunctious little tykes . . . listening in on the party line." He paused, as though savoring the memory before resuming. "With each letter, we grew to know each other a little better, and as we grew to know each other, we grew to love each other. You know someone so much better through letters than you ever do through conversation.

The letters are so much more meaningful. I know I will cherish those letters from Faby for the rest of my life."

"So, what prompted you to get married?" Ed said, dispensing with the last bite of his sandwich.

"I couldn't live without her," Louis said. "It wasn't so much that I was lonely. I wasn't, really. I was just lonely for her, and I wanted her with me."

Neither Ed nor Shirley had any response to that. "Well," Louis said, unfolding himself and getting to his feet, "enough of this palaver. We're here to play cards. Five Hundred all right with you?"

Shirley and Ed both assented with a nod and a shrug.

Louis reached into the inside pocket of his jacket and took out a deck of playing cards, which he handed to Ed. "Here, why don't you start shuffling these while I dig a sweater out of my suitcase? This room is beastly cold." He crossed the room and unsnapped the clasps on his suitcase. "You pay good money for a room, the least they can do is give you some heat, chiseling bastards." He returned to the group clad in a thick turtleneck sweater, his head seemingly disembodied.

After rejecting Shirley's suggestion of playing boys against the girls, Louis took the cards back from Ed, shuffled them, and began dealing the first hand. "Now Ed, here, is a piano man. Broke his mother's heart, it did, after she scrimped and saved to pay for years of piano lessons, when the ungrateful whelp thumbed his nose at the great concert halls of Europe and went into vaudeville instead. You should hear him play. As long as it's ragtime, jazz, or Tin Pan Alley he is a virtuoso on the ivories—nobody can touch him. He can play *anything*—as long as the fellow who wrote it isn't dead."

Ed said, "Beethoven is overrated," and bid four no trump. Faby wondered if he was just playing along with Louis. She couldn't imagine *anyone*, jazz musician or no, who would make the claim that Beethoven was overrated. When Ed played the Jack of clubs and said, "Bach was a hack," she knew he was being facetious, and in all likelihood he was classically trained.

By the time each couple had won two games, Ed and Louis had consumed the entire box of crullers between them, and it had gotten dark outside. However, the men couldn't leave it at a tie, and they played one more hand. As soon as Shirley and Ed won the hand, Shirley got up from the bedspread, stretched, and smoothed her clothes. "We should be going along. Faby must be getting tired. Actually, you're looking a little pale, dear."

Faby was not feeling well, and Shirley's remark confirmed her fear that she might be coming down with something. After Shirley and Ed left, Louis said, "Are you feeling all right?"

Faby shook her head. "Not really. My stomach hasn't felt right all day."

"Maybe you should go to bed early, see if you can fight it off."

"I think that's a good idea." She undressed, put on her nightgown, and crawled under the covers. When Louis asked her if she needed anything, she said no and closed her eyes.

"All right, then," he said. "I'm going to go down to the lobby and see if I can find a comfortable chair and a newspaper while you rest. I'll be back up in a couple of hours to go to bed."

Faby felt a little better once she'd been alone in the room for a few minutes. As quiet as the room had been when she'd woken up that morning, she was surprised at the number of different noises she was able to discern through the walls, now that it was dark: water running and passing through pipes, men's voices, doors opening and closing, footsteps coming up the stairs, other footsteps going down the stairs, a woman laughing, a child crying. At one point, she thought she heard a piano playing softly in the distance.

When Louis returned to the room, she was still awake, and her stomach hurt. She moved away from him when he got into bed, as close as she could get to the edge of the bed without rolling off onto the floor. Before she finally fell asleep, her stomach hurt enough that she considered rolling off the bed to sleep on the floor, which would remain flat and stationary when Louis stirred in his sleep.

The cramps and nausea woke her at first light, and she rushed into the bathroom, not knowing whether she should kneel before the toilet or sit on it. Her bowels made the decision for her, and she was able to grab the wastebasket from under the sink just as the retching started. When the first wave had subsided and most of the shaking had stopped, she dumped the rejected contents of her stomach into the toilet, rinsed the wastebasket out as best she could, and cleaned herself up. She went back to the bed and lay down gingerly on top of the covers to wait for the next round. Louis appeared to be still asleep.

The second round woke him, and he spoke through the door which she'd had just enough time to pull closed. "Ugh, sounds like you've got it good." She was too sick to respond, and he didn't try to elicit one or open bathroom the door.

When she returned to the bed, he was fully dressed and putting on his coat and hat. "Sorry, doll. You've probably just got food poisoning. The ham may have been a little off, and in your condition, your system couldn't handle it. I just can't take a chance, though. If you've got the bug, and I catch it, I'll lose another couple days' pay—and we've only got enough money to make the jump to Scranton."

By the time he'd finished his explanation for leaving her, she was back in the bathroom, and when she got out he was gone. She was just as glad of it.

She spent most of the morning in the bathroom, at one point just lying on the floor with a towel under her head to wait for the next round of cramps and vomiting instead of risking the passage from the bed to the toilet. By the middle of the afternoon, she was able to doze between bouts, grateful to drift away from the nausea for a few minutes to her bedroom at home, until cramps forced her to open her eyes again.

When the light began to fail in the room, a knock came at the door. She wondered if it could be Louis come to check on her. She said, "Come in," but whoever was on the other side of the door must not have heard her because the knock came again. "Faby? Are you all right? May I come in?" A woman's voice. Faby said, "Come in" again and waited. A key scraped in the lock. The door swung open to reveal Shirley. "Louis sent me to check on you," she said softly, approaching the bed. "How are you feeling?" She put the back on her hand to Faby's forehead. "You poor bunny. You look just miserable. Can I get you anything? I have Sterno heat in my room. I could heat you up some beef broth."

Faby shook her head and whispered, "No, thank you."

"Are you sure? You need to keep your strength up."

Faby shook her head. "I don't feel up to eating anything."

"Well, all right, then. I'll be back to check on you later."

After Shirley had closed the door behind her, Faby heard the sound of a key in the lock before drifting off to sleep once again.

True to her word, Shirley came back at nine and again shortly before midnight, Faby wondering groggily why she would have come so late to interrupt the sleep of someone who had been sick all day. Shirley didn't mention Louis again, but Faby assumed he must have sent her.

After vomiting only intermittently during the night, Faby woke the next morning feeling better, perfectly content to lie in a strange bed in a strange room that had now become oddly familiar and comforting, watching pure white clouds shift against the blue sky of a sunny winter day. When she finally had to empty her bladder, she left the bed reluctantly, pausing after she washed her hands to fill a glass with water to sip on as she lay in bed. She was still weak and shaky, so she would wait to take a bath.

A little while later, when she heard a key in the lock, Faby knew it would be Shirley, and sure enough it was. Shirley was wearing a powder-blue belted cardigan over a white pleated skirt, the belted cardigan showing off an enviably small waist. "Well, you're looking better this morning! How are you feeling?"

"Much better, thank you."

Shirley glided to the bed and adjusted the pillows so that Faby could sit a little higher. "Good, good. Are you ready for that broth, now? It's canned, of course, but I can heat it for you, and it will be wholesome."

"Yes, I think I'd like that." Then, seeing Maman's stock pot simmering on the back of the gas stove, she said, "You can heat broth in your room?"

"Heating beef broth is nothing. You'd be surprised what a resourceful person can cook in a hotel room with a can opener, an aluminum pan, and Sterno heat. You just need to remember to stuff some towels under the door first—although you'll want to go easy on the sautéed onions and garlic, if you don't want to bring the proprietor running up the stairs with a trashcan for your contraband. The first time I got caught, I actually shoved a skillet with bacon and eggs under the bed and tried to lie my way out of it. Since the bedspread didn't go all the way to the floor, that didn't work so well."

Faby smiled, pleased and surprised that Shirley had taken the time to include a little story with her concern.

"Before I fix your broth, would you like me to help you take a bath? It should make you feel better."

Faby was ready for a bath. Ready for a bath in the worst way—and a clean nightgown. But there was no way she was going to let Shirley see her naked.

When Faby didn't respond, Shirley said, "How about I run your water and wait in here while you take your bath just in case you slip and fall?" She pushed the sleeves of her pretty blue sweater above her elbows and trotted off to the bathroom without waiting for Faby to respond. As the water was running, she came back into the room and said, "Can I get you something clean to put on?"

"Oh, that would be lovely, thank you. There's a clean nightgown in my suitcase over in the corner. It's not locked."

Shirley opened the suitcase, lifted out a folded garment, and held it up as she got to her feet. "This it?"

"Yes."

"Hmm, flannel. Pretty."

Shirley went into the bathroom with Faby's nightgown and turned off the bathwater. As Faby turned back the bed covers, Shirley was at her side, helping her out of bed and supporting her by the elbows as she led her into the bathroom. "There, a nice, hot bath should be just the ticket." Shirley turned to leave the bathroom. "I'll just wait for you out here to make sure you're all right."

"Thank you, I won't be long." Faby pulled off her nightgown and gingerly eased herself into the steaming water. Even though it had been only a few days, her rounded belly looked larger than it had the last time she had a taken a bath. She wondered if she had made the baby sick as well. He wasn't completely formed, of course, but he must be formed enough to feel sick. How frightened he must have been yesterday.

"You all right in there?" Shirley called out.

"Yes, I'm fine." Faby soaped herself thoroughly, ran the washcloth free of soap under the tap, and rinsed herself with it. As she dried off, she steadied herself with one hand on the towel rack. When she slipped her clean nightgown over her head, she was surprised to discover that it still smelled of hanging on the clothesline outside, even after being in her suitcase since she'd washed it at Mrs. Thompson's boarding house. She would enjoy the clean smell of it and the clean feel of it, a little stiff against her skin, for just as long as she possibly could.

"Now you're on the trolley!" Shirley exclaimed as Faby emerged from the bathroom. "I'll just help you back into bed and go fix you that broth."

Shirley returned with the broth in less than half an hour. "Here you are," she said, handing Faby a thick white cup. "You sip on this slowly, and if you want more later, I'll fix it for you."

The white cup in which the salty broth steamed looked somehow familiar, as if Faby had seen one like it before, but she couldn't place it.

"Yes," Shirley said. "I took the cup from a diner, a little place in Massachusetts, Ipswich, I think. They're perfect for the road, indestructible. I walked out with it in my hand while it was still half-full of coffee. If anyone saw me, I'd just apologize for my absent-mindedness and hand back the cup."

Faby couldn't help but feel shocked. She didn't think she'd ever known anyone who had stolen something as an adult. She bent her head to take her first sip of the broth, half expecting it to just the same as Maman's, but of course it didn't.

"I brought you some Melba toast, too," Shirley said, setting a small packet on the nightstand. "I always keep a couple of packages in my suitcase in case I get hungry and there is no food to be had anywhere. They don't spoil."

"Thank you," Faby said, taking another sip of the broth. "You're very kind."

"Think nothing of it. I have to get going, but I'll be back in a little while to check on you again."

With Shirley gone, the room seemed very empty, but Faby decided that she didn't really mind it so much, knowing that Shirley would be back. She opened the package of Melba toast. Impossible to eat something so crunchy without getting crumbs in the bed, but obviously the sheets would be changed for the next guest, so it didn't matter. She wondered if Louis would return to the room, once Shirley told him that the worst of the illness was over. Since Shirley had last checked on her the previous night, the thought of Louis had not once crossed her mind.

When Shirley returned, a couple of hours later, she was carrying a stack of magazines. She perched on the bed and fanned them out next to Faby. "Something to pass the time while you're recuperating. You might as well keep them for the train. I'll be getting new ones at the next station with a decent newsstand."

"Oh, thank you. I love *Photoplay*. It's my favorite."

"Mine, too."

"Oh, what's this one?" Faby picked it up. "There are other movie magazines besides *Photoplay*?"

Shirley laughed, although not unkindly. "Of course. The fans can never get enough of their favorite players. And news of the latest up-and-comers."

"Oh, look, Harry Houdini! Do you know, Louis met Harry Houdini once? In a restaurant in New Jersey. Mr. Houdini was sitting at the table right next to Louis's, eating spaghetti and meatballs. He was gracious enough to autograph a menu for Louis. Louis snuck it out under his coat."

"Did he now?"

"Oh, yes, he told me all about it and showed me the menu."

Shirley got up from the bed, "Well, Faby, I'd better be getting back to my room. I should work on my act before we get to Scranton, thin walls and other guests be damned. You'll be all right here by yourself for the rest of the day?"

"Oh, yes. I'll just stay in bed and rest—and I have these to pass the time." Faby patted the magazines.

After Shirley left, Faby was surprised at how tired she felt, and she closed her eyes for a brief nap. When she opened them again, some time had passed, and her broth was cold. She spent the rest of the afternoon looking through the magazines and dozing. When the light outside the windows began to fail, Shirley returned with another of the thick white diner cups, this one filled with chicken noodle soup. She had changed her clothes from earlier in the day, now wearing a long black dress embellished with blue and red braid on the sleeves and an elaborately braided belt to match.

"I'm on my way out to dinner," Shirley said after handing Faby the cup and a spoon. "Next time, you'll have to come with us." She gave a gay little wave as she left the room, revealing a diamond bracelet.

Faby wondered who Shirley meant by "us" because she hadn't said who she was going out with, but Faby figured it must be Ed. She ate the soup with little difficulty, accompanied by a piece of the Melba toast Shirley had brought earlier in the day. When she was finished with her light meal, she turned on the bedside lamp and went back to the magazines, now needing to read the articles in earnest, as she had already scrutinized every detail of every photograph. She fell asleep, waking up later to use the toilet and brush her teeth. When she fell asleep again and awoke with the light still on, she fumbled on the nightstand for her wristwatch to see what time it was. After midnight, and she was still alone in the room. She wondered where Louis was and why he hadn't come back.

Chapter 26

Someone was in the room. Faby opened her eyes. Louis was coming out of the bathroom with his toiletry case. He knelt in front of his suitcase and snapped open the clasps.

"Ah, you're awake," he said, straightening up. "How are you feeling?"

"Much better, thank you. Shirley looked after me."

"It's always better to have a woman looking after you when you're sick. You'll need to get these cups back to her, but for now, I'll just wash them out and stick them in my suitcase." When he came out of the bathroom, he said, "Come on, get a wiggle on. We've got a train to catch, and I don't want to pay for another day on this room."

Faby didn't have time to think about what she would wear. She found clean underwear and put on the same jersey dress and sweater she'd worn to play cards. While she was brushing her hair, Louis made one last circuit of the room to make sure they hadn't forgotten anything and went down to the lobby with their suitcases. When Faby entered the lobby, a few minutes later, Louis was settling up the bill. When he was finished, he said, "We can get a streetcar to the station. The stop is a few blocks from here, but the walk shouldn't be too bad."

The streetcar stop was more than a few blocks, and they were facing into the wind. "Good God, what a miserable place Buffalo is in the winter," Louis said, his shoulders hunched from the weight of the suitcases. As Faby struggled to keep up with his long strides, she didn't know which was worse: her precarious footing on the snow-covered sidewalk or the biting wind in her face, not daring to grab onto Louis's arm for fear of upsetting his balance with the suitcases.

The warmth of the train car was a welcome relief, and Faby slipped off her coat. Before long, the train left the station and began moving through the snow-covered landscape. "Now, this is more like it," Louis said, looking out the window. "Clear tracks ahead and not a cloud in the sky . . . of course, Scranton isn't the most glamorous destination in the world . . . but at least it's not Buffalo."

"Have you been to Scranton before?" Faby said.

"Oh, sure. I've played Scranton five or six times. Now, *here's* an interesting fact for you. I'll bet you didn't know that the Scranton Button Company is the primary maker of phonograph records."

"No, I didn't know that. Why would a button factory be making phonograph records? Did they stop making buttons?"

"They made shellac buttons."

"I see." It was time to read a magazine.

Louis stood up. "All right, then, time for a smoke. I'll leave you to your magazine."

Faby opened the magazine to a series of letters to the editor discussing Rudolph Valentino's limited acting ability, but as the train rattled and shook, she found it increasingly difficult to concentrate. She couldn't get the thought of where Louis had stayed for the past two days out of her mind. He said he was short on money, having missed out on the pay he was expecting from the Buffalo date. He said he had only enough money to get them to Scranton. So if he didn't have enough money to get another hotel room, where had he stayed? When she realized that of course he must have stayed with Ed, she resumed reading the magazine article, now fully able to enjoy it.

After several minutes, she looked up, sensing that someone was standing in the aisle next to her seat. "Why, hello, Shirley! Are you in this car?"

Shirley shook her head. "No, I came looking for you. Ed's in the smoker playing cards, and I don't know anyone else in the car. Besides Ed and Louis, I haven't seen any one else I've played with before. Mind if I join you?"

"Oh, no, of course not! Please sit down."

"Thanks." Shirley carefully smoothed her skirt and sat in Louis's seat. "You must be feeling back to your old self?"

"Pretty much."

"Good. Other than getting sick, of course, how do you like being on the road with Louis?"

"I like it well enough. I enjoy being able to see a show whenever I want."

"So tell me more about how you and Louis got together. Did he give us the straight story? His version of events seemed just a wee bit . . . um . . . fanciful."

Faby didn't answer, her face flushed hotter than it had ever been before in her life. Shirley smiled and patted Faby's hand. "No need to be embarrassed. You're not the first girl to be swept off her feet by a charming man."

Faby's face grew even hotter. Is that what had happened? She had been swept off her feet? She wondered if Shirley had been swept off her feet by old Whatshisname. When she'd described their flirtation act, she had seemed so fond of him. What could have happened to split them up?

"Penny for your thoughts," Shirley said.

"Oh! Actually, I was wondering what had happened between you and Whatshisname."

Shirley raised her eyebrows. "Whatshisname?"

"The partner you did the flirtation act with in Bennington."

"Oh, *him!* Whatshisname. He had a wandering eye . . . which I could put up with, but not when the rest of him went wandering along with it."

"I couldn't imagine anyone stepping out on you. You're so beautiful."

Shirley shook her head. "That's sweet of you to say, Faby, but for some men it doesn't matter how beautiful the woman they're with is. They're going to go after someone else, just because she's someone else."

"What are you two hens clucking about?" Louis had returned. "You need to get back to your seat, Shirley. The conductor's coming through for tickets."

Shirley got out of Louis's seat and stepped aside to let him in. "See you later, Faby."

"What was that all about?" Louis said, sitting down.

"She came to find me when Ed went to the smoking car. She doesn't know anyone else on the train. I like Shirley. I think we could become friends."

"Do you now?"

"Yes, she was so kind to me when I was sick. She brought me broth and chicken soup and magazines. And Melba toast. She even let me keep the magazines for the train, so that I would have something to read."

"Yeah, Shirley's a peach all right," Louis said.

"I would love to see her act in Scranton. She's so beautiful, and I'll bet she's really clever."

"I suppose," Louis said. "I haven't seen her new act, but, sure, I'll get you a ticket if you want to see the show. Will you stay to see my act?"

Faby hesitated before responding, but then Louis smiled, and she knew that he was just teasing.

When the curtain rose for Shirley's act in Scranton, the backdrop depicted a small nightclub with several men playing saxophones and a young woman in a pale pink frock dancing by herself. Shirley was center stage wearing the same filmy pink dress—dancing to the ukulele introduction of the song before getting to the point of the lyrics: "T'ain't No Sin to Take Off Your Skin and Dance Around in Your Bones." As Faby bounced along to the rhythm, she wished with all her heart that Josephine were sitting in the seat next to her to enjoy it. This was a song to be sung for days afterward at top voice while dancing around one's bedroom, until one's grandmère pounded on the ceiling below with a broom handle.

The backdrop for Shirley's next number was very clever, a gaggle of young women dressed in bright flapper clothes leaning towards a snazzily-dressed young man who had his back turned to them, his arms crossed, and his nose in the air: *Everybody loves her baby, but her baby don't love nobody but she.* The song was nothing special, but Shirley's flapper outfit—V-neck dress, hat, scarf, shoes—looked like it was right off a movie screen.

The curtain came down momentarily, then rose on a completely dark stage. As the orchestra began to play the first sweet strains of "What'll I Do," a faint blue light came on and gradually revealed Shirley in a long dark dress, seated on a stool looking so melancholy someone should have told the audience to look away out of respect for her privacy. As the last note faded, Faby knew the sound would stay with her forever.

Chapter 27

The following night, after spending the day working on her review of the show, struggling for just the right words to describe how Shirley's performance had moved her, Faby fell into an uneasy sleep, one insufficient word after another having been considered, then rejected.

She was awakened several hours later by the light from the bedside lamp shining in her face. Squinting, she looked up to see Louis standing above her smiling and disheveled.

"I'm sorry. Did I wake you?" Before she could respond, he answered the question himself. "Well, of course I did. I shone a light in your face." His overcoat was unbuttoned, and he slipped it off and let it fall to the floor. "Not a very gallant thing to do, admittedly, but I can't wait till morning to tell you my news."

"News?"

Louis plopped himself down on the bed to sit cross-legged next to her as she struggled into a sitting position. "I'm booked for the Delmar Circuit. *Finally.* I can't tell you how long I've been trying to get on Delmar Time. Finally, *finally,* after that fiasco in Buffalo, I get the wire I've been waiting for."

"Is the Delmar Circuit the Big Time?"

"Uh uh. Delmar is still Small Time, but it's Small Time where it's *warm.*"

He vaulted off the bed and picked his overcoat up off the floor. "We won't be needing these much longer. Where we're going, Panama hats are de rigueur, and woolen overcoats are outlawed." He hung up his coat in the tiny alcove that served as a closet. "I'm never going to be able to sleep. Will you stay up with me? I know you need your rest, but you'll have all day tomorrow to sleep."

"I'm awake now," Faby said, pushing the covers aside and getting out of bed. "Just let me use the toilet." She slipped out of the room without bothering to get her bathrobe. When she got back, Louis was lounging on top of the bedcovers, wearing pajama bottoms and his turtleneck sweater. "The first performance is in Norfolk, Virginia, and from there we start making our way south. Let's see, we're booked for Nashville, Charleston, Atlanta, Hattiesburg, Baton Rouge, New Orleans, Birmingham . . . and a few others I can't recall off the top of my head. You must be sure to take good photographs for the family album. You will want to get just the right shot of each place to remember it by."

"I will," Faby said. She picked up her wristwatch from the nightstand and checked it for the time. It was three o'clock in the morning.

"Best of all," Louis went on, "we will end up in sunny Florida, the Land of Enchantment. And enchanting it is, with balmy breezes, white sand beaches, palm trees swaying languidly over broad avenues, magnificent sunsets over the water, and equally magnificent sunrises at dawn the next day. If you haven't been there before, you can't possibly imagine what it's like."

Faby nodded her head. He was right; her imagination could no longer stretch that far. "Have you been there many times?"

"Oh, no, just once, with an Army buddy of mine from Boston, when the war ended." He turned to get his cigarettes off the nightstand. "By the time we left France and got to back to the States, it was the week after Christmas. After we were processed out of the Army in South Carolina, the thought of sitting on a train for two days with a bunch of doughboys who would stay half-drunk the whole time was about as appealing to us as being shipped back to France. And the thought of Boston in the wintertime was as unappealing as the journey to get there." He lit a cigarette and set the ashtray on his stomach. "Seeing as we were already most of the way there, we pooled our money to buy this broken-down Hupmobile roadster off some fellow we met in a bar-room and headed down to Florida in search of adventure. It was grand! The war was over. We had all our limbs, money in our pockets, and nobody to answer to. Our plan was to just follow the coast down the Atlantic side and back up the Gulf side before making our way back to Massachusetts. For two weeks, we spent our days on the beach sunning and swimming, as playful dolphins cavorted just out of reach in the clear turquoise waters."

Louis stopped speaking, an expectant look on his face, but all she could think of to say was, *You must have gotten terribly sunburned,* which was not the reaction he was waiting for, so she said, "Go on," instead.

"The hotels were a sight to behold, with that Old World Spanish architecture which goes so well with palm trees. But even though we could never afford to stay in one of those places and play golf and tennis all day with the other swells, we weren't the least bit envious of those who could. After spending the day on the beach, we'd throw on a shirt, run a comb through our hair, and head out for the nearest joint with a dance band, in search of fun, if you know what I mean. And fun was not hard to find, kind of like Revere Beach, without all the rides."

"Where did you stay, then?"

Louis looked surprised at her question. "In a pup tent on the beach. I suppose there were cheap places where we could have stayed, but we wanted to make sure we had enough money for booze."

Faby wanted to reach out and turn off the bedside lamp, which was still shining in her face, but she didn't dare to with Louis smoking in bed.

"Speaking of Old World," he went on, "coming upon Saint Augustine nearly stopped us dead in our tracks. It was like stepping back in time, with Spanish moss festooning the trees and narrow streets with quaint, overhanging balconies. Every time we turned a corner, we half-expected to see a Spanish cavalier standing there. There was even an old stone fort to guard against pirates."

Louis paused to take a drag from his cigarette and blow out the smoke. "Of course, the Ponce de Leon Hotel was the grandest of them all, like a medieval castle big enough to hold an entire village, with a gated entrance, towers and turrets, and all manner of embellishment. So, naturally, before we left Saint Augustine, we decided it would be a lark to go into the dining room and see how long we could stay without being asked to leave."

"You caused a disturbance?"

"Indeed we did! We were in our shirtsleeves. Turned the poor maitre-de apoplectic. We laughed ourselves sick all the way to Daytona Beach. Now, Daytona Beach was a sight to see. They actually race cars on the beach. Can you imagine that? Talk about a boffo show! There is nothing like a fast car to get a fellow's blood pumping. Beats the hell out of riding on trains."

As Louis continued the story of his Florida odyssey, Faby's attention began to wander as she tried to bring his news into closer focus. It was good that for a time he wouldn't have to worry about getting new bookings, and the warmer weather would be pleasant, but for her there would still be the trains, rattling and clattering, blowing hot cinders in her face as she got on and got off, swaying from side to side as they took her closer and closer to the birth of her child and farther and farther from her mother. As she drifted off to sleep, she found herself in her own bed with Maman at her bedside stroking her forehead and offering soft words of comfort, only to be awakened a short time later by a man's voice.

"The Hupmobile finally gave up the ghost a few miles south of Miami, and we had to pick fruit for a month to earn train fare to Boston, but I didn't regret a single minute of it." Louis stubbed out his cigarette. "Of course, I had to lie to Mother about when I'd gotten discharged from the Army, which I didn't really like to do, but she would never have forgiven me for arriving stateside and not coming home right away."

Faby turned away from him, trying not to cry.

Chapter 28

They were on the train again, making their way down the Del-marva Peninsula on the way to Louis's inaugural performance on the Delmar Circuit. The train began slowing down as the next station came into view. The depot was even smaller than the one in Enosburg, and Louis noted that it was barely worth getting off the train for. "But we should at least get off to stretch our legs—and you look like you could use some fresh air."

Faby stood up to follow him off the train, surprised that he had noticed. After her interrupted sleep the night before and with the baby's increasing weight, she was feeling decid-edly groggy. Some fresh air *would* do her good.

As they walked up and down the platform, Faby was sur-prised at how cold she felt. While there was no snow on the ground, a cold, raw wind blew off the surrounding fields that seemed to go right through her heavy woolen coat. She took Louis's arm, as though walking closer to him would warm her. "I thought Virginia would be warmer. Isn't Virginia in the South?"

Louis patted her hand on his arm. "Yes, but not the *Deep* South. You'll find it warmer once we get to Georgia."

Before Faby had a chance to respond, the conductor called "*All aboard!*" and they got back on the train, with Faby stopping first at the ladies' room. The train started moving just as she reached Louis's seat, and he caught her under the arms to keep her from falling as she stumbled. "You need to be more careful," he scolded as he helped her get settled in her seat. "You mustn't fall and hurt yourself."

"I know. It's just hard to get used to having this weight in front of me." She gestured with her hands on her belly.

"Mmm. You seem to have gotten quite big quite fast. Your face seems to have changed shape, too. It seems a little fuller."

She didn't respond, and Louis brought his hands down on his thighs. "Well. Time for a smoke."

Louis stayed in the smoker until the train approached Cape Charles, where they would board a ferry to take them to Norfolk. The Cape Charles train depot was adjacent to the water, with the ferry docked right next to it. "Ready?" Louis said, taking Faby's overcoat from the rack and holding it open for her. Even though the walk to the ferry was only a few yards, the wind coming off the bay was cold, tearing at her hair and catching in her throat as she hurried after Louis.

Once on board the ferry, she found that the interior was well-heated. "I've never been on a ferry boat before."

"Oh?" Louis said. "I'll find us a seat near the deck, so you can look out. Even though it's pretty windy, there doesn't seem to be much chop on the water, which is good." He steered Faby to an upholstered bench seat and helped her off with her coat. "We'll have a little bit of a wait while baggage is transferred from the train to the ferry."

"I don't mind. I've gotten used to waiting."

"Atta girl!" Louis draped her coat and then his own over the back of the seat.

Running a comb through his hair, he launched into a story of backstage rivalry between two female acts that ended with switched sheet music and an entire act done a capella out of spite. He had just finished his story of Ned the stage hand falling to his death from his perch in the flies as he tried to look down the blouse of a woman performing on the stage at the Wells Theatre in Norfolk, when the floor beneath Faby's feet started throbbing.

"Ah!" Louis exclaimed. "We are on our way to Delmar Time!"

As the ferry maneuvered away from the pier, Faby said, "I think I'd like to go out on the deck to get a better view."

"Are you sure? The wind is going to be even colder than it was on shore."

Faby stood up and put on her coat. "I know. I just want to get a better view."

"Suit yourself."

Out on deck, the wind was blowing as hard and as cold as Louis had predicted, but she was not about to go back inside. Turning up the collar of her coat as best she could and shoving her hands in her pockets, she stood at the railing watching the shore slide by, a narrow strand of sandy beach against a backdrop of evergreens. Before long, the ferry was out in the bay and the shoreline was no longer visible, just an endless expanse of water with no discernible horizon.

When her teeth began chattering, she went back inside, but Louis wasn't sitting on the bench. She had a momentary feeling of panic, thinking she'd come in the wrong door and they'd actually been sitting somewhere else, but then she saw that his overcoat was still draped over the back of the seat. He'd probably just gotten up to stretch his legs. Sitting on the bench, she left her coat on until her teeth stopped chattering, first unbuttoning it, then waiting several more minutes before she slipped it off. She had just relaxed and settled back for the rest of the ride when she heard a woman's laughter from immediately behind her.

"Good Lord, Faby! What have you done to your hair? You look like you've spent the day in a wind tunnel."

Faby turned to see who was speaking to her, and there was Shirley, as stylish and slim as ever, turned out in an embellished wool dress with a fur collar, her face framed by a sleek gray cloche. Faby reflexively put both hands to her head. "Shirley! I didn't know you were on the ferry. Where are you going?"

"To Norfolk, of course. I'm playing on the Delmar Circuit."

"You are?! So is Louis!"

"Yes, I know. I ran into him as he was coming out of the gents. He told me where to find you." Shirley held out her hands and gestured for Faby to get up. "Here, let me have a look at you." She helped Faby get to her feet. "Look at you— you've gotten so big! I guess I hadn't noticed when we met in Buffalo." She took a step back. "But what on earth are you wearing? It looks like it was pieced together from two different stage costumes . . . not flattering at all."

Faby's eyes filled with tears. "Louis asked one of the girls with the show to make it for me, along with another one so I'd had one to wear and one to wash. I've gotten too big for my other clothes."

"Of course you have, poor bunny." Shirley's fingers brushed Faby's cheek. "I'm not trying to hurt your feelings. I just meant that Louis should do better by you. Here, let's sit down, get you off your feet. You can tell me what you've been up to."

Faby quickly brushed away a tear. "I really liked your act in Scranton." She hesitated, then continued softly. "I wrote about it in my review of the show."

Shirley removed her cloche and deftly restored the waves in her hair with her fingers. "You wrote a review?"

"Yes, I write a review of opening night for every town we're in . . . I'm calling it *Reviews from the Road.*"

"How sweet!" Shirley exclaimed, "How utterly charming. What does Louis think of it?"

"I haven't told him."

"Ah," Shirley said, putting a manicured finger to her lips. "It'll be our little secret, then."

Chapter 29

Waiting for the opening night curtain at the Wells Theatre in Norfolk, Faby could not stop herself from openly gawking at the ornateness of the décor by which she was surrounded: marbleized walls, gilded plasterwork, heavy velvet draperies, and murals painted on every surface of the vaulted ceiling, not to mention the profusion of sparkling chandeliers. Six semicircular box seats were suspended at dizzying heights along each of the side walls. If this is what the Delmar Circuit promised, then Louis's excitement at being signed had not been misplaced.

One could not help but enjoy performances given in such plush surroundings, and Faby found that none disappointed, from the first to the last. By the time she settled back for the closing act, the Buster Keaton short, "One Week," she was already composing her review in her head, noting how the pianist's bouncy accompaniment was so sophisticated when compared with Blanche Martin's frantic scrabbling at the keys whenever anything mildly amusing appeared on the screen. Faby had seen the short before, but it was just as funny the second time around, and she stayed until the end, after the majority of the theater patrons had cleared out, leaving only herself, a handful of families with children, and an elderly couple who had both fallen asleep by the time Buster attempted to move the house from the wrong lot across a set of railroad tracks, and the house got demolished by a train.

When the house lights came back up, Faby was surprised to see so few people left in the theater. How could anyone resist a Buster Keaton short? After looking at her wristwatch for the time, she gathered up her coat, then hesitated. Where was Louis? He hadn't said where to meet him after the show. She didn't know where the stage door was, as one side of the theater abutted another building, while the other side was set so close to the building next it that a door would have no clearance to open. The stage door must be at the back of the building, but she had no idea how she could get there, other than go backstage, which of course she couldn't do.

It had been hours since she'd last eaten, and she needed to use the toilet, but still she hesitated, peering at the stage, waiting for Louis to emerge from the wings, vault off the apron, and lope up the aisle to offer his arm and take her to supper. Then she remembered that of course he would have to take off his greasepaint and change into his street clothes. And there was no denying that Louis was a man who took pride in his appearance.

When she reached the ladies' room, she actually had to wait for a toilet, as the families who had let their children stay up late to watch Buster Keaton weren't about to take them home again without using the toilet first. Two little girls in matching smocked dresses and white sweaters were still waiting, one fretful, the other whiny, their mother half-heartedly trying to shush them. Faby looked down at her belly and frowned. Oh, she would not like it if her child were fretful or whiny. She would not like it at all. She wondered how one could prevent it. Take the Neale children, for instance. As many of them as there were, you didn't hear them whining and fussing. On the other hand, maybe that was because they just ran wild, whooping and shrieking and losing their shoes. Well, as long as her baby was inside her belly, he would go where she went and do what she did and not have a thing to say about it.

Back in the lobby, she found an upholstered bench against the wall, where she could wait for Louis. She hoped he wouldn't be long. Her back was hurting something fierce. Faby shifted her position on the bench and looked at her wrist-watch. It was well after eleven o'clock. What could be keeping Louis? She looked around the lobby and saw no one. The lights were still on, though, so there must be someone else there.

Without the buzz and chatter of other people, she felt completely exposed under the coffered ceiling of the lobby, the chandeliers directing a myriad of small spotlights on her. She was as exposed as the breasts of the toga-clad maidens emerging from the columns supporting the ceiling. Louis couldn't still be in the theater, and he wasn't coming for her. As she stood up to put on her coat, she thought she heard a gasp, but she wasn't sure until a man in a belted gray overcoat and matching hat appeared at her side. "God *damn,* you gave me a start! What are you doing here? The theater's been closed for nearly an hour. I've just been tallying up the box office."

"I was waiting for my husband."

The man frowned. "He left you here?"

Faby shook her head. "No, I had to use the toilet."

"I see. Well, I can check inside the theater to see if maybe he fell asleep while you were in the ladies' room."

"He wouldn't be there. He would have gone to his dressing room."

"His dressing room. He's part of the show, then?"

"Yes. Slim White."

"Slim White." The man inhaled sharply and held his breath a moment before letting it out. "Well, all right, then.

Slim White isn't here, and there's no point in waiting for him any longer."

Faby tried hard to blink away the tears as she looked down to button her coat. "I was just getting ready to go."

When she got the first two buttons fastened and looked up, leaving the third button undone, she met the man's gaze as he looked at her. "Are you expecting?"

She nodded, and again the man inhaled sharply and held his breath before letting it out, although he didn't say anything right away. Finally, he asked in an odd, soft voice, "Where are you staying?"

Faby wasn't sure if she should answer him. He'd asked the question in such an odd, soft voice, a voice she'd never before heard anybody use. She looked from the man to the door leading to the sidewalk. "At a hotel."

"At a hotel," the man repeated. He took off his hat and ran his hand over his hair before carefully settling the hat back on his head.

"My husband must be waiting for me in the room." As soon as the lie was out of her mouth, Faby realized that of course that must have been what had happened. When Louis came into the lobby while she was waiting in that long line in the ladies' room, he naturally would have thought that she had returned to the hotel. He was waiting for her in their room at the hotel.

She started for the door, but the man stopped her with his hand on her arm. "No, you don't. You're not walking back to any hotel by yourself at this time of night. I'll drive you."

Again, Faby gauged the distance from herself to the door, and this time, she bolted, only to be stopped by the door, which was locked. The theater manager reached around her with his keys in his hand. "We can't have people wandering in off the street after closing." He didn't unlock the door. "Look,

I understand you don't want to get into a car with a stranger. I'll just walk with you to see that you get to your hotel safely. Would that be all right?"

Faby didn't know whether it would be all right. The manager seemed nice enough, a little older than her father, with thinning hair and a receding chin, but she just didn't know. He unlocked the door and held it open. As soon as she felt the rawness of the night air on her face, she started walking, not waiting for the manager, not telling him yes or no, just walking. She heard the clunk of the bolt as he locked the lobby door again and his quick footsteps as he caught up to her. "I'll just walk with you." He didn't try to take her arm, and she didn't slow her pace. If she just didn't say anything, she should be all right.

While all the businesses were closed, the street was not deserted, the occasional couple scurrying by arm-in-arm, cars passing by, the sidewalk illuminated by streetlamps. As fast as she was walking, the heels of her shoes resounding against the sidewalk, Faby felt even colder than she had on the ferry, the wind seemingly passing through her heavy woolen coat unimpeded, through her dress to her skin, through her skin to her bones, through her bones to their marrow, until she no longer noticed that the theater manager was still at her side, the sound of his shoes against the sidewalk a counterpoint to hers.

By the time she reached the hotel, she had a stitch in her side, and she had to use the toilet again. As she slowed her pace by the entrance, the theater manager said, "Is this it, then?" She nodded. Just as she was wondering whether she should thank him for seeing her safely to the hotel, he tipped his hat and turned to walk back the way they had come.

Inside the hotel was blessedly warm, and as she pulled the warm air into her lungs, the stitch in her side started easing itself out. She hurried up the stairs, hoping that Louis would not be too angry with her for making him wait, but when she got to the room, no light shone from beneath the door. Could he have already gone to sleep? He hadn't waited up for her? On the other hand, maybe he'd fallen asleep without intending to: he would be tired after doing three shows. Turning the handle, she discovered that it was locked. Could have locked her out? Why would he lock her out? She knocked. No answer. She knocked again. Still no answer.

And now she had to use the toilet.

She went back down the stairs to the lobby, retrieved the room key from the night clerk, trudged back up the stairs, unlocked the room, and flipped on the light switch. The room was empty. Louis was not there. She did not know where he was or if he would be coming back.

She went into the bathroom to use the toilet. As soon as her bladder emptied, she felt as if the bottom of her stomach had dropped out. She was ravenously hungry, but this late at night, she was not going to be able to get anything to eat. There was nothing for it but to go to sleep and wait until morning. She brushed her teeth and drank two full glasses of water. She would end up having to get up several times during the night, but the water should ease the gnawing in her stomach long enough for her to fall asleep.

After undressing and putting on her nightgown, she crawled into bed, beyond the point of caring. The sheets were cold, and she curled on her side, trying to get warm. After a few minutes, the sheets began to warm, and she eased her body into a more natural position and cried herself to sleep, only to awaken a short time later with the bedside lamp shining in her face and Louis sitting on the bed, smelling of soap and bay rum, his hair neatly combed. "Tell me, how did you like the show tonight?" He sounded like his usual affable self, which was a relief, but it was the middle of the night, he'd abandoned her at the theater, and as hungry as she was, she wouldn't be able to eat until morning.

"I have to use the toilet."

Louis got off the bed to let her up, and she went into the bathroom and locked the door. After emptying her bladder, she considered whether she should just stay in the bathroom for the rest of the night with the door locked but decided against it. When she opened the bathroom door, Louis was sitting on the bed in his underwear. He stood up and pulled back the covers. "You get back into bed now and get some sleep. I'm sorry I woke you." Faby did as she was told, getting back into bed while Louis brushed his teeth and used the toilet. After he had settled in beside her, his hand resting on her hip, it occurred to her that he had not said why he was so late, where he'd been, or why he had left her at the theater alone.

Chapter 30

They were on the train again after a month on the Delmar Circuit, Faby dutifully attending every opening night and writing her review the next day, dutifully taking snapshots to represent the towns where Louis played: avenues of live oaks trailing Spanish moss, houses with deep verandas stacked one atop the other, houses with columns, squat brick churches missing their steeples, an iron bridge over the Mississippi River, a glimpse of mountains from a hotel window.

Now they were on the train again, and Faby was desperate to find a conversation worth eavesdropping on as Louis sat next to her engrossed in a month-old copy of *Variety*.

". . . biggest diamonds and dirtiest underwear I'd ever seen."

"Shocking to others, perhaps, but a fella has to keep his priorities in order!"

Faby found herself smiling, until she remembered that the responsibility for keeping Louis's underwear clean fell to her.

". . . then one time I was playing Jackson, Mississippi with Eddie Ashton—we were known as Ashton and Raines then, until we got a bad notice from some hack in some Godforsaken hamlet that managed to make the rounds of the booking agencies, so we changed the act to Payne and Murphy."

"I hear ya, brother. If you stop to think about it, don't it seem confounding that the fortunes of the truly talented can be dashed, ground into dust, based on the ignorant opinion of some third-rate hack who don't know shit from Shinola?"

"And how! Anyways, this one time, we were playing Jackson, Mississippi, and there was this one sketch about a wife who has a fellow in her bedroom when her husband comes home unexpectedly to catch her—only you don't see the other fellow— he's supposed to be hiding behind the draperies. The husband bursts into the room from stage right waving a pistol around. He points it at the draperies and shouts, 'Come out of there, or I'll shoot!' Big dramatic moment—but nothing happens. Thinking the fellow behind the draperies missed his cue, he shouts even louder, 'Come out of there, or I'll shoot!' Still nothing, and a-course the wife has been stuck on her mark this whole time, hands to her face, mouth agape. The husband, desperate by this time, screams, 'Come out of there, damn you, or I'll shoot!'—and you hear the voice of the stage manager from the wings, 'Go ahead and shoot. He's down in his dressing room asleep'."

When the laughter of the two men subsided, the one being told the story said, "Oh my God, don't tell me the fellow supposed to be hiding behind the draperies was Fred Spicer? I played with him once in Boise. Terrible drunkard. Fell asleep on stage on opening night."

"Bushwah! He did not fall asleep on stage. Nobody falls asleep on stage, no matter how bad they are. Mind you, I've heard of people dying on stage—and I don't mean flopping, I mean *dying,* falling in the traces, so to speak."

"No, he really fell asleep on stage, I tell you. It was supposed to be one of those drawing room comedies—you know the type—some cake-eater in a white sweater, holding a tennis racket for no good reason and calling everybody *Old boy* and

Old sport. Those bits never go over in the sticks. In any event, Spicer wasn't the cake-eater with the tennis racket. He was the cake-eater's n'er-do-well brother, squandering the family fortune on gambling and loose women and such. He was sprawled on a sofa when the curtain rose, but he didn't have his first line for several minutes while the cake-eater engaged in witty repartee with his sister and his mother. Well, the witty repartee goes on, and in the course of it, Spicer falls asleep. But nobody notices, seeing as he's been sprawled on the sofa all languid-like right from the beginning. His cue comes and goes. Mother says 'And what do you think, Frederick?' and he's supposed to say 'As little as possible!'. Lucky for him, Mabel Bernstein was playing the mother, and when he missed his cue for the second time, and she realized he was asleep or dead, she didn't miss a beat. She just started ad libbing, and by God if she didn't ad lib the rest of the first act, writing him right out of it as if he was just another piece of the furniture. She saved the play, but Spicer was fired as soon as the curtain came down. Mabel Bernstein was the best ad libber in the business. I've never seen a quicker mind. But that's a story for another day."

As Faby smiled at the story, the thought occurred to her that Mabel Bernstein really could not have been certain whether Fred Spicer was sleeping or dead. She would have been too far away from him to be able to tell unless he moved. He really could have been dead for all she knew, but she didn't stop the play for someone to check his pulse and try to rouse him. She continued right on with the scene and kept it going. Faby had never really understood what was meant by the old saying, *The show must go on,* because it had seemed so obvious. Maybe it wasn't so obvious after all.

Louis had shifted in his seat and leaned forward to join the conversation. "Say, fellows, I actually did see someone die on stage one night."

The two men turned around in unison, and in unison said, "You did not, Slim."

"I most certainly did. Do you remember George Blackton? Billed himself as Feodore Gruzinsky, always closed his act with 'The Song of the Volga Boatmen'? He was huge in the '90s, played all the best theaters in New York and Chicago, sold out European tours, and even had a successful tour of the Orient. In his heyday, he had a *basso profondo* that would make the ladies wet their pants. He was handsome, too, which is unusual for an opera singer. They're usually bearded and run to fat. At any rate, Feodore would come out in his Russian peasant costume, belted tunic, pants tucked into tall boots, and the ladies would swoon before he even opened his mouth. However, by the time I ran into him, after the war ended, he was on his way down playing Small Time. He was getting on in years, and at some point he'd contracted TB. He would check into a sanitarium during the off season to rest, but it was never long enough before he had to be back out on the road. The night he died, I was actually in the audience. I'd been given the deuce spot at the last minute, after being promised the fifth spot when I was booked, and I was really steamed. After I did my act, I decided to sit in the audience to see what surefire show-stopper had knocked me off my spot on the bill. It was Feodore Gruzinsky. I will never forget it. He looked so ghastly, you wouldn't be off the mark describing his appearance as gruesome. He was shockingly thin, and you could see the dark circles around his eyes through the greasepaint. He looked so bad, the audience actually gasped. But he'd been booked to sing 'Song of the Volga Boatmen' and by God, sing it he would. He managed to get through the first chorus reasonably well. Then his voice strained and cracked. He coughed twice and when he coughed again, a gush of blood flooded from his mouth all down the front of his tunic, and he crumpled to the stage as if his bones had just turned to dust. For a brief moment, the audience just sat there in stunned silence. Then a woman let out a scream, and all hell broke loose. The curtain came down, the stage manager started screaming for a doctor in the house, and the ushers rushed in to hustle the audience out of the theater. Old George stopped the show all right. Talk about an ignominious end. George Blackton will be forever remembered for coughing his lungs onto his shirt in front of a half-empty house in Birmingham, Alabama. Nobody deserves to go out like that."

"I've played Birmingham more times than I can count, and I never heard anything about that."

"Of course not," Louis said. "As superstitious as actors are, you think any theater manager would let them get wind of a player dying on his stage?"

Chapter 31

At some point, Faby must have fallen asleep because she came awake not knowing where she was while someone said her name. Her head was resting against Louis's shoulder, and it felt very heavy as she raised it, blinking, trying to get her bearings. The train appeared to have stopped, and there were people in the aisle, moving about. "Where are we?"

"Birmingham."

"What time is it?"

"Mmm, half past one. Here, get your coat on."

Faby let him help her with her coat, shuffling after him as the passengers began leaving the train, wishing there were a way she could close her eyes and still see where she was walking.

Inside the train station, the waiting area appeared set up as a cathedral where one sat in a high-backed pew of polished wood and contemplated the immensity of the domed ceiling while waiting for one's battered suitcase to be hauled off the train. She didn't think she had ever felt so exhausted.

"How you holdin' up, doll?" Louis said.

"I'm okay."

"It's going to be a while longer before we get to our room. Do you want to put your head on my shoulder and try to sleep?"

Faby nodded and let her body ease against his. However, closing her eyes did not bring sleep as the baby began squirming, trying to insert himself between his two parents, and the train's wheels passing over the points in the track still sounded in her ears, and countless bright lights from countless train stations penetrated her eyelids.

Then Louis collected their bags, and they were outside. The air was surprisingly mild for the middle of the night. Louis put his arm around her shoulders. "Our room isn't but a block or two, but I'll see if I can get us a taxicab. You're dead on your feet. Wait for me here while I run over to the taxi stand."

The taxicab pulled up to where she was standing, with Louis in the back seat. Before he could make a move, the cab driver had jumped out, opened the rear door, and helped Faby into the taxi, solicitously clucking about her condition. She barely had a chance to get settled in her seat when the taxi came to a stop in front of a large two-story house. "Here we are," the driver said. A dimly lit sign on the small patch of grass in front read, "Rooms to Let: Nightly, Weekly, Monthly."

As they stepped onto the porch, the front door opened and a small man in a voluminous bathrobe said, "You must be the Whites. Come on in. I'd offer you something to eat, but the wife's asleep."

"Don't trouble yourself," Louis said, taking off his hat. "We've gotten in very late."

"This way, then," the man said, gesturing towards a well-trod staircase, then bending down for their luggage before leading them up the stairs. "You're the second door on the right." He pushed the door open and turned on the overhead light to reveal a small narrow room with a metal bedstead at one end and a washstand at the other, both of which looked as though they had recently been hauled down from the attic. "The room is all made up for you. Towels on the washstand, bathroom at the end of the hall. Breakfast is at seven." Without waiting for an acknowledgement, he turned and closed the door behind him.

After setting Faby's suitcase on the bed, Louis surveyed the room. "Well, I've definitely seen better, but, then again, I've seen worse." He grimaced. "Hideous wallpaper, though."

The next morning, Faby awoke to mid-morning sun in her face, the limp lace curtain covering the window behind the bed doing nothing to diffuse it. She struggled to a sitting position, groaning as she swung her legs over the side of the bed. After getting up during the night every hour to use the toilet, she had to use it again.

Returning from the bathroom, she gradually became aware of the muffled sounds of a train yard: the hiss of escaping steam, the clanging of warning bells, the squeal and thud of metal on metal, all with a deep undertone of rumbling engines. She went to the window and pushed aside the curtain to look out. The rooming house was much closer to the train station than she'd realized. She let the curtain fall back into place and sat down on the bed. She just felt so very tired.

A knock came at the door, followed by a soft, viscous voice. "Mrs. Whaht? Are you all raht?"

"Yes, I'm all right." When she didn't hear footsteps receding down the hallway, she reluctantly got off the bed and opened the door.

An older woman wearing a gingham housedress covered by a gingham apron stood in the doorway holding a tray. "Well, bless your heart!" she exclaimed. "If you aren't in the family way!" Faby stepped aside to let her enter the room, still exclaiming. "Now that explains all those trips to the commode last night!" The woman paused to sweep her gaze around the room, as though looking for clues to the character of its temporary occupants. "When it got to be noontime and you didn't come down to see about getting you something to eat, I got to worrying. I figured I better come up and check on you."

Faby eyed the tray the woman held in front of her, unsure of what exactly was on the plate. It appeared to be a milk gravy with some kind of ground meat in it. "You didn't have to bring me breakfast."

The woman advanced on the bed. "Now, you just get back in the bed and have you some nice biscuits and gravy. And don't be shy about asking for seconds. There's more left over, and you're eating for two."

Faby did as she was told, surprised after taking the first bite just how hungry she was and equally surprised when the woman sat herself down at the end of the bed and kept on talking. "I'm Maisie Budd. My husband Carl and me run the place. You would have met Carl last night. He sometimes works swing shift at the plant, so he's used to odd hours."

Faby chewed and swallowed before responding. "Yes, he was very nice."

"Not always, but thank you for saying so. Your husband asked me to keep an eye on you when he left this morning, but he didn't say why. Now I know! You want a glass of milk to go with that?"

Faby nodded, chewing. Maisie bustled out of the room and soon returned with a brimming glass of milk. She stood beside the bed until Faby had drunk enough of the milk to keep it from spilling, then sat back down on the bed.

"So your husband's with the vaudeville show, is he? I've always enjoyed the vaudeville show. We have plenty of the big acts come here to Birmingham. When Carl and me were first married, we saw Eva Tanguay perform on several occasions. Wore these outlandish costumes and Sang 'I Don't Care'. Well, I guess that would be about right, seeing as she couldn't possibly care about other people's opinions, dressed like that.

She was the biggest name in vaudeville for a right long time, although she must be getting on in years now. Why, she's got to be as old as me—and I'm much too old to go prancing around in front of the public half naked!" Maisie paused as Faby finished the last of her biscuits and gravy. "Here, let me take that from you while you finish up your milk." Maisie reached for the tray and set it on the floor. "When are you due, Faby, if you don't mind me asking a personal question?"

Faby hesitated. "Pretty soon, I think. I don't know exactly." She really didn't know, just that it had to be soon.

"This your first?"

Faby nodded.

"I thought as much, young as you are. First babies tend to be late. I don't know what that husband of yours is thinking, dragging a girl in your condition all over the countryside when she should be home with her mother making preparations for her lying in."

"Preparations?"

"There's the layette to be got ready, of course, and pads for yourself, along with getting the room ready. Just make sure you don't let any doctor talk you into a hospital birth. They'll give you that ether, and you'll be sick for days."

"I guess I hadn't thought about how the baby is actually going to get born." There had been no time for Maman to make preparations for little Guillaume, only clean-up afterwards and arrangements for burial.

"Probably just as well," Maisie said. "You'll find out soon enough." She stood up and bent down for the tray. "Well, I'd best be getting to my washing. After you get dressed, why don't you come downstairs and keep me company?"

After Maisie left the room, Faby was surprised to find that she didn't feel nearly as tired as she had earlier, and she got up to make the bed, speculating as she smoothed the quilt into place where each scrap of fabric had come from and what had happened that it was unable to fulfill its original purpose.

She spent a pleasant afternoon with Maisie chatting about this and that as Maisie filled the washing machine with water, threw the lever to agitate the clothes, emptied the tub of water, and ran the clothes through the wringer before taking them outdoors to be hung on the clothesline to dry. As she was pushing a bed sheet through the wringer, it occurred to Maisie that Faby and Slim might have dirty drawers they would like washed before moving on to the next town, Faby affirming that they did and collecting them, taking care as she walked down the stairs to keep a firm grip on the railing with one hand. By the time all of the laundry was washed and hanging on clotheslines, it was time for Maisie to prepare supper for Carl and the boarders, who would soon be coming home hungry from the plant.

Faby joined them at the crowded dining room table, cheerfully passing platters of fried chicken and bowls of riced potatoes this way and that, happy to be eating her evening meal in someone's home. After the dessert of shortcake and canned peaches, she excused herself from the table to take a nap before going to the theater for opening night. It took her no time at all to fall asleep, but when she awoke, the room was dark, and Louis was sliding into bed next to her. "Are you awake?" he whispered.

She opened her eyes, sighed, and got out of bed.

When she returned from the toilet, Louis pulled the covers aside for her to get in "You missed opening night." He pulled the quilt up over her shoulder.

"I don't know what happened. I came upstairs to rest before getting ready to go to the theater, and I must have fallen asleep. How was the show?"

"Good, good. We had a full house. My act went over big. Shirley's did, too."

"I'm sorry I missed them."

Louis was silent for several minutes before speaking again. "Maybe it's time to start thinking about sending you home to have the baby."

"What do you mean?"

"Well, I've been talking it over with some of the fellows, and they're telling me that a girl your age should be with her mother when her time comes."

The thought of lying in her own bed with Maman and Josephine at her side, Maman Aurore hovering nearby to offer the assistance of a third generation seemed almost more than she could hope for—but only if Louis were downstairs in the living room with Papa waiting anxiously for the process of birth to run its course. "Do you really think I should?"

His hand caressed her cheek. "Yes, sweetheart, I do."

Chapter 32

So there she was, trundled onto a train for the two-day ride north, Louis's fellow players having taken up a collection to pay for a Pullman ticket and meals in the dining car. She could feel the long reach of the locomotive's engine, thrumming and throbbing, as it built up enough steam to pull the string of cars back through the Deep South, up through the Carolinas, around the Delmarva Peninsula, and finally up into New England, like a motion picture playing in reverse, the end of the film coming loose from the reel in Saint Albans, flapping around and around and around until the projectionist finally stopped it.

Louis hadn't seen her off, the departure time for her train conflicting with his call time for the matinee. Maisie had called for the taxicab and stood at the curb to wave goodbye as it pulled away, and at the station, the cab driver had found the porter to see to her suitcase.

As she waited for the train to pull out of the station, Faby scanned the faces of the people on the platform, looking for one that regretted the departure of his loved one, wanting nothing more than to see her step off the train and run back into his arms. But all seemed indifferent, turning their backs to walk away before the train had even begun to move. Even so, she continued to watch the platform, waiting for someone to turn around and wave, someone to cry out, *I'll miss you!*

After several false starts, the train began to move, drawing away from the platform, making its way through the maze of tracks in the train yard, warning bells clanging, *We're leaving, we're leaving!* By the time conductor came through to punch her ticket, they had left the begrimed Birmingham skyline behind, factory chimneys obliviously disgorging black smoke.

Passing through Alabama to reach their first major stop in Atlanta took a surprisingly short time, as the train sped through acres of stubbled farmland, the brittle remains of the previous year's crop unidentifiable, here and there being turned under by a lone man behind a mule and a plow. After the train had come to a stop at the Atlanta station, she stood up with the other passengers to get off, needing to walk to try and ease the swelling in her feet and ankles. As she stepped off the train, she misjudged the distance and stumbled. If there hadn't been a porter there to catch her, she would have fallen.

"Is there someone with you, Missus?" he said as he stood by her side to ensure she had regained her footing.

She shook her head. "I'm traveling alone."

"There should be someone with you, Missus," he said, turning away to finish his sentence as he helped a woman with two young children, "in your condition."

On second thought, it was probably not a good idea for her to go wandering through Terminal Station by herself, unable to see her feet or locate her center of gravity. She would walk along the platform instead. However, scarcely had she begun when the porter who had helped her off the train approached her. "Begging your pardon, Missus, but you shouldn't walk so close to the edge. You could fall." She let him help her back onto the train, but instead of going to her seat, she waddled up and down the length of the car, steadying herself with her hand on the backs of empty seats until the other passengers returned to claim them.

Once the train got underway again, it was time for lunch, and she was seated at a table with a pleasant young woman named Ernestine who had an encyclopedic memory for motion picture storylines along with an apparently irresistible impulse to relate them scene by scene to strangers. As Ernestine prattled on about romance, scandals, and near-death escapes from every manner of disaster—train wrecks, swirling rapids, unexpected cliffs, vampires—Faby's own story receded further and further into the background, and she was sorry to see the lunch end.

She spent the rest of the afternoon watching the train cut a never-ending swath through the pine trees lining the South Carolina railbed until the low country pines gave way to the more mountainous terrain of inland North Carolina. When it was time for dinner, Ernestine was nowhere to be seen, and Faby found herself seated across from a woman with an unfortunate overbite that caused her to speak with such a pronounced lisp it took all of Faby's concentration to respond to the woman's game attempts at small talk without asking her to repeat herself.

Later, when the porter came through the car to make down the berths for sleeping, Faby began to worry that she would not fit in the narrow space allotted to her, that she and the baby would protrude into the aisle to be jostled by every single man, woman, and child making their way to and from the toilet.

As it turned out, the berth accommodated both her and her belly, although not at all comfortably. As she pulled the curtains closed to button them, she knew she was in for a long night, what with the confined space, the clacking of wheels over points in the track, and the sounds of so many strangers in close proximity making night noises in their sleep that shouldn't be overheard by others.

As the train sped through the unseen night, every mile it traveled took her closer to White River Junction where she would change trains for Saint Albans. Once in Saint Albans, she would have to get off and wait for the next train to Enosburg, which ran only twice a day, once in the morning and again in the afternoon. In all likelihood, she would wait for several hours in the Saint Albans depot, by herself, with no husband beside her, visibly pregnant, wondering how it had all gone so wrong.

She slept fitfully as she tried to imagine what her homecoming would be like, walking up Depot Street lugging her suitcase, only to find the once towering maple trees now twisted skeletons decaying on the ground, their bark scabrous, their brilliant foliage reduced to leaf mold. The Neale children would be scattered to the four winds, their mother having become too sick and downtrodden to care for them, the eldest boy now in prison. Sally the beagle would be dead, one day having mustered some misguided impulse to waddle off the porch, down the front walk, and into the street to be run over by one of the few cars driving down the street that morning. The Bergerons' hysterical terrier would be buried in their back yard, having hurled itself at last through the bay window in a spectacular shower of broken glass to die bleeding on the lawn.

Faby came awake the next day to the early morning sounds of other people, shifting in their berths, clearing their lungs with morning coughs, murmuring to travel companions above or below them. When she returned from breakfast, the porter had all of the berths tucked neatly away, and she took her seat, looking out the window to see how far they had come during the night. While she couldn't tell exactly where they were, the passing landscape was as familiar to her as her own name: faded red barns, muddy, snow-mottled fields, trees hung with hooded metal buckets. She was back in Vermont.

Chapter 33

All too soon, the train began to slow for the stop in White River Junction, navigating the complex network of tracks to the platform where the passengers would disembark. When the train came to a complete stop and the passengers began to gather their belongings, Faby didn't move. She would wait until the other passengers in the car had gotten off before attempting to maneuver her unwieldy self to the door.

Directly across the aisle, an elderly woman held two little boys by their wrists, pleading with them to accompany her off the train. The boys looked about four and five years old, possibly a year older, both trying desperately to wriggle out of her bony grasp, their feet braced against the seatback in front of them. They weren't arguing or fussing, instead focusing all of their energy and strength on breaking her grasp, their little jaws set, their round eyes narrowed.

Faby wondered what horror could possibly be awaiting children so young that they would refuse to get off the train with their elderly caretaker, who for her part, was frantically looking this way and that as first one boy then the other set himself to shrieking.

A man bearing a passing resemblance to the two boys appeared in the doorway and advanced on the little group, saying in a clear, firm voice, "That will be enough of that, now." The boys stopped shrieking, the elderly woman dropped their wrists, and the three of them followed him meekly off the train, leaving Faby by herself in the car with no option but to follow them herself. Looking at her wristwatch, she saw that she had just enough time to use the toilet before boarding the train to Saint Albans.

The train left White River Junction at an alarming rate of speed, flashing past the freight warehouses adjoining the train yard to head north. Faby watched helplessly through the window as dairy farms flew by, barnyards mired in mud, smoky steam trailing from hilltop sugar houses. Small enclaves of villages rushed by, schoolhouses sheltering unwitting children, opera houses shuttered and unseen. Stops at the larger stations in Montpelier and Burlington provided the only relief from the headlong careening to the northern part of the state, but all too soon each respite ended and the train resumed it inexorable hurtle north, the rivers still blocked with ice, the trees still withholding their buds.

When Saint Albans came into view, the sun was low in the sky, cold shadows cast over the mountains on the horizon. As the train pulled into the immense train shed, Faby knew that she had missed the afternoon train to Enosburg. She remained in her seat, watching the other passengers preparing to leave, as if she were not one of them: a chubby little boy stuffed into a double-breasted coat for the cold walk to the car, his mother pulling on her gloves; a young couple bundling their baby into pink bunting; a scowling man with a clipped mustache who appeared not to trust that his wife had come to the station to meet him.

Straggling behind the last person off the car, Faby went to the ladies' room before joining the cluster of people waiting for their luggage to be taken off the baggage car. Oddly, none of their faces looked tired or impatient after waiting for countless miles of track to pass beneath them, only to get off the train and wait some more. The chubby little boy, now held by his father, beamed from his new vantage point, while his mother smiled up at them. Assorted relatives surrounded the young couple with the baby, chucking her under the chin as they eagerly awaited their turn to hold her. The scowling man was scowling no longer, his arm around his pretty wife's waist.

When she was able to retrieve her suitcase, Faby was surprised at how heavy it seemed, before realizing that from the time it had first been packed in her bedroom on Depot Street, it had never once been necessary for her to lift it herself. She let the suitcase drop and straightened up to ease her back. As she bent over to try again, she heard a man's voice behind her asking what she thought she was doing. She hesitantly turned around, unsure whether the man was speaking to her or to someone else. Indignant eyes in a sallow face glared at her from behind round spectacles.

"What do you think you're doing? You mustn't lift heavy objects in your condition. Wait for your husband."

Before she could think better of it, she blurted, "My husband's not with me."

The man's eyes widened. "He's not with you? Where is he then?"

"Birmingham." Faby wondered why she felt strangely obligated to tell the man the truth. "Alabama."

"Alabama? What kind of man sends his wife off on a train by herself in your condition? What's he doing in Alabama?"

"He's with the vaudeville show."

Behind their round spectacles, the man's eyes were now incredulous. "The vaudeville show . . . "

Faby nodded.

"Oh, for Christ's sake!" he exclaimed in disgust. "Don't you people have any sense at all?" He abruptly turned on his heel and walked off, leaving Faby alone to contend with her overloaded suitcase, hoping that their exchange had not been observed by others in the station as creating a public scene. Before she had a chance to recover her equilibrium, the man returned, mumbled an apology for his rudeness, carried her suitcase to a bench in the waiting area, and got in a parting shot. "Someone is coming to fetch you, right?"

As Faby sat next to her suitcase on the bench, watching the people who had been on the train leave the station to be replaced by the people arriving for the next one, she gradually became aware that she needed to eat. Before leaving the bench for the small restaurant at the other end of the depot, she checked the clasps on her suitcase to make sure they were securely locked, checked her purse to make sure she had the key, then left the suitcase on the bench and walked to the restaurant. She ordered the blue plate special, which turned out to be a stick-to-your-ribs pile of meatloaf and mashed potatoes. Were it not for the fact that some manner of brown gravy had been dumped over the whole thing, the food would have stuck to her gullet, unable to make it down as far as her ribs.

After the meal, she returned to the bench with her suitcase to settle in for a very long night. For several hours, she was able to occupy herself with people-watching, getting up from time to time to ease the pain in her back and use the toilet, occasionally making eye contact with passersby directly in front of her, wondering if she might see anyone she recognized. By one o'clock in the morning, she was alone in the waiting area, huddled on the bench with her suitcase of homemade clothes she could no longer wear, wanting more than anything in this life to lie down and go to sleep, but knowing that she couldn't: While the seat could accommodate her lying down, the baby would be suspended over the floor in the fragile hammock of her skin with nothing solid beneath him. She spent the rest of the night with her arms on the back of the bench, her head on her arms, dozing when she could and responding to intermittent voices asking if she was all right.

By daybreak, dozing had become unbearable, and she opened her eyes to watch the dawn through the tall arched windows across from her, the sky tentatively lightening from gray to lavender before opening up a glowing array of variegated color soon gone. Unlike the day before, the sky was clear, sunlight coming through the windows in shafts that would grow stronger as the morning wore on. In March, Faby knew, sunlight could be deceiving. Until you actually opened the door and left the house, you could never tell whether the day would be as cold as the hard frost the night before or a warm harbinger of spring.

Returning from the ladies', she thought about getting some breakfast when the restaurant opened, then thought better of it. She would rather just stay hungry until she was able to eat something Maman would cook for her.

She bought her ticket, a porter appeared at her elbow for her suitcase, and she was on the train. In less than an hour, she would be back in Enosburg, while America's Favorite Hoofer danced the Black Bottom in Birmingham, Alabama without her.

Chapter 34

As Faby waited for the train to leave Saint Albans, her breath began coming in short gasps. Even though there was only one other passenger in the car besides herself, she quickly turned to the window to hide her face. The other passenger, a well-dressed woman in a fur-trimmed coat, appeared much too stylish to be on the same train as Faby. Maybe she'd gotten on the wrong train in Saint Albans; she thought she was actually on her way to Montreal.

As the train picked up speed, the wheels clacking at regular intervals over the points in the track, Faby's breathing calmed, and she relaxed in her seat, clearly envisioning each farm from Saint Albans to Sheldon in her mind before it reached her sight. When the train arrived at the Sheldon station, she briefly considered getting off to stretch her legs, but she knew there wouldn't be enough time before the train left again. However, the well-dressed woman and her fur-trimmed coat did get off. When she didn't come back before the train continued on to Enosburg, Faby couldn't imagine what there could possibly be in the village of Sheldon that would be of interest to such an obvious woman of the world. Unless you wanted to count several cemeteries, Sheldon held nothing of note but the train depot and the poor farm, which attracted no visitors. If your circumstances were such that you ended up in the place, you had no one in this world who cared enough about you to visit you there.

The railbed from Sheldon to Enosburg followed the path of the Missisquoi River, its frozen surface at times visible from the train, at times briefly obscured by the rolling landscape, the serene mountains on the horizon always in view. As the train drew closer to Enosburg, Faby was surprised to notice subtle variations in the shading of the ice on the river, variations indicating that something had shifted, something had changed, and although the surface looked solid, it was no longer safe to walk across. She was surprised she could still read the river ice after being away for so long, as surprised as she was to find herself at the Enosburg depot, sitting on the train with no one accompanying her and no one on the platform to meet her.

She got as far as putting on her coat and hat, but then she was unable to leave her seat. The thought of stepping down from the train in her condition after only four months of marriage, as brazen as a young woman who has misplaced her drawers, shamed her to the roots of her hair. Across the street, the Opera House stood blank and closed, obliviously peeling its dove gray paint. Just as she was thinking she needed to turn away from the window so that no one passing by would see her face, someone spoke her name.

"Faby!" Gardner Croft had entered the train car in his shirt sleeves and was advancing on her. "Faby Gauthier! What are you doing here? Can't you see that we have passengers waiting to board? What are you doing still on the train?"

"Can't I sit here a little longer?"

"Of course not, child. We have a schedule to keep. Come, come." Gardner put out his hand to help her up, making no attempt to hide his surprise as she stood to her full height. "Well, well, look at you now! Well!"

Faby followed him the short distance to the door of the train with her head down, keeping it down as he helped her off the step, keeping it down as she followed him into the depot to wait for her suitcase, all the while thinking that if only she weren't so big, she could turn tail and run, suitcase be damned. She could run out of the station all the way up Depot Street to the house, all the way up the stairs to the refuge of her bedroom.

"You sit right here and rest while I see to your suitcase," Gardner said, leading her to the bench against the wall with his hand at her elbow. "You do have your suitcase, don't you? But where is your young man?" Before she could respond, Gardner bustled off to the baggage car. When he returned with her suitcase, he repeated the question— *Where is your young man?*—and this time he expected an answer.

"He didn't come with me."

"He didn't come with you?" Gardner's face assumed an indignant expression. "Where are your parents, then? Why aren't they here to meet you?"

"They don't know I'm coming." Faby stood and picked up her suitcase. "Thank you for helping me with my suitcase, Mr. Croft." She started for the door, the suitcase seemingly two steps behind her, but still in tow.

"Where do you think you're going?" Gardner stopped her at the door, just as Clyde Geraw came through it. As Clyde entered the station, seeming not to recognize her, Gardner grabbed the door and held it closed. "Where do you think you're going?"

"Home."

"Oh, no, you're not." Gardner grabbed the handle of the suitcase and pulled it out of her hand. "Not in your condition." He hesitated, her suitcase in one hand, his other holding the door closed. He yelled over his shoulder, "Clyde, get over here!" Clyde

296

crossed the small station to join them, his face nearly a caricature of surprise when he recognized Faby. "What is it, Mr. Croft?"

"You here for the train to Saint Albans?"

Clyde nodded yes.

"You have your car with you?"

Clyde shook his head. "Uh uh, timer went. She may be a goner this time."

"Well, Faby here needs someone to carry her suitcase and walk her home. She's in no condition to carry it herself." Clyde looked unsure, as Faby silently willed him to say no. If she had to drag that suitcase up Depot Street an inch at a time, it would be less humiliating than having to face the boy she had turned down for the holiday dance the year before.

"I'll hold the train for you," Gardner said, and Clyde brightened. "Sure thing, Mr. Croft, as long as you're holding the train for me." Clyde picked up her suitcase, held open the door, and offered Faby his arm once they were outside, which she took reluctantly, so as not to hurt his feelings after turning him down for the dance. "Gosh, Faby. I haven't seen you in ages. How've you been? *Where've* you been? I heard you married someone from the vaudeville show last summer. Watch the puddle."

"Yes, I did," she said letting go of Clyde's arm to sidestep the puddle. "He thought it best that I come home. He's finishing out the Delmar Circuit."

"I see, sure. On the road, eh? Kind of like being in the Army, is it?"

Faby didn't respond, grabbing his arm when she slipped on a patch of ice as they passed the Touchettes' house.

"Be careful!" Clyde scolded. "You mustn't fall. What is the Delmar Circuit, anyways?"

"The show gets booked to play at different theaters in the South."

"The South, you say? I hear that Florida is really something, like a tropical paradise."

"I don't know. I only got as far as Alabama."

They had reached the Neales' house, and Faby couldn't stop herself from looking to see if any of the Neale children were peering out the window at them.

"You'll have to tell me about Alabama some time, what it's like to see all those grand plantations," Clyde said. "Wait, your front walk's icy. Let me get your suitcase up on the porch, and I'll help you."

When Clyde had gotten both her and her suitcase up on the porch, he rang the bell before she could reach for the latch to the storm door, realizing in that moment that in fact ringing the doorbell was the most appropriate thing for Clyde to do because this house on Depot Street was no longer her home. She was a guest—an uninvited guest at that. As she and Clyde waited for someone to answer the door, she looked down at the mat beneath her feet, a worn hooked rug that had outlived its usefulness as a cheerful spot of color in an otherwise drab room, now relegated to holding the dirt and wet that people stamped off their feet. There would be another one, a little less worn, just inside the door.

The door opened to reveal Maman, her dress covered by a faded apron, her face flushed from the stove. Faby met her mother's eyes through the storm door, silently pleading with her to push it open, even as her mother's expression so clearly read, *Oh, cher. What have you done?* If that storm door didn't open, she had nowhere else to go. Unless her parents were willing to swallow their pride and talk some obliging relative with a spare room into taking her in, she had nowhere else to go. Even if she managed to acquire the money for train fare, it was too late to rejoin Louis on the Delmar Circuit. Her pregnancy was too far gone.

Clyde broke the silence, asking through the storm door, "Where would you like me to put Faby's suitcase, Mrs. Gauthier?"

"Oh! Clyde. I didn't see you standing there." Maman pushed open the storm door. "Please just set it inside by the door here." As Clyde set the suitcase down, Faby heard Maman Aurore's voice from the top of the stairs. "Who is that at the door, Yvette? Who is here?"

Clyde touched Faby's shoulder and said, "I better get going. Mr. Croft is holding the train for me. Will you be all right?"

Faby nodded. "Thank you. You were very kind to walk me home."

Clyde shrugged and blushed. "Maybe I'll see you around some time." He left the porch, and Faby turned back to face her mother, who was still holding the storm door open. "Come in! Come in out of the damp."

As Maman closed the front door, Maman Aurore exclaimed from the bottom of the stairs, "Faby! You've come home for your lying-in! I've been making preparations."

Faby quickly looked at Maman, but she seemed not to have noticed, intent on getting Faby's overcoat off her and onto the hall tree without dislodging the precarious load of coats and jackets it already held. "You can tell us what's happened after we get you warm and fed. How far did you have to travel to get here? How long did it take you?"

"Two days on the train. We were in Alabama." The front hall was filled with the smell of cake baking.

"All the way from Alabama," Maman murmured, taking one of Faby's hands in hers.

"Two days on the train," Maman Aurore murmured, taking Faby's other hand in hers and rubbing it.

Faby's chin quivered, and she wished she could have her hands back to cover her face.

The furnace kicked on.

"We need to get you cleaned up," Maman Aurore said, giving Faby's hand one last pat. "What on earth is that you're wearing? You look a sight."

"Never mind about that now," Maman said, still holding Faby's hand. "Let's go into the kitchen where it's warm. I'll make you some cocoa."

Faby let her mother lead her into the kitchen, with Maman Aurore right on her heels. When Maman went to the icebox for the milk, Maman Aurore led Faby to the wide rocker by the window. "Here, you come sit in my chair while your Maman fixes you some nice cocoa." Faby stood dumbly looking down at the rocking chair. She had never, ever sat in Maman Aurore's chair, nor had she ever seen anyone else sit in it, the black paint on the seat worn through to the wood in the shape of Maman Aurore's ample buttocks. "Don't just stand there like a lost sheep," Maman Aurore said. "Sit down."

Tentatively positioning her arms on the armrests, Faby watched from Maman Aurore's rocking chair as Maman poured a little milk into a small saucepan and set it on the stove to heat as she mixed in sugar, cocoa, and a pinch of salt. She continued to stir as she poured in more milk. "Shouldn't take but a minute for it to heat."

As she sat in her grandmother's rocking chair, Faby looked around the kitchen, surprised to see that nothing had changed. Standing in the front hall earlier, with her mother and her grandmother on either side holding her hand, she had expected the kitchen she remembered to somehow have disappeared, or changed into something else altogether. But no, it was just the same. The cookstove, the icebox, the washing machine, the sink. The stamped tin ceiling, the cupboards and shelves, the linoleum rug on the floor, the pattern nearly worn off from scrubbing, Maman making her something hot to drink.

In the meantime, Maman Aurore had taken the kettle off the stove and was standing at the sink running water into it. "I'm going to heat you some water for a nice sponge bath in front of the oven."

"I don't need a sponge bath." Faby took her hands off the armrests of Maman Aurore's rocker and rested them on her belly. "I'm not sick."

"Of course you're not," Maman said, testing the temperature of the cocoa with her finger. "But you're past the point of being able to take tub baths."

"What do you mean?"

"Childbed fever," Maman Aurore said, holding the kettle perfectly steady as it grew heavier and heavier with the weight of the water.

Faby didn't dare ask for further clarification.

"How have you been feeling?" Maman Aurore said, her hand gripping the handle of the kettle as though pressing down on it would make it boil faster.

"I've been feeling all right. I had stomach flu in Buffalo, but that's the only time I was sick."

"Hmph, probably food poisoning," Maman Aurore said.

"All right, that's enough of that," Maman said, opening a cupboard and taking out a cup. "You're here now and you're just fine." She poured the cocoa and crossed the room to hand Faby the cup.

"Thank you, Maman."

"You're welcome, *cher.*"

Maman Aurore still stood at the stove watching the kettle. "You drink that down, and I'll give you a nice sponge bath after your mother takes the cake out of the oven."

Faby tried to catch Maman's eye as she quickly washed up the saucepan, dried it, and put it away. "The bathroom will be fine for Faby's sponge bath, Maman Aurore."

"All right, then," Maman Aurore said as the kettle began to whistle. "I'll just pour this water in the tub to warm it up before Faby gets in." She lifted the kettle off the stove.

"Let me help you with that," Maman said. "You mustn't carry boiling water up the stairs by yourself."

"Mustn't I?" Maman Aurore turned to leave the room. "I've managed heavier things in my time."

Maman rolled her eyes at Faby, who was forced to stifle a giggle. Maman was still Maman, and Maman Aurore was still Maman Aurore. "You must be tired from your long trip."

"A little," Faby said cautiously, fearful of giving away too much. She hoped Maman would wait a while for her to get her bearings before asking about Louis. At least for a little while.

"I'd better get that cake out of the oven and start the biscuits for lunch." Maman went into the pantry and came back with a broom straw to test the cake for doneness. "Just right," she said, reaching for potholders and taking the cake out of the oven. She brought flour and shortening from the pantry to the scarred work table in the center of the room and began to make biscuits.

"What are we having?" Faby said, as if she were still a schoolgirl and what they were going to eat for lunch actually mattered.

"Pea soup and honey biscuits."

"Do you have any jam?"

Maman looked up from her biscuit dough. "Of course we have jam. I put up strawberry, raspberry, blueberry, and rhubarb. You were here when I made it. What would give you the idea that we would have no jam?"

"I don't know. I guess I thought you might have eaten it all."

Maman shook her head and went back to her biscuit dough. Maman Aurore entered the kitchen with the empty kettle. "We need to get upstairs for Faby's sponge bath before the tub cools."

"Just let me get these biscuits in the oven."

"We don't have time for that. Besides, you'll need to watch them so they don't burn."

"No, I'm going up to help Faby with her bath." Maman went to the sink and washed the dough off her hands.

"You leave that dough, the biscuits won't rise right." Maman Aurore said.

Faby struggled to get up from the rocker. "I can take my bath by myself."

As if they hadn't heard her, Maman and Maman Aurore pulled her the rest of the way out of the rocker and walked her up the stairs, Maman in front of her in case she should trip and fall forward, Maman Aurore right behind her in case she lost her balance and fell backward. To avoid either eventuality, Faby kept one hand firmly on the banister as she navigated the stairs.

In the bathroom, as Maman and Maman Aurore unbuttoned her dress and pulled it over her head, Maman Aurore muttered under her breath, but loudly enough to be heard, "The man couldn't get you something decent to wear while you're carrying his child?" She dropped the dress on the floor. "Here, Yvette, cover her with this towel while I find something for her to wear after we've cleaned her up. I must have an old flannel nightgown and wrapper that would fit her." Maman Aurore left the bathroom, continuing to mutter to herself as her footsteps echoed down the hall.

Maman draped a bath towel over Faby's shoulders, holding it closed for her. "It's not that bad. I'm sure he did his best."

Faby nodded. "One of the singers made it for me out of an old stage costume when I couldn't fit into any of my clothes. She didn't have to. It was very kind of her."

"Of course it was," Maman murmured as the sound of Maman Aurore opening and closing drawers came from her bedroom.

"Here," Maman said, "put your hand on my shoulder so I can get your shoes and stockings off." She struggled momentarily. "My, your feet are very swollen."

Faby didn't respond as she stood shivering on the bath mat, one arm wrapped around her breasts, the other across her belly in a vain attempt to cover it while she struggled to maintain her balance.

"Your drawers are in tatters," Maman murmured as Maman Aurore reentered the bathroom. After they helped Faby over the high side of the tub, Maman quickly washed her as Faby crouched miserably in the bottom of the tub, shivering, struggling to maintain her balance, wondering all the while how repulsed they must be by the changes to her body that Louis had caused.

"When was last time you saw a doctor?" Maman said as they helped her out of the tub and toweled her dry. She put up her arms for them to slip Maman Aurore's nightgown over her head.

"Not since I've been gone. Should I go see one in Saint Albans?"

"Oh, no, you don't," Maman Aurore said. "That baby has dropped, and you're not riding on no train to Saint Albans."

"No, *cher,*" Maman said, buttoning the nightgown. "Dr. Ballard can attend the birth. Saint Albans is too far away."

"But everyone will know if I go see Dr. Ballard."

"They will know soon enough," Maman Aurore replied. "We can't very well hide you in the attic, now, can we?"

Chapter 35

Back in her bedroom tucked into her own bed, Faby slept through lunch, not waking until Josephine brought her supper on a tray, as the light from the day was fading. "There you are, sleepyhead, awake at last!"

"Josephine!" She struggled to sit up. "What time is it?"

"Nearly five o'clock. You've been asleep all afternoon. Maman says you were two days on the train to get here."

Faby nodded. "It went by fast, though. Well, except for last night, waiting for morning in Saint Albans."

"You were all night in the train station? How dreadful!"

"It wasn't so bad. I've gotten used to waiting in train stations."

Josephine did not look convinced. "Where's Louis?"

"Birmingham."

"He didn't come with you?"

"No, he's playing the Delmar Circuit. They must be on their way to Knoxville by now." Faby looked down at her hands. "It could be his big break, you see."

Josephine still held the tray in her hands. "Goodness, I don't know where to put this. You have no lap. Scoot over, and I'll sit here and hold the tray steady for you while you eat."

"Let me use the toilet," Faby said, relieved that Josephine appeared ready to leave the subject of Louis's comings and goings for another time and move onto the more immediate concern of supper.

Settled back in bed, Faby looked with more interest at the tray Josephine had brought up. "Mmm, ham in maple syrup. And pickled beets, my favorite."

"Maman opened a new jar for you."

Faby snatched up her napkin, the cloth floppy and limp from laundering. "Oh, look, my napkin ring! I remember when Papa carved these for us. I never could figure out exactly what kind of a bird it was supposed to be, seeing as it didn't have any wings."

"I remember. You were very put out that it had no wings."

Faby took a bite of ham. "Have you already eaten?"

"No, we'll eat with Papa when he gets home. Maman wanted to be sure and get some food into you since you missed lunch. I've been coming up here every fifteen minutes to see if you were awake."

"You could have woken me up."

"Oh, no, I couldn't! I never would have heard the end of it."

Faby smiled and tried some of her beets, pleased that they were as good as she remembered. Josephine was right, of course; she never would have heard the end of it had she rushed upstairs to wake her sister upon hearing the news of her arrival home, what Faby herself would have done if the shoe had been on the other foot. "So how have you been, Josephine? It seems like ages since I've seen you. I've missed you terribly. You received my letters?"

"Oh, yes, and I read them aloud to the family. Many times over."

"I tried to make them entertaining."

"Indeed you did. The trip sounded like quite a lark, traveling from town to town, a new place every week."

"Twice a week!" Faby forked up some riced potatoes swimming in butter. "But what about you? What have you been doing? Are you still working at Asletine's?"

"Oh, yes. I'm still working on my trousseau—" Josephine stopped speaking, so abruptly that Faby paused with her forkful of potatoes halfway to her mouth to ask her what was wrong.

Josephine shook her head. "Nothing. I just lost my train of thought. I was so surprised when Maman told me you were here! Why didn't you tell us you were coming?"

Faby set her fork down. "I didn't know I was coming myself."

"You didn't? What do you mean? You hadn't planned to come home for the birth?"

"No, I thought I would stay with Louis."

"Why didn't you?"

"I don't know. Everything was fine, and the next thing I knew, Louis told me I needed to go home for the birth and I was on the train. Please don't tell Maman and Papa he sent me away."

"Don't be silly, Faby. Louis didn't send you away. He's just watching out for you and the baby, to keep you both safe and healthy. I give him credit for that."

"I suppose." Faby finished her meal as Josephine continued to hold the tray steady for her. When she was finished, she said, "Does Papa know?"

Josephine set the tray on the floor. "About the baby? I don't know. I don't know if Maman would have called him at work or whether she's waiting till he gets home to tell him."

"Do you think he'll be mad?"

Josephine looked thoughtful. "Was Maman angry when she saw you?"

Faby shook her head, and her chin quivered. "No. She looked surprised. But not angry."

"Well, then, I think you can expect the same from Papa."

Just then, footsteps sounded on the porch and the front door opened and closed. Immediately following the front door's closing came two sets of footsteps.

"They must be telling him now," Josephine whispered.

Faby held her breath, but no shouts or thunderous curses sounded, just the deliberate sound of her father's footsteps on the stairs. When he appeared in the doorway, he walked straight to Faby's bedside, took hands, and kissed her cheek. "So good to have you home, Faby, so good."

Chapter 36

Later that night, Faby was awakened by the sound of Maman Aurore's treadle sewing machine, whirring and clanking, the sound reminiscent of all those trains passing over all those points of track, day after day after day, from station to depot. After breakfast, when Faby went upstairs to get dressed and fix her hair, Maman Aurore followed her up and presented her with a new dress, a simple smock of light blue chambray with a middy collar. "We had to throw out that awful thing you were wearing when you got here."

The new dress her grandmother had stayed up so late to make was pretty, even dainty for something so simple, but all Faby could think of was the other dress, the one that someone she had never even met had so thoughtfully pieced together out of her own costume trunk. And now it was gone.

Faby spent most of the day resting in her bedroom, listening for the ordinary sounds of housework getting done and meals being prepared, as water dripped from the eaves outside the windows when the sun grew warm, melting the snow on the roof. Whenever the house grew inexplicably quiet, she read from the book of best-loved poems Josephine left on her nightstand.

That evening, as soon as Papa had swallowed the last bite of his supper, Maman Aurore demanded that he go out in the garage and search for an old wicker rocking chair which the previous owner of the house had abandoned after determining that it was no longer fit for service on the front porch. After supper, while Faby and Josephine helped Maman with the dishes, Maman Aurore dragged the chair into the pantry and cleaned off years of disuse with a scrub brush, hot water, and carbolic soap.

The next morning, when Faby came down to the kitchen to help with breakfast, the wicker rocker was clean and dry, its cushions newly decked out with slipcovers made of blue and white ticking. Even more startling than its appearance was its position, right next to Maman Aurore's rocking chair by the window.

"There," Maman Aurore said as Faby stood gaping at the chair with a bread knife in her hand. "Now you can stay warm until the baby comes, right here in the kitchen with your maman and your grandmère."

So she spent the next week sitting in the wicker rocker in the kitchen next to Maman Aurore, waiting out each day in a peculiar state of anxious lassitude. As her body grew heavier and heavier, she waited for it to give some sign that the waiting would end, some sign that would tell her why Louis had sent no word.

Her labor to bring Sonny into the world came upon her as stealthily as his conception. When she awoke that day, she had a hard time getting out of bed and very little appetite for her breakfast, barely managing a few bites of toast and a scant cup of tea. When she pushed her chair back to get up and help clear the table, Maman said, "You look a little pale, *cher*. You should sit and rest. I'll take care of the dishes with Maman Aurore."

After she settling herself in the wicker rocker, the newly refurbished cushions easing her back, Faby began to feel a little better. As the sun streamed through the windows onto the spotless worn linoleum, she began to gently rock herself. The baby shifted, like a sigh before sleep. Maman passed through the kitchen to the pantry, retrieving the carpet sweeper to get up the breakfast crumbs in the dining room, while Maman Aurore scraped plates and got the dishes ready for washing. Odd, how she had to wash them in a predetermined order.

When all of the dishes had been washed, dried, and put away, Maman turned from the cupboard and said, "Can I get you anything, *cher,* before I start the washing, maybe a nice galette? You barely touched your breakfast."

Faby shook her head. "I'm really not hungry, Maman."

"Are you feeling all right?"

Faby winced. She'd been feeling fine until Maman had asked her if she was feeling all right. "My back's hurting more than usual."

Maman Aurore stepped up. "How much more?"

"Not so much. It comes and goes."

Maman Aurore put her hands on her hips. "We need to get her room ready, Yvette. That baby's coming any time now."

Maman looked at Faby, considering. "You may be right. We can tend to the washing after we've gotten the room ready, tomorrow, if need be."

Faby said, "What do you need to do? Josephine and I have the baby's basket all ready."

"Oh, there's more to it than that. Giving birth is a messy business," Maman Aurore said as Maman glared at her.

"What do you mean?" Faby said.

"Never you mind," Maman said, nudging Maman Aurore's shoulder to move her along. "Your grandmère likes to exaggerate."

Faby hoped that's all it was. She hadn't actually thought about the process by which the baby would be born. She held him inside her body now, and sometime in the near future, she would hold him in her arms, but how he would remove himself from her body she hadn't been able to envision. Perhaps he would just choose to stay where he was, perfectly content to remain upside down for the rest of his life, never getting any bigger, never to be touched by the cold light of day.

She shifted her position to ease her back. The sound of footsteps above her had given way to what sounded like furniture being moved, bumping and scraping. She couldn't imagine what they could possibly be doing. She thought about getting up from the rocking chair and going upstairs to investigate, but the effort didn't seem worth it, and she stayed where she was, not realizing that she was dozing until they came back in the kitchen to prepare lunch.

"Can you help me up, Maman? I think I've been sitting in this chair too long. My back hurts."

Maman bent down and helped Faby out of the chair, still holding onto her when she was on her feet. "Better?"

Faby took a deep breath and straightened up as much as she could. "Yes, actually. May I help you with lunch?"

"Of course, *cher,* if you feel up to it."

Although opening cans of salmon and setting the table didn't do anything for Faby's appetite, she was happy for the simple tasks and even happier when Papa and Josephine arrived home for lunch, the Spavin Cure factory having been granted a brief reprieve from its steady decline with an order from a large Morgan horse farm downstate, Mr. Asletine in an absolute state after being forced to mark several shopworn bolts of taffeta. "What did he expect?" Josephine said, buttering a biscuit. "Who in Enosburg wears taffeta?"

After lunch, Maman set Faby up in the living room with a card table and a picture puzzle of the same print that hung over the sofa. Over the course of the afternoon, as Faby pieced together first the edges, then the supine girl wearing ancient garb, then the younger girl standing over her wearing nothing at all, the pain in her back had become periodic but perfectly bearable cramping, which then began working its way down and across to her belly as she sorted the pieces for the two columns.

When she declined to come to the table for supper, Maman bade the others begin eating and sat next to her on the sofa. "How are you feeling, *cher*? Are you having contractions?"

"I think so."

"How far apart are they?"

"I don't know, about every fifteen minutes, I guess, maybe longer. Does that mean I'm in labor?"

Maman nodded. "We'll know for sure when they start coming closer together. I know you probably don't want to eat, but will you come sit with us at the table?"

Faby shook her head. "I'd rather stay here."

"All right, but you'll need to keep your strength up. I'll fix you some broth to sip on while you work on the puzzle."

A few minutes later, Josephine appeared in the archway with a steaming cup in her hand. She set it down on the card table and joined Faby on the sofa. "Maman and Maman Aurore are doing the dishes, so I can sit with you." She hesitated with her hand over the table. "Would you mind if I helped you with the puzzle?"

"Of course not. Why should I mind?"

Josephine responded, "I didn't know whether you would want to put it together by yourself," when of course she meant, *I've never seen you in labor before.*

By the time the branches of the trees overhanging the two girls were well-leafed and fully-flowered, the cramping was really starting to hurt, and Faby had to stop and wait for it to pass before she could place the puzzle piece she was holding. Just as she was wondering what could be keeping Maman and Maman Aurore in the kitchen, they entered the room, Maman Aurore carrying her knitting basket, Maman holding a piece of white flannel featherstitched on one side in red. Faby felt a flash of relief when each sat in her respective armchair and bent her head to her work rather than stare at her waiting for her face to signal that the baby's arrival was near. However, when Papa appeared in the archway, his eyes registered that he was gazing upon an awkward tableau, his firstborn on the sofa about to deliver, his wife hemming a receiving blanket at breakneck speed to catch the baby in, his mother desperately knitting something, *anything* to keep the baby warm. "I'm going to head on up to bed. Can I get you anything, Faby?"

"No, thank you, Papa. I have everything I need."

He seemed to hesitate before turning toward the stairs. "All right, I'll say good night, then."

The mantle clock chimed eleven just as Faby and Josephine finished the puzzle, looking up to meet the gaze of Maman and Maman Aurore, who had raised their heads when the clock chimed.

"Are they coming any closer together?" Maman said.

"About every ten minutes or so."

Maman got up from her chair. "I'll call Dr. Ballard and see what he'd like us to do."

There wasn't much to Maman's end of the conversation, except her initial reporting of the contractions, so she must have been receiving instructions. When she came back to the living room, she said, "He said to call him when your water breaks or your contractions are five minutes apart, whichever comes first. In the meantime, he says to give you a soapsuds enema and a sponge bath and get you into a clean nightgown."

Faby had never had an enema but she knew what it was, and as she painfully made her way up the stairs accompanied by the other three women in her family, she couldn't help but wonder if this was what it felt for a condemned prisoner to ascend the gallows to her execution. Maman administered the enema, as gently as she could, but still Faby cried out in pain, as hard as she tried not to, and when Maman set her on the toilet to let the enema do its work, she felt as though her bowels were turning inside out and dragging the rest of her insides out with them. When she let her mother back into the bathroom, an eternity later, Maman had tears in her eyes as she sponged Faby clean and gently patted her dry.

When Faby entered her bedroom, she immediately noticed that the furniture had been rearranged. Her bed had been moved away from the wall and placed in front of the windows so that it was clear on both sides. Underneath the bed had been spread a large piece of oilcloth, an incongruous blue with strawberries on it. A small table been moved into the room, with a clean white cloth spread over it. On the table were arranged neat stacks of clean linens: towels, sheets, washcloths, and what looked like pads of several different sizes. A bottle of grain alcohol and an unopened bar of carbolic soap were set next to the same enameled basin that had caught her morning sickness all those months ago, these supplies making her impending motherhood more real that it had ever been before, more real than the vomiting, more real than the outward changes to her body, more real even than the marriage, the miles spent sitting by Louis's side, the dark nights spent in strange beds listening to the sound of his voice as he painted the images of all the places he'd been of which she had no part.

"Well, don't just stand there like a senseless chicken," Maman Aurore said, "get into bed."

315

"It's all right," Maman said, folding back the covers. "You should sleep while you can. We've put a pad on the bed in case your water breaks."

"Don't worry," Josephine said, pulling hairpins from her hair. "I'll be right here next to you if you need anything."

"And I'm right across the hall," Maman said, but still Faby couldn't move to get into the bed that had been moved from where it belonged, the floor beneath it protected from whatever was waiting to gush forth from her body without warning. A contraction finally moved her feet from where they were rooted to the floor, and she crawled into bed.

Maman tucked the covers around her shoulders. "When the contractions start coming closer together, you wake Josephine to come and get me."

"Should I stay up, Maman?" Josephine said as she braided her hair for sleeping.

Maman shook her head, "No, Faby will wake you if she needs you." She turned to Maman Aurore, "Let's get some sleep while we can. I expect we'll be up again before the night's out."

Maman Aurore nodded. "I expect you're right, Yvette." She bent over Faby and kissed her on the cheek. "You get some sleep now."

They left the room, and Josephine got into bed. "I don't think I'll be able to sleep. I'm too excited."

Faby lay curled on her side. She didn't dare answer, and she didn't dare close her eyes.

After several minutes, Josephine whispered, "Are you frightened, Faby?"

At last, someone had said it, so she could acknowledge it and drift off to sleep. "Yes."

After she'd been asleep for two hours, she was awakened by a crushing pain so relentless it couldn't have come from inside her body; there had to be some outside force bearing down on her. She clenched her fists and tried to squirm away from it, but she couldn't, and the crushing force went on and on as she felt someone's hand on her closed fist trying to open it. "Are you all right, Faby?" Josephine was crouched on the floor next to her, trying to take hold of her hand.

She shook her head and continued to squirm as Josephine's hand tried to gain some purchase on her clenched fist. The pain gradually receded, like water trying to find low tide.

"It's passed," Faby said.

"Will you be able to sleep?"

"Yes, go back to bed."

"No, I'll stay here next to you. Just let me get my bathrobe."

And so it went for several hours, a never-ending cycle of punishment and reprieve, retribution and release, until she could no longer tell where one left off and the other began, and Josephine and Maman and Maman Aurore were all in the room. They were dressed for the day even though it was still dark, and Dr. Ballard was in the room, and it was no longer dark, and the bed was wet and the pain bore down hard enough to meld the baby's features and the poor creature would be born without a face.

Then someone was holding her legs and exhorting her, and the pain slithered from her body to lie mottled and wet on the bed between her feet, tethered to her body by a kinked cord.

"You have a baby boy, Faby," Dr. Ballard said, bending to tend to him as his arms and legs flailed and his desperate cries filled the room. Faby had never before seen anyone look so frightened to be where he was, and his tears ran down her face.

Chapter 37

Even though she still hadn't heard from Louis, Faby didn't dare name the baby without his father's blessing, so she called him Sonny. When he was a week old, Maman and Papa came up to her room looking very serious.

"You must name the baby, Faby," Papa said. "Dr. Ballard has been calling us every day. He needs to register the birth. You have to give the boy a proper name."

"Louis and I haven't had a chance to agree on a name."

"Louis isn't here now, is he?" Papa said so harshly Faby flinched. "He's left it to you now, hasn't he?"

Maman put her hand on his arm. "Don't, Joseph."

Faby looked down at the basket by the bed, where her son lay swaddled in a receiving blanket in an uneasy sleep, before awaking to nurse fretfully at her breast.

"Of course the boy's father should name him," Papa said, Maman's hand on his arm unable to dissuade him. "Do you know where he is?"

"He's on the Delmar Circuit."

"You've told us that, but do you know where he is? How can you get in touch with him? Can you at least get a message to him?"

"Stop badgering her, Joseph," Maman said. "If she doesn't know where he is, she doesn't know where he is."

"He could at least have called her. He sent her here; it isn't as if he doesn't know where she is."

Just then the baby woke up and started squalling.

"Now, look what you've done," Maman said. "He'll be wanting to nurse now."

Papa said, "I'm sorry, Faby." He seemed about to say something else, then hesitated as though thinking better of it and left the room. Maman picked up the baby and settled him in Faby's arms. "Don't mind your father. He didn't mean what he said."

"Yes, he did."

"Surely, Louis's mother must know how to get a message to him. We'll call her."

"No. You can tell Dr. Ballard that I'm naming the baby Sonny."

Maman looked at the back of the baby's head doubtfully. "Are you sure? That's the name he'll carry for the rest of his life. I can't really see a grown man named Sonny."

"I'm sure. His name is Sonny. And if he doesn't like it when he's a grown man, he can change it."

"Oh, Faby." Maman turned and left the room.

Faby touched the soft spot on Sonny's tiny warm head as he nursed. "Sonny's a perfectly fine name, isn't it, little one?"

Before long, Faby heard Maman Aurore's heavy footsteps coming up the stairs. She was in for it now.

"You can't name that baby Sonny."

"Leave me be, Mémère."

Maman Aurore advanced on the bed. "No, I'm not going to leave you be. If you name that baby Sonny you'll live to regret it."

"I'm sure I'll live to regret a lot of things, but naming my son won't be one of them."

Oddly, Maman Aurore looked more sad than angry as she turned and left the room without another word.

Sonny was nearly a month old when his father finally sauntered up the porch steps of the house on Depot Street to ring the
bell with much more vigor than was necessary to get someone
to answer it. Faby saw him from the window coming up the
front walk, and she ran to answer the door before anyone else
could get to it.

And there was Louis, standing on the mat, a fistful of
flowers in one hand and in the other a teddy bear that bore the
stunned expression of someone who has just been hit in the
head. Louis's lantern-jawed face wore the same jovial smile as
when Faby had first met him, the night of the vaudeville show
at the Opera House. She felt her stomach drop.

Louis's smile didn't waver. "Aren't you going to invite
me in?"

Faby stood aside to let him in. "I'll get a vase for those."

When she entered the kitchen, Maman Aurore was already out of her rocker, and Maman was slipping off her apron.

"Is that him?" Maman Aurore said grimly.

"You know it is," Maman said.

"Don't——" Faby said. She tried to maneuver around
Maman Aurore to get to the pantry. "I need a vase for these
flowers."

Maman reached for the flowers, removed a clean Mason
jar from the dish drainer, and ran water into it. "If you must
put them in water, you can use this."

Relinquishing the flowers, Faby returned to the front hall
where Louis was waiting, Maman Aurore right on her heels.

"So," Louis said, waggling the teddy bear, "What do we
have?"

"You have a son," Maman Aurore said coldly.

Louis's face lit up as if he had received a standing ovation.
"A son? I have a son?"

Faby nodded.

"I was hoping for a boy!" Louis said, peering this way and that. "Well, where is he? I must see him!"

Faby felt a surge of hope in her chest, and she grabbed for Louis's free hand. "He's just upstairs in his basket. I'll take you to him." She held tight to Louis's hand as she led him up the stairs, not even caring that Maman and Maman Aurore were following close behind.

In the bedroom, Faby let go of Louis's hand to lift Sonny's basket from the floor and set it on the bed.

Louis bent down to look and whispered, "He's sleeping."

"For the moment." Faby reached for Louis's hand as she searched his face for some reaction, some indication that even though Sonny was new to the world, Louis recognized him as his son—but Louis gave no sign as the four of them, mother, father, grandmother, and great-grandmother, stood by the bed looking down at the little bundle that was Sonny.

"Would you like to hold him?" Faby whispered, letting go of Louis's hand and bending over the basket as though he had already said yes.

"All right, if you're sure I won't wake him."

Faby lifted Sonny from the basket and gently set him in Louis's arms. "Support his head, now."

Sonny squirmed a little and opened his eyes, but instead of howling outright or even whimpering, he looked his father full in the face and held his gaze until Louis looked away. "He looks like a Gauthier."

Before Faby could respond, Maman Aurore said, "Well, who did you expect him to look like, the iceman?"

Faby took Sonny from his father and laid him back in his basket. Maman made to leave the room, while Maman Aurore stayed right where she was. "Maman Aurore and I have work to do downstairs, so we'll leave you two alone. I'm sure

321

you have a lot to talk about." She left the room, with Maman Aurore following reluctantly behind her.

When they were out of earshot, Faby said softly, "When I didn't hear from you, I named him Sonny. I think it's too late to change it. Dr. Ballard has already registered the birth."

Louis smiled. "It's never too late to change your name. Just look at me. I had two other stage names before I settled on Slim White."

"You did? You never told me that."

Louis shrugged, his smile unchanged. "Didn't I?"

"So, you don't mind that his name is Sonny?"

"Uh uh. Sonny is a perfectly fine name."

Faby waited from him to continue, to tell her where he'd been since dispatching her and their unborn son from Maisie Budd's boarding house in Birmingham, Alabama for the two-day trip to this bedroom on Depot Street, why he hadn't written or telephoned or wired her, what unimaginable obstacles he had been unable to overcome on the Delmar Circuit that had kept him from her.

Louis took both of her hands in his and sat her down on the bed. "Faby, you know that I care for you. We've had some swell times together, and I'll always hold a special place for you in my heart. And Sonny, too, of course. But the fact of the matter is that you caught me on the rebound, doll. I'm back with Shirley now, and we'll be wanting to get married."

Faby said nothing as she removed her hands from his and, for all the good it had done her, pulled off her hand-me-down wedding ring as Louis said, "I never meant to hurt you."

Chapter 38

The following year, Josephine married Leonard Paradis and moved into her own home, the Ramsdells' old house on Orchard Street. Faby was able to make it through Josephine's wedding without crying, her face as stoic and proud as Maman's when the organ music swept Josephine down the aisle on Papa's arm, the rustling of her dress mingling with the hushed whispers of the guests marveling at how beautiful she looked.

Faby shed no tears at the reception: not a tear for the receiving line, when guest after guest wished Josephine and Leonard well and predicted a long and happy marriage; not a tear for her own marriage ceremony in her parents' living room, the memory of the lie they told Father Messier flushing her face with shame still, not a tear for poor Sonny, looking cunning in short pants and sturdy little shoes but a boy growing up without a father nonetheless.

It was only after Josephine and Leonard left for their honeymoon, after Faby had bathed Sonny and gotten him settled in his crib, after she had taken a bath and gotten ready for bed herself, that the tears started. When Faby entered her bedroom after taking her bath, Josephine's bed was empty, the pillow fluffed, the tuck beneath it perfect, the bed neatly made only that morning. The top of Josephine's desk was now clear except for a reading lamp. On the top of her bureau, only the starched white dresser scarf remained.

In his crib, Sonny lifted his head as Faby stood between the two twin beds, tears running down her face, unable to move. Sonny continued to watch her from his crib, frowning. He pulled himself up and, steadying himself with his hand on the rail, reached out to her with his other hand. Faby walked across the room to his crib and lifted him off his feet to lay him back down. He struggled to remain standing, but when she spoke to him, "Time for sleep, little one," he stopped moving and let her cover him with his blanket, although he did not close his eyes. Faby could feel his eyes open all that night as she lay awake wondering why Josephine had married so young. Every so often, she heard Sonny blink his eyes, the sound like a camera shutter closing, then opening, a sound she had never heard a person make before. Josephine could have waited to marry.

Sonny didn't learn to talk until he turned two, nearly a year later, and, even then, he didn't talk much. "That's all right," Papa would say, when Maman Aurore fretted and fussed. "If the boy has nothing to say, there is no need for him to speak." Faby wondered if Sonny might just be confused about which language was actually his to use, his mother speaking to him in English, his grandparents speaking to him in French.

Once Sonny started school, Papa fitted the tiny storeroom over the kitchen with a cot, a small dresser, and a discarded wicker laundry basket to hold toys—and that was where Sonny spent his childhood, under the eaves, until he enlisted in the Army the day after he graduated from high school and left for basic training. He never lived with his mother again.

Faby continued to live in her parents' house on Depot Street, contributing to the household income with her job at the telephone company, working next to young girls waiting for someone to marry them, each year some of them leaving and new ones coming to take their place, while Faby stayed behind. She gave little thought to her circumstances one way or the other, nor to the years passing, until first Maman Aurore died, then each of her parents in turn. After Maman died, Faby inherited the house, as Josephine had long been well-established in her own home and Faby's prospects for a second marriage grew dimmer with each birthday.

Everything in the house spoke to Faby of loss: Maman's apron hanging on the back of the pantry door, the faded cloth still streaked with batter from the last chocolate cake she had baked before dying; Papa's pipe resting next to the humidor in the living room, the stem white from his teeth, Faby unable to knock the dottle out of it, much less get rid of it; and even Maman Aurore's knitting basket, which still rested on the floor next to her big empty rocker in the kitchen by the window, in the same place it had always been, in the days when she showed her disapproval of Maman's housekeeping skills by how fast her needles clicked, as yet another mitten or sock took shape beneath them.

Worst of all was Faby's own bedroom, still outfitted with two twin beds made up with matching spreads, a shared nightstand between them; two chests of drawers, one filled with Faby's clothes, the other empty; and two small desks, both tops equally scratched and stained with ink, one laid out with Faby's toiletries, the other bare.

Still having an adolescent's diffidence about staying in the room where her parents had lain together in bed every night, Faby moved into Maman Aurore's old room, but it didn't help. She managed to remain in the house for six months after Maman's death, until she could bear it no longer and sold the house to a young couple from East Enosburg who wanted to live in the village so that their children could walk to school.

The week before she closed on the house, Faby moved into a small three-room apartment in the Perley Block on Main Street, into what had once been part of a larger, grander suite of rooms when Enosburg was prosperous, before the Spavin Cure factory went out. The room that overlooked Main Street, the living room, was the only room in the apartment with windows, the bedroom behind it in perpetual shadow, the kitchen dark. Where original walls remained, they were graced with beautiful walnut woodwork, the newer dividing walls trimmed in a poorly-stained attempt at matching it.

Faby's first night in the apartment, she was unable to sleep. She was in her own bed, which Leonard had set up for her earlier in the day, with her nightstand and lamp by its side, but when she opened her eyes for a comforting glimpse of the night sky, whether shadowy with clouds or bright with moonlight, it wasn't there—which made her keep opening her eyes and looking for it all the more. She could hear the occupants of the apartment next door bumping about for hours, walking from room to room, playing the phonograph, dropping heavy objects on the floor. When they settled down at last, she could hear them talking through the wall, their bed obviously positioned in the same place in the room as hers. Even when their voices dropped to intermittent murmurs, then stopped altogether, she was unable to sleep. She finally gave up and turned on the light to read as the building creaked and popped, and the radiators gurgled and sighed.

After a year or so, she became accustomed to the apartment's quirks and could even call it home without feeling a pang of disbelief or betrayal in her stomach. It was, after all, fitted up with the familiar furnishings of her childhood: the sofa from the living room, her father's Morris chair, her mother's tea cart for plants. The remaining furniture from the house on Depot Street was stored in Josephine and Leonard's garage, earmarked for whichever of their children married first. The pictures on the walls in Faby's living room were also from the house on Depot Street: fading scenic vistas that in all likelihood depicted the New England landscape but could actually be just about any place that wasn't tropical or barren.

Saturday became the best day of the week for her. Saturday was the day that Josephine came over to spend the afternoon with her. As soon as she arrived, Faby would brew a fresh pot of coffee for them to drink, with cream and plenty of sugar, as they shared their news of the week, Josephine having more news to impart by virtue of children and a husband, Faby's week always the same: Monday through Friday up early to get ready for work, then the brisk walk to the telephone building in good weather and bad to sit at her switchboard, plugging and unplugging the village's conversations, some petty, some of life-changing import, the telephone traffic increasing as the yearly Town Meeting day approached, when farmers and elderly widows bemoaned the current property tax rate, begrudging every dime that went to teachers' salaries, every nickel that went towards school books, every penny for paper and chalk, then the trek back to the Perley Block at day's end and back up the stairs to her apartment, the smell of stale cooking odors lingering in the stairwell oddly comforting.

Josephine's week was always more interesting than hers, her three children winning awards and saying clever things, the latest meeting of the Ladies' Village Improvement Society a free-for-all of petty grievances over wilting petunias and impassioned discussions of discarded cigarette butts, Leonard not only successful but thoughtful, painting the bathroom her favorite shade of blue, cooking supper when she wasn't feeling well. Yet, Josephine never lorded it over her, and Faby enjoyed her Saturday afternoon visits more than she could ever say, Josephine's voice as she shared the details of her week indistinguishable from when they had shared a bedroom as girls and talked late into the night about school and boys and what their lives would be like when they were grown.

Chapter 39

The day of Sonny's wedding, Faby awoke encased in a headache, as though her head had burst through a car windshield and she lay shattered and bleeding beneath a tree just sending out its first tender spring buds. She covered her eyes with her forearm, but the morning light, dim as it was around the edges of the closed draperies of the unfamiliar hotel room, still exploded beneath her eyelids. The thought of having to rise from her bed, pull a hairbrush through the exposed nerve endings of her hair, and put on her new taffeta mother-of-the groom dress that would erupt into a clamor of rustling every time she moved brought sudden nausea and the nearly-forgotten image of poor Maman Aurore vomiting into the gutter as Faby stood rooted to the sidewalk between getting her grandmother safely home and joining her new husband at the train depot.

Groaning, she turned on her side, picked up the telephone receiver, and asked the front desk to connect her with Josephine Paradis's room.

When Josephine's voice came on the line, Faby rasped, "I don't think I'll be able to make it to Sonny's wedding."

"What's wrong?"

"I have the worst headache I've ever had. I'm sick to my stomach."

"Let me get dressed. I'll be right there."

A few minutes later, a knock came at the door with Josephine's voice. "Come in," Faby said weakly. The knock came again, Josephine's voice louder now. "The door's locked, Faby. I can't get in."

Faby rolled out of bed and cautiously made her way to the door to open it. As soon as it opened, Josephine exclaimed, "You look terrible, Faby! Are you going to throw up?"

Without waiting for a response, Josephine got Faby to the toilet and held back her hair as she retched. "You must have a migraine," Josephine said. "Let's get you back into bed, and I'll get the house doctor up here to give you something to make you sleep."

"It's Sonny's wedding day. If I don't go, he'll never forgive me."

On the phone with the front desk, Josephine didn't respond. Putting down the receiver, she said, "The doctor should be here in about fifteen minutes. I'll go and get a cold cloth for your forehead. It might help a little bit until he gets here."

The cold cloth did help a little, and Faby found that if she lay perfectly still and barely breathed, she could almost just bear the pain behind her eyes. When the house doctor arrived, about twenty minutes later, his jovial manner was almost as difficult for her to endure as the headache. "Now, what have we here?" he said, lifting the cloth from Faby's forehead. "I hear tell you have a massive headache. Any vomiting? You'll need to open up those peepers, so I can have a look."

"Yes," Josephine responded. "About half an hour ago. Faby, please open your eyes for the doctor."

He shone a penlight into each of her eyes, setting off more explosions. "Well," he said cheerfully, "you're not having a stroke." He clicked off the penlight and dropped it into his

330

medical bag. "Looks like you've got a garden variety migraine headache. Shot of Demerol should fix you right up."

"What time is it?" Faby said. "My son's getting married at one o'clock."

"Ah," the doctor said, taking a syringe and a small vial out of his bag. "You wouldn't want to miss that, now would you?" He pierced the membrane of the vial with the syringe and began drawing out the fluid. "You taken Demerol before?"

"No."

"It's going to make you sleep, but I'm giving you a lower dose that should start wearing off in time for you to get to the wedding. No guarantees about dancing till dawn, though. You can toast the bride and groom, but you'd better stay away from any other alcohol. Pull up your nightgown. This is a fanny shot."

"Thank you, Doctor," Josephine said as he closed his medical bag after administering the shot.

"She should be fine, but if she runs into any trouble, just give the front desk a shout, and I'll come back."

"Irritating man," Faby mumbled as the door closed behind him.

"Are you sure you're up to going to the wedding?" Josephine said. "Everyone will understand if I tell them you've been taken ill."

Faby's eyes had become very heavy. "I didn't tell Sonny."

"I'll tell him you're not well, and we're waiting a few hours to see how you do with the medication."

"Not that. I'm going to the wedding. I didn't tell Sonny about Louis."

As Faby sank into the narcotic embrace of the Demerol, she heard from a long way off Josephine's voice saying, "I'll check on you at 11:00," and Louis's voice, "He looks like a Gauthier."

Three hours later, when she slowly surfaced into consciousness to see Josephine sitting in a chair next to her bed, the headache was gone, in its place a surreal kind of grogginess, as though the headache were still there even though it no longer hurt.

"How's your headache?" Josephine said.

"Gone."

"Are you feeling all right?"

"Yes, just kind of groggy."

"Let me run you a bath, and then I'll call down to room service and order you some toast and hot tea. We won't be eating until at least two o'clock. You should have something on your stomach in the meantime."

After eating tea and toast in her bathrobe, Faby took the new dress she'd chosen for her role as mother of the groom out of the closet. She probably should have gone for a solid rather than a print, but it was such a lovely shade of purple that she hadn't been able to resist it. "Do you think this dress is too frumpy?"

"Of course not. It's not at all frumpy, and you're going to look lovely in it. You are such a silly old thing, Faby."

When the usher led Faby to her reserved place at the front of the church, she was surprised to see how simply the church had been decorated, with two brass vases of white lilacs on the altar and several more strategically placed on the deep sills of the stained glass windows. While the vases shone with fresh polish, the flowers looked as though they could have been taken from the Neales' front porch earlier that morning with no attempt to change their natural shape with the fussy ministrations of a florist shop. Margaret must be a sensible girl, and her mother must be equally sensible not to demand that the father lay out a king's ransom for flowers to impress their friends and relations for barely an hour's time.

Dressed as a groom in an off-white tuxedo jacket and black trousers, Sonny stood at the altar with his groomsmen, his eyes never wavering from the open church door as he waited for his bride. Faby had never realized until that moment just how handsome he was, with his French coloring and dark wavy hair, with nothing of his father in him. As Sonny waited for Margaret, Faby hoped against hope that he would be so enraptured with his bride he wouldn't notice that Louis hadn't come to the wedding after he'd promised he would. Josephine squeezed her hand. "Are you feeling all right?"

"Yes, I'm fine. The wedding should be about to start, shouldn't it?"

When Margaret came through the church door on her father's arm after her bride's maids had solemnly processed to the altar, Sonny's face radiated such joy that Faby's breath caught in her throat. She had no idea that her son would be capable of such happiness. After the ceremony, she stood proudly by his side in the receiving line as he and Margaret accepted the handshakes and kisses of a never-ending stream of well-wishers. Even so, she couldn't stop help herself from sneaking furtive looks at him to see if he realized that his father had never arrived to see him be married.

After the obligatory round of photographs, the wedding party joined their guests for the reception dinner in the parish hall. Surely, when they were seated at the head table, Sonny would notice that his father's place was empty. Yet when they all were seated, there was no empty place. She couldn't understand it. Sonny had told her specifically that his father had accepted his invitation. Had Louis cancelled, and no one told her? Not that there was any need to tell her. They had been divorced for so long they might as well never have been married.

Sonny's best man, an Army buddy of his from the war, stood up to make the first toast to the happy couple, relating the most charming anecdote of how Sonny and Margaret had first met, when they both were working at a Goodwill summer camp for underprivileged children and struck up a friendship that quickly blossomed into love.

After the raised glasses were lowered and the best man had sat down, a young man at one of the guests' tables tapped his fork against his glass. As he got up to make his toast, Faby had to stop herself from gasping as Louis stood there before her: his tall, thin frame, extravagant blond pompadour, and lantern-jawed smile just the same as the night she had met him after the vaudeville show. Only this version of Louis was younger, barely old enough to shave.

"To Sonny and his lovely bride," Louis said, raising his glass. "A fellow couldn't ask for a better big brother." His glass still raised, he looked around the room, blushed, and abruptly sat down.

The cheerful din of conversation and cutlery against china seemed to recede and reverberate as Faby sat incredulous that anyone looking so much like Louis could ever be at a loss for words.

She heard Sonny's voice close to her ear. "You look a little pale, Maman. Let me take you out to get some air." As Sonny helped her up from her chair, Faby was surprised to see Margaret give her a genuine smile of encouragement to leave the room with her son. Sonny offered Faby his arm, and she let him lead her out of the parish hall to stand together in the new spring sunlight on the front steps of the church.

"Are you all right, Maman?" Sonny said as Faby put up her hand to shade her eyes from the brightness of the sun. "You looked as if you'd seen a ghost when Louis stood up to give his toast."

"It gave me such a turn, seeing him like that."

"Oh, no, I'm sorry. Of course it would have, after what happened."

"After what happened?" She took her hand from her eyes. "Who told you? They left it to me, but I couldn't bring myself to tell you of your father's death two weeks before you were to be married. I just couldn't do it."

"I'm sorry, Maman. Louis told me. He called when he didn't see me at the funeral."

"Why would he have done that?"

"Because he's my brother."

Faby stopped herself from saying *half-brother,* and they stood in silence on the front steps of the church as Faby's new daughter-in-law waited patiently for her husband to return to her.

Sonny broke the silence. "I never told you about the day I met Louis, did I?"

Faby looked up at him, surprised. "No, I don't think so. No, you didn't. I would have remembered. You were, what, twelve years old?"

Sonny nodded. "That day was the happiest day of my childhood."

"Why didn't you tell me?"

"I thought that telling you my father had given me a special day would hurt you. May I tell you about it now?"

"Yes, please tell me."

"It was the first time I'd ridden any real distance on the train by myself, and I felt very cosmopolitan, changing trains in White River and striking up conversations with perfect strangers. I spent the night at Grandmother Kittell's house in my father's old bedroom. When I went upstairs after supper, I found a small trunk on the bed. The lid was open, so I figured that Grandmother must have set it out for me. Inside were my father's vaudeville memorabilia. I must have been up until nearly midnight going through it all: sheet music, photographs, scripts, newspaper clippings, theater programs, everything you can imagine, even worn-out shoes.

"The next morning, Dad drove up from Connecticut in a shiny new Desoto. As soon as I heard the car in the drive, I ran out to meet it, and there was Louis, kneeling on the front seat with one hand on the dashboard waving like mad with his other hand. You wouldn't know it to look at him now, but he was a chubby little fellow back then, just as cute as he could be in short pants and a Dutch boy haircut. Standing on the front steps as the car pulled up, I thought I cut quite the dashing figure of a big brother in my long pants and black beret.

"I slid into the front seat next to Louis, and the three of us were off to Jamaica Pond for a picnic. I remember Louis was so thrilled to meet me! He kept saying, *You're my big brother? You're really my big brother? I really have a big brother?* Once we had that settled, he was on to the questions: *What grade are you in? How much do you weigh? Can you play baseball? What kind of hat is that? Can I try it on?*

"When we got to Jamaica Pond, our father surprised us by renting a row boat. The three of us piled in with the picnic basket, and he rowed us the whole circumference of the shore with little Louis shouting at every person he saw, *Look at us, look at us, we're in a boat!*, our father laughing so hard he had to rest on the oarlocks a couple of times to catch his breath. Then he rowed us out to the middle of the pond to drift as we ate our picnic. I'll never forget that picnic lunch: brown bread and cream cheese sandwiches, cold baked beans, and hermit bars. Louis's mother had put in grape soda for the two of us, which we both refused to drink after the first swallow. Our father tried it for himself, declared it vile, and agreed to share his Thermos of hot coffee with us as long as Louis didn't tell his mother. As much cream and sugar as it had in it, it was pretty much coffee for children anyway.

"After we'd finished eating, our father pulled a camera out of the picnic basket, and we took turns taking pictures of each other in the boat. When we got back to shore, our father took a picture of Louis and me together. Would you like to see it? I keep it in my wallet."

Sonny took out his wallet and handed Faby the snapshot, which showed him in long pants and the beret he used to wear, standing behind a chubby little boy with light hair. Sonny's hands were on the boy's shoulders. Never before had Faby seen such happiness on her son's face, not until today.

Faby didn't see Sonny much as the years passed and the children came, he and Margaret having moved to North Carolina after their honeymoon for him to take a teaching job he hadn't really expected to get, while Faby remained in Enosburg, plugging and unplugging the conversations of village folk she now barely knew, as removed from their concerns as her apartment in the Perley Block was removed from the house on Depot Street, yet every year when the lilacs bloomed, their fragrance would bring to mind the joy on Sonny's face on his wedding day, and for a few brief moments, she could stop regretting that she had once been a girl who loved the vaudeville show.

About the Author

Elizabeth Gauffreau grew up a child of the 1960s in northern New England before spending twenty years in the South as a Navy wife. Currently, she teaches critical inquiry courses at Granite State College in Concord, New Hampshire, where she is the Director of Liberal Arts Programs. In addition to academic advising, teaching, and higher education administration, her professional background includes assessment of prior experiential learning for college credit. Much of her fiction is inspired by her family history, and lately she has developed an interest in writing about her family's genealogy. She lives in Nottingham, New Hampshire with her husband; their daughter has flown the nest to live in sunny California.

CPSIA information can be obtained
at www.ICGtesting.com
Printed in the USA
BVHW031142270219
541314BV00001B/28/P

9 781949 180510